Copyright © 2016 by Natasha Preston
All rights reserved.

Visit my website at www.natashapreston.com
Cover Designer: Dalliance Designs
Editor and Interior Designer: Jovana Shirley,
Unforeseen Editing, www.unforeseenediting.com

No part of this book may be reproduced or transmitted in any form or by any means, electronic or mechanical, including photocopying, recording, or by any information storage and retrieval system without the written permission of the author, except for the use of brief quotations in a book review.

This book is a work of fiction. Names, characters, places, and incidents either are products of the author's imagination or are used fictitiously. Any resemblance to actual persons, living or dead, events, or locales is entirely coincidental.

ISBN: 978-1530083602

Copyright © 2016 by Natasha Preston
All rights reserved.

Visit my website at www.natashapreston.com
Cover Designer: Dalliance Designs
Editor and Interior Designer: Jovana Shirley,
Unforeseen Editing, www.unforeseenediting.com

No part of this book may be reproduced or transmitted in any form or by any means, electronic or mechanical, including photocopying, recording, or by any information storage and retrieval system without the written permission of the author, except for the use of brief quotations in a book review.

This book is a work of fiction. Names, characters, places, and incidents either are products of the author's imagination or are used fictitiously. Any resemblance to actual persons, living or dead, events, or locales is entirely coincidental.

ISBN: 978-1530083602

dedication

I couldn't have finished this book without the constant help of a good friend, Hilda. Not only have you been there to encourage me, but you've also sent me so many gorgeous teasers, album covers, and book cover options. I don't know how, but you always seemed to know just when I needed something visual to keep me going. Your enthusiasm for this book has gotten me through many late nights and a lot of doubt!

TEXAS
MONDAY, MAY 4
OXFORD, ENGLAND

I roll over on my bed, stare up at the ceiling, and sigh down the phone. "If you fancy telling me how I'm going to get through this tour, Peyton, that'd be awesome."

"Um…"

Best friend? Yes. Good at advice? No.

Probably doesn't help that I've not told her absolutely everything yet. It's hard to say aloud what's happened between me and Kitt because then I'll have to talk about what happened after.

And I won't talk about what happened after.

"Yeah, Pey, I'm going to need more than that."

"You'll be fine on tour. You love it on tour. No one is better suited for looking after six grown-ass man-children than you."

Ugh, ass.

She's getting all Americanised, out there in LA.

"Ha, they do act worse than kids."

"But Kitt"—even the sound of his name has me breaking out in a sweat—"is the object of your desire, and being around him makes you feel like your vagina is going to explode," she says.

"I…what?" I make a face even though she can't see. "Your vagina feels like it's going to explode when you're around a guy you like?"

I can practically see her twirling her finger around her blonde hair. "Well, not literally but yeah. In a good way."

A good exploding vagina. Of course.

"I think I'm scared of you right now, freak."

"You love me long time, slut. Now, stop stressing about Kitt, and enjoy seeing the world. Again."

I roll my eyes. Everyone seems to have that misconception. Touring isn't all that glamorous. I don't get to sightsee everywhere and try local cuisine. I'll see lots of roads and lots of arenas and eat lots of room service."

"You get some time off, right?"

"A couple of days here and there and then a bit of time between the bus tour and flying out to places like America and Australia. We *have* to meet up in the States."

"Duh. I'm trying to swing a couple shows closer to home, too. Not sure yet, but I'll do my best."

I sit up. "Oh my God, do that! It's been so long, Pey. I hate that you're off being a superstar actress in LA. And, you know, also super proud," I add with lots of enthusiasm.

I *am* proud of her, but I miss her like crazy. She's the only girl I like, and I'm not exaggerating.

"I will do my best. I miss you and the boys."

"Yeah, want to spend the night perving on my band with me?"

My band? Yes. They are mine. If it wasn't for me, they would have missed at least five appearances. Unorganised lazy shits. I love them to death.

Especially Kitt Daniels—AKA the kiss ninja. One minute, he's there with his lips all over mine, pinning me against the wall, and the next…poof, gone.

"I don't know how you haven't slept with all of them yet. Honestly, they might well be whores, but"—she wolf-whistles—"they're all *gorgeous*."

I'm one hundred percent biased, but every member of Filthy Sound really is beautiful, all in completely different ways. It's like they were sent from the rock gods to break the heart of every woman—from Kitt Daniels, who is heavily tattooed and has dark hair, to Jack Cooper, who's blond and lightly tattooed, to Milo Sterling, whose hair is the colour of black ink and whose skin is pristine and untouched.

"Right," I reply.

But there's only one of them I want to sleep with—and, well, marry—and he doesn't feel the same.

"Is your panic over?" she asks, having about as much time for girlie drama as I do.

"Yeah, I'll figure something out. I'm getting to be a pro at pretending I feel nothing for him."

"Aw, Texy."

"Ugh, shut up. We're not doing the teenage boy-drama shit, I swear. Tell me something awesome you've done recently."

"I went on a date with Chad Galley."

My jaw falls onto my chest. "I hate you so much."

She laughs. "Don't be jealous. He plays some incredible characters on-screen, but trust me, he's *very* good at acting."

"No! He's boring?" This isn't the first time that Peyton Best has ripped apart my celebrity fantasies. I hate it when you meet someone, and they're nothing like how you want them to be.

"Watching-paint-dry boring. I could've fallen asleep. Do you know what chassis goes in different cars?"

"No."

"Oh, I do."

"Ouch."

Nothing is worse than being trapped on a date with someone who's making you fall asleep. I'm not brave enough to walk out. It feels rude. Plus, "Ignorant Texas Knight" would be all over the Internet by the time I got home, and there's enough untrue rubbish in the world about me as it is.

"Yep. Mum thinks I should give him another chance because it could've been nerves, but I'm not going to waste anyone's time."

"How is your mum?"

Peyton and her mum have been on their own since Peyton was a baby. Her dad took off to find himself shortly after she'd turned one. So far, he's not found anything. Well, at least that she knows of because he's never had any contact with her since. Her mum, Fern, thought maybe he'd be in touch now that Peyton is a superstar, living in LA, but they've heard nothing.

Growing up, we kind of shared each other's parents. It's probably why we're so close. Then, the bitch moved across the world for a part in an ongoing TV series surrounding an American high school, kind of *One Tree Hill-* and *90210-*style, and I miss her every day.

"She's good. She hates America still."

I laugh and shake my head. Fern doesn't *hate* America. She hates that they don't all drive on the other side for her or add tax to the prices on show.

"So, tell me something awesome *you've* done recently, Tex," she says.

"I ate a whole share bag of M and M's and Maltesers in one sitting while watching three seasons of *The Big Bang Theory*."

Peyton is silent for a long time, but just as I'm about to ask if she's still there, she clears her throat. "Time well spent."

"Yeah, I think so."

Deep down, I know I need to do more epic shit, but what this epic shit will be I have no idea. My dad's a rock star, my mother's a supermodel, and my best friend is a TV star. I have a lot to live up to, and I don't know where to start.

For now, I'm content to tour for the summer, and then I'll figure something out.

Swinging my legs over the bed, I get up and throw my favourite T-shirt in my case. I should've started packing earlier, but that never changes. I've got no time for that. And we do have a little time before we leave.

"Anyway, Pey, I need to go. Call me as soon as you can fit me into your busy schedule," I tease.

"Mmhmm, I'll try to pencil you in next week."

"I hate you."

"Love you, too, whore," she sings before hanging up.

Chucking my phone down on my bed, I finish packing the last—I hope—of my things.

I zip up the case as Dad walks into the room. He rubs the dark stubble covering his chin.

I look like Dad—minus the facial hair, of course. We have the same shades of medium-dark brunette hair and hazel eyes. Mine have more green in them though, and that can be attributed to my mother. She's all blonde hair, dazzling green eyes, and miles of legs.

He leans against the doorframe, like he's in a Calvin Klein ad, which he was asked to do a few years ago. They wanted rock star Mark Knight on their campaign. Thank God he turned it down because I would've had to get myself emancipated. No one wants to see their dad in underwear on billboards and on TV.

And if they do, they need to reevaluate their life.

"Want to see if you can meet up with your mum before we leave?" he asks.

I raise my eyebrow. My mother, the woman who pushed me out and then left me with Dad thirty-six hours later. She didn't even try for two days.

I give him a sarcastic look. "No."

"Texas, you won't see her for a couple of months."

"Then, nothing will change," I reply as I shrug.

I generally see her once every three months. Being on tour won't change my relationship with her at all. Christ, moving to the North Pole wouldn't do that.

Mother Dearest is a supermodel, household name, and ex-reality TV star. I'm so glad I refused to be on *Living with the Star* when she had the film crew at her house for almost a year.

To be fair, she's damn good at what she does. Jennifer does high-fashion and runway shit, wearing stupidly expensive clothes that look as uncomfortable as they are impractical. I'm a shorts-and-T-shirt kind of girl most of the time.

I don't think there's a glossy magazine she's not been on the front of. All of that success is great, but she sucks at being a mum. My dad, nanny, his band, and his entourage have brought me up, and they've done a pretty awesome job.

Dad sighs. He knows how I feel about Jennifer, and while he doesn't disagree that she's not even fit to look after a plant—which she kills regularly—he doesn't like to say anything bad about her to me. Growing up, he made so many excuses for her. I knew the real reason she was rarely there. She didn't want to be my mum, plain and simple.

"Okay, just give her a call then." He throws the house phone down on my bed, like I don't have a mobile, and walks out.

I know I should call her and let her know I'm about to go on tour with Dad, but she already knows. She still follows Dad's career, like she did back when she was an eighteen-year-old groupie—only now, she Googles him.

Mum was one of Dad's first groupies when his band was just starting to get big. She followed him everywhere, and I'm proof that he screwed her—just once though. In my head, it is only ever once. About nine months after their romantic evening in a grimy bathroom in Texas, I was born. Yes, of course, my dad—being left alone with a baby and having no clue that baby name books existed—named me after the state I had been conceived in. Lovely. It could have been worse, I suppose.

I scroll down the list on the home phone until I come to Jennifer Star—not her real surname but she needed to match the ego.

In my mobile, she's down as The Oven.

"Texas, darling," she says, drawing out *darling*, like she's an extra in *Absolutely Fabulous*.

Lord, help me.

"Hello, Mother."

"Oh, don't call me Mother. You make me sound old."

You are thirty-eight. I want to say it, but it's not worth the hassle. Plus, thirty-eight isn't old.

"Sorry, *mum*."

I honestly would rather call her Jennifer to her face, but after the long, drawn-out lecture Dad gave, I caved. Jennifer hadn't been ready to be a parent, and apparently, I shouldn't be too hard on her. Sorry, not my fault. She'd opened her legs, so she should have dealt with what came out between them.

Dad seems to think I'd have a better relationship with her if I told her how her abandonment made me feel. I don't want to have that conversation with her. We don't discuss feelings with each other. She's never even told me she loves me, so why should I try?

"How are you, sweetheart? Daddy told me you're learning to drive." She sounds surprised, like she didn't realise I'm older than eleven now.

"Yep," I reply.

At nineteen, I'm two years behind passing my test, but you know, touring with rock stars totally takes precedence. And besides, we have drivers, so I can sit back and chill while being driven around.

I'm not as princessy as that sounds. Honestly.

"Has he bought you a car yet?"

I turn my nose up. "No, he won't even talk about it until I've passed my test."

"Oh, you leave that to me. I've just bought a nice little Mercedes CLK, and you'll absolutely love it. How cute would it be to have matching cars?"

7

Nope. Not cute at all.

I want to tell her not to worry and that I'll be happy with whatever Dad gets me—which, no doubt, will be a sensible, safe car—but I really like the sound of a CLK. Plus, Jennifer lives in Notting Hill, and we're an hour away from her, so no one would see our matching cars.

Jennifer likes the *idea* of having a daughter—now that I'm an adult—more than the reality of it. She wants the fun stuff, like getting made up together, going out, having our nails done, and buying me expensive things. Tough luck for her that I'm not girlie.

Growing up, I just wanted a mum.

"I don't know if Dad would like that."

She has as much right to buy me whatever she wants as Dad does, but I would never encourage anything I knew he wouldn't be cool with. He is the most important person in my life, and nothing will get in the way of that.

"Leave it to me, Texas. Have I ever let you down before?" She makes it sound like a joke.

I blink in shock, my heart sinking. *You heard that right, right?* There is nothing I can reply that's not all the time, so I glue my lips together. Dad taught me to shut up if you're not going to say anything nice.

"We're going on tour soon."

"Yes. How exciting."

"Uh-huh."

"I believe it's for Filthy Sound and your dad's supporting, yes?"

She knows that already. There's no doubt in my mind that she Googled *Enigma's tours* long before now. Crap band name, I know, but they were young and drunk at the time. At least, I hope they were.

And I am one hundred percent sure, deep down, that she knows about my massive *thing* for Kitt—lead singer of Filthy Sound and my future husband.

I haven't seen him properly since *that* night, the one where we kissed. One earth-moving, life-affirming kiss that he hasn't

bloody mentioned since. I wanted him to propose the second we broke apart. He didn't.

Is that really too much to ask?
Selfish bastard.

I sigh. "Yeah."

"That Milo is into you," she says.

So, I was wrong. And so is she.

Milo is into blondes, lots of them. Plus, as Enigma's lead singer's nephew, Milo is practically family.

And I want Kitt.

"No, he's not, Mum." I sense she's about to say something, so I quickly add, "Anyway, Dad's calling me. Gotta load the bus up. Bye."

I hear her say, "Bye," right before I hang up.

Speaking to her is exhausting.

Dad passes by my door and looks back in. "How did it go?"

"Fine. She's the same." *Not changed in the nineteen years I've been alive.* "You packed?"

Frowning, he lazily shrugs one shoulder. "I think so."

"Plenty of condoms? We don't want you knocking up another groupie now, do we?"

He glares.

Truth hurts, I guess. I'm far too old to have a little brother or sister now, and Dad's just old.

"One time, that happened, munchkin."

I smirk. "It only takes one time."

"Apparently so," he mutters dryly. "We should hear about your grade soon. Gina will let us know."

Gina is—was—my personal tutor. She's been with us since I was five. Because Dad is on the road a lot and not wanting me to be away from him, he hired a nanny and tutor to come along with us. Of course, she stopped the nanny bit a long time ago, but she is a bloody genius and the reason I finished my studies a year ahead.

Hopefully, I'll soon have a degree in forensic psychology. I've always been addicted to true-crime shows and serial killers, so I chose to study something I knew I'd enjoy rather than what I needed to. Also, I don't know what I need because I don't have plans. I'm not sure what I'd do with my degree career-wise, but I loved the course, and I'm confident I could make someone disappear and never be caught.

My life has been quite sheltered. Actually, it's been *very* sheltered. I've never been to a proper high school or made many friends and mortal enemies, but I've met Guns N"n' Roses, so none of that normal stuff matters.

"I'm sure I rocked the degree."

"I hope so. I don't enjoy wasting money."

"You even noticed it's gone?" I fire back.

"Will you notice if I take it from your bank?"

"Good luck trying to convince the bank you're a nineteen-year-old girl."

"My plan is to stop any further payments from being made to you."

My face falls. *Damn.*

"You agree I win?" he asks. His mouth triumphantly tilts up at the side.

Not yet. I don't want to give in yet. "I can live off of what's in there."

"Texas Knight."

Full name alert.

You're nineteen. That doesn't have to scare you still.

But it does because you're a baby.

"All right." I hold up my hands. "You win. Happy?"

His smile widens. "Yes. Now, be downstairs in ten. The guys are coming over for pizza and beer."

Ah, pizza and beer. It's the start to every tour.

Enigma began the tradition back when they were playing in local social clubs, pubs, and bars. They still do it. Filthy Sound adopted the theme, too, because…well, pizza and beer.

"*All* the guys or just your lame band?"

I know the answer to this. It's Filthy Sound's tour, so obviously, they'll be here, too, but I don't want them to be.

They've been locked up in the studio for months, so I've not seen Kitt since the Christmas party.

Dad's eyes narrow at the mention of his band—or maybe it's because I called them lame. "All. Now, hurry up, Texas. You're on drink duty for that."

My heart slams in my chest.

No, I can't go downstairs if Kitt is here. He completely ignored the fact that we kissed, acting as if it'd never happened at all.

How am I supposed to be around him?

You can't. You'll make a tit out of yourself.

I raise my hand to my forehead. "But I'm sick, and I think it's really serious. I should stay in bed because it definitely feels like influenza."

"You're fine. Get downstairs. I'm serious," he replies, grinning like he just won another Grammy.

Dad leaves my room, and I know he'll be up again if I don't go. I can't get out of this.

It's fine. You're okay. You can do this. Don't stare at Kitt, and don't let him know you've thought about that kiss every second since it happened. Don't let him know that every day that passes without contact from him kills you a little bit more. Don't let him know that you're falling in love with him and terrified that your heart is going to be trampled.

Drink beer. Hide the sinking feeling behind a flawless smile. Be normal. Pretend you're okay with being just a friend.

Laugh. Joke. Pretend, pretend, and pretend.

I take a deep breath and force that bloody smile onto my face.

KITT
MONDAY, MAY 4
OXFORD, ENGLAND

Mark had headed upstairs to tell Texas to come down, so we'd let ourselves into the living room.

Their house is massive, far too big for two people, but it feels like home. Pictures of Texas, from a tiny baby to now, are everywhere. She has an expressive face, always smiling or pulling a funny expression, and just by watching her, it's hard not to feel like the whole world is okay.

If Cynthia, the housekeeper, didn't clean it a few times a week or do their shopping, they would probably call for takeaway every night. Neither of them has any time at all for cooking.

"I'm starving," Milo complains.

It's been at least twenty minutes since he ate last, so of course, he needs feeding again.

"Think Cynthia's been around today?" he asks.

"Jesus, man, we're ordering pizza soon," Cooper, the idiotic member of Filthy Sound, replies. I love him like a brother but Milo is definitely easier to live with. "I'm after the beer. It's a damn shame Mark doesn't have an open house. I didn't get laid last night."

Mark's place definitely isn't a party house—outside the seven of us anyway. It always pisses Coop off because the dickhead needs sex at least five times a week, and this is the place we usually hang out. But Mark won't have shit like that around Tex regularly.

"Why can't we order now? We know what everyone wants," Milo says, sitting on the largest sofa and kicking his legs up onto the footstool.

Coop walks past him and pushes his head. He heads straight for Tex's swivel chair. She won't be happy that he's sitting there, and that's exactly why he's done it.

Immature prick.

Wish I'd gotten there first.

I chuck myself down on another of the four huge sofas in here. Their living room is large but separated into two zones—a seating zone and a music zone. Beyond the sofas, coffee table, and TV are bookshelves, a long bench seat below the window that stretches the entire length of the room, and an awesome grand piano.

We're here to start the tour off right. *Our tour.* My stomach is filled with electric excitement. I want to be out there now. This is what I was born to do, and we're finally getting our shot at the big time.

Sinking back into the cushions, I flick on the TV. *Let's just get tonight started.*

"Porn?" Coop suggests.

I roll my eyes and settle on one of the Fast and Furious movies. Cars and races. Safe for everyone.

Cooper runs his hand through the front of his hair, making me and Milo laugh.

"Beautiful, sweetheart," I tease.

"You look gorgeous," Milo adds in a feminine voice.

"Fuck off, both of you."

I look at Milo. "Isn't he precious?"

"Damn cutest thing I've ever seen."

Coop growls and balls his fists. "I hate you wankers."

Will and Jimmy, the final pieces of Enigma, walk through the door as we're ripping on Cooper for playing with his hair. He's worse than a teenager.

Will is Milo's uncle, and that connection got us our first break. The second was Mark seeing our potential.

Mark spent hours, days, weeks, months with me, helping me hone my craft. I've never been shy or lacked confidence—I'm fucking brilliant—but Mark has taught me so much about the industry and my personal performance that I *know* I can't fail.

I could never do enough to repay him.

Enigma is the reason we're where we are today. This tour—our first tour—wouldn't be happening without them. We owe them *everything*.

So, when I decided to kiss Texas at Christmas, I fucked up on a monumental level.

I don't know what I was thinking. We'd both had a few, and she had been dancing around in this dark red dress that slightly flared out. It perfectly hugged her waist and breasts and showed off those killer legs. She doesn't often wear dresses, so I was screwed from the get-go.

I had been turned on from the second I saw her. It had been torture all night. I couldn't help myself. She had gone upstairs to her bathroom, and when she'd come out, I had been waiting. No one had gotten me that crazed with a kiss before. I'd never been so hard or so needy as I had been when her legs were wrapped around my waist, her hands all in my hair, and her mouth glued to mine.

Shit.

I rearrange myself while Milo and Cooper are saying hello to Will and Jimmy.

Thinking about that night gets me off quicker than any girl bouncing around on top of me.

15

Mark would do his nut if he found out.

I'm a dick. It was one drunken kiss, and as much as I wanted it, it shouldn't have happened. Tex is one of the most amazing people I know, the best probably, and I can't mess around where she's concerned—not even if I know it would be mind-blowing.

I've not spoken to her about it, and she's not mentioned it in the couple of times we've texted since. That's for the best. We need to chalk it up to being drunk and move on. She's not a casual shag. Mark would go crazy if he knew we'd kissed. I'm not ready for a relationship, so nothing can happen again.

Right now, I'm living the dream and enjoying the women who come along with that dream. There are a lot of them, and they're always so eager to please.

"Kitt, what are you having?" Milo asks, looking over one of the pizza menus left on the coffee table. He knows exactly what he's having and what the rest of us want.

"Meat feast—" I almost finish my sentence before Cooper interrupts by laughing, waving his fist back and forth in a wanking motion. "Really, dude?" I ask.

"You were thinking it, too," he says, kicking his legs up on Tex's footstool.

I deadpan, "No, I wasn't."

"You three need an adult with you at all times," Will says. "Spoken to your mum today, Milo?"

He groans. "Tomorrow. Forgot."

"Make sure you do, or I'll get it in the ear, and I've had years of my sister's whining, all right?"

Milo salutes.

"You idiots ready then?" Jimmy asks, flopping down next to Milo.

"We're ready," I reply for all of us.

We are. We are *so* ready for our own tour. This one is all about us even though I'm sure thousands of people will buy tickets because Enigma is supporting us. They sell out arenas in seconds and have to add dates to fit demand.

"Yeah, don't think you'll puke your guts up onstage?" Will asks, trying to psych us out.

"Once!" Coop snaps. "And I had food poisoning."

It was a long time ago when we were playing in a pub. Still funny though.

"Food poisoning is caused by too much Jack?" I ask.

"Fuck you. It was the curry."

"From three days before?" Milo says.

Coop narrows his pale eyes. "It's not too late for me to leave the band. Then, where will you be?"

I smirk. "Performing on a clean stage."

"I don't need this from you tossers," he hits back, scowling like a kid.

Milo laughs. "We're definitely ready for this. And we'll make sure Coop doesn't drink too much before each show."

I don't think I've ever been more ready for anything. Since I was old enough to hold a toy guitar, I've wanted to perform. I grew up listening to my grandad's old-school rock albums. When I met Milo and Cooper in high school, we formed a band, and I knew this was it. Whatever happened in my life, I had to play music.

It's been a dream my whole life and not one I ever thought I'd achieve, but here I am. As soon as we started playing for parties and in small clubs, I knew we had to pursue it.

Then, Milo started talking to his uncle.

Enigma and Tex came to see us one night, and they all loved us. I gave them a demo, and a few days later, we were taken under their wing. Eventually, we were asked to be one of two supporting acts on their tour last year. It wasn't like we'd turn that down. It was a pivotal time for our career.

We performed to crowds of thousands. It was one thing to have Enigma on board, but if the fans didn't like you…

But they did, and then we were signed with the same label who'd snapped Enigma up twenty years before.

I crash back against Mark's enormous sofa.

We've fucking made it.

Nothing compares to this feeling.

I hear footsteps outside the living room and look up.
Jesus.

I see her before she enters the room. She's looking toward the kitchen and not in my direction, which is good since it takes me a few seconds to fully take in her beauty. It's like being whacked by something really fucking hard every single time.

Texas is stunning.

She purses her full lips in the way she does when she's thinking hard about something. Her hazel eyes look greener in this light. She runs her hand through her long dark hair, pushing it out of her eyes.

Then, she turns toward the living room, and I force myself to look away.

TEXAS
MONDAY, MAY 4
OXFORD, ENGLAND

I'd stomped downstairs, but by the time I reached the bottom, I was embarrassed by my behaviour.

You're not seven. Get a grip. You'll be fine seeing Kitt. You're stronger than this.

Thank God no one saw me. I freeze and grip the chunky wooden banister when I hear his sexy, rough voice.

I might be strong, but Kitt makes me feel so weak.

Kitt is in the living room. His voice travels along the hallway. My heart instantly starts to thump hard. He gives me butterflies. *Great. Why does that still happen even though I'm over the age of thirteen?*

It's okay. Just breathe. You don't even like him anymore. He ditched you after the Christmas party. He's the enemy now. The bastard enemy. You. Do. Not. Like. Him.

I step into the living room, and my mouth goes dry. There he is. Kitt Daniels, in all his perfect glory, is sitting on the sofa, his ankle resting across his knee, with his arm thrown over the back of the cushions. His brown hair is stylishly messy on his head, slightly shaved at the sides, and he has tattoos covering his skin. My body is instantly hotter than lava.

Okay, maybe you like him a little.

"About time," Kitt says, smirking. His gorgeous deep blue eyes turn all logical thought to gibberish.

Kiss me.

The rest of the guys are talking about the tour, not even realising I'm now in the room, but they've been warned that when they enter our house, they have to keep the crude talk to a minimum. They never do.

I shrug. "Was busy." *Yep, I'm playing it cool. Totally ice-cold cool.*

You kissed him, but it doesn't matter because you only want to be friends with him anyway.

Even when I see his perfect come-to-bed midnight-blue eyes, sculpted jaw, cheeky smile, dimple, and light stubble, I still only want to be friends.

Definitely just friends.

"Hmm, a lot going on in *Made in Chelsea*, was there?"

Glaring, I show him my middle finger. "Bugger off."

He chuckles. *Damn, that sound.* "I love it when you're feisty."

I squirm inside as his words go down south.

I've had sex with one guy before. It was a year ago when we all were home for about eight months. I'd tried to do the relationship thing, and for a little while, it was great. But I didn't *want* him in the way I wanted Kitt, so I called it off before anything real started. Right now, I'm very much ready to see what Mr Daniels is like in bed.

"There's my girl," Coop says, giving me a Cheshire Cat grin that makes his light eyes shine. He's on *my* chair, but I don't care right now.

Jack Cooper—although the last person who called him Jack got a black eye—is Filthy Sound's guitarist and joker of the group. I love him but in the only-ever-a-friend way. Don't get me wrong, if he's shirtless, I'll be looking because the guy has an awesome body, but I would never go there.

"Cooper," I say, returning his infectious smile.

He's the guy who has the power to always cheer you up, usually by doing something stupid. But he's funny, so I've never discouraged him from jumping out of a moving vehicle—at slow speed. I don't want the dude to die—or from putting bulldog clips on his nipples. I was the one who had bought the bulldog clips.

"I've still not had my answer, and, let me tell you, Tex, that stings."

I smirk and tilt my head. "All right. If neither of us is married by forty, I'll marry you."

That's likely, too, since Kitt is being an arse, and Cooper has never been on a date.

"Texas, beers," Dad says from behind me.

"Dad, fine."

I turn on my heel and walk into the massive restaurant-size stainless steel kitchen that's ridiculous because neither Dad nor I can cook. We could chuck out everything but the fridge, kettle, and microwave, and nothing would change.

I grab the large cooler and open the freezer to pack it full of ice cubes. There's no way I'm playing beer bitch all night. I'll do one cooler, and then they're on their own.

"Want a hand?"

I jump at the sound of Kitt's voice and turn to see him leaning against the granite counter with his eyes firmly on my butt.

A hand with what exactly?

"Sure, you can start by looking at my eyes and then grab some beer from the fridge."

He laughs and gives an innocent shrug. "But your arse looks incredible in those shorts."

See? This is the rubbish that frustrates me. Is it just harmless flirty banter, or does he want more? Does he want to take me against that cold, hard worktop, like I want him to, or not?

I play along because that's really all I can do. "Hmm, you should see it in my lacy French knickers then."

His eyes bulge, and his mouth parts. It's so sexy that I feel like I've been electrocuted down there.

I give him a look. "Seriously, Kitt, beers!"

He salutes, opens the fridge, and grabs a handful of beers. Silence falls over us, and it grates at my skin. I've never felt like that before. It's usually comfortable.

It's because you kissed.

Kitt doesn't seem to care though. Everything is the same for him—the way he acts, how he is with me. Nothing has changed for him at all. It's me who's slowly going insane.

I grit my teeth.

"God, I haven't had a Becks since the Christmas party," he says, filling the cooler.

The Christmas party. That's what he's calling it. I prefer to remember it as The Kitt Kiss Night, but whatever.

"Yeah, me neither actually."

I don't think I can have one. I still remember the taste of it on his mouth.

"Have you drunk at all since then?"

I frown. *Have I? Not that I can remember.* I feel like I want to daily. "No, don't think so."

"Well, we've got all summer on tour for that." He winks and walks out.

For what? Drinking or kissing? Or drinking and kissing. I growl inwardly and throw ice in the cooler, like it's burning me.

Kitt is a total mindfuck.

When I've calmed down, I join the guys in the living room and hold a beer up, so Dad can see it. With my best pout and puppy-dog eyes, I silently ask him if I can join in tonight.

You're nineteen, for Christ's sake.

He frowns, so I flutter my eyelashes and mouth, *Please.*

It's not like I want to get off my face—well, I do after my conversation with Kitt in the kitchen, but I won't. It's not hard to understand why Dad's so against me drinking, but double standards isn't something I'm okay with.

"Your limit for the night is three," he says sternly.

I know he means it. There is no way I will get another one out of this, but I did only expect one, so I'm getting more than I thought already.

"Score!"

"*Three*, Texas." His hazel eyes darken as he bores a hole into me.

Holding up my thumb, I reply, "I got it, Dad."

He's seen so many celeb teens with drinking problems that he's obsessed with me not adding to the statistic. He must stress about raising me to be a well-rounded, normal person at least ten times a day. If Dad could see me at after-parties once he'd left, he would crack down even more. Thankfully, Kitt, Cooper, and Milo know when to keep their mouths shut.

"You know, you're a bit too old to be getting a limit from daddy," Kitt says, smirking.

I smile as sweetly as I can. "Bugger off."

Kitt is right, but my relationship with my dad is a little…different. For the last nineteen years, it's only been us, and he's busted his arse to make up for the fact that Jennifer isn't really interested. That's kind of left us in a place where I'm still a child to him, and I automatically seek permission. It's unhealthy, but that's where we are.

"Open it, please," I say, handing him my bottle.

Kitt pops the lid with his teeth and hands it back. There's a bottle opener in Jimmy's hand that I could have used, but I wanted it in Kitt's mouth.

See? Totally well-rounded and normal.

"Thanks," I say before taking a swig.

"So, on a scale of one to pissing your pants, how excited are you right now?" he asks.

"Pissing my pants," I reply. "What about you?"

"I'm holding it in."

"You know you get moodier every time I see you, right? Be more enthusiastic."

"I thought I was supposed to? Goes with the territory and all that."

I shake my head. *Not on my party bus.* "It's absolutely not allowed. No one wants to travel with miserable, so please cheer up."

"I'm not miserable." He puts his beer down and holds his hands up. "Right now, I'm just not…"

"Pissing yourself?"

Laughing, he replies, "Exactly. Pissing will commence on the bus, I promise."

"I really wish your scale wasn't so disgusting. We could have a scale of one to bursting into impromptu song in a mall."

"You're such a girl."

"Thanks for noticing." Sometimes, it doesn't seem like he does.

His eyes flick down to my chest. There is nothing casual about it, and he doesn't even make an attempt to try to conceal his perv. Kitt goes for it every time. He's so sure of himself. I clear my throat, sweeping the room to see if anyone is looking. Thankfully, no one is. Kitt looks up, grins, and shrugs one shoulder. He doesn't care that I caught him because he'd intended me to.

"I apologise," he says, grinning in a way that's clear he's not at all sorry.

This is what we're like all the time. There's a lot of banter and flirty moments that mess with my head. Then, he'll turn cold or go distant, and I won't know why. But at least the awkwardness—on my part—in the kitchen is over.

We spend most of the night sitting on the sofa together, talking and occasionally chatting with everyone else.

Tonight though, most of our focus is on each other. A little while ago, he started to lean in closer, so now, our arms are touching.

"Okay," he says, "what's the first thing you're going to do in…France?"

"Easy. Eat cheese."

"Italy?"

I don't even need to think. "Ice cream. Or crepes. Or both. America?" I ask.

"Shit, that's a hard one. Corn dog."

"Pancakes! Hershey!" I say.

"Oh my God, will you two stop talking food?" Cooper says. "We're going on tour to *rock*, not to make some lame cooking show, you boring fucks."

I laugh along with Kitt. Coop really has a way with words. Kitt makes a wanking gesture with his hand and then grabs another beer from the cooler off the coffee table.

As soon as Coop goes back to listing names of celebrity women he wants to bed, Kitt starts another conversation about things we're going to do on tour. He sits even closer to me, his arm firmly wedged against mine. I feel warmth wherever he touches me, and it's starting to drive me insane.

You can't kiss him. It won't end well.

I smile up at him, desperate not to look like I'm completely crazy about him. He bumps my shoulder and sips his beer, like nothing is wrong.

Same as always.

Texas is in love with Kitt.

Kitt only likes Texas.

TEXAS
TUESDAY, MAY 5
OXFORD, ENGLAND

I stand beside the massive tour bus in the cool night air and sigh. As much as I love our house, I also love being on tour. I don't get to see a lot of the countries we visit, but I love the freedom of traveling.

Jimmy bought the bus a couple of years back and had it heavily modified. Upstairs has bedrooms and a shower room, and downstairs has large seating areas and a very small kitchen. The bedrooms are small cupboard-size singles, but we all get a bed and the privacy of having a door rather than the typical bunk-bed style with curtains. The two drivers and two full-time security guys have the bunk beds, but they each have a door.

"You ready, Texas?" Will asks.

I blink up at him. "Yeah, sorry."

He smiles. "In your own little Kitt world." And then he disappears back on the bus.

He just said...oh God, no! No, no, no. Not good. He knows. Does my dad know? And Kitt?
I want to die. I want to throw myself under the bus.
This is bad.

No, Dad doesn't know. He would've brought it up for sure. We would've had many conversations about not getting caught up in the whirlwind of Kitt's impending success and saving myself for someone I'm sure of. Someone who will never let me down or hurt me. Someone who isn't famous. They're safer apparently.

Would've been for Jennifer.

"Texas, will you get your arse on the bus?" Coop shouts out the window.

I don't want to now, but I still step on and make my way to the seating area behind the driver's seat. Two big half-moon–shaped sofas face each other, both with a table in the middle. Hanging from the wall is a large flat screen TV that's playing some football match.

Everyone besides Milo is in the living room area. He's in his room, mentally preparing himself and running through the set list in his head. He's a worrier and always scared he'll start drumming along to the wrong song and embarrass Filthy Sound and himself. Either that, or he's doing something else I really don't want to know about. Gross.

I sit down and try to catch Will's eye.

Does anyone else know I'm hopelessly in love with Kitt? I need to know. The thought of them talking about me liking Kitt behind my back makes me feel sick. *Do they think it's just a phase, and it'll pass?*

Because that's what I thought...two *years* ago.

I shouldn't still like him, let alone love him. But who gets to control that? If I could've stopped, I would've done that after the first time I had seen him with another girl.

We had been at a club in central London where they were playing. I'd just started talking to my ex, Xander, keeping things friends, only because I liked Kitt. Then, I had seen him

with his tongue down some girl's throat, and they'd left together.

My heart aches at the memory, equally as hard as it did that night. I told myself I was done, and I gave things with Xander a chance. We didn't even last a year. I couldn't stop myself from loving Kitt, so I ended it.

The bus rumbles quietly and pulls away as we head off on the two-and-a-half-hour journey to Dover to get a ferry to France. We have a ferry booked to Calais, and then it's a three-hour drive to Paris.

Flying would have been easier, but Jimmy hates to fly. It's the reason he bought the massive bus and had it pimped.

There is no way he is *"being shot toward any-fucking-where in a tin can"* if he can reach it by car or boat.

Even with all the cases of sinking ferries, he still refuses to fly. *"I can swim, Texas, but I can't bloody fly."*

So, we drive where we can. It takes a lot longer to get places, but some of my best memories are on the tour buses. And we'd all rather drive than listen to Jimmy's constant bitching with death-by-plane-crash statistics.

"What are you drinking?" Kitt asks, knowing full well that alcohol is off the cards for me since my dad is right there.

Besides, it's too early to start—or too late.

"Coke, I guess."

"Good choice, Tex," Dad says.

"*Only* choice, more like," Milo teases. He sits down with us after finishing whatever he was doing.

Narrowing my eyes, I give Milo the finger. "I hate you all. I hope you know that."

"Hmm," Dad mutters at my action.

He wants me to have a clear head at all times, I think. He and Jennifer drank *a lot* when she was following him around. She was desperate for Dad's attention, and she didn't care about the consequences. I won't be the same because I know better. There is no way I would ever put myself in the position Dad and Jennifer were in. No one should be an unwanted child. I'm lucky that Dad wanted me.

"Whatever. I don't need to get drunk to have a good time," I say.

"Of course not. Look at the company you keep," Kitt says, jamming his thumb into his chest.

"Right. You're a treat," I reply.

"You have no idea how good I taste, Tex," he murmurs low enough not to be heard.

My throat dries, and I lick my lips. *Don't let him see that he affects you.* "Oh, yeah? Come chocolate, do you?"

He laughs, throwing his head back. The neckline of his T-shirt is stretched, revealing one of the many star tattoos that cover his body. His Adam's apple bobs as he swallows. Even that is sexy.

You need help.

"Well, I've never had any complaints."

No, of course not. When you're the lead singer in one of the hottest rising bands at the moment, you're not going to hear women complaining.

I force a smile. The thought of him with other women makes my skin crawl.

"Maybe none that you've heard, but there's not a Facebook group for unhappy KD conquests for no reason."

His face falls, and I pretend like I've said too much.

I sit up straighter. "Oh God...you didn't know."

"You're joking," he says slowly, narrowing his eyes.

From the look on his face, I know he thinks I'm being serious. He grabs his phone from his pocket and starts desperately tapping on it.

Part of me hopes there really is one.

While Kitt frantically searches for his own name on Facebook, my phone rings. It's Jodie, Filthy Sound's manager. She usually deals with me if she's not here because the guys are kind of forgetful and mostly always drunk. Jodie wouldn't be caught dead on a bus. She has flights booked for each stop she'll attend.

"Hey, what have they done?" I ask.

She laughs down the phone. "Nothing yet. I just want to check that you have the up-to-date schedule for the tour."

"If it's the one you sent yesterday, I do. Don't panic. I'll make sure they attend every engagement on time and fully dressed. Besides, Carl will be with us."

Carl is Enigma's manager, and he is so efficient that he makes everyone else on the planet look lazy as hell.

"The radio interview in Paris—"

"Is an early one. I got this. Believe me, I've already planned at least five different ways of getting them up on time."

Out of the corner of my eye, I see Coop make a fist and move it back and forth, pretending it's a blow job.

I tilt my head to the side and mouth, *You wish.*

"Thank you, Texas. I know Carl can handle everything in my absence, but I do appreciate your help. You have the dates where I'll be joining you, and you can call anytime you need."

"It's fine, Jodie. I enjoy it. I like to help."

"You're a godsend, girl. I'm trying to add a few more dates when I can join you in America, but I don't know if I'll be able to swing it."

"Carl and I have it covered."

"I know. I know. Remind me to hire you! Okay, I've got to run. Call me if you need anything."

"Will do. Speak soon."

"Bye, darling."

As much as I love Jodie, I like it when she's not here. It gives me purpose to be able to contribute something to the tour. Plus, I really do enjoy waking them up, especially Cooper. He is *not* a morning person.

So far, I've used water, their own instruments, shaking them, and jumping on them. Tomorrow, if they're not up, I might try screaming to watch them wake up scared and on high alert.

"What did she want?" Kitt asks.

His eyes are wide with... *fear?*

Every time I take a call from Jodie, he looks terrified, like he thinks she's calling to tell us they've made a mistake, and the tour is off. They've put an obscene amount of money into this, so that's obviously never going to happen, but he still panics.

It's cute. Shows how much this means to him. I love seeing his passion for music. It makes me like their songs and him even more.

"Just making sure I have your schedule, and I'll get you lazy bastards up on time."

He raises an eyebrow. "Like I'd forget anything. The more PR shit we do, the more people will turn up at the show." He smirks, and his eyes turn playful. "Then, the more women I get after the show."

I feel sick.

"Right. It's all about the women," I say sarcastically, unable to keep the hurt from my voice.

He doesn't flinch. His eyes keep a sparkle that's gone from mine. At least he didn't pick up on how his words had kicked me in the stomach.

He makes me want to run away and hide, and he doesn't even know it.

It's fine. You know he sleeps around. This is nothing new. Just breathe.

"Not *all* of it is about the women."

"Great," I reply tightly.

Shit. Stop it. I'm too hot, too angry, too hurt. I feel like I'm swallowing fire.

Kitt doesn't owe me anything, so I shouldn't let it get to me, but that's way easier said than done. Without realising it, he hurts me so much all the time.

I take a much-needed breath and pray my stomach settles before it empties.

You. Are. Fine.

"Hey, if you ever want a go..."

A go?

My heart cracks at the casual way he asked me to let him know if I want to be another notch. I stare at him, willing myself not to cry. I can taste bile.

My God, that hurts.

There is nowhere for me to hide away either. There's only so long you can stay in a smaller-than-a-prison-cell room before you lose it. I don't have anywhere to go.

Looking away, I purse my lips and rub the throbbing ache in my chest.

I want him so badly, but I could never be just a shag.

One night with him, if that's all I could ever have, would be incredible. To have his hands on my body, his lips against mine—it's what I think about before falling asleep. It's what I long for, right down into my fucking bones. But, damn, I would be broken when I woke up alone.

How could I be around him, knowing I'd had him *once*? I couldn't. Things would get messy. I can hide what I feel for him, but I know I couldn't hide the level of heartbreak I'd feel after being another one of Kitt Daniels's one-night stands.

Nope.

I can be strong. I can resist him because I can't handle losing him.

And I can get drunk—when my dad's not around, that is.

"All right, no shagging talk," he says, his mouth lifting at the corner.

"I'm not one of the guys, remember?"

"Right. Occasionally, I forget."

"Wow," I mutter. Yep, that hurts, too.

"No," he says, laughing. "Come on, I didn't mean it like that. I don't see you as a guy. But I'm just...really comfortable around you. Never had that with a girl before."

That's something, right? *Right?* I think so. Unless he's thinking *comfortable*, like an old slipper. I want to be his *everything*, not his slipper.

"That's good?" I ask cautiously. My heart is sprinting with nerves. This is a conversation that could go either way, and so far, not much with Kitt has gone the way I'd like.

33

"It's good," he confirms. "It's just a little new, and sometimes, I suck at being your friend and remembering you're a girl."

Yep, didn't go the way you wanted.

I blow out a breath. "Well, this has been enlightening. Drink?"

I need to get away from him for a minute.

"Er, sure. I'll take another beer, please."

Forcing a smile that probably looks like I want to kill him—I'm not far off—I get up and walk to the little kitchen area.

Hold. It. Together.

I jump when Will stands beside me. He's far too close. *He must have heard. Great.*

"Are you okay?" he asks, lowering his voice so that no one else can hear.

"I'm just dandy."

"Texas..."

I shrug and grab a beer for Kitt. "I'll be okay. It's nothing I didn't know already." That's a bit of a lie. I knew Kitt didn't want more because he's been pretending our kiss never happened, but I didn't think I was just a girl version of Milo and Cooper to him.

"Are you sure you're all right?"

I give him a smile, and with a pinup-model bottle opener, I pop the lid off Kitt's beer. "I'm fine."

Never has a person who has said, *I'm fine*, ever been fine.

I sit back down, but this time, I'm opposite Kitt—for safety reasons. Thankfully, the conversation has moved away from Kitt not thinking of me as an actual woman. They're going over their set, making a couple of changes to a new song that I already think is perfect. Will is beside me with Dad and Jimmy next to him around the table.

This is what I love.

Beers are scattered around the table, two each at a time. *Pissheads.*

I bite my lip, barely able to hide my excitement, even after what's just happened. The tour bus is like a home away from home. I don't care what anyone says; traveling by bus is cool—but not a public transport bus. I imagine that would suck.

"Excited, Tex?" Kitt asks, smirking at me from behind his beer.

The very tip of the glass bottle grazes his bottom lip, and I gulp.

I nod. "You know I love being on the road."

And this one is a four-month tour. I do wish Jimmy's wife were with us though. But I suppose I don't mind being the only girl. It's been that way before.

"Right," Coop says. "Same bet. Same stakes. Closest one to banging thirty girls wins."

Ah, the bet, the one that Cooper starts when he goes...well, anywhere. He really is a pig.

"Obviously, excluding Jimmy," Cooper adds. "Saskia would have his balls. And Kitt's out, too."

Seconded.

Kitt laughs. "And why am I out?"

If his question wasn't laced with humour, I'd want to throw something at him.

"Because you don't take the game seriously, man."

"Does anyone?"

Yes, some do—Will, Cooper, and Milo, to be exact. They know women throw themselves at them, and they lap it up. I actually think that's why Will hasn't settled down.

Coop swallows loudly. "Are you going to take part properly, Kitt?"

No. The answer is no.

Kitt turns his nose up. "No, thanks."

I immediately brighten, and Will tries not to smile. The temptation to tease me over my crush is probably very strong, like it was when he found out I liked Chad Michael Murray. I was thirteen at the time, and Will found great pleasure in making cardboard cutouts of Chad's face and changing my screen saver to shirtless pictures of him.

If Will starts to do that with Kitt, I'll throw him off the bus.

"Suit yourself, but one day, you're gonna get old, and it'll fall off. Or worse, you'll get a girlfriend, and you'll wish you'd screwed around more." Coop picks up his beer and takes a long swig.

"Oh, Jesus, you're going to be one of those sad, dirty old men, screwing your way through the local university in your sixties, aren't you?" I say.

"Texas," Dad scolds.

I roll my eyes.

"Damn right I am!" Coop replies.

Lovely.

"Come on, we all know Coop's future after the band," Kitt says.

Yeah, we do. He'll be exactly what I said, and he'll love every second of it.

"I can't wait," Cooper says, grinning all crazy-like.

I turn away, wishing there were at least one girl with me at this moment. Being around so much testosterone is sometimes like bashing my head against a wall, especially when the younger ones are all about women and not a lot else.

"Are you okay, Texas?" Dad asks. "You've gone quiet. It's unlike you."

"Oh, ha-ha. I'm fine. The guys are grossing me out—as usual."

"Am I doing the right thing, bringing you?"

"And the award for the dumbest question goes to…"

"I'm serious, Texas."

"So am I! I love it here, and you know it. The last place on earth I want to be stuck is at Jennifer's, so stop stressing. Sometimes, I just need a little break from the who's-sleeping-with-how-many talk."

Dad laughs. "We all need a break from Milo and Cooper from time to time."

"Kitt, too. And Jimmy. Actually, you're all pretty gross. Except you. You gave all that up when you impregnated Jennifer."

Milo laughs. "Right, so that woman leaving your hotel room before Christmas was a figment of my imagination, was she?"

Ew. No. I turn my nose up and hold my iffy belly. I so don't want to think about my dad with a woman, or I'll puke.

"Let's *please* not talk about it. Also, Dad, remember to be careful."

Dad shakes his head, discouraged, but he really has no room at all to say anything. We don't want another mistake landing on his doorstep.

"She was a hottie, too, Mark. High five," Milo says, holding his hand up.

Dad reaches out and high-fives him, and I've suddenly changed my mind about being here.

"Old man's still got it," Kitt adds for my benefit.

I glare at him. *Arsehole.*

"Yeah, I'll be in my room," I say, leaving them to it.

Of course I know my dad has sex, but I don't *ever* need to hear it. As long as he wraps it up and keeps them away from me, we're cool. Not that he would ever parade his conquests in front of me. I've only met one woman in my whole nineteen years, and that was by accident.

"Oh, Texy, come back," Cooper says.

"Not a chance in hell!" I shout back, rushing up the stairs, taking them two at a time.

That's not a conversation I'd ever hang around for. I would rather drink acid.

My room is tiny. It just fits a single bed, small wardrobe, and minuscule dressing table. But it's mine, and it's somewhere I can escape to when needed. This is absolutely one of those times. I grab my bag and pull out my iPad. We have Wi-Fi on the bus, but it's temperamental. I hope it's good enough for me to get through a couple of episodes of *The Walking Dead* on Netflix because I need a distraction.

Plus, I can pretend the zombies are the idiots out there, drinking and talking about my father having sex.

5

KITT
TUESDAY, MAY 5
DOVER, ENGLAND

We've just entered Dover, and we will soon be at the port.

The fucking bets have started to come in. So far, the first one to catch an object—preferably underwear—will get a grand from the others, and the first one to puke from drinking has to do the windmill at an after-party.

I guarantee both will be Coop.

We're sitting around the table on the lower deck, drinking yet more beer. I was buzzing before the beer, and now, I'm half-cut. It's stupidly early— 4:03 a.m.—but I'm not at all tired. No one besides the second driver has been to sleep yet, so it's only a matter of time before we crash hard.

Right now, we're hyped up on pre-tour excitement and booze.

Coop punches his arm in the air. "Right. Three grand to the first person to do two in one night."

Obviously, he's referring to having sex with women. It's a game we've played since the start. None of us have any trouble getting laid, but since the band formed, it's been ridiculous. And I mean that in a good way. No matter when I want sex, someone is always more than willing to give me what I need.

I'm living the fucking dream.

"Why three grand?" I ask.

We usually stick to an even thousand.

"Does it fucking matter? You're too much of a pussy to join in."

Lying back against the seat, I give him the middle finger. "I don't want to embarrass you."

Coop's pale eyes darken, and he barks out, "Fuck that! You're in. We'll see who pisses over who."

"You're all disgusting," Texas says before taking a sip of my beer while Mark's in the bathroom.

At nineteen, Tex has been legal to drink for over a year, but Mark seems to get stricter with her, the older she gets. And that has everything to do with the fact that she's now the same age Jennifer was when they had her. And Tex is touring with three guys around the age Mark was when he knocked Jennifer up.

"Help yourself," I mutter, taking the bottle out of her hand.

"You want in on the bet, too, Tex?" Cooper asks.

Fire courses through my veins. I want to bash his face against the table. Tex isn't that kind of girl, and she isn't someone we can mess around with. I feel this primal protectiveness when it comes to her. We owe Mark, and she's the most precious thing in his life.

And you think she's amazing. And since Christmas, you've been constantly hard around her.

"Watch it," Milo says, beating me to the punch.

Coop rolls his eyes, and the corner of his mouth turns into a cocky smirk. "She knows I'm kidding. You're still a virgin, right, Tex?"

Her eyes widen, and she looks to me and Milo for help. She turns her nose up. "Awesome. We're discussing this."

That isn't an admission or a denial. I want to know even though it shouldn't matter to me.

It doesn't matter to you.

Yes, it does. She had a boyfriend for almost a year, so she's probably not still a virgin. Until I know otherwise, I like to think no one's been there.

You want to be there.

"If you want to rectify that problem, we can go to my room," Coop says, wiggling his eyebrows.

This time, Milo doesn't beat me to it. I swing my arm and crack him around the back of his skull.

Fucking idiot.

Texas smiles at Cooper, smug to have me and Milo defending her against him. Deep down, I know Coop would never touch her. None of us would.

Except for me. I've already crossed that line. Actually, I jumped over it, feetfirst.

Now, I can't forget how she tasted, how soft she felt, and the way she reacted to my every touch. I can't stop myself from wanting to do more, to go further and bury myself deep inside her.

Fuck. I'm getting hard.

I sit forward and try to focus on something else.

Mark walks back into the room, and Coop's expression changes instantly. Gone is the hunger to wind her up because he knows he'll be beheaded by her dad. Mark is overprotective of Tex. I get it, and I'd be the same, but sometimes, I look at her, and I can see a strong woman fighting to get out and find her own way.

"Daddy got your tongue?" Milo teases, jabbing Coop in the ribs.

"Fuck off. Are we on for this bet or what? I understand if not. We know I'll win."

Coop is competitive and hates it when he loses. His parents spoiled him, growing up. His Christmas photos look

41

like they were taken in Toys "R" Us. They let him win every game, and now, he has to face off with me and Milo, people who won't let him win. It makes him hotheaded, which is always amusing.

"Not this again," Mark says, laughing and shaking his head.

Mark and Jimmy never join in, but Will does, sometimes beating his nephew's score, too. The man is an absolute legend, and I have a feeling that one or more of us will end up just like him. Cooper, for sure. Milo doesn't have any aversions to settling down. He just knows he doesn't want to do it while he's young and getting laid multiple times a day by multiple women. He left his high school girlfriend of three years when we started to get big. He's really not an arsehole. They'd both known their relationship was changing, and they had been growing apart. Sometimes, I think he believes he made a mistake, like when I catch him looking at a picture of Lexi, but he's adamant he did the best thing for them both.

"I'm betting on Milo," Texas says. "Dad, you have any money on you?"

We all laugh. Milo grins proudly.

Mark stares at her, dumbfounded. "No, Texas. You're not betting on this shit!"

"And, Tex, really? Don't you already have *all* the money?" I tease.

Mark is worth billions, and Jennifer is, too. As their only heir, Texas stands to be one of the wealthiest people in the UK.

She narrows those pretty hazel eyes and pouts. Her lips are full, pink, and I'm desperate to see them spread around my cock.

Don't think of that.

"You would think so, but *someone* doesn't want me to be spoiled." She gives her dad a pointed look.

"How ridiculous," Milo says with exaggerated surprise.

"It is. Like I'm going to be a total bitch whore from hell just because I have access to more money."

"It'll ruin you," Coop says.

She laughs. "It'd ruin you."

Cooper grins like a Cheshire Cat on coke. "Oh, I'd hope so."

I turn away from the idiots I consider family and look out the window. The sun is starting to break the darkness, but it's still hard to see much of anything. Here, I feel content. I love being on tour. The open road is filled with possibility and adventure.

Growing up, I never really went anywhere. After the deaths of my parents when I was a baby, I was raised by my nan and grandad. They're incredible people, and I owe them everything. Because money was tight, we didn't get to travel. They're both my biggest fans, and nothing makes me happier than when they're watching me at a concert. They will be at every one in England when we eventually get back.

"Kitt, you fucking listening, man?" Milo says.

I turn back and shrug just as Mark sits down, making Texas have to scoot closer to me. Her arm touches mine, and the effect it has on me is like she's just palmed my dick through my jeans.

"What?" I say.

"The bet. Are you in?" Coop asks.

"No, thanks."

Coop scoffs. "So, it's just me, Milo, and Will? That's hardly a contest."

"Screw you," Milo says.

It's a good thing Mark doesn't get pissy at bad language around Texas, or he'd be spending all his time chastising us. There are a few banned words—one, in particular, beginning with a C—that only gets brought out when we're in male-only company.

"Do you really think you'd win?" Texas asks when everyone else is busy arguing among themselves. She tilts her head, eyeing me with suspicion.

I cock my eyebrow. *What a stupid question.* "I know I'd win. Fortunately for them, I'm in this more for the music than the women."

It's the truth, too. I love women, don't get me wrong, but music was my first love, and it's all I've ever wanted to do. Women are just an added bonus. A very happy bonus.

She purses her lips. "They love the music, too. That's their main motivation."

I nod. "I know. But I'd rather work on the next song the morning after, and the boys would rather go again."

She narrows her eyes. "Nice. And you regularly have another go the next morning." Her face pales. "I've heard."

"I'm not a monk, Texas." With a smirk, I add, "Besides, it'd be selfish to keep a body like this to myself."

"Oh, so by having random, meaningless sex, you're pretty much providing a public service."

"Exactly. But one for beautiful women."

"You only hit on the beautiful ones?"

"Who doesn't? If you're looking for a one-night stand, you look for someone you're attracted to."

"Oh…so you've never hit on me because you think I'm ugly?"

Silence.

The whole fucking bus is now silent and watching. Even Mark is amused as he looks on at me while I'm digging my own grave. Saying Texas is ugly is like saying I'm bad in bed. She's the most beautiful thing I've ever seen, and I'm killer between the sheets.

"Not at all. The reason you've not been in my bed is because your dad would kill me."

"Correct," Mark says.

Texas scoffs. "Cocky much? The reason I've not been in your bed is because you're not my type."

I laugh, loving the banter between us. "Texas, baby, don't tell lies and embarrass yourself." I wink and flash her a smile that makes her try to kill me with one look. "Not your type," I mutter, shaking my head.

"Is it really so hard to believe that someone doesn't want to get in your pants?"

No, of course it isn't, but this is fun. When we're messing around like this, I feel a sense of peace I've never experienced before.

"Yes," I reply.

She scoffs. "You're a pig, Kitt."

"Texy, Texy, Texy, just admit, I'm your type, and we can move on."

She shoots daggers at me from her eyes. "I will as soon as you do."

"Fine. I'm totally my type."

Tex stares on at me with a blank expression.

"Oh, come on! Tex, you're *everyone's* type."

"See?" she says, throwing her hands up. "That wasn't so hard to admit, was it?"

"And you think I'm cocky…"

"Everyone thinks you're cocky."

I shrug. "Doesn't bother me."

"Helps, I suppose."

"With?"

"Being a rock star," she says, like it's the most obvious thing on the planet. "Anyway, how come you're really not taking Coop's bet?"

I lower my voice and say, "Honest answer, or cocky answer?"

"Know your audience, Kitt."

"Fine," I reply, smiling. "I kind of feel like…I'm not sure of the right word. Sleeping with women for a bet is…"

"Dickheadish," Texas offers.

"Yeah, I guess that's a good word for it. Just doesn't sit right with me anymore. If I'm sleeping with someone, it's because I want or need to get laid, not just because I want to have more than Cooper."

"Wow, you just went up in my estimation."

"Thanks. That doesn't mean I don't sleep with more women than him though."

"And back down you go again," she mutters sarcastically. "I should just be a lesbian. Men are horrible."

"But you don't like women."

Tex has one female friend, and that's it. Peyton is cool though, not like many of the materialistic girls Tex grew up with.

"Ugh, no, I don't. I can't deal with women-hating-on-women shit and who's skinnier or prettier. Maybe I'll just get cats."

"You're allergic to the fur."

"God, Kitt, can't you let me have anything?"

I grin. "I'll let you have something."

"Nice."

"Jäger bombs!" Milo shouts, interrupting everyone.

Texas slumps back in her seat, knowing she'll be allowed *one* shot—and that's only if she bats her eyelashes at her dad for long enough.

Last year, after performances and events, Mark started letting Tex stay out at after-parties with us because she'd turned eighteen. I saw a whole new side of her then. It's what started my downward spiral, which ended with me kissing her like I was dying while dry-fucking her against her bedroom door.

"Daddy," she says, going straight in with the puppy-dog eyes and everything.

"Oh, I don't think so, pumpkin."

Their argument goes on for two rounds until he finally gives in, and she joins us for a few shots.

I wouldn't be able to say no to her either.

And I have a feeling that's going to screw me over.

TEXAS
WEDNESDAY, MAY 6
CALAIS, FRANCE

I wake up after napping for about three hours, and we're in Calais. We still have a little over four hours until we arrive in Paris, but I'm happy to be here. It's early—well, it's 7 a.m., which is early for the entire lack of sleep I had yesterday. Or I should say, this morning.

Rubbing my eyes, I head downstairs to make about a hundred coffees. Kitt and Will are the only ones already up, and they're drinking beer around the table.

Yeah, beer.

"Seriously?" I say, reaching for the coffee.

"Ninety percent of you is caffeine," Kitt says.

"Ninety percent of you is alcohol," I reply. "What's your point?"

They both laugh, and Will cracks open another bottle. They're crazy. By midday, they're going to be dead.

"Have either of you two actually slept?" I ask, putting the beans in the machine and flicking it on.

Oh my God, I need caffeine so bad. My eyes are stinging because I'm so tired.

"Be more specific," Kitt replies, raising his eyebrow.

"Have either of you slept in the last twenty-four hours?"

"That would be a no."

And I see it. They're both glossy-eyed and smiling. They've gone past the point of being tired, but the slight shadows under their eyes tell all. Kitt's beautiful dark blue eyes are marred by a light redness, but he's still perfect.

Over the years, Will's eyes, which were almost black, have lost some of their pigment and lightened. He thinks it's cool and not at all due to the fact that he's aging. Today, they look dark because he's substituted sleep with beer.

As well as his eyes lightening, Will's black hair is starting to grey around the sides. Apparently, it's a sign of a well-lived life. I call it too much alcohol and too many women.

"You do know that you both have to be fully functioning humans today, right? We all have a club to be at tonight—which you need to remove my dad from early, Will. I'm cutting you off after that one, and you're switching to coffee."

"God, she sounds like my mum," Will teases. "And don't worry. I'll have him home nice and early, so you can do whatever it is you do when there's no adult supervision."

His eyes flick to Kitt for a brief second, and my heart stops. But he wouldn't dare say anything, and thankfully, it goes unnoticed by Kitt.

"I don't care if I sound like your mum. You two look like shit, and that will give a bad impression in the papers. We don't want that. And thank you, Will. I won't be too bad, promise."

"Don't promise that, love. In your late teens and twenties, you're supposed to be bad." He gives me a wink and takes another swig of beer.

Will looks a lot like Milo—dark hair, dark eyes—which is not surprising since the men in the Sterling family look similar.

Will is like a surrogate dad—only, he's much more laid-back about me having actual fun, and he is always telling my dad to lighten up and let me make my own mistakes. Will is into learning through experience, but if I ever needed him, I know he'd be there to pick up any pieces lying around.

"I'll have to remember that one for when I screw up and have to answer to my dad."

"Ouch, you'd throw me to the lions like that?"

"Damn straight. He's the one who has the power to stop my allowance."

Kitt laughs, knowing I don't really care about money. "Tex, he could cut you off right now, and you'd still live a very comfortable life. Probably in a castle."

He's right. My bank account is...well, seven figures. Unless I need new clothes, I think I spend about twenty pounds a week, and most of that is spent at Starbucks.

"I might invest in a castle, you know," I say. "Could be fun."

"You're so spoiled," he replies in jest.

I shrug. "You know I'll end up in a tiny flat. Less to clean."

"You won't have staff?"

"Piss off," I say, throwing a small bottle of ketchup at him. It was the closest thing to me.

Kitt catches it with no trouble and puts it down on the table. I watch the muscles in his arm flex and blush as Will lifts his eyebrow.

Bugger. He caught me perving.

Now that he knows, he's going to do things like his little look constantly. I'll really have to watch myself around him. It's one thing if he thinks I have a little crush on Kitt, but it'd be something else if he knew just how deeply my feelings ran.

"Sorry, Tex," Kitt says, laughing.

He's not sorry at all, of course, but I let it go. I'm not going to lie and say that I don't like the money because that's crazy, but it's not everything. Stuff doesn't make you happy.

The rest of the guys get up an hour later, and Jimmy cooks his famous bacon, cheese, and egg baguettes for everyone. Cooking on the bus is a little difficult since the kitchen is tiny, and with security there are eleven people, but we make it work. It's better than some of the service-station crap, that's for sure.

We arrive at the hotel, and Carl is waiting. He's also not a fan of the bus, so he flies wherever we go most of the time. Honestly, he and Jodie don't know how to have fun. Getting up close and personal to rock stars—my dad and the old ones excluded, of course—is the best.

Ted, head of my security, gets out in front of me and is immediately on high alert. He gets out his phone since he's been liaising with the temp security team, who will be here…soon, I guess. He's the head of Enigma and my security.

Security has been stepped up because there are seven people who will most likely scatter, especially to and from after-parties. I try to ignore the extra people as much as I can because dwelling on my lack of privacy is a little depressing sometimes. It helps that Ted has been with me and Dad since I was nine, so he's like family.

Hank looks after Filthy Sound, and I don't think I've ever seen a bigger man in my life. He has a buzz cut, no neck, and his muscles have muscles. If I didn't know him, I'd be terrified.

Carl gets us checked in, and we're shown to our suites. Ted follows me until I'm in my room, and then he goes to his next door.

My suite is massive, as usual. I'm the only one staying in here, and I have a large open-plan kitchen and living area and two bedrooms. *Why do I need two bedrooms?* When booking accommodation, I swear, the label just go with what they think I should have rather than what I actually need.

There's a loud bang on my door. I put my bag down on the bed and walk over to the door. Looking through the peephole, I see it's Kitt.

Damn, I bet I look a mess. I fluff my hair up, but there's no time for anything else.

I open the door and see his shocked expression. "What's wrong?"

"Tex, my room is bigger than my flat."

Bless, it's his first time with this level of treatment.

His eyes are wide, and I'm kind of surprised that he's surprised. Filthy Sound signed a *very* good deal with the label, and Enigma is supporting them. Obviously, they weren't going to be booked into a hostel.

"Yep. Get used to it, rock star."

"The mini bar, which isn't all that *mini*, is fully stocked, and I can have whatever I want... for *free*."

He's so overwhelmed. I love it.

I nod. "Yes."

He scratches his jaw. "Think I can eat and drink it *all*?" He sounds naughty, and it takes great effort on my part not to laugh.

"Er, that's what you're supposed to do. I used to have contests with Dad, Will, and Jimmy to see who could finish theirs first. But you have to leave a note, or housekeeping will stock it right back up, and you'll have to start again."

"I can have it all?"

"Kitt, you're expected to have it all. You know, you have to stop this uncertainty. It's very un-rock star of you."

He grins, and it's the most adorable thing I've ever seen.

Oh, wow, he really thought he'd be in trouble for racking up a bill on the room. I doubt anyone even looks at the bill. It's just paid because the label make a killing off of Enigma and they want to keep everyone happy.

Well, actually, my dad used to look at mine to see if I'd consumed any alcohol, so I would go to a shop and buy it. Thankfully, he's eased off that now.

Kitt leans against the doorframe, and his posture changes drastically. Gone is the shy uncertainty from a few minutes ago, and the old him is now back, smirking.

"So, can I come in? Or are you busy?"

I step aside. "Not busy. I was just about to get started on the chocolate."

"Do you have the mini bar bet on?"

"We've not said, but you can never be too careful. It takes me longer to finish it, so it's good for me to get a head start. Want to help?"

I've let him in again. He unknowingly hurt me earlier with the women talk. I should be trying to maintain some sort of distance. Instead, I'm inviting him in to share my food and drink. I can't help myself, and it's kind of annoying.

He's annoying.

And beautiful.

And I'm in love with him.

You need help!

"Want to grab some drinks, and I'll get the junk food?" I say. "We have to meet with Carl at seven p.m. though, and after that, you guys are on the radio. You can't be drunk for that."

"Noted. Five beers, max."

Five? I'd be on the floor after three.

I give him a smile. At least there are only six beers here, so all I need to do is drink two. "I'm cutting you off at three," I say. "Jodie will not be happy if I let you get drunk before the interview."

"And you're her assistant manager now?"

"No, I'm just helping. I'm good at organising your lazy arses."

"You are."

He steps into my personal space – and I would gladly share more of it with him in bed, too. His eyes are serious, and they're already dragging truths out of me.

"But do you enjoy it, Tex?"

I shrug. "I guess I do. I'm good at it, and it's nice to feel useful while I'm here. When I was in full-time education, I didn't feel like a freeloader. Now, I'm an adult and trying to work out what the hell it is I want to do with my life. I'd feel like a bum if I wasn't contributing."

Kitt frowns. He wants to tell me I shouldn't feel that way, but he can't because it's true. There are plenty of people who would be happy to live off their daddy's money forever. I'm not one of them. I mean, I already have a lot of it, but that doesn't mean I don't want to earn my own or do something more than be his daughter to deserve it.

"You know I'm right. Please do what I say, so I don't feel like the early Jennifer."

My mother followed Enigma around, so she could sleep with my dad and get drunk off his money.

I won't be a groupie. I won't be a groupie.

Obviously, I'm not talking about my dad here because *vom*, but you know what I mean.

"You're nothing like her. You could never do what she did."

"You know, I'm not even angry about her leaving me. Well, I am, but I can understand her being too young and not ready, but not once has she apologised or even tried to talk to me about it. Who does that? I'd be totally happy if she just acknowledged our past."

"She's probably scared to. I can't imagine it's something she's proud of."

"I hope not. I'm her daughter though. Shouldn't she love me more than she wants to save face?"

He shrugs and takes a swig of beer. I watch his lips circle the bottle.

Stop perving. You can't do it subtly.

I force myself to look away because I really am horrible at *admiring* Kitt's form without staring.

"Why don't you bring it up to her?"

Oh no. No, no. "That's never going to happen. I think I would rather chop off a limb with a rusty saw. I've *never* done touchy-feely with Jennifer, and we don't talk. She's not someone I can talk to, and I wouldn't feel comfortable opening up about how she made me feel over the years. Besides, it's over now. I'm all grown-up."

"It's not over. You might be older now, but it's not something that'll disappear. It's a conversation you should have with her."

"Maybe."

He smirks. "You're not going to, are you?"

"Not unless hell freezes over."

"Chicken."

I shove his shoulder in good spirit. "Bugger off!"

"Only trying to help. You only get one mum, Tex."

Cringing inwardly, I put my beer down and twist to face him. "I'm sorry. That was insensitive of me."

"No, it's okay. It was a long time ago, and I'm all right."

"Yeah, but—"

"Don't. Neither of us has had nearly enough alcohol for this conversation. You meant nothing by it, and neither did I. My parents died, and growing up without them was hard, but I have the best grandparents. I didn't miss out, and I'm not messed up, so please don't stress. Although, if you're feeling bad, I know one way you can make it up to me."

I lift my eyebrow, waiting, and Kitt grins. His eyes are lit with mischief.

"You could take your top off. No one is unhappy after seeing tits."

"And here I was, thinking we were having a deep and meaningful conversation."

"There's nothing shallow or meaningless about your breasts."

Yep, moment over. It was nice while it lasted.

I don't know how he can change between Serious Kitt and Jokey-Slutty Kitt in a nanosecond. And he only does it around me—that I've noticed anyway. I don't tend to watch him when he's flirting with other women because it makes me feel sick.

"Yeah, thanks. Drink your beer, and then we should get Milo and Cooper before the meeting." My voice is icy, and although I want to be better at concealing how I feel, I don't really care this time.

"What's up your arse?" he asks. "It was only a joke."

"Why is everything a joke to you?"

Oh my God, Texas, shut the fuck up! What are you doing? Christ, sometimes, you have no filter between your brain and mouth.

I really don't want to do this with Kitt.

It's okay. Keep calm, and laugh it off. You can do this. Bring it back to a normal conversation. Stay cool.

He rears back in shock, and his eyebrows flick up. "I don't think everything is a joke. What just happened, Texas? One minute, you're cool, and the next, you're acting like my pissed off wife!"

Oh, he did not just joke about that.

I grit my teeth as my body heats with anger.

Bastard!

"I am not acting like your bloody wife! You're not even planning on getting married, idiot. You just want to shag your way through all the women."

So, apparently, you can't do cool. Nice one.

"I have no idea what my fucking future holds, but of course, I don't want a fucking wife yet! What the fuck does it matter to you anyway?"

Oh God, he's dropping F-bombs all over the place. I've really done a fabulous job at messing this up.

He slams the bottle down on the table, and beer rushes out the top and spills over the side. "Fuck, Tex!"

I'm stunned into silence. His breathing is heavy, and he looks half-mad and half-confused. We stare at each other, neither of us knowing exactly how we got here or what to do next. Kitt's eyes are intense, and I feel naked under their scrutiny.

I don't know if he's angry still or if he wants to kiss me. He's flitting through so many emotions so quickly that I can't figure him out.

Taking a deep breath, he shoves his hands through his hair, closes his eyes, and groans, like he's been worn down. "I don't want to do this with you. Not you," he grumbles.

"Neither do I. We shouldn't argue," I whisper.

We shouldn't argue because we have no reason to. But we often find ourselves like this. It's stupid.

If we're nothing and he only wants us to be friends, then why does it feel like more to me?

I shouldn't build dreams around a fantasy. At the moment I don't know if he wants anything more.

Kitt places his hand over mine, and I take in a sharp breath. I feel alive every time his skin touches mine. It's an intense charge that heats my whole body and makes me want us to be more. So, so much more.

"I'm sorry, Tex. Can we forget it?"

Like we forgot the kiss, like we forget every look, every fight.

Our whole relationship feels like one big cover-up. Either that, or he's being straight up and honest, and I'm the delusional one reading more into it.

At this point, I have no idea. I've spent such a long time thinking Kitt feels something for me, I've questioned and second-guessed his actions and words a million times over, and I've obsessed about every situation so much that I don't know what to think anymore.

Instead of saying everything I want to say and everything I *should* say, I take the coward's way out. "I'm sorry, too, and it's forgotten."

Kitt gives me the briefest smile, and then he picks up his beer again. The bottle is wet, but it's stopped foaming now, so he takes a long swig. He's tense still, and I don't know if he's forgotten it or what, but he's not back to normal.

Has he finally realised that some things can't be easily forgotten? Or am I reading too much into this again?

I definitely should crack open something stronger.

After a few drinks and a lot of junk food, we head down to one of the meeting rooms Carl booked for the afternoon, so we can run through the next few days. My calendar is full of notes, so I know what they need to be doing at every second of the tour.

Jodie and Carl have given me an opportunity to step up, and I'm determined to make it work. I'll be the only one consistently with the bands through the whole tour, so it's important I don't mess this up.

After the meeting that Kitt, Milo, and Cooper couldn't wait to leave and radio engagement, we head outside, so Hank and Ted can drive us to one of the local clubs. Dad is taking the temps. He always has Ted go with me because he trusts him the most.

Dad, Jimmy, and Will decided to go elsewhere in the end, which just means they want to behave like rock stars but don't want to do it in front of me. As long as I don't see a picture of my dad pawing at some girl tomorrow, I'm cool. Plus, it means I can enjoy myself straight off.

Me and Filthy Sound are the back of the car as it whizzes along the pretty streets of Paris. Coop is trying to make me feel uncomfortable by staring at me. It's an impossible task now. I know him too well.

I have on a short black dress, which is pretty plain but shows off my legs. Those bad boys have gotten me into a lot of places I shouldn't have been in before.

Kitt, Milo, and Cooper are dressed casually, and even if there's a dress code, we won't be refused—mainly because the manager of the club has invited us. Filthy Sound being photographed outside the club is good advertising for them.

Cooper turns to us. "Ready to get fucked up?"

After today, I have never been more ready.

KITT
WEDNESDAY, MAY 6
PARIS, FRANCE

There is no denying that I'm drawn to Texas, but I sure as hell can fight it.

I owe it to Mark to fight it.

She seems to unknowingly make it as fucking difficult for me as possible. Every time she looks at me, I remember the way she looked at me that night. Every time she gets pissed off and raises her voice, I want to shut her up with my mouth. Every time I hear her voice, I hear her moaning my name.

And she's wearing a dress tonight.

The woman is the devil. She's testing my strength to its breaking point, and I don't know how much longer I can hold off.

"I'm so ready to get off my face," she says, swatting at Coop's hand lying on her knee.

He grins at her. I don't need to intervene because she's got this covered. But it does piss me off.

Concentrate on all the women you can have tonight, not on the one you can't.

France is full of beauties, and there will be many, many models at this club.

You do like models.

"Glad to hear it because we're not going back to the hotel until sunrise," Milo says.

"We're here," Coop says, pulling on the back of the driver's headrest. "Are you two insisting on coming with?" he asks Ted and Hank.

He knows the answer. Where Tex goes, Ted goes, and Hank has his orders, too. It's the smart thing to do, but having someone there almost all the time we go outside takes some getting used to.

We're not used to it yet, but Tex never bats an eyelid.

With humour in his eyes, Hank looks at Coop in the mirror. "What do you think, hotshot?"

"Fine, but stay back. You guys need to give the master space to work."

Milo snorts. "Master of what? Being a complete knobhead?"

"Fuck off. You're jealous because you know I'll score first."

"Keep dreaming, lads. The first one is mine," I say, hopping over Milo and opening the back door.

Hank and Ted are quick to get out now that the door is open. For blokes as big as they are, they can shift it fucking fast.

"Suppose you're my shadow tonight?" Tex says to Ted.

"Unless you end up somewhere private, and I can wait outside, yes."

She links her arm with his, which makes his job easier. "Yeah, yeah, I know the drill."

The only time Ted will leave her is if she's at a private after-party or event. I want them both to leave us alone tonight, so we can be normal, but it won't happen. We don't get normal anymore. It's a small price to pay, but it's still a price.

We walk to the entrance, and the bouncer nods us through on sight.

"Fuck yeah!" Coop says, raising his hands. "Let the shagging begin." He thrusts his pelvis and ducks inside the club.

"You must be so proud to share a band with him," Tex says, laughing, as Coop runs ahead.

"We felt sorry for him," Milo replies.

We turn the corner, and fuck, the club is insane. Everything is blood red besides golden cages hanging from the ceiling.

Cooper is in his element as girls in bikinis dance in the cages. He's looking up and, I think, praying.

"Grab a table. I'll get drinks," I tell Milo and Tex.

Coop wanders off, following a beautiful blonde in killer heels. He loves this.

I head to the bar, keeping one eye on where they go. The lighting in here is intentionally dark, like the walls, giving a sexy and exclusive vibe. Only the golden cages are bright to draw your eye to what's happening up there, but people seem more interested in their drinks than the dancing above their heads.

Along the bar is another stunning blonde who Coop will be after if I'm not quick. She's exactly what I need on a night where a certain brunette is dressed to have men falling at her feet. I've been there and done that, and it's not something I can repeat even if it makes my balls ache like fuck.

I step next to her and offer a smile. I don't know who she is, but she must be *someone* if she's in here. The place is apparently full of models most nights, and judging by the look of this girl, she is one of them.

"*Bonjour*," I rasp.

She giggles, and I know I'm in.

"*Bonjour*. That wasn't bad for a Brit." Her French accent makes the English language sexy.

"Thank you very much."

"You're Kitt Daniels."

I flash her a smile and bump my side on the bar, so I'm facing her. She mirrors my action.

Don't look at her cleavage before you get her a drink. You'll look like a pervert.

"I am."

"I'm Angèle."

I take her hand and place a kiss on her wrist. "Pleasure. Can I buy you a drink, Angèle?"

She leans forward and places her hand on my chest. Her breasts press against my body, and my cock springs to life. "I would love a glass of champagne."

I order our drinks with Angèle attached to my side, and I'm told someone will bring them over because I couldn't possibly carry five glasses anymore. To be fair, I didn't even need to come to the bar. Servers are everywhere.

I lead Angèle to our table, and we're met by a frosty Texas. Milo is off dancing with someone already, and I can no longer see Cooper, so God knows where he followed that girl.

Angèle introduces herself to Tex, and while she's polite, I can tell she doesn't like someone else coming to our table straight off. *Or coming to our table with me?*

"I love it," Tex replies in answer to Angèle asking if we're enjoying Paris so far.

I get the feeling she added, *Until you came along*, in her head.

I look at them sitting next to each other, and all of a sudden, Angèle's beauty is questionable. She's pretty, don't get me wrong, but Texas is out of this world.

What the hell are you doing?

I rub a building ache between my eyes. I can't want her. *Why do we want what we can't have?*

I force a conversation with them both, and the whole time, Tex is avoiding eye contact with me. But Milo rescues me minutes later. Angèle is making Texas uncomfortable, and I don't like it. Milo sits on the chair next to Angèle, so while he's talking to her, I slip over to the one next to Tex.

I instantly relax. *This is where I'm supposed to be.*
Fuck it!

Tex looks over at me. She looks hurt, and I want to go up and throw myself from one of those cages. It's like a knife to my chest.

I'm sorry. You have to forgive me.
Jesus, what are we doing here?

It's like we're opposite ends of magnets. I can't help it. I need to be near her. Nothing feels more right than when we're together. Since Christmas, something has drastically changed even if neither of us will admit it aloud.

"Are we getting drunk tonight?" I ask, slinging my arm over her chair. It's a territorial move as well as one to show Angèle that she should absolutely keep flirting with Milo because I made a big mistake. This is where I need to be.

"We?" Texas wants me to clarify. In her mind, I'm already shagging Angèle.

I lean a fraction closer. "Me and you, Tex." *Always.*

There's a glimmer of forgiveness when her lips turn up into a beautiful little smile that lights up her eyes.

You. Are. Perfect.
And you are going to hell, Daniels.

"I can be corrupted."

Oh, I hope so.

The server arrives with another tray, and I pass a drink to Texas. "To us getting drunk," I say.

"To not being able to stand later." She necks the drink and looks longingly at the empty glass, wanting another.

That's my girl.
My girl?

Two hours later and it's just me and Tex around the table. She looks up and her eyes bulge. "Cooper is in a cage!"

Milo has left the club with two girls—I've never seen anyone smile so much—and Cooper is apparently in a cage.

I swing my head up, and sure enough, he's being straddled by a girl in a cage. The dancers are gone now, so everyone else is allowed up there to dance.

I won't be going.

Coop's shirt is undone, and his arms are stretched out to either side as he holds on to the bars. The blonde is going for it, rubbing her arse in his crotch and giving the dancers a run for their money.

Tex shakes her head. "How can she dance so sexily and elegantly in a swinging cage? I can't even walk properly on a sloped path."

Laughing, I chuck my arm over her chair. "I'd make a dick of myself up there, too."

A slow grin spreads across her lips. "Want to come up with me?"

"Nope." I take a swig of my beer.

"Come on. This club is invite-only, so there won't be people taking pictures. Besides, no one is really looking up there."

"You did."

"Because I saw Cooper going up there. I dare you, Daniels."

Maybe I will be going.

I stand up and see panic in her eyes. She didn't think I'd go through with it. I love our bets, and I never back down.

She gets up and keeps her back straight to appear confident, but her breath wavers with nerves.

Angèle comes over from her table of friends and stops beside us. "Are you dancing, Kitt?"

Tex's face falls, and she goes to sit down. Without thinking, I step closer to Tex, my hand circles her wrist, and I haul her into my body. I don't want to dance with Angèle. I want Texas.

I always fucking want Texas.

"We are," I say, giving Angèle a polite smile so that she knows me and her isn't happening.

She looks at Texas and back to me. Her eyebrow quirks, like she doesn't think Tex is good enough, and then she walks off.

I grit my teeth. Now, I don't give a shit about what people think of me, but there is no one better than the girl leaning on my chest, looking up at me.

"Ready?" I ask.

Instead of responding, she stares, and it silences the whole room. There is no noise and no people. Just me and her.

"Take me then," she whispers.

I groan. Fuck, I would love to hear her moan that in bed. Doesn't even have to be in bed. Anywhere. Literally.

I snake my hands around to the small of her back and tug her flush against my chest. "Are you sure?"

Her lips part, and I want to dive in. I'm unimaginably hard, and all I can think about is getting my mouth on hers. Last time was intoxicating. This time would be explosive. I can feel it.

Laughing, I twist her around and walk us toward the stairs. She doesn't move far ahead in front of me. We're still touching, and although it's awkward, I'm getting off on the fact that my dick keeps grazing her back. And I get the impression that it's intentional.

Little tease.

I want to show her what I do with women once they finish playing that game.

Two of the eight cages are empty, so we head for the one in the corner. It's more private. I shouldn't even be doing this, so privacy here is key.

Texas grips the sidebars and tentatively steps into the cage. Fuck knows how they get away with health and safety here because there's about a foot gap between the edge of the walkway and the cage.

It swings gently as she walks inside, but the whole thing is held to the ceiling tight, so it's not too bad. I don't think it would swing past five or six inches either way.

She turns and smirks. "Your turn."

I'm not backing out. I just needed a minute because my self-control is almost out the window. She looks entirely too beautiful in there. Without taking my eyes off her, I grab a bar with one hand and step inside before closing the door behind me. The cage sways a little more but not enough to make us stumble.

"Now that you have me in here, what are you going to do with me?" I ask.

Her eyes burn a hole in me. In the dim light, they look browner.

Silently, she raises her arms and holds on above her head. Stretched out, her breasts are pushed up and straining against the material of her dress.

Fuck. Me.

She watches my reaction as she starts to sway to the music.

I suck in a breath. I'm so jacked up that I could come in my fucking jeans. I have to grip on to the bars on each side of the cage to stop me from grabbing her. Letting go, she wraps her arms around my neck, and the second her chest touches mine, I groan.

"Shit," I hiss as she arches herself into me. I take one hand off and wrap it around her back, cementing her to my body.

"Kitt," she whispers, letting her head drop on my shoulder.

I feel like a fucking volcano ready to erupt. I'm so horny that if she's not careful, I'm going to fuck her in this cage. Consequences be damned.

Her head lifts, and her lips are so close, too close.

Fuck it!

I dip my head and mould my mouth to hers. She moans and presses her body into mine. I trail my hand lower and cover her arse, pulling her onto my dick.

I'm instantly on edge, and from the way her tongue dives into my mouth, I can tell she is, too. Our kiss is hungry and urgent. It's a battle, and right now, I don't care who fucking wins because the way she's grinding herself on me is making me lose my mind.

"Oh God, Kitt," she murmurs into my mouth.

I growl. I'm wound so tight that my balls ache, and all I can think about is the end goal.

She's attacking every one of my senses simultaneously. I've never been this desperate to come before. I grip her tight, sinking my nails into her hips, and I pull her into me harder while I devour her mouth. Her fingernails cut into my scalp, and she bites down on my lip.

She's coming.

Fuck. So am I.

I moan long and deep as my body shudders. My fist clenches a bar so hard that it feels like it's going to snap. If I wasn't holding on, I'd collapse.

Texas breaks the kiss, but she doesn't move away.

Finally letting go of the side, I wrap my arms around her. Neither of us speaks, but we hold each other, trying to catch our breaths.

We fucked up. Again.

But I can't regret it.

KITT
THURSDAY, MAY 7
PARIS, FRANCE

I can't get my mind off the cage last night. It was singularly the most erotic and sexiest thing that has ever happened to me, and I didn't even enter Texas. I came harder than I'd thought was fucking possible and nearly passed out.

A replay of that night is on a loop in my head. I keep seeing her grinding herself into me. I can still taste the champagne on her tongue and feel the softness of her lips. When I wash my hair, I feel the sting from the tiny half-moons she cut into my scalp. I want to do it again. I want her pressing herself against my cock. I want to do it without the clothes.

Filthy Sound have just finished our last appearance of the day on another radio show. Now, we're heading back to the hotel for a chilled night. Well, I am. Coop and Milo are meeting up with two models they met at the club.

I'd love to take Texas back to that cage, but she's been avoiding me all day. She woke Milo up and told him to make sure Coop and I were awake and ready to go.

Apparently, Texas isn't feeling well.

It's bullshit.

She's not ill. She's embarrassed about us getting each other off in a public place.

It's a hot day in Paris today, which means Cooper is perving out the window and scoring women on a scale of *I'd shag them once* to *I'd do them all week long*. Milo's mind is off somewhere else, and he keeps tapping on his phone every five seconds.

It's probably a girl. It's probably his ex, Lexi.

We get back to the hotel, and Hank follows us up to our floor. Milo and Cooper are going to shower, change, and go straight back out. I hesitate outside Tex's door. She won't want to see me; she's made that clear, but I can't leave things like this.

I miss her.

Before I can pussy out, I reach up and rap on her door.

She opens the door just as I'm about to give up. Her cheeks are pink, and she's having a hard time looking me in the eyes.

"Hi," she says.

"Hey. Are you okay? Milo said you're unwell."

We both know the truth.

"Um, I'm okay now. Thanks." Her fingertips are turning white where she's gripping the edge of the door so hard.

I breathe heavily through my nose and grit my teeth. She's lying to me, and I can't stand it.

"Texas," I seethe.

"What?" Her posture turns defensive, and she takes a small step back.

"I'd rather you tell me not to touch you ever again than you lie to me. Ignoring me isn't an option."

"All we do is ignore."

She's right. Since Christmas, before even, so many things have happened between us, and I'm not talking about the physical stuff. There's been the sexual tension, the looks, the flirting, the way we can be in complete silence and it's still the most comfortable I've felt, and the way we feel so right.

But we have to ignore this.

"Look, I'm sorry about last night. We both got carried away, and I shouldn't have let it go that far."

Her head tilts, and she looks at me like I've just grown another head.

"You know what? I'm sorry, too, Kitt. You're right. It was a mistake, and it won't happen again."

She can't promise that. We should be able to, but we both know if we're in that situation again, she'll be moaning my name as she comes.

"Can I come in? I hate it when we're not okay."

"Okay."

I walk into her suite, and she slams the door shut.

I'm not really sure what to do now. I'm clearly not good at this. So, I do all I know. "Coop's very put out because the girls made each other come faster than he could."

She laughs. "Good. He needed to be taken down a peg or two—or seven. His ego has been getting out of hand."

I made you come in minutes—without touching you.

The thought makes me harden.

"I think that did it. Although he's out with someone else right now."

"One day, he's going to catch something."

"He's probably already had everything."

The fire in her eyes is back, and she laughs. "Probably. Want to drink all the beer? It's been restocked. I forgot to leave the note."

"Sounds good to me."

It sounds perfect actually.

She walks past me to the fridge and bends over.

Shit. Her arse is incredible. And those legs...

The memory of my hand on that arse, yanking her closer, as she ground against me invades my brain. I can still feel the desperation as we both battled to get off as soon as possible.

Her hand flashes by my face, far too close.

I look over and frown. "What?"

She hands me a drink and wiggles her fingers toward me. "I was talking, and you were off in whatever land you were in."

The land where her mouth was glued to mine, and she was clawing at me.

"Sorry," I say.

Her lips purse, and I want to launch myself at her.

"What did you say?" I ask, putting down my drink.

"I just offered you a blow job, but don't worry about it."

Oh God, don't say that.

"I would've heard that if I were on Mars, Tex, but please feel free."

Her hands cover mine as I go to the belt on my jeans.

Chuckling, I pick up my beer and take a swig. "You can't offer something you're not willing to go through with."

Rolling her eyes, she pulls my hand away from my now straining erection. If she noticed it, she's not letting on.

"It was a joke, Kitt."

"Blowies are no joke."

"I'll remember that for next time."

I arch my eyebrow. "Next time?"

"You know what I mean."

I shake my head, half to tell her that I don't know and half to clear the filthy thoughts swirling around in my head.

She. Is. Off-limits.

We should've gone out with the guys. Being in a group is safer. Right now, I feel like an alcoholic in a brewery.

"So, the BJ is a no-go then?" I ask, smirking down at her as we walk to the sofa.

I can't help myself.

She smiles over her shoulder. "Sorry, I'm not giving it up for nothing."

"Hey, I wouldn't come and then leave you hanging. I'd repay the favour."

I would *love* to repay the favour. Fuck, I'm rock solid, and it's becoming too uncomfortable. I want to lay her down and trace my tongue over every inch of her body. I want to taste her before I bury myself inside.

Enough. You need to focus on being her friend and forget whatever physical attraction you have with her. She's just a girl. There are plenty of those for you in every city in every country.

We sit down, far too close for our not-so-innocent friendship. She gently thumps me on the arm and then traces the dragon wrapped around my bicep. She's so easily distracted.

"I want a tattoo," she says.

"Yeah? You're going to mark that virgin skin?"

"I don't know what I want or where I want it, but I like them. And it's been a while since I realised I have something virgin."

"Ah, the dickhead ex."

Her ex was an absolute twat of a man. He was boring and soft as shit. If he called her honey one more time, I would've punched him.

"There was nothing wrong with him."

"Oh, please. With people like him, you know *exactly* what your future would be like. You don't fit that mould. You'd go insane."

She shrugs one shoulder and then shuffles back and twists, so she can kick her feet up onto my legs. "I know. We weren't compatible at all, but that doesn't mean there was anything wrong with him. He was happy to be still, and he was content with what he had, whereas I need to keep moving and find something new."

"Still is dull."

"For people like us, it is." She leans in closer, and her legs press into my crotch.

Is she doing it on purpose or what?

I lick my dry lips and grip the beer bottle with two hands.

You can't touch her again.

Tex puts on a movie, and we watch it, hyperaware of each other and not really paying attention to the screen. I feel like I'm being pulled toward her, like a greater force is at work.

Keep your fucking hands to yourself.

The movie is wrapping up.

Tex lays her head back and tilts it in my direction. "Do you ever wonder what your life would have been like if something major had or hadn't happened? I occasionally wonder where I'd be if Jennifer had taken me with her."

"Where's that?"

"Ugh. I would've grown up as her mini me. She would've dressed me in kid versions of her outfits and done mother-daughter photo shoots to sell her own line of clothes. There was talk about it, but I think she realised she can't design shit."

"I often think about my parents. I was too young to remember them, but I sometimes wonder if I'd be here now. My grandad is the rocker in the family. If I wasn't raised in his house, I might be somewhere completely different."

"I'm glad you're here," she whispers.

"Yeah, me, too."

I can't help it. She's looking at me like she wants me to kiss her, and there is nothing else in this world I'd rather do right now. I dip my head, and her lips part. She wants this as much as I do. My heart is hammering harder, the closer I get.

Fuck everything.

I'm going to kiss her, but before I get close, her door swings open and slams back on itself. *I'm so fucking glad Milo has a spare key...* Texas and I jump and look over the back of the sofa. Cooper struts in without paying attention, but Milo sees us.

"Just in time," Milo says, lifting his eyebrow.

I lean away slightly. "We were just discussing Cooper's threesome fail." *About two hours ago. Believe me, Milo.*

He's looking too hard, and I'm afraid the truth is obvious.

I can't lie to myself anymore, so how can I fool a guy who knows me better than anyone else?

Cooper is the joker, and Milo, I can talk to. I've never discussed Tex with him, and he doesn't know about our first kiss or last night, but something tells me that I might have to talk to him soon.

"It wasn't a fucking fail, dickheads. I'm grabbing a Jack, Tex."

She waves the back of her hand at him. "You sleep with some models then?"

Milo grins. "Of course. What've you boring wankers been doing?" he asks. His question sounds innocent, but it's laced with accusation.

"Movie and beer." I reply.

"Mmhmm. Mind if we join?" Milo looks at me with judgment in his dark eyes.

Tex shrugs a shoulder but still doesn't move her legs. The way Milo is watching me, he might as well have me on the other side of a table, shining a light in my eyes. His hard what-the-fuck-are-you-playing-at look is demanding a thousand answers to a thousand questions that I don't even want to think about.

I don't know what I'm doing.

I've never really wanted someone before. Tex is the first, and it's fucking with my head.

Awkwardly, I sit up a little straighter, and she drops her legs. The bastard's made me self-conscious of my *friendship* with Texas.

You know it's gone further than that.

Not even Mark would've batted an eyelid at how we were sitting. It wasn't different to how we'd sat a thousand times before, but everything is different now.

"You two are still sober. How is that possible?" Texas asks, suspiciously eyeing them.

She's right. Cooper doesn't believe in being sober ever, and Milo always gets shitfaced when he's out.

Milo grins. "We peaked early. Then, we got bored."

By that, he means, they each slept with a model and got their fill, and now, they're ready to chill with more alcohol.

I shake my head. "No stamina. I feel sorry for those women."

"Hey, she came like a fucking train," Cooper says before swigging from the bottle.

"Cooper, for fuck's sake!" Texas shouts, pointlessly launching a cushion at his head. "I don't want to catch your STD when I drink JD!"

"I'm clean, sweet cheeks. Wanna try?"

"What? No, I really don't want to try to catch chlamydia from you."

"Clean," he replies slowly, frowning at her. "You can't be spreading that shit around."

"But you can spread that shit around?" she hits back, nodding toward his dick.

He runs his hand over his hair, but I can't be bothered to rip him for it. "I'm a very giving person, Texas. I like to share."

"I'm sure they appreciate it," she replies sarcastically.

Cooper grabs his dick through his jeans. "Anyone would."

"I hate boys."

Oh, she does not.

I raise my eyebrow, and she narrows her hazel eyes.

Liar, I mouth while the other two are pouring different drinks.

She bites her lip, and her cheeks redden.

Fuck.

I'm done for.

9

**TEXAS
THURSDAY, MAY 7
PARIS, FRANCE**

Milo and Cooper duck out after two drinks because they're lightweights. I'm flat-out exhausted, and it's closing in on one a.m., but I don't want to sleep. And Kitt doesn't seem to want to leave yet either.

Things are good right now, and I want it to last. I can pretend.

"Are you going to sightsee tomorrow?" he asks.

"I want to, but I won't have time."

"Should've come with us today. We could've hit up the Tower after."

My mind is instantly back in the cage, and my body is on fire. All day, I've been trying to ignore what happened.

"Should've," I mutter. *Please, let's change the subject!*

"If you hadn't been hiding out in your room all day…"

"I wasn't hiding."

"Really? So, you weren't avoiding me because of the cage?"

Oh, great! This he talks about! Everything else is pushed away, but giving me the most intense orgasm of my life is the one thing he doesn't want to paper over.

Perfect.

Cringing in embarrassment, I look away. I might want him to leave this room, but my body doesn't. The mere thought of him getting me off has me breaking out in a sweat.

"No." My bloody voice betrays me. I sound like a terrified chipmunk.

Kitt leans in, and it frazzles my mind. The smell of his cologne wraps around me.

"You're sure? I don't want awkwardness between us, Tex. I'm sorry if I made it that way."

That sounds an awful lot like, *It won't happen again.* My heart is as heavy as lead.

It shouldn't happen again. I can't handle being rejected by him over and over.

"I don't want that either. Can we forget it? I thought we'd forgotten it." Might as well get in there first, I suppose, while I have an ounce of dignity left.

"Right," he replies. "Okay. Good."

We sit inches apart, watching each other. The atmosphere could be cut with a knife, and even I'm not sure if it's awkward or sexual.

I chew on my lip. God, I hate this back and forth.

Do something. You can't leave it like this.

He sighs. "I don't want to do this tense shit. Would you like another drink?"

I dip my head, refusing eye contact. "No, thanks. My tummy is still iffy from last night. I can't do another drop."

He laughs. "You did have a fair bit. I had to carry you back."

Kitt carried me? I don't remember much after the cage because I upped my alcohol intake, but I assumed Ted would've brought me back to my room.

"You did?"

"Er, yeah. I already had you when I met Ted, so"—he scratches the back of his neck—"I kept you and put you to bed."

He kept me.

"I promise, I didn't even take a peek at the good stuff." He thumps his heart with his fist. "Perfect gentleman."

And we're back to normal.

And my headache is back.

Kitt orders some room service. Who cares about the time?

Thirty minutes later, I'm uncomfortably full, so much so that I can't move.

Kitt puts his plate on the side with mine and groans.

"Does it hurt you, too?" I ask, rubbing my bloated belly.

"Nope. Did you eat too much again?"

Whimpering, I nod.

He's sitting so close to me. We're less than an inch apart, and every time he moves to get his drink off the coffee table, we touch. I don't know why he doesn't keep hold of it rather than going back and forth all the time.

Don't read too much into it.

"I ate far too much." I really need to remember that just because room service is on the label, I don't have to eat *everything*. "Why did I do it after last time?"

Kitt laughs and nudges my shoulder, which isn't helping my stomach. "Because you have no self-discipline."

Now, that is not true. I have it in truckloads. If I didn't, I would've made a fool of myself over him a long time ago. "Ugh, we should've gone out for the evening. I'm dying."

"You're the one who wanted to stay in and veg."

"I made a terrible mistake."

"We won't get much time to relax once the shows start."

He's right, and I would have felt bad for making him traipse around Paris when he has a crazy summer ahead, but sitting and eating was a bad choice.

"Yeah, I know."

"If you want to do something more...exhilarating, I have a few ideas," he says with a sexy smirk that I've seen him use to score a fucking harem of women before.

My heart clenches so hard that I almost pass out. I got a taste of that last night. He got me off without even touching me, and it was the most intense orgasm I had ever had.

Jesus, what would having him inside me be like? Okay, I can't think about that because, pretty soon, I'm going to be begging him to work last night's magic on me.

"Oh, yeah? What ideas would those be?" I ask, glancing up in an attempt to appear sexy. I probably look like a creeper.

"Mmm," he murmurs, leaning in closer.

His eyes are white hot, and it makes me quiver. Kitt does sexy *really* well. His lips part a fraction, and he looks like he's about to devour me.

I can't breathe when he's this close.

Having no idea what he's doing to me, he lifts his eyebrow in that hot, cheeky, charming way, and I want to kiss him so bad that I'm positive I'll burst into flames any second.

If I'd ordered more alcohol with room service, I probably would have had enough courage to go for it. At least then, I could have blamed it on the drink when he pushed me away.

"Actually, I can think of about a million different ways to liven things up."

Wow. I believe him, too.

I've not had much experience—though I'm definitely not a nun—but I know he'd be able to show me a few things. More than a few things actually. The thought of it makes me throb like crazy.

Compared to the women he's been with, I might as well not even know what a cock is. He's probably used to women doing things to him that I can't even pronounce.

I subtly grip my stomach, feeling sick. *Why do I do it to myself?* There is never a need for me to think about Kitt with other women. Like ever. But I still do.

"A million really?" I say sarcastically.

"You doubt me?"

No, not at all. That's the problem.

"No, I don't doubt it, but I want you to list them and prove it, Casanova."

"You'll only get embarrassed."

I glare and resist the urge to kick him. "I'm not five, Kitt. I do know what all the parts are and where they go."

He looks off ahead, and his mind goes somewhere. "Hmm, I guess that's true."

"Do you think of me like a child?" I squeak out like an idiot before my brain engages and realises how desperate that sounded.

"No, of course I don't. I just haven't ever thought about…" he mumbles, stopping right before he says what he means.

I hate when he quits talking right when I want him to continue.

"Oh my God, you're uncomfortable, aren't you?" I tease, elbowing his side.

It really doesn't bode well for me that he's finding it so hard thinking about me and sex at the same time. Still, I enjoy his awkwardness. Small victories and all that. Plus, after last night, he must think about me in that way. The thought alone has my stomach flipping over.

"Please, Tex, I'm not uncomfortable. If your dad could hear you now though…"

"Why is my dad in your head right now?"

Bloody hell, my father is constantly screwing me over where Kitt is concerned. If I were brave enough, I'd tell Dad how I felt about Kitt, but I couldn't see him being thrilled and telling me to go for it.

Kitt frowns, and his eyes look troubled or maybe grossed out. It's hard to tell. "Good point. Take your top off, and we'll rectify this."

"You first," I blurt.

It's not like he's going to get shirtless with me in my hotel room. He slaps Cooper on the back of the head for even joking about it. Although he did kiss the hell out of me on

Christmas, and he got me off last night. He must want me a bit, right?

I stare him in the eyes. There's no way I'm going to back down and look like a child. I can give as good as I get.

Kitt's hand fists the bottom of his shirt, and he starts to pull it over his head.

My heart lurches in surprise and excitement. "What are you doing?" I want this, obviously, but I didn't think he would do it, and now, I'm scared he'll make me.

"You challenged me, Tex. Are you pussying out of your own dare?"

"Yes! Are you crazy?" *Oh God, please take your jeans off as well.*

He shrugs, and my attention is brought to his shoulder and arm. *Those tattoos.* I want to see them all. Now. I want to trace them with my tongue.

"Is it crazy to follow through with a bet?"

No. I'm the crazy one. I don't think there's any doubt about that.

Jesus, my hands are shaking, and I think I'm going to throw up.

With trembling fingers, I grip my top and take it off. Kitt's eyes widen and hone in on my lace-covered breasts.

He didn't think I would do it, and I'm a bit shocked at myself, too.

What am I doing? I don't randomly take my top off, especially not for a bet.

"Tex...what..." he mumbles, his eyes still glued on my chest.

Thank God I'm wearing a nice bra rather than a boring plain one.

"Oh, I'm going to burn in hell. I can't..."

The hunger in his eyes turns my insides to jelly. I want him so much that my body is throbbing.

I clear my throat. "Are you okay?"

He scrubs his eyes and finally looks at my face. "Wanna take a dare on you getting that bra off?"

Tilting my head to the side, I reply sarcastically, "I would, but unfortunately, you're not wearing one."

"Got a spare? I can quickly put one on and whip off."

It is the most tempting offer I've had in a long time. I want to do it because seeing Kitt in a bra would make my whole life, but then I would have to take mine off, and I'm so not doing that.

When...or *if* Kitt ever sees me with nothing on, I don't want it to be because of a bet.

"I don't think I could handle seeing you like that."

"Ah," he says, nodding once. "Get too turned on?"

"Oh, yeah, I'm sure that's it."

"So, is that a no to the bra coming off?" His voice is rougher than usual, kind of like he has a sore throat.

Sexy as hell.

I roll my eyes and shove his chest hard. Yeah, I did that just to feel that six-pack. This touchier, get-shirtless Kitt is definitely more fun, but I know it's going to be over soon, and he'll pretend it never happened.

I need to remember that tonight is nothing but us messing around. Kitt is naturally flirty, and he does it with everything that has breasts. I'm not exaggerating.

Whatever this is, I need to enjoy it. I feel like my time with Kitt is limited. Filthy Sound won't always tour with Enigma. Soon, Kitt will be off all the time, rarely coming home. He might even move far away. LA seems to be the relocation of choice for celebs. It'd be cliché as fuck, but it could happen. Peyton did it.

As much as it pains me to think about it, my friendship with Kitt has a sell-by date. Our connection is my dad's band, and I'm scared that if the bands go their separate ways, Kitt won't have a reason to see me again.

Deep down, I know I'm being ridiculous. We're friends, and we have been for a few years now, so we'll probably stay in touch. Kitt is one of the few people I trust, but the music industry and fame can change a person. I've witnessed that multiple times.

"Kitt, would you ever move to LA?" I blurt out before thinking.

"What? Do you remember our last trip to the US? I couldn't get beans with my breakfast, finding a decent tea was like looking for the meaning of life, and they put a mash of cream and milk in their coffee. I couldn't live there."

His words soothe something inside me. Whatever happens, at least we'll still be in the same country.

"Why did you ask that, Tex?"

I shrug and try to pretend like I wasn't just holding my breath and panicking. At some point, I'm going to have to try to get over this thing with him, but it feels a lot like forever, and I have no idea how to deal with that without it exploding in my face.

"No reason. It just seems to be the *done thing* with rock stars and other celebrities."

"You know I don't like doing the done thing."

"Yeah, is that why you're sitting here, half-naked, with me?"

My dad gave a lot of warnings about any member of Filthy Sound messing around with me, and he was very graphic as he went into the consequences if that were to happen. Kitt is quite clearly choosing to ignore that because, right now, he's breaking Dad's rules big time. Again.

Kitt's Adam's apple bobs as he swallows hard. "You're different."

He makes me feel different, too, like I'm not just another woman to mess around with, like I'm special. Sometimes. Then, there are many, many occasions when he makes me feel like I'm falling into a bottomless black hole.

At this moment, I feel like there's no one else. I don't want to hide my body away. He wants to see me, and I want him to as well.

"How am I different?" I ask.

"You're not a game I'm playing, Tex."

Well, that's good to hear. If he were just pushing the limits with me because he had a problem with following the rules, I'd lose it.

"Then, what are you doing? Because this definitely wouldn't be okay with my dad."

"I'm not looking to strip for your dad. Right now, I only care about what you think…what you want."

"You're asking what I want?" Best to not go there. "Are you going to regret this in the morning, Kitt?"

"Regret? No. Will I feel guilty as hell when I look him in the eyes tomorrow? Yes. But remembering one major detail makes it easier."

"What's that?"

"You're an adult, and you'll never be a one-night stand."

Bloody hell. My lungs deflate—in a good way.

If we did this, it'd be the start of something. It's dangerous to think about more with him. It could end so badly for me. I should be smart and think it through. But I can't. When I'm around him, there is no thinking, no logic, and no consequences. It's a bad combination, and I know I should stop.

But with Kitt, I can never stop.

10

TEXAS
FRIDAY, MAY 8
PARIS, FRANCE

The morning before a show is a chilled one, which is good because I'm so tired that I feel like my eyes are bleeding.

Last night, Kitt and I stayed up until four a.m. We fell asleep on my sofa. No funny business happened. It was nice. Thankfully, we were up in time to get back on the bus. We'll be at a different location in Paris tomorrow, so we checked out of the hotel, and now, we're heading to tonight's venue.

There's a lot to do throughout the day to prepare, especially since Enigma and Filthy Sound like to have a hand in everything, but the mornings are for eating good food and drinking your own body weight in coffee.

As the tour goes on, it'll be harder to get them all up, but I do it every time. While we're all together, it's not always easy to spend quality time when about a hundred things are happening all at once.

I turn the bacon and sausages, bumping along to Kings of Leon. What I really want to listen to is one of Filthy Sound's numbers, but I'm already failing big time in keeping my feelings for Kitt under wraps.

No need to add to it. Desperation doesn't look good on anyone—except for Kitt when he was kissing me in the cage.

Don't think about that, Texas.

Kitt is the first one out of his room, which isn't unusual. I don't think he went back to sleep when we hit the road for all of the thirty minutes.

Lazy musicians this morning. Jimmy used to get up early with me, but since Kitt's been around, he's been sleeping in, no longer feeling bad that I might be alone. It wouldn't have bothered me anyway, but I did appreciate his company.

"I think I'm dying, Tex," Kitt groans.

"Did you, by any chance, drink too much of my minibar?"

Jamming his fists into his eyes, he nods.

He changed his T-shirt. This one is white and plain. It doesn't do much to hide his tattoos, which kind of turns me on. We've not even slept together, and I want him all the time.

With my ex, Xander, it was never like that, and we'd had sex. I was self-conscious with Xander, but I let Kitt maul me in public. He makes me feel sexy with one look. It's unintentional, and he probably does the same to every woman he looks at. It's those come-to-bed deep blue eyes that do it.

Yeah, you really need help.

"You okay, Tex? You've not moved in a while."

"Right," I say, turning so that he doesn't see the colour of my cheeks. My face feels like it's on fire, so no doubt, my cheeks are red. Thank God he doesn't know he just witnessed me imagining having sex with him.

You're tragic. Get a grip.

Nodding my chin toward the coffee pot, I say, "Coffee is ready. Can you pour me one, too, please?"

Caffeine will help clear my dirty thoughts. I hope.

"Oh my God!" I spin around. How could I forget?

He's far too close. For a split second, we're back in the cage, and desire pools between my legs.

Clear head, Tex.

"I'm such an idiot. Today is huge for you. First show on *your* first tour. How are you feeling?"

He takes a little step closer, and his chest is centimetres from mine. The floor whips away, and I'm free-falling. I want him to kiss me so bad. My lips...yes, my lips *ache*.

Gulping, he clears his throat. "I'm fine besides a headache. I'm excited and nervous and anxious all at once. I want to be out there now." He's animated, and it makes his whole face light up.

I can't help from getting swept up in his excitement. He comes alive when he talks about music and the band. I love his passion. And I don't just mean his passion for music.

A part of me wonders what he'd do if I came on to him. Like properly. *Would he take things further than we've already gone?*

"I can't wait to watch you." My voice is too quiet. I sound ridiculous.

"Well, I can't wait for you to watch me."

Okay, where is this going? Because I would really like to watch him.

"Eggs?" I ask, mentally whacking myself with something hard.

Nice one, Texas. Now, you look like a total moron.

Kitt laughs. "Eggs sound good. Your bacon is going to burn soon, by the way."

Gasping, I spin around and take the pan off the heat. There's not a whole lot I can do on tour besides trying to keep them in check, so I want performance day breakfasts to be perfect.

While he's still laughing behind me, I hear Kitt grabbing two mugs for our coffee.

"Is there anything else you need me to do?" he asks.

There's plenty but nothing I can say aloud.

"Nope. I think I'm good. Thanks. You just sit and wait for food."

I turn the heat down, so the food will take a little longer because I don't hear any signs of life coming from the bedrooms above.

Taking my drink, I sit opposite of Kitt at the table, and my phone buzzes with a text.

Darling, wish the boys good luck. XOXO.

It's Jennifer. She could text Dad, but since she hit the big time, she doesn't need him anymore. Having his child was enough to rocket her career to the top. Things she wants to ask him go through me now.

"You going to reply to that?" Kitt asks.

He's read it, too, because my phone is lying on the table, and I didn't bother to pick it up.

"Doesn't really require a reply. Good luck from Jennifer."

Dipping his head, he picks up his mug and correctly chooses to leave the topic of Jennifer alone.

My mother is kind of a sore subject. I wouldn't change my life or the way I grew up. Dad's the best, and he made sure I never felt unwanted, but some real and meaningful interaction with the woman who brought me into this world would have been nice.

Why should I go out of my way when she can't be bothered?

"After-party tonight," he says, grinning.

"Now, *that*, I'm looking forward to."

He laughs, and his eyes turn lava hot. "Me, too," he rasps.

He's thinking about the cage. Oh my God!

After breakfast, I wait in the bus with Ted while the guys go off to do a final sound check and familiarise themselves with the venue. There's no reason for me to be there quite as early, so I have a quick shower, change, and lie down on my bed.

I'm tired and aching, so a nap is everything right now. Because no one can nap before reading the entire Internet, I scroll through Twitter.

There is tons of support for Filthy Sound. In fact, they're trending! There's a lot of *#MarryMeKitt*.

Get in fucking line, darling.

And people are saying they want Cooper's children and to have sex with Milo on the stool he sits on while playing the drums.

When they're in the media more, there's an increase of photos. I hate photos. Kitt will never refuse a fan a picture or autograph, and it always comes back to bite me on the arse, especially when he takes slutty photos with the women he wants to feel up. They never have an issue with his tongue down their throat or his hand inside their bra or on their arse. In fact, they often actively encourage it.

Not that Kitt needs any encouragement.

I bite down on my tongue as I torture myself by flicking through some of them. Kitt's not mine, I'm fully aware of that, but it still hurts every time I see him with someone else. We might have kissed and whatever a couple of times, but that doesn't mean anything, not really. He's done more with countless women, and they're never seen again.

Kitt has called me beautiful before, he's admitted he's attracted to me, we've kissed twice, and we've shared something much more intimate, so I know there's something between us.

Is it just my dad, or is Kitt not that into me?

Nothing would make me change my dad, no chance, but it would be nice if his status didn't matter so much. Peyton couldn't care less. I wish Kitt could say the same.

He's not holding back because of who your dad is. It's who your dad is to him. Still doesn't help you though.

I turn my nose up. So many selfies of women with the Filthy Sound hashtag are flooding Twitter.

Filthy Sound is getting the recognition they deserve, and I love that, but I really wish the women would love them a little less. Jealousy is an ugly emotion but one of the hardest to control. I've learned that a thousand times over since I met Kitt.

I try hard not to let it bother me, but by now, I know it's pointless to push myself. I feel what I feel, and until I stop loving Kitt, I'm going to want to scratch the eyes out of every woman he gropes. Or I'll start drinking the harder stuff more often.

A text from Kitt flashes across the banner, and I'm a little too mad at him to want to look, which is ridiculous and makes me borderline insane.

When are you coming?

That's weird. Right? Isn't that weird?
The show isn't for hours yet, and he knows I planned on getting there closer to the start. I don't see why he needs to know an exact time...unless he wants me there.
He doesn't want you there. He probably needs something.
But he might just want you with him.
I type a quick reply.

Why? What's up?

My heart is in my mouth as I wait. Turns out, I don't do playing it cool well—internally anyway.

I'm bored. Coop's a nightmare. Milo wants to switch up the set.

Okay, that's kind of like he wants me there because he wants to spend time with me. *Right?* I'll take it. But I'm not getting up yet. Just because I want him above, like, breathing doesn't mean I'm going to let him know that.
Smiling to myself, I reply.

Sorry, busy. I'm in the bath.

It's a small lie. I'm lying down. I'm just not in water.

Naked selfie?

I bite my lip as I read his last message a few times over. Kitt has never seen me naked before. The idea of it makes my body burn and not just from the temperature of my pretend bath.

I'm a good girl, Kitt.

So, be bad.

I consider what to send next when I get another text from him.

Fuck, I'm hard.

Holy...
Is it possible to faint while lying down? Right now, I'm thinking yes.

I press my legs together, but it only heightens the throbbing.

I made him hard. Again. He was hard the night he slammed me against my wall and kissed me like his life depended on it. He was rock solid the night he made us come in the cage.

You're a guy. You're always hard.

I said that because I might want him to tell me it's not because he wants to get laid but because he wants *me*.

Not true. Are you sending me this pic? I'll send you one first if you're shy.

What?
I sit up so fast that I almost fall back down.
Oh my God. What the hell? Is he serious? Oh, please be serious.
Wait.
Kitt is very anti pissing my dad off, so I'm not convinced he's sending those messages right under my dad's nose. At the Christmas party, he didn't follow me upstairs until after Dad had left to drive Cynthia home from the party.

Coop?

I send the text with trembling fingers and swallow bile. My body is ice cold. I don't want it to be another one of Cooper's jokes, but this has a Cooper prank written all over it.

My phone starts to ring, and it's Kitt. Well, it's his number. I'm not sure if it'll be him on the other end of it. I press Accept and hold the phone to my ear.

I'm nervous. My heart is beating rapidly as I grip the phone so hard that the tendons in my wrist pop up.

"Are you telling me, you want Cooper to send you a pic of his dick?" Kitt hisses.

Sweet mother of...

It was him!

And he sounds pissed.

I open my mouth and quickly close it again. My brain has turned to mush, and I can't think of one thing to say.

"Texas?"

"Um…no."

"Um, no? That's all you have to say?"

Okay, what's happening right now? "No, I mean"—I sigh—"I don't want to see a picture of Cooper's anything. Your last message…I thought maybe he'd taken your phone."

"Why?" he questions. His voice is low, and it echoes, so he must be locked away in a bathroom or somewhere like that.

"I didn't think you'd offer to send me what you actually offered to send me."

"Well, I did." He groans like he's just realised what he was about to do. "Fuck."

In my need to save face because I can't have him rejecting me again, I say, "I know. Forget it, okay? We were just messing around. No harm done."

There's a pause on his end of the line, and I feel the tension growing and taking physical form. My pulse is thudding in my ears. He's annoyed because he thought I wanted Cooper.

"No harm done. Right. When are you coming over here?" he says. He's reserved, and he sounds like he's doing that neck-scratch thing he does when he's uncomfortable.

"Er, I'll get ready and have Ted drive me."

"Fine."

I frown and stand up to grab my leather jacket. "Are you okay?" I almost don't want to ask because I can see it turning into an argument.

He had that tone in his voice. For some reason, I can wind him up in a second.

He clears his throat. "Yes, I'm great. I've got to go. Carl's calling me."

Kitt hangs up the phone.

Carl wasn't calling him. Kitt just lied. He was desperate to get off the phone.

Did he see where this was headed, too?
How did we go from almost sexting to barely talking?
He's so frustrating!

Being around him and all this back and forth and up and down is like being on a terrifying roller coaster ride, and the worst part is, I don't even want to get off—the ride, that is.

KITT
FRIDAY, MAY 8
PARIS, FRANCE

Since my phone call with Texas, I've been frustrated and pissed off. *Why did I even go there?*

A beautiful girl tells me she's in the bath, and my dick immediately takes control over the situation. I didn't think. There is no fucking bath on the bus! She's making me lose my mind.

She'll be here soon. It's been almost an hour since we spoke on the phone.

What would I have done if she'd sent that photo? It terrifies me how far I might take it when I'm not thinking clearly, which is all the time she's near or when I'm thinking about her.

I need to make it stop.

Tex is off-limits, and that's hot as hell. It's like putting sweets in front of a kid, saying not to eat them, and then leaving the room. They won't be able to resist, and I'm not sure I will if she offers herself up.

I'm in my dressing room, sucking down whiskey like it's water.

Milo would be pissed if he saw how much I'd had already. We've got hours before we go on, so I'll sober up in time, but he will definitely have a few things to say about my behaviour.

And he'll be right.

This is our first show. The first damn one! I need to be on top of my game, not have my head screwed over by some unattainable girl. Shit, I can have anyone I want. After the show, there will be plenty of women willing to come back to my dressing room or hotel with me.

Why do I want inside the pants of the one I can't have?
Who am I? Cooper?

I need Texas out of my system. If I could just have one night with her, things could go back to how they were before I started to wonder what she felt like.

You don't believe that.

Closing my eyes, I fist the glass to the point where I feel it could give way.

It can't happen. Get a-fucking-hold of yourself.

Someone knocks on my door.

I down the last of the whiskey, drop the tumbler on the table, and shout, "Yeah?"

Texas walks in, looking like my own brand of perfect. Her hair is in a messy plait to the side, her lips are red, and she's wearing skintight jeans, a plain grey top, and a leather jacket.

I want to push her over the dressing table and hold on to nothing but that hair.

Clearing my throat, I smirk. "So glad you could make it."

She narrows her eyes and puts her hands on her hips, which makes her top stretch over her breasts.

Fuck. Me.

"Shut up. I don't need to be here early. And I hope that was apple juice."

"Of course it was."

Smiling, she shakes her head. "You're terrible, rock star. Are you crippled with nerves yet?"

She closes the door and sits down on the large sofa with a grin. Her legs are stretched out in front of her. I want them wrapped around my neck.

Shut up. Resist. You can't go there. Tonight, you can have any girl you want—more than one if you feel like it.

I might just do that.

"Nope, I'm fine."

"Hmm, all thanks to the whiskey?"

"I've only had a couple."

"Keep it that way. You can get drunk after."

"Plan to. You're still coming to the club, right?"

I don't know why I'm asking. Of course she's still coming. She loves the after-parties almost as much as Coop does.

"Duh. I plan to get so drunk that one of you arseholes will have to carry me to my room."

"I might be busy," I say, wiggling my eyebrows so that she knows what I mean, not that she wouldn't. "I'll be sure to let Milo and Coop know."

Ted would get her home, no matter what, but we've always looked out for her. We made a promise to a man who's given us everything. Protect Texas. Included in that is, don't fucking touch her. *Two out of us three is good, right?*

I'm a bastard.

"Lovely," she says, turning her nose up. "You know, it's not a requirement to sleep with *all* the fans."

"No, but it sure is fun."

She rolls her eyes, and then they settle on disappointment. It makes my gut clench.

"Come on, Tex, if you'd had me before, you wouldn't be trying to keep other women from experiencing this." I gesture to my dick with my hand.

"If you're going to keep this up, I'll go and see if Carl needs me to do anything. But if you want to switch back to my normal Kitt, I'll stay."

Her normal Kitt.

I can't play stupid and pretend like I don't know what she means. I didn't intend on talking about women with her. It's like a defence mechanism. If she really, really knows that I'm fully happy with sleeping around—which I am—then she won't flirt back.

Of course, it would be easier if I didn't flirt first or if I didn't fantasise about being inside her quite so much. But since I'm incapable of doing those things, I need something to keep her at a distance. Turning her off is the only thing stopping us from making another mistake. And that's what it would be—a mistake. It might be one I want to repeat over and over, but that doesn't change anything.

Sex with her would be the best kind of wrong.

I hold my hands up. "Sorry. I'll save that talk for the guys."

"Thank you. Got anything good to eat?" She purses her lips and checks out the food on the side table.

I requested more than what I've got, but that'll be here a bit later. We're early because it's our first show and because Milo is like a worrying old woman.

She picks up a bag of giant milk chocolate buttons and opens it without asking—not that she needs to ask, but you know, be polite. But we've gotten way past the point where we need to ask. We're at the point where we could very easily share orgasms under clothes.

The door bursts open, and Coop strolls through with Milo a few paces behind. They each have a beer in their hands.

I push the whiskey bottle behind my hair shit. "Fuck do you two want?"

Milo gives me the middle finger. "You seen the stage recently? I nearly came, bro, I swear!"

Texas fake gags and eats more chocolate.

"It looks good," I agree. I'm playing this down because if I acknowledge just how big it is, I'll be plagued with nerves, and I need to keep myself in control. This means too much to let anything ruin it. I need a clear head. I need to think of it as another supporting gig.

And I need to expel Tex from my mind.

"Maybe you shouldn't eat those," Tex says to Coop as he tips a handful of giant milk chocolate buttons into his palm.

Milo laughs. "Yeah, don't want to puke everywhere."

"Fuck off," Coop growls.

"You fuck off."

Tex and I share a look. They're like an old married couple most of the time.

"Let him eat them. It'll be funny," I say, sticking my middle finger up.

"You can fuck off, too."

"Someone take me to see the stage," Tex demands.

She stands up, and I can't help but let my eyes follow her.

Coop throws the pack of chocolate down. "I'll take you."

There's definitely an innuendo in there, but she doesn't bite.

Milo's eyes are on me the entire time. He waits until they've left, and then he cocks his eyebrow.

"What?" I ask.

"You two have been pretty cosy recently."

"We're friends."

"Mmhmm."

Prick.

"If you have something to say, Milo..."

"Out of the two of us, I think you're the one who should be talking. Last night, she was practically lying all over you, and today, you're eye-fucking her. What's going on?"

I bend over on the chair and cover my face with my hands. "Fuck."

"How far has it gone?"

"Too far," I reply, groaning.

"You've slept together?"

My head snaps up. His dark eyes are wide.

"No. Not *quite* that far. We've kissed a couple of times, and there was this thing." I try so hard not to smile, but I can't force the muscles around my mouth to stop lifting.

"What thing?"

"Doesn't matter. Let's just say, it was hot as hell. And it shouldn't have happened."

"I'm sorry. Have you lost your tiny mind?"

I laugh. "Yeah, I really think I have."

"This isn't a game, Kitt!" he snaps.

"Believe me, I know. Do you think, if I could help it, it would have happened? I don't want to need her, Milo, and I've tried to stop. We kissed at her old man's Christmas party, and since then, I haven't been able to get her out of my head."

"Jesus," he breathes.

"I don't know what's going on between us. We don't want to fuck things up with Mark. I swear to you, I won't do anything to lose what we've got, man."

He narrows his eyes and folds his arms over his chest. "You think that's what I care about? You're my brother, Kitt. I care if you and Tex are okay. You've never been cut up over a girl before. You like her."

"Yeah, I do."

"You want to be exclusive?"

"Exclusive…" I say, testing the word. It used to leave a nasty taste on my tongue. Now, it conjures the picture of Texas in my head. "Oh, shit. I want that."

Milo's smug. He tilts his head and smirks. "Good luck, man."

He's the only one of us who's been in a relationship, one that lasted longer than a couple of months anyway. Milo and Lexi were together for three years.

"Are you subtly trying to tell me relationships are shit?"

My question wipes the smile off his face.

"No, they're not." He doesn't say more than that, but there are so many things left unsaid that I start to worry about him.

"Do you miss her?"

"We've been in contact."

"Oh. And?"

He shrugs. "Two years have passed, Kitt. I thought I was over her."

His admission isn't a huge surprise. The way he's been going through women though, I assumed he'd moved on.

"How is she?" I ask.

I always liked Lexi, but the more time Milo had to spend on the road, the more they grew apart. Lexi started to resent the band. She was never nasty and would *never* ask him to leave. She'd break her own heart before she tried to kill his dream.

"She's doing really well," he says, sounding genuinely happy. "She's opened her own boutique where she sells her designs. I guess all that sketching has paid off."

"That's great, man. Are you going to meet up with her?"

He shakes his head, and his jaw clenches. "She's with someone."

Damn. "I'm sorry."

He shrugs, but his eyes wince with hurt. "I let her go. I can't be pissed when she's found someone who wouldn't."

"Did she say she doesn't want to meet?"

"No, she wants to get coffee."

"You should."

"No, I don't mind talking to her on Facebook occasionally, but I'm done with her. We ended a long time ago, and I'm looking to the future. Lexi is the past."

She doesn't sound very in the past.

"All right." I pour whiskey in my glass and hand it over.

He doesn't want to talk, and that's fine. He knows where I am.

He takes the glass and downs the amber liquid. "Cheers."

Texas and Cooper come back in minutes later. They both look like they went to do coke, not look at a stage.

Tex bounces on her toes and shoves her phone in my face. "Look how awesome it is! I can't wait!"

Milo puts the empty glass on the table.

"Come on, let's fuck shit up and then get laid," I say. Coping mechanism.

Texas spins around and jumps on Milo's back. He laughs and grips her calves.

Fuck, I love seeing her like this. But I wish her legs were wrapped around me.

At least Milo is smiling again though.

Mark, Jimmy, and Will are legends. I stand backstage, watching them from the wing. Mark's stage presence is undeniable. They finish up on one of their most popular songs, and it'll soon be our turn.

I can't believe we're about to start our opening show of *our* world tour. It's still so surreal. There couldn't have been a better place to start than Paris. The love and support we've received from our French fans is mind-blowing. The date sold out within hours, so we had to add a second show.

I'm buzzing so hard that you'd think I'd been on a cocaine binge. Milo and Coop are standing closer to the edge of the stage with beers, enjoying the show, but I'm a little farther back with Tex.

Mark's voice carries through the entire stadium, owning it. If I get to be half as good as him, I'll consider my career a huge success.

Tex takes my beer from my hand and helps herself to a sip before handing it back.

"Thanks," I mutter.

Smiling brightly, she replies, "You're welcome. Are you nervous?"

"A bit. This is what I'm good at, and I know I'll fucking rock, but I don't want to mess this up."

"You've never messed up a set before, and you've done *tons* of shows."

"I know, but I don't want to let the guys down. Tonight is kind of a big deal."

"You need to calm down. You've gone white," she says, placing her hand on my forehead.

I have?

"Don't puke—at least, not until after the show."

"Thanks. That's helpful."

She laughs and puts a stray stand of hair behind her ear. "All right, just pretend this isn't your tour. You're supporting Enigma. By the way, do you think that band name is lame, too?"

I chuckle. "You're a terrible daughter."

With a shrug, she wraps her arms around my waist. Milo is suddenly finding this more interesting than watching Enigma. I don't care right now.

"You're going to be fine, Kitt. You've got the sexiest, most incredible voice I've ever heard, and you rock the guitar. You guys are my favourite band. Stop worrying, okay?"

I pull her against my chest and hold her close. She's the only girl I feel comfortable enough to do this with. The rest of them want something. Tex doesn't care about the fame, what I do, or how much money I have. She just wants me, and that makes resisting her ten times harder.

"You think I have a sexy voice?"

"Don't let it get to your head, rock star. Everyone knows you do. Your voice is kinda rough, and when you sing, you sound…"

Laughing, I offer, "Filthy?"

"Yeah," she replies, looking up at me. "Massive ego thing to name your band after your sound, by the way."

"Not really. It's *my* band."

"You could've had anything."

"You don't like Filthy Sound?"

She shakes her head and squeezes my middle. "No, I do."

"What would you have called us?"

Giggling, she pulls away and stands straight. "It changes often, depending on my mood and how idiotic you're all acting."

"Wow. So, only bad things, huh?"

"Pretty much. Hey, they're almost finished with the last song. Are you ready to rock, Daniels?"

"Fuckin' right I am, Knight. You'll be watching?"

"Of course! Sing my favourite loudest."

I drop my arms and bow, which makes her laugh. "Anything for my number one fan."

"Hmm, anything, huh? I'll think about that. Now, go! Cooper looks like he's about to rip your head off."

Just as Tex finishes her sentence, Coop shouts, "Come the fuck on, Kitt!"

She raises her eyebrow. "See? Go."

Before I think about what I'm doing, I lean down and kiss her forehead. It felt right. Clearly, she thinks so, too, because she smiles and bites her lip. I back away and take a deep breath. It wasn't a smart move, but it's done now.

She's here, and she'll be watching. You've got this.

I'm not usually nervous, but we have to do this right. The fans deserve the best, and Enigma doesn't have to do things, like support our little band. They're far too big for that. We can never let them down.

We stand at the edge while our instruments are changed over. People are everywhere, fussing around and making sure everything is ready.

Jodie arrived a while ago and is back to firing encouragement at us.

I look back at Tex as I swing my guitar over my head, and she gives me a shy smile. She is my calm in all this crazy.

You are so fucking screwed.

Mark joins her, and I look away.

"Are you ready?" Jodie asks.

Milo bounces up and down. "Oh, yeah!"

"Let's get out there," I say, itching to start playing.

The lights on stage go out, and everyone screams.

I take a moment before I follow Milo and Coop out. This is so overwhelming in the best way. Adrenaline pumps through my veins as I walk out, and the lights flick on. I raise my hand in acknowledgment of the audience, and the noise reaches a deafening point.

Damn, I want to do this every night.

The atmosphere is electric.

Every time, I get this huge rush that I can't get enough of. But this, tonight, is something else.

"Good fucking evening, Paris!" Cooper shouts down his mic.

There's another wave of screams. People are shouting to us, but together, it's just noise.

"If you want us to start, I'm gonna need to see some titties! Right, boys?" He turns to us.

I laugh. *Here we go...*

"He's right, ladies," Milo says.

Chuckling, I shake my head and scan the audience. There are a few hotties I wouldn't mind having a peek at. It takes less than a second for dozens of women in the front few rows to lift their tops.

This is Coop's favourite part of each show, I'm sure.

"You ladies look fucking beautiful tonight," I say, earning massive screams. "So...are you ready?"

The noise kicks up.

"He said, are you fucking ready?" Cooper bellows.

I close my eyes and grip the mic.

12

TEXAS
FRIDAY, MAY 8
PARIS, FRANCE

"They're awesome, right?" I say, tugging on Dad's arm.

Laughing, he nods his head. "There was never any doubt, pumpkin. I wouldn't have taken a chance on just anyone."

"Kitt looked nervous before they went on. None of them want to let you and your rubbish band down. Or everyone out there."

Dad cuts me a look. "As ever, Texas, your support is heartwarming."

I giggle and hug his arm. I feel like I'm drunk, and it takes me a second to realise that it's because I'm so bloody proud and excited for the guys. For Kitt. "Do you still get nervous?"

He thinks for a minute before slowly shaking his head. "No. I think I've been doing it too long to get nervous. Being on the stage is second nature to me now, as natural as breathing."

"Well, you've definitely been doing it for too long," I quip.

"You do know my career is the reason you're living this life. A life you love?"

"Totes, Daddy. I'm not saying you're not awesome, but you're *definitely* past it. Hey, I'm still happy to be seen with you."

"Thank you for not being too embarrassed by me."

"She is, man. We just pay her," Will says, winking at me.

Ha, I love it when they join in.

"Right. I don't think you could afford to bribe her," Dad replies.

"Ah! He's got you there, Will," Jimmy adds.

There is a lot of money talk where I'm concerned, and I don't know why. I'm not expensive to keep! At least, I don't think so anyway.

"I'm not embarrassing," Dad argues.

Will smirks and dips his chin in my direction. "Not to us, but to a teenager..."

They start a full-blown argument about which one of them is the least embarrassing to a teenager—the answer is none—and I tune it out in favour of watching Kitt, Cooper, and Milo perform. Without thinking, I let go of Dad and step closer.

Kitt's voice calls me, beckoning me forward.

He is beautiful up there onstage. The way he moves his body is so sexual that I feel myself getting hot. I'm sure I'm not the only one. The women I see out in the crowd are all bidding for his attention, trying to get him to notice them. He sings to everyone, individually, all at once.

Kitt owns the stage. The way he handles the guitar at the same time as singing his heart out is magnificent to watch. I can't tear my eyes away. He demands the attention of every person. Including me. Always me.

A heavy arm rests on my shoulder, and Will chuckles. "They're going to be bigger than us."

"*Going* to be?"

"Hilarious. I just hope your head is screwed on when it comes to Kitt."

Yeah, I don't like where this is going.
"I don't expect anything, Will. I'll be fine."

Only, I know I won't be fine. We've never been together or done anything more than kiss and…dry-humped, but my feelings are real. I would love to turn them off because loving someone who doesn't love you back is heartbreaking.

And Will is right. They're going to be huge, and I'll still be little Texas, daughter of an aging rock god. It's pitiful really.

Finding something I'm good at and that I want to do needs to be shot to number one on my to-do list, even above bingeing on every season of *American Horror Story*.

"I hope so, Texas, because I don't like it when you're hurting."

"He can't hurt me. We're not together."

Lies, lies, lies.

Will knows it, and I know it. We look at each other with the understanding that I'm talking out of my arse right now.

I sigh. "All right, fine. It's cool though. I know the score. I'm not some idiot, expecting the world from someone who's currently trying to conquer it."

"What you expect and what you want might be two different things, but that doesn't mean it'll hurt any less."

Awesome. This conversation is uplifting.

"Got it, chief. I'm all good," I say lightly, playfully punching his stomach.

"All right, girl." He kisses the side of my head.

We watch the rest of their set in silence, occasionally singing along. Kitt does sing my favourite song louder than the rest, and it makes my heart ache. Through the whole thing, he sings out into the crowd, but it's for me. He holds the mic with two hands when he doesn't need to play the guitar and sings like his life depends on it.

It's the best I've ever heard that song, and it brings a tear to my eye.

Yep, this is going to really hurt.

My heart is racing as he bellows out the lyrics. I'm falling harder, and it's terrifying. I'm completely overwhelmed by him.

After the show, we head to a local club.

Dad's been to enough after-parties to know that the later you stay, the better they get, but he, Jimmy, and Will still move on elsewhere most of the time. He trusts me, and more importantly, he trusts Ted, who would never leave me, no matter how much I beg him to.

Will is the first one to leave because he's made a female friend for the night. Jimmy has spent most of his time texting Saskia, so he and Dad head out to a quieter venue where they can talk about things old people talk about to other older celebrities.

Kitt throws his arm over my shoulder as we watch my dad leave. "Now, you can play properly," he whispers in my ear.

His breath tickles my neck and makes me shudder. His eyes are flirtatious and alluring, drawing me in and making me hot with desire.

I think my ovaries just imploded.

"Hmm, how does one do that then?" I ask, putting on a posh accent.

"Well, darling, one simply gets fucked up," he replies.

"All right." I turn to him, laugh, and link my arm in his. "Fuck me up real good, Daniels." Double meaning there.

I try to keep a straight face, but his sharp intake of breath drives me wild.

He leans even closer, and his lips brush my ear.

Oh God.

"Be careful with your choice of words, or you could get something you've not bargained for."

That would be nice.

"Oh, really?" I say, tilting my head the way Peyton's character does when she's being sexy. Bet I look like a tit doing it.

This is a dangerous game I'm playing. He doesn't know it, and I don't want him to, but he holds all the power. I want him. It's his choice if anything happens between us. It's my heart that has the potential to be crushed.

I can't take this too far.

Self-preservation mode: On.

Back out of this.

"Are you buying me a drink or not?" I ask, moving over so that he's not almost on top of me.

No more flirting. It won't end well.

He'll probably be shagging someone else in a matter of hours. My heart aches at the thought of him leaving with another woman. I've seen it so many times before, and it never gets easier. When he touches them, kisses them, tells them how pretty they are, I want to die—or rip their fingernails from the beds.

He stands straighter and nods. "Let's find Milo and Coop and do some shots."

Taking my hand in an innocent gesture, Kitt leads me through the VIP area where we look for the two amigos on the prowl. My hand feels so right in his. Everywhere he touches me, even accidentally, comes alive.

I hate how much I want him, and I hate that I can't stop it. No matter how hard I try, no matter how much it hurts me, I can't stop him from being my heart.

I love him.

I'm in love with someone who doesn't love me back.

"Texas!" Cooper shouts across the room.

The music is loud, but everyone still heard him. He bounds over and picks me up in a bear hug.

"Oh my God," I squeak as his arms crush my chest. "Put me down, pisshead!"

"Dance with me," he says, carrying me toward the dance floor.

I don't have a choice. Laughing, I slap his back and give Kitt a wave. Looks like I'm dancing with Coop for a bit.

Cooper puts me down and tugs me against his chest. I wrap my arms around his neck as we move to "Bang Bang."

He's a good dancer, and when he's wasted like this, he's even better.

Over Cooper's shoulder, I notice Kitt at the bar with a girl. Seeing him lean in and smile at her is like swallowing fire.

Don't look.

I focus on Coop and the music.

You knew this was going to happen. It isn't a surprise. This is what you two do.

I'm getting pretty sick of what we do.

I want to stop loving Kitt.

I will make myself stop loving him—right after I get off-my-face drunk.

Rubbing the ache in my chest, I say, "Coop, let's do shots until we can't walk."

He pulls back and stretches his arms up. "Texas Knight, I love you!"

Even though my heart feels like Kitt is taking frequent stabs at it, I still laugh. I can ignore him and his conquest for tonight. I can have fun with a guy who doesn't hurt me.

"Please just get me drunk. Right now."

Coop grabs my hand and pulls me to the bar. Thankfully, he doesn't spot Kitt, and we end up in a space farther down. I don't want to make small talk with them.

I want to pretend he doesn't exist.

"We'll take ten shots of tequila, please," Cooper says to the stunning girl behind the bar. He speaks to her chest, but she doesn't seem to care.

"Ten? I want to be drunk, not dead."

He gives me a lopsided smile. "I know. That's why I'm only allowing three for you. It's all you need, little lightweight."

"Great. I'm carrying your arse home…"

"Kitt will do that. Looks like he'll be spending most of his night shagging than drinking."

More frequent stabs. I force myself to smile, and it takes great effort.

You need to find a way to stop this shit. It's getting out of hand. But how?

13

KITT
FRIDAY, MAY 8
PARIS, FRANCE

The blonde has been all over me, like a fucking rash. She's one of the more enthusiastic ones, and I know she will do *anything* to please me. It turns me on. I love it when a beautiful woman's only goal is to make me come. Who wouldn't?

Since Texas went to dance with Coop, he's been her favourite. I know I'm being a dickhead, and this is my fault, but we have to try not to slip up. This is the best way I can think of to do that.

We're now in the car, and Ted is driving us back to the hotel. Texas is in front of me with Cooper, and the blonde and I are in the back row. Her hand is cupping my dick through my jeans as she kisses my neck.

Tex hasn't moved since we got in the car, not even an inch.

She reminds me of when I was about five, and I'd see boys playing football with their dads at the park. I'd get so upset that I didn't have my dad that I'd freeze, thinking it would somehow reverse time. It was like, if I sat so still and concentrated so hard, then he'd walk up to me with a ball under his arm. It was stupid.

I didn't do it much after I'd told my grandparents why I was a statue. They realised I was at an age where I understood the loss of my mum and dad more, and they helped me come to terms with it. And that weekend, my nan packed up a picnic, and we all spent the day at the park, playing football and eating cake.

Is Texas a statue because she's hoping it'll stop this from being real?

No, of course not. You are reading way too much into this. She's probably asleep.

The blonde—fuck, I wish I'd listened when she told me her name—is trailing kisses along my jaw, and I start to get rock solid.

Because you're looking at Texas. This is wrong, you sick fuck.

We arrive at the hotel, and Ted ushers us inside. There's no one about at this hour, and since we went straight from yesterday's hotel to the arena to the after-party, no one knows this is where we're staying.

"Coop, you're walking Tex back, right?" I say as we approach my suite on the eleventh floor.

My room is near the lift while Texas's room must be farther on. The guys are somewhere in between.

"I can make it," she says with sarcasm.

There's a tightness to her voice that doesn't suit her. She looks like an angel, and her mouth sometimes forgets it.

"I got it, man," Coop replies, picking Tex up and throwing her over his shoulder.

She immediately starts shouting and thumping his back, but that wouldn't bother Coop.

He's probably turned on by it. My eye twitches.

"Come on, baby," the blonde coos, rubbing me through my jeans.

I get more turned on when Tex looks at me. We're in the middle of the corridor, but that doesn't seem to bother her. And I couldn't care less about anything right now because I'm pissed off.

Why am I so fucking obsessed with Texas Knight?

Forget her, and lose yourself in this girl. There are no consequences if you shag her. No one cares. Except you.

I slot the card in the door, and it clicks open.

"Night," Ted mutters, laughing, as he follows Cooper to Tex's room.

Pushing the girl into my room, I give Ted the middle finger over my shoulder. As soon as the door is shut, she yanks at my jeans, as if she's strong enough to rip through the material. I have a spike-studded belt on. *Ain't gonna happen, love.*

Gripping the tops of her arms, I remove her from me and smirk. "I'm all for you ravaging me, but let's get down to the good stuff first. Clothes off."

Just do it. You'll feel much better after.

No, you won't.

You're hurting Texas.

Fuck.

I rear back, and the blonde looks confused.

I can't do this when I'm hurting the girl I care about. "Sorry, you need to go."

"What?"

"You heard me. I can't do this right now. I'm sorry. Do you need me to call you a taxi?"

She scoffs and wrenches my door open. "You're a fool."

Don't I fucking know it?

I wince as she slams my door so hard that the painting on the wall almost drops. I turn and jam my fist into the wall. Thankfully, I don't put a hole in it.

What the fuck? I should go to Tex's room right now and tell her to stop whatever she's fucking doing to me.

But that'll make things worse because then she'll know I can't stop thinking about her.

So, I opt for whiskey. Lots and lots of whiskey.

SATURDAY, MAY 9
PARIS, FRANCE

In the morning, I head to Cooper's suite because he's ordered everything on the room service menu, and I'm starving. Milo and Texas are already here. I still feel like absolute shit, and I've had a few hours of sleep.

My head is banging so I head straight for water and to find something to kick this headache.

"Morning," Texas says loudly. She smiles, like she knows I'm suffering.

Wincing, I hold my hand up. "Shh."

"What's wrong?" Her voice is no quieter than before.

She's enjoying this, and she should. I'm an arsehole.

"Tex, please. I think I drank too much."

I definitely drank too much.

"Your after-the-after-party activities probably didn't help either." Her voice is full of accusation, and although she's being nicer than I deserve, her eyes are cold and distant.

"No, but that was a lot more fun than drinking."

Don't tell her that. Tell her you sent the girl packing.

"Whatever," she mutters. She turns away, grabbing her coffee.

I swallow regret.

"Can you break your dick?" Coop asks.

All eyes are suddenly on him.

I look to Milo and Texas, but neither looks like they're even going to attempt this one.

"I'm sorry. Can you, what?" I ask.

"Your dick. Can you break it?"

"Are you asking me to?"

"No, tosspot. This girl was rough the other night, and I'm a fan of rough, but fuck knows what she did. It doesn't feel right."

"Oh my God!" Texas snaps. "We're eating here, Coop! If your little slut broke you, go to a doctor. Or better still, why don't you all show some fucking restraint? You don't have to sleep with everything!" She slams her coffee cup down and storms out.

We all jump as the door bangs shut.

"What just happened?" Milo asks.

I happened.

"Er, I don't know, but I nominate Kitt to go find out," Coop says.

"Seconded," Milo adds. "Good luck, Kitt."

"Why me?"

Milo folds his arms over his chest, making it clear that he's not going anywhere. "Because you two are closer." He gives me a pointed look. "She talks to you more."

I give him the middle finger. "I'm not handling an emotional woman before coffee and food."

He gestures to the food laid out on the trolleys. "Then, get to eating."

After consuming bacon rolls, pastries, and cereal, I suddenly find myself in front of Tex's suite. I knew I couldn't put it off forever, but I did eat very slowly.

I raise my hand and knock on her door. I can perform to thousands of people with barely a care in the world, but one girl has me nervous as hell.

In the two years I've known her, our friendship has been easy. Now, I feel like I'm walking a tightrope. Blindfolded.

She opens the door and bites the inside of her cheek. Her eyes look slightly to my side, like she can't quite meet my eyes.

"Hi," I say.

"Hi."

"Can I come in, Tex?"

She doesn't say anything, but she takes a step to the side. I'm not sure if I want to have this conversation or not. Today should be epic. We should all be on a high, and this is doing nothing but bringing me down.

"Are you okay?" I ask when she closes the door behind us.

"Yeah." She sighs. "I'm sorry about before."

"What was that?"

"Um, I don't really know."

I give her a look. "Don't lie to me, Texas."

I step closer, and her eyes widen. She looks like she wants to run. I'm not going to give her the opportunity to run from me. She backs up until she's pressed against the door. There's nowhere else for her to go.

"I'm not," she whispers.

"You did it again. Don't. Fucking. Lie."

Why the hell does her honesty mean so much to you? People lie about shit all the time.

"I think you should go," she says, straightening her back.

I'm so close to her now that I can feel her rapid breath. She's just inches away. Her body trembles, as if she's afraid, but I know that she's not.

"I'm not leaving." *Why am I not leaving? Why can't I just leave?* "I don't like it when things are like this, so let's move past it. I'm tired of this shit."

"Fuck you," she whispers.

"Fuck me?" I lift my eyebrow. "Is that the problem, Tex?"

I push my body against hers, and her mouth opens.

I groan, and she closes her eyes.

"Kitt, you can't. What are you doing?"

Good question. It's one I don't have an answer to because I usually know exactly what I want and what I need to do to get it. With her, I don't have a clue. I don't know what I'm thinking, what I'm doing, or what I want. She makes my fucking brain short-circuit. She takes away all logic and reason, and all that's left is what my goddamn body wants.

I step closer, and her body is flush with mine. She feels like heaven.

Her eyes flutter open, and she breathes long and deep, like she's trying to control herself. I clench my fists and grit my teeth so hard that they almost crack.

If I sleep with her, there's no going back, not even if it'll help with all this sexual tension. The guilt will still be there. I'll still know I betrayed Mark even if he never finds out.

"What's wrong? Finding it difficult to admit to yourself that you want me to fuck you?"

Her expression falls, and she looks devastated.

Fuck. I've hurt her. Again.

She sucks in a breath, and her eyes fill with tears.

I step back, like I've been shocked, and I shake my head. "I shouldn't have…I'm sorry, Tex. I didn't mean that. Shit, I don't know what I'm doing here. I don't know why we do this."

It's more than that. We could never just shag.

"You should leave." Her voice is low and thick with emotion that she won't allow herself to embrace in front of me.

I should leave, but I don't want to because I know she's going to cry as soon as I do.

"No." I feel desperate. Everything inside me is screaming for me to fix this, to find some way of taking it back. "I can't leave it like this."

"Fine. I forgive you. Now, please leave me alone."

That sounds more permanent than I can give her. A few hours, I can do, but she sounds like she wants me out of her life. Not only is that impossible in our current situation, but I'm not willing to even try. My life without her isn't a life I want.

I rub my forehead. "What is happening? What are you doing to me?"

Using my moment of confusion against me, she slips around me, and now, there's a lot of distance between us.

She's stronger. Her back is straight, her head held high. "I'm not doing anything. I had a moment back there, and I apologised for it. Let's blame estrogen."

"I don't want to blame something that isn't at fault."

"Then, blame me or yourself. Whatever, Kitt. I don't really care anymore."

"Yes, you do!" I explode, shocking myself. "Oh my God, you're frustrating." Gripping my hair, I take deep breaths and pace. I don't know if I want to kiss her or kill her.

"You need to leave."

"You need to stop lying to me!"

"Why? It doesn't matter. I don't have to tell you every little fucking detail. You don't need to know everything about me."

"Yes, I fucking do!" I snap.

What? No, you don't. Friends can keep secrets. You don't need to know everything.

Yes, you do.

Fuck.

"I don't know what you want from me," she says.

"Neither do I," I whisper.

Inside, I'm raging with myself. I hate not knowing what's going on in my own head. I hate how much she can get to me. It shouldn't be possible. Right now, I have everything going for me, and here I am, allowing a girl to get so deep inside my head that I don't have the first idea how to get her out—or if I even want to.

I feel like smashing something, then grabbing her, and burying myself so deep inside her that I'll forget everything.

"Okay. Then, can we leave this? I would really like for us to go back to normal now," she says.

"Until you ran out a few minutes ago, I wasn't aware that we weren't." I'm lying now.

She folds her arms. "Really, Kitt? When I'm telling you I want things to be okay between us, you come back with that?"

"Sorry." I hold my hands up. "I'm sorry, okay? I don't know why I'm being a dick."

"Have you eaten?"

"Yes," I reply.

"Then, I don't know why either."

Lie.

We both know. Deep down, we both fucking know.

"I know that I need some space though..." She lifts her eyebrow and looks at the door, giving me my cue.

Leaving feels wrong even though I've done a bang-up job of screwing this up.

"Right. I'll see you later?"

"Sure," she replies, not committing to anything.

If she had any intention of seeing me again today, she would be a little more enthusiastic, so I don't expect anything.

She won't have a choice tomorrow. She's accompanying us to some bullshit chat show we have to do. I get that we have to do all these appearances, but I'd honestly rather just play music.

"Okay. See you later," I say as I turn around. My hand hovers over the handle.

This is so wrong. I don't want to leave her. There is so much I want to say, but I don't have any clue what or in which order. I don't know what any of it means.

She doesn't reply, so I walk out, having no idea if I've screwed things up permanently or if I can fix this.

14

TEXAS
SATURDAY, MAY 9
PARIS, FRANCE

I'm in the green room, waiting for Filthy Sound to appear on a chat show here in Paris.
　　Last night and this morning was horrible, and I'm done.
　　So, I'm sitting here, pretending I'm not completely focused on Kitt.
　　Milo is distracted on his phone, so I'm chatting with Cooper—or I'm pretending to. It hurts to watch Kitt, but I can't stop looking. It's like witnessing a car crash. Only, I feel like the car is going to plough into me.
　　"These things are piss boring," Coop complains.
　　"Piss boring?"
　　Lazily shrugging one shoulder, he adds, "Why do we have to do it at all?"
　　"Er, to promote the tour."
　　"It's already sold out, Texas!"

"So, talk more about the album, Coop. You're not a complete rookie anymore."

"I feel like it. All I want to do is play music and get my end away."

Charming. I really wish there were female members in Enigma or Filthy Sound. Being the only one is tough.

Coop grins at my expression. "This isn't news to you."

"No, it's not. I think I'd enjoy it more if one of you were a gentleman rather that sex mad animals."

"Kitt's the closest. Go sit with him."

Yeah, fucking right! I'd rather stick needles up my nails and rub bleach in my eyes than talk to him at the minute. And that man is *no* gentleman.

"No, thanks. I'm happy here."

"Oh, Texy, he'll ditch that chick to chill with you."

He makes a face, and I turn my nose up.

"So not what I mean." *Lie.* It is, but I don't want anyone to know Kitt's flirting with other women bothers me. I don't want to have feelings for him. I'm working on getting rid of them. Only, I don't know how to do that.

The girl Kitt is talking to laughs.

I know her name, but I don't wish to acknowledge it, so I'm going to refer to her as Slut Y because that's about where we are on the alphabet. Kitt has slept with way more women than that, but I've not had to endure all of them.

Turning my head, I make sure I can't see them at all.

It's fine. You'll be fine. You've been through this many times. You're a seasoned pro.

But just because I've done this time and time again doesn't mean it hurts any less. As soon as I'm over him, the better. He makes me feel weak, and I hate that *so* much. My dad brought me up to take on the world while giving it the middle finger, and one guy can bring me down.

What the hell is up with that?

Cooper kicks his feet up onto the coffee table and grabs a handful of chocolates. He lies back and shoves them in his face, having no idea about my inner struggle, not that he would.

I've not exactly told anyone about how much I like Kitt.

Except for Peyton. I miss her now more than ever.

Behind me, Slut Y laughs.

Because I can't see them, I'm imagining what's happening, and I don't know what's worse.

Just keep smiling, and keep breathing. You'll be out of here before you know it.

I need to put some distance between me and Kitt because this isn't healthy for either of us. I constantly feel like my stomach is in knots, and I'm exhausted—physically, mentally and emotionally.

If I could have any wish right now, I'd wish to be completely over Kitt.

Actually, that's a lie. It would be for him to want me as much as I want him.

This. Sucks.

Filthy Sound is called out. They won't need luck. The show will. Cooper is kind of a loose cannon, and when they're all together, they're not easy to control.

"Don't swear, Coop!" I remind him.

"Don't try to change me, baby!" he shouts over his shoulder, raising his arm in the air.

Kitt swings his arm out and slaps his stomach. Then, the door closes behind them, and I breathe a sigh of relief.

I'm left with Ted, Slut Y, and her security team. I have Ted with me, and she has five bodyguards. *Five.*

How incompetent are the first four?

Whatever. It doesn't bother me.

"Are you enjoying the tour, Texas?" she asks.

Perfect. She knows who I am.

"Yep. Congrats on the movie, by the way."

It's recently been announced that she's a lead in something I no longer want to see.

"Thank you," she replies.

Ugh, she's even sincere. Why can't she be bitchy, so I can hate her?

Oh God, I'm the bitchy one.
Fuck you, Kitt Daniels.

She's not doing anything wrong. She doesn't know what's been happening between me and Kitt.

I put on a smile and engage in conversation. "So, are you coming to one of the shows?"

"I think I might have to now!"

Slut.

"Yeah, that'd be great. I'm sure the guys will love to see you there."

Kitt will. Obviously. Because he's incapable of keeping it in his pants, and he sleeps with everyone who isn't me.

She flicks her shiny rusty-red hair over her shoulder. "I hope so. There any gossip you can tell me about him?"

Herpes. That's all you've got to say to make this problem go away.

"Well..." I pause, weighing up my options. "Um..."

She purses her lips as she waits. Lips that will be on Kitt later.

"He has herpes."

All right, I never claimed the high road was for me.

Her mouth pops open, making a gross smacking sound.

Oh, shit, I can't actually do this. Kitt does not need that rumour floating around.

I make myself laugh. "I'm kidding!"

"Oh God! I thought you were serious. I should've known. You've got quite the rep for being funny and playing jokes."

Hurry up, guys, I want to leave.

Standing up, I give her a fleeting smile. "I need the bathroom. Please excuse me."

"Of course." She turns to talk to one of her security guys, who looks like Johnny Bravo with his massive blond quiff.

As soon as I'm in the corridor, Ted is right beside me, watching me as I walk. I really hope he bumps into something.

"If you keep staring at me like that, I'm going to fire you."

"You can't fire me. You didn't hire me."

I grit my teeth. "I fixed it, Teddy. You saw that, too, right?"

"Oh, I saw it all."

"I hate you."

"I'll be right outside."

Gripping the door, I turn to him. "Oh, don't worry. I'm never coming out again."

I hear him laugh as I go inside the bathroom. *Wanker.* This isn't funny.

Nothing about me and Kitt seems very funny anymore. I miss that.

After the interview, which I hid in the bathroom for most of, we head back to the hotel to prepare for the show tonight, which will involve beer and food. For me, it's going to be drinking my body weight in alcohol, so I won't think about Kitt or what he and Miss Movie Star Slut Y will be up to later.

If there weren't something wrong with me, some part that must like getting hurt, I'd leave and go home. It would be much easier. But I need to be around him.

My God, you are so screwed up.

Even though I know he's going to be shagging someone else tonight, I still won't bloody leave. That's not right. Maybe I should put an SOS call in to Peyton. She'll have me on the next flight out of Paris.

We go our separate ways when we're back at the hotel, and I dial Pey's number as soon as Ted wiggles the door handle on the other side to make sure it's definitely locked.

I have three male rock stars and a bulky bodyguard who've had a hand in bringing me up. I shouldn't be this bad with Kitt.

How were you raised by four men and still suck with guys?

You're a special kind of fail.

"What have you done now?" Peyton says down the phone.

"Piss off, bitch. I've not even said anything yet!"

She laughs. "You don't need to. You're in close contact with Kitt every day, so something is bound to have gone wrong."

"And you immediately think it's because of me?"

"Well, yeah."

"Why?"

"Because you *lurve* him and because he…" She stalls, not wanting to hurt my feelings.

Honestly, it's nothing worse than I've had direct from the source a hundred times over.

"Because he doesn't like me in that way," I say.

"Oh my God, Tex, do you want me to go?"

"No. I want you to come here."

"I wish I could. Portugal, I promise."

"Can't wait."

"Are you going to the show tonight?"

I groan. "Yep."

"Are you going to tell me what's happened with him?"

Cage, dry-humping. I don't think so.

"We kissed, and it's a big mistake that should've never happened." Apparently.

"I'm sorry."

"It's fine. Just be prepared to get me shitfaced when you're here."

"Like that wasn't going to happen anyway."

I love her.

"Anyway, do you need more moral support? Only, I'm on set, and I'm fucking tired. If we don't wrap this up, I'm going to kill someone."

"Wow. Go act your little heart out, and I'll speak to you soon."

"Be careful, Tex," she says before the line goes dead.

Her warning is a little late.

Enigma is kicking things off, like, right now, so I run toward the back entrance. I'm bloody late! My dad might well be past it now, but I'm not missing his performance.

with the Band

I stepped outside for a second because my stupid phone wasn't getting reception, and I had to return Jennifer's call. Turned out to be nothing besides her asking how it was going.

A member of security folds his arms over his bodybuilder-style chest as I approach. I expect him to step aside, but he doesn't.

"Excuse me," I say. "I need to get inside."

"I'm sure you do. Ticket holders need to use the front or side entrance. If you don't have a ticket, you're not getting in."

Well, of course I don't have a bloody ticket. "I'm Texas, Mark Knight's daughter. Can you let me in, please? I really don't want to miss the show."

Whoa, he does not believe me at all. His overgrown eyebrows rise higher than I ever thought possible.

"That's a new one. I'll give you that. Sorry, love."

"What? I'm not making it up. Look, just go get him or anyone else—literally, *anyone*—and they'll tell you," I say, looking past him into the building.

"I don't know how you got around here, but you need to leave. Now."

"I got around here because our fucking car is right over there," I snap, pointing to the vehicle he can't even see in the dark. "Come on, please. I promised my dad I'd watch, and I want to see him before he goes on."

"Do you think I was born yesterday?"

"Right now, I do, yeah," I reply through gritted teeth. "Why would I make up being Mark's daughter?"

"To get inside."

I sigh sharply. "I'm not lying. I'm with the band."

"Of course you are, darlin'."

Fine, he asked for it.

"*Dad!*" I scream at the top of my lungs, making the guy jump.

"What the hell are you playing at?" he shouts as he reaches out for me.

I jump back and hold my hand up. "Don't touch me!"

Cooper pops his head around the door, and I want to kiss him.

"Tex, you okay? What the fuck are you doing out there?"

The bouncer's face drops as he realises he's made a mistake. He looks like he's scared for his job. If I were a total bitch, he should be. But I'm not, so I won't say anything.

"Excuse me, *please*," I say.

He steps aside, muttering an apology.

Cooper slings his arm over my shoulder and kisses the side of my head. "He giving you a hard time?"

"Nah. He just assumed I'm a groupie."

"Anytime you want to give that role a try—"

"I'll speak to Milo."

"Ouch, girl. Why Milo?"

Because saying Kitt would send me paranoid that Cooper might joke about it. I can't handle Kitt knowing how I feel about him. I mean, he probably knows, but it's not been confirmed. I don't want it to be confirmed.

My life is one big fucking picnic.

"Why not Milo?"

Cooper stops and pulls my arm, twisting me around so that he's facing me head-on. "I'm much better-looking, and you know it."

"Better-looking than who?" Kitt asks from behind me.

My breath catches. I was not ready for him.

"Nothing. Good luck out there." I dash off to Ted, who's standing down the hall.

My heart is in my stomach. I can't be around Kitt.

15

TEXAS
SATURDAY, MAY 9
PARIS, FRANCE

I love the part of the after-party when my dad fucks off. It only ever happens if Kitt, Milo, and Cooper are with me because, without them, I would obviously be murdered or whatever other scenarios my dad stresses over.

It only took five shots to get me drunk. Or was it six? Whatever. I had shots, and I'm buzzing. The atmosphere is awesome, and everyone is being friendly. And, so far, there has been no drama. I think it helps that the only sober people are security and staff.

I'm at the bar with Kitt, Milo, and Jessica LaRoux, who I'm kind of fangirling over because she's a mega awesome actress and she has kissed many beautiful leading men. I want to quiz her on them, but you should always be able to relax at an after-party, not have more crazies hounding you.

She's probably going to be sleeping with Milo tonight because there have been many, many *looks* between them. And his hands have been on her all night.

"So, you want to dance, handsome?" she asks Milo, tilting her head to the side in a sexy and seductive way.

Smirking, he hands Kitt his drink and backs Jessica up to the dance floor.

Kitt necks Milo's whiskey and slams the empty on the side just as Cooper storms over to us.

"Uh-oh," I mutter.

He looks pissed off and frustrated.

"What happened?" Kitt asks.

"I've just had boring sex." He scowls.

"Maybe you're losing your mojo," I tease.

His baby-blue eyes instantly darken, and if I wasn't a girl, I think I would've been floored by now. Beside me, Kitt laughs.

"That is *not* it, and if you're going to say shit like that, I'm going to take you over the bar to prove you wrong."

I shrug. "No, thanks. I don't like boring sex."

"Kitt, sort her out."

Kitt shakes his head.

Coop's eyes narrow. "Why not?"

"Funny."

I grin and raise my eyebrows. "See? He's on my side. Why was this last girl boring then? She just lie there, like a sack of potatoes?"

"Not exactly. Just didn't feel right."

"You had it in the right hole, yeah?" Kitt asks.

"Fuck off," Coop replies. "She was…you know…"

"A man?" I say.

"You two are dicks!"

"Ah, come on. What was wrong with her?" Kitt asks.

"I'm not one to be rude about people's bits and pieces, but she was big down there, like no-point-in-doing-it big. Seriously, it was like chucking a sausage down a tunnel."

Kitt laughs, but I do not.

What the fuck is wrong with Cooper?

"Jesus! I have the worst mental image," I groan. "You're a terrible person, Coop."

"You *both* asked me what was wrong with her."

"And aren't we regretting that?" Kitt probably isn't actually. He's still laughing.

They're going straight to hell.

"How do you know it's her and not you? You might be tiny," I say.

I know he isn't, and I don't mean that I've been there, but almost everyone has seen Cooper's penis. He's not at all shy.

"You're cute, Tex."

"You're a pig, Coop."

"Who's your conquest for the evening?" he asks, ignoring my gibe.

"Yeah, I'm not like you guys."

"Ah, come on. I've pulled already. It looks like Milo is about to, and Kitt likes the blonde in the red dress. What about you?"

Kitt likes some slut in a red dress?

Gritting my teeth, I look around the room, pretending I'm not affected by Kitt's perving over someone who is not me. "Not sure yet."

"You're not playing, Tex," Kitt says.

He sounds very authoritative, and it's bloody annoying. *How dare he try to dictate what I can and cannot do, like my dad does.* I know Dad told them to look out for me, but this is ridiculous.

Unless he likes you...

Nope. Don't go there. It always backfires.

When we shared those kisses, the cage, every look, and every near miss, I thought something might come of it. I can't keep giving a piece of myself to him, only to have it thrown back.

"I think I'll do whatever I damn please. Thank you very much. Who isn't a dickhead in here, Cooper?"

Throwing his arm around my shoulders, he scans the room. "Well...I don't know many of them. Or I do, and I was drunk the last time." He flashes a smile. His liver is probably shrivelled. "I think Isaiah is pretty down though."

"Hmm," I murmur, looking Isaiah over. "He's gorgeous."

"Cooper, what are you doing? Mark will have your balls if you introduce her to—"

"Funny enough, Kitt, I hadn't planned on telling him," he replies.

"You need to stop. I'm not a fucking kid, and if I want to see someone, I will," I snap.

Who the bloody hell does he think he is?

Kitt holds his hands up and turns around. I instantly regret what I said, which pisses me off even more.

Forcing myself to look away, I say to Cooper, "Introduce me."

I don't really want to do this, but maybe meeting someone new is what I need to finally get over Kitt. To be fair, I'd be bloody over the moon just to stop thinking of him constantly.

We are never going to happen, and I have to accept that.

You can't accept that because you're so in love with him that you'd rather have your heart pummelled than walk away. You. Need. To. Seek. Help.

Cooper takes my hand and marches me through the throng of gyrating bodies on the dance floor. I recognise most people here, and I'm a little starstruck by some. Everyone is drinking champagne, and laughter is buzzing off the walls. It seems like Kitt and I are the only ones not jumping with happiness tonight.

Coop squeezes my hand as we get closer. I know of Isaiah and his band, The Kings. They're a little more mainstream than Enigma and Filthy Sound, but they're good. This is my first time meeting him.

He turns as we approach, and when his amber eyes land on me, he smiles. At least he seems interested. Isaiah is very good-looking. His chiselled jaw and dusty-blond hair are enough to melt hearts and have women lift their skirts. He's tall and muscular, and he has a killer smile.

Even though he's the whole perfect package, I can't help but compare him to Kitt. I do it with every man.

And, of course, Kitt never loses.

"Isaiah, hey, man," Cooper says, slapping him on the shoulder.

"Great show tonight," Isaiah replies.

"Thanks. This is—"

"Texas Knight," Isaiah finishes. "Pleasure." He leans in and kisses my cheek.

Bit forward, but Kitt is backward, so it's a nice change.

"Hi," I say before biting my lip.

He smells good. It's a woodsy smell I recognise from the vast amount of guitars we have at home and on tour.

"Gotta go. Milo's calling me," Cooper says before ducking out.

Milo obviously hasn't called him or anyone. He has his tongue down Jessica's throat.

I wince. "Yeah, Coop's not so subtle."

Isaiah laughs, and his voice is deep and sexy. "No, he's really not. So, how are you finding things on tour?" He frowns. "I'm a dick. Forget I said that. You've been on tour since you were in nappies."

Who would've thought this rock star was actually awkward? It's endearing.

My rock stars are cocky little fuckers.

"It's better now that I'm of drinking age," I reply.

"You didn't drink underage?"

"Oh, I did, but since I turned eighteen, my dad's been a bit more relaxed about leaving me with Kitt, Cooper, and Milo."

I've no idea why. He's met them.

"Your dad is my fucking hero. I grew up listening to his music and miming along at his concerts. And you can never tell him I told you that."

I salute. "Your secret will die with me."

Isaiah laughs and nods his head toward the bar. "You want to get a drink?"

I've probably had enough, but I really want to spend some time with him. It's healthy since we seem to have a mutual like for each other so far.

"I'd love to."

He places his hand on my hip as we dodge the people on the dance floor. Kitt is at the bar, too, so this might get a little uncomfortable.

"What are you having?"

"Sambuca," I reply, smirking.

His light eyebrows rise. "Oh, yeah? Well, it'd be rude to make you take shots on your own."

"Plural?" I ask.

"You only want one?"

I shake my head.

Yes, this is exactly what I need. Getting wasted with a beautiful man is about my favourite thing to do.

"Good," he replies.

Isaiah and I clink glasses before downing the first shot.

"What's next for the band then?" I ask.

He steps closer, so we're in each other's personal space. "Oh, you've heard of me then?"

Biting my lip, I nod, hoping it looks sexy. It must because Isaiah's mouth parts, and he presses his chest against mine. His chest is hard and muscular. He towers above me, but he looks good from this angle. My heart isn't all over the place, like it is with Kitt, but I'm definitely attracted to Isaiah. I mean, I have eyes.

"I happen to quite like your band," I say.

His lips pull up into a crooked smile. "I'll have to get you backstage next time."

"Yes, you will. I'm not a groupie though, Isaiah."

Chuckling, he wraps his arms around my waist. "Believe me, I know."

"You're kind of confusing."

He looks genuinely surprised. "I am?"

"Yes. One minute, you're shy and borderline awkward, and the next, you're forward. Which one is the real Isaiah?"

"You'll have to spend some time with me and find out."

"Mmhmm, but I'll be gone in the morning."

"So, we have, what? Seven hours?"

"About that. If we don't sleep."

This is moving speed-of-light fast, but it's a nice change of pace.

"Texas!" Kitt shouts.

Isaiah's eyes light up. "Kitt Daniels. Man, awesome show."

Kitt grinds his teeth. "Thanks. We're leaving in ten, Tex."

"Fine. I'll see you at the hotel in the morning."

"Do you really think that's going to happen?"

I'm burning with anger. My skin feels hot and tight, and I want to slap him.

Glaring, I stare him down. He doesn't budge. His eyes bore into me, and his face is completely blank. I don't know if he's jealous or just being a prick.

Isaiah puts his arm over my shoulders. "It's cool, man. I'll make sure she gets back okay."

"See? I'm fine with Isaiah."

I tug his wrist, and he takes the hint. We walk away from Kitt and head toward a table in the corner.

Kitt is being fucking ridiculous. My hands are shaking. I'm so angry with him.

"You good?" Isaiah asks, sitting down on a stool.

Be fine. Isaiah is gorgeous, too, and you're having a nice time with him.

"I am."

He smiles and pulls me between his legs. I don't feel what I feel when I touch Kitt, but I'm not hopelessly in love with Isaiah, so there's no reason I'd feel the same. Plus, I'm not looking to marry the guy. We're just having a few drinks together.

"Glad to hear it. So, if I were to ask you to dance, what are the odds you'll say yes?"

"Hmm, I think your odds are pretty good."

His eyebrows lift. "Interesting."
He takes my hands and puts them around his neck.
Yep, I'm going to enjoy tonight.

16

KITT
SATURDAY, MAY 9
PARIS, FRANCE

I take a swig straight from the bottle I made the bartender give me. I'm past the point of having the patience to wait for single glasses. Texas is pissing me the fuck off.

"What's up with you?" Cooper asks, leaning against the bar. "You look like someone's left you high and dry. The blonde not up for it?"

"I didn't talk to the blonde."

The brunette's driving me crazy.

"So, why this look?" he asks, wiggling his fingers in front of my face.

"I'm tired."

"So? Sleep when you're dead. You're a rock star, dipshit. Start acting like one."

"There's more to it than sex."

He looks me dead in the eyes for the longest time. "No, there's not."

I roll my eyes. "Fuck off, Coop."

"Nah. Where's Milo?"

I raise my eyes to the exit. "Left with Jessica thirty minutes ago."

"Nice. She's a solid nine. Texas?"

Gritting my teeth, I tilt my chin toward a booth. Texas and Isaiah are drinking together, sitting far too close. I fucking hate him, and I hate her.

No, you don't hate her.

If he touches her leg one more time, I'm going to cut his fucking hand off. My chest is tight. Everything is too fucking tight. I'm grinding my teeth so hard that there will be nothing left. All I can feel is rage.

"Ah, go get him, girl," Cooper murmurs. He sounds proud of her.

"Why are you encouraging that shit?" I bark.

"Why wouldn't I? She's a big girl now. If she wants to have sex with a rock star, she can."

I want to punch him in the gut.

And since when has it been okay for Texas to sleep around?

Double standards. You're hardly saving yourself for marriage. You didn't even save yourself until it was legal for you to have sex.

"You know who she is, Cooper."

"Mark knows she's not going to stay a virgin forever. Heck, she's probably not a virgin now."

My hands shake. I slam the bottle down and clench my fists. "We should get her back to the hotel."

Coop's mouth turns up, and he folds his arms. "Are you jealous, Kitt?"

Jealous? I don't get fucking jealous. I can have whatever I want, whenever I want.

"I'm just looking out for her—you know, like we promised Mark. Or have you forgotten everything he's done for us?"

You sure have.

"Not forgotten, but she's fine, bro. She can flirt and do whatever the hell she wants. We're here to look out for her, but that doesn't mean we're her babysitters. It means, we'll make sure she's safe, and she gets home safe. What she chooses to do in the meantime is up to her. Now, again, are you jealous? Is there something going on with you and her? Because you're not usually this uptight."

"Of course there's nothing going on."

"Then, calm the fuck down. She's having fun."

Too much fun.

I feel sick.

"Nah, I'm beat. I'll see you back at the hotel." I push off the bar.

Cooper grabs my arm. "Are you making her go with you?"

"Yes."

She's lucky I've waited this long.

"I can get her back just fine, too, you know. She's enjoying herself."

Leaving Cooper alone with Texas when they're both drunk is one of the worst ideas I've ever heard. Many times, he's fallen asleep in a bar, and security has had to bring him back to the bus or his room. Or he's stayed out with some girl and woken up in a strange house, having no idea how he got there or which hotel he was staying at.

"You're kidding, right? Only a few weeks ago, you tried to let yourself into a room in the wrong hotel."

"But I had the right room number," he says, as if it's something to be proud of.

I'm all up for having a good night and getting wasted, but I've always been able to walk at the end of it. "I'll be taking Tex with me. See you tomorrow."

He rolls his eyes. "Whatever, man."

I leave him to it. No doubt, he'll see his next victim soon and forget all about Texas anyway. My muscles protest from the effort of trying to slow myself down. All I can see is her with Isaiah, and I need it to stop.

Neither of them looks up as I approach. Isaiah brushes Tex's hair out of her face and leans closer.

Fuck no.

I stop dead when his lips touch hers.

Instead of pushing him away, like she should, she kisses him back. I feel like I've just had the air knocked out of me by something big and hard smashing into my chest.

"Texas!" I snap. I make my legs move and finally reach the edge of their booth.

Stay calm.

Jumping, she looks over her shoulder. "Kitt, what's wrong?"

"We're leaving. Now. Cooper is looking for his next conquest, and Milo's already gone. I'm not leaving you with a guy you've known for three minutes. No offense, Isaiah."

He smirks. "None taken. I understand the situation."

No, you don't.

"But I don't want to leave, Kitt."

"Well, life's a shit sandwich, Texas. Get up."

"You're being an arsehole," she growls.

"Say good-bye. I'm sure you'll see Isaiah again."

"I'm sure she will," he replies, stroking her cheek.

I look away and ball my hands.

Why does this *hurt*?

"Fine," Texas says. "Thanks for the awesome evening, Isaiah." She stands up without kissing him again.

I snatch her hand and pull her closer to me. "Bye, Isaiah."

As I practically pull her outside, she yanks on our connected hands, but I'm too strong. I can't let go.

"What the bloody hell is wrong with you? That was so rude!" she says.

We smile as we leave the club because we know exactly what's going to be out there. I release her hand and wrap my arm around her back, opening the door with the other hand. She won't run because it wouldn't look good.

Lights flash like strobe lighting the second we're outside.

"Kitt, have you had a good evening?"

"Kitt, how's the tour going?"

"Kitt…"

"Kitt…"

I zone them out and concentrate on getting Texas into the waiting car. Ted is on the other side of Texas, making sure no one can reach her. He opens the car door, and we get in.

Tex sighs as Ted slams the door closed. Her smile falls. She's itching to shout at me again, but she won't do it with Ted here. I'm sure that'll be reserved just for me later.

"Are you okay?" I ask.

She purses her lips and nods once.

I hand her a bottle of water from the fridge. "You're going to need to sober up a little. Mark might still be up."

She snatches it from my hand and mutters a pissed off, "Thanks."

I groan and rub my eyes. "Don't be angry, Tex."

Stealing a glance at Ted, who is on his phone and deep in conversation, she says, "You acted like a moron tonight, and I don't understand why. Kitt, you're usually…I don't know…fun."

"I'm not fun anymore?"

You've noticed that, too.

"Tonight, you weren't. I don't like it."

"I'm sorry, okay? I just don't want to see you make a mistake."

She screws the cap back on the bottle and twists her body. "A mistake? I was only talking to him. We had one kiss. I'm not a child. If I want to talk to someone, I will. If I want to kiss someone, I will. If I want to have sex with someone, I will."

Her words rub across my skin like sandpaper.

"I understand all of that."

"Then, what?"

Yeah, what?

I look out the window and close my eyes. If I had the answer to that question, I have a feeling that things would be so much easier. I don't want to be like this.

She turns her body, and out of the corner of my eye, I see her determination. She wants answers.

"Come on, Kitt!"

"Mark," I say, as if that's the answer to everything. "What if you'd left with Isaiah and been photographed with him, and your dad saw, huh? He doesn't know the guy, and he sure as hell wouldn't be happy if your sex life was splashed all over the press."

She narrows her eyes, knowing I've got her there. Mark isn't an idiot. He must know that Texas isn't a virgin after her relationship, but no one wants to see their child's about-to-have-a-one-night-stand picture.

"My dad would've been fine. He knows I date."

"Dating and casual fucking are two different things, and despite what you say, I know you don't want him to know if you chose to sleep around."

"Fuck you. It was *one* guy, and nothing even happened. You make it sound like I'm with someone new every night. That's you!"

"That's not what I meant, and you know it."

"Oh my God, why are we even talking about this? Let's forget it because you're making me hate you right now."

Fuck.

She is the only person with the power to bring me to my knees with her words.

"I…" I mutter, like a fucking idiot. "Don't hate me, Tex," I whisper.

She groans and turns her head. "Don't use your eyes like that. It's not fair!"

"Come on." I smile now because I know she's already forgiven me. "I'm sorry, okay?"

When she looks up, her shoulders relax, and her face softens. "Okay."

I need to fix this. Somehow, I need to fix something I unintentionally broke, but I have no idea how to repair it.

With the Band

Once Ted hangs up, I lean forward and whisper in his ear. He chuckles and nods his head, letting me know he understood and is on board.

I hope she likes this because, right now, I'm nervous as hell.

"What was that?" she asks.

"You'll see in a minute."

"Come on! I hate—"

I nudge her shoulder. "Don't be a brat."

"Bugger off."

Smirking, I lean over and kiss the side of her head.

Why does that feel so right?

Tex looks up and gives me a smile that stops my heart.

Jesus.

She turns and looks out the window as Ted drives us in a different direction. No doubt, she's trying to figure out where we're going at 1:38 a.m., but her knowledge of Paris is limited.

After fifteen minutes of silence, Ted parks the car and turns to me. "I can give you a bit of space."

"Thanks, man."

Texas is staring, open-mouthed, as she finally realises where we are—the Eiffel Tower. For the next hour and fifteen minutes, the lights will be on and will twinkle on the hour for ten minutes.

"You getting out, Tex? We need to walk the rest of the way."

She finally snaps out of her trance. "You've brought me to the Eiffel Tower?"

"Looks like it. I'm happy to watch from the car."

"Right. Get out, idiot" she mutters to herself. Giving me a long look, she opens the door.

"Wait in the car, Ted? We won't go far."

"Kitt…"

"I won't let her get hurt. Please?"

"I said, I'll watch from a distance. That's the best I can do."

I give him a nod, knowing I was asking too much. Security is something we have to take seriously, especially with her. I round the car, and somehow, my hand finds hers.

Friend zone's fucked.

She feels like answers to questions I'm not ready to even think about.

We walk across the grass in silence. There are quite a few people around, locals and tourists, but it's so easy to forget everyone when she's around. It's dark out, but the area is lit. The vastness of the Eiffel Tower takes me by surprise, and the lights make it even more incredible.

Pictures do not do it any justice.

"Wow," Tex whispers. This isn't her first time here, but this isn't something that gets less exciting, the more you see it. "How come you brought me here? I didn't think we'd have time," she whispers.

"That's why," I say. I've got a lot to make up for. "We have time now, and I thought you'd like to see the light show."

"Oh my gosh! I forgot about that." She squeezes my hand in excitement and picks up the pace.

I'm not sure how close she wants to get because I imagine it's better if your view is of the entire thing. I don't really care as long as she loves it.

Why is everything suddenly about her? Why do I want to move the fucking earth if it'll make her happy?

Texas stops just before it starts to become difficult to see the whole thing in one frame. "It's so beautiful at night. Remind me to move to Paris one day."

Pushing my luck further, I let go of her hand and wrap my arm around her.

I need her closer. It's not enough.

She lays her head on my chest, and my heart starts to thump loudly.

Get a grip.

She tilts her body into me while looking up at the lit tower. Nothing has ever felt more right or more important.

Something, everything, inside me shifts, and I have the urge to hold her tighter and never let go.

This is so, so wrong, and I'm taking things too far. I can't pretend this is innocent. There has never been a less innocent embrace in history. This is full of promises and hope and future.

No matter what happens from here on out, Texas will have a piece of me that I'll never get back.

Fuck. She is the first girl to have my heart.

I rest my head against hers and close my eyes. This won't last forever. No matter what I want to happen after tonight, it can't. This moment with her is perfect, and I'm not going to spend a second of it stressing over my moral dilemma.

We'll always have tonight. Always.

She takes a sharp intake of breath, and I know that means the lights will be twinkling. I want to open my eyes, but I know nothing will be better than holding her like this right now.

"Kitt...it's amazing. So beautiful."

And she has no idea how my whole world has moved. She's happily watching the light show, and I've just had the floor whipped from under my feet.

It's terrifying. My legs are ready to run, but my arms can't let go.

"Are you watching?" she asks.

I open my eyes when her head lifts.

"Yeah. It's incredible."

That's putting it mildly. And I don't mean the tower.

"Thank you. This is...everything."

The reflection from the lights makes her eyes the most stunning shade of green. I can already feel myself moving closer. There is nothing I can do or want to do to stop me from kissing her. The need is in every part of my body.

Unlike last time, she doesn't show any signs of alarm. She doesn't back up. She does nothing but continues to stare at me, like I'm some sort of grand prize. I want to warn her that if she doesn't want this, she needs to push me away, but I can't. Nothing will stop me from tasting her.

Her mouth parts a fraction when I'm an inch away. I pull her closer with one arm, and with the other hand, I stroke her hair from her face. She's soft and delicate, and touching her skin does more for me than any other girl I've been with.

This kiss is going to be more than I'm ready for, and even knowing that, I can't stop myself from leaning in that last bit and pressing my mouth against hers.

She is perfect.

I moan as she kisses me back, long and slow. The last two kisses we shared were frantic and desperate. This kiss is full of as much need and emotion as those, but it's still worlds away.

This is everything.

This is...love.

As she presses her body against mine, she wraps both arms around my waist and holds me so tight that it's like she's scared I'll change my mind. *Not happening.*

I kiss her harder, bruising our lips with the need to be as close as I can. Texas opens up a little more, and I slide my tongue against hers.

Fuck.

Fuck!

Our hips meet as we mould closer, devouring each other. I never want this to end.

Moaning again, I begin to worry that this is turning into a porno, not that I'd mind. But Texas probably wouldn't want this to go viral.

It takes every ounce of self-control for me to pull away from her. My body wants to kick my arse in protest. I'm painfully hard, and all I want to do is kiss her until we can't breathe.

She opens her eyes and looks up at me. We're still clinging to each other.

The lights on the tower have stopped, but she doesn't seem bothered that she saw maybe only thirty seconds of the ten-minute show. Actually, it doesn't look like she's even noticed it's over.

"That should've been our first kiss," she whispers.

"I don't know. I'm kind of fond of that first one."

"Yeah? You've never mentioned it before."

"I couldn't. It's not something I regret, but it wasn't my best move."

This is.

She bites her lip. "Because it was at my dad's house?"

"That, and we were both drunk."

"It was a Christmas party. Of course we were drunk."

I laugh at her explanation and because I'm so fucking happy right now. "I should get you back to the hotel."

"You should."

She gives me a knowing smile, and I kiss her again.

It's every bit as passionate during the second pretty much sober time around. I run my hands up her arms and over her shoulders, and then I cup her face. She responds by moaning, and the sound vibrates right down to my dick.

"Yeah, we should go," I say, grinning wider than the way I did after the first time I'd touched a boob under the bra. This is one of those life-changing moments that everyone goes through. And it's happening way ahead of time and with the worst person.

And I can't bring myself to care.

"Okay."

She snuggles into my side as we turn around and head back to the car. I hold her the entire way. This is how we should've been since Christmas.

17

TEXAS
SUNDAY, MAY 10
PARIS, FRANCE

Two things.

One, tonight has been the best night of my life.

Two, I think Kitt is bipolar.

I'm not trying to be a bitch here, but his behaviour swings from one extreme to the next with absolutely no notice and seemingly no reason. I think we're good and maybe getting somewhere, and then the barriers go up, and he acts like I'm an annoying little sister.

It's giving me a headache.

But the way he kissed me tonight, right in front of one of the most romantic places on earth, has given me hope. We can't go back to how things were, not after tonight. Right now, we're good. Kitt is like the most fun and scariest roller coaster ride I've been on, and although I know, for the sake of my sanity, I should get off, I can't.

He made it impossible for me to give up when he turned on the romance.

"She's going to die. So is she. And him," Kitt says.

The movie has only just started, but it's a horror, and the teens will start getting picked off soon. His arm is around me, and I'm tucked into his side. It's the most natural position we've ever been in together.

"Yeah, and she's going to be the sole survivor," I add, curling my arm around his chest. If I'm wrong, I'm going to be pissed off. As much as I love it when a film breaks the rules, I hate it, too. I let myself like the one I think will survive, and when that person dies…

It's the reason I have to have someone hold my hand while I watch *The Walking Dead*. They don't give a shit who they kill.

"Are you going to get angry if you're wrong?" Kitt asks, smirking. He knows me well.

I lazily bump his shoulder with my head. "Yep."

He laughs and presses a kiss to the top of my head.

See? This is more than friendship.

"Thought so. You hate to be wrong about this stuff."

"Of course. You'd hate to be wrong about something musical."

"TV isn't your career, Tex."

Might as well be.

I squeeze his middle again. I like it, like how he feels. "So, Mr Rock Star, are you happy with the way things are going? All I see on social media is how awesome you guys are."

"It's amazing," he says against my hair where he places yet another kiss.

I'm so not getting bored of that anytime soon. It feels too good.

"I never thought it'd be like this. You know, I was always happy with where we were. Earning enough through music has been my goal. Of course I wanted to sell out stadiums, but as long as I was doing what I loved for a living, I was content. This is so much more than I could've imagined."

"You deserve it. I love Filthy Sound, and you all work *so* hard."

He kisses my head again.

Don't jump him.

"Thanks. I love it. I really do."

"I wish I had something I really loved. I still have no idea what I want to do." I'm surrounded by people who knew their dream careers from when they were in the bloody womb. In my nineteen years, I still haven't figured it out.

Every day, I'm with successful people, and I'm over here, proud that I can watch an entire series on Netflix in a few days. That's my life.

I need more.

But what?

Unless Netflix is hiring, I don't know what to do. I don't know what I'm good at.

Maybe Netflix is hiring. You need to check on that.

"Go find it. You have so many opportunities, more than others, but you've not had the opportunity to explore them."

"Is this your way of telling me that you don't want me on the tour?" I joke, making light of something that is so on point that my stomach rolls with discomfort.

There are people who would kill to be in my situation, and I've been wasting the chances I have. I'm in a unique position. There's not much a phone call couldn't get me, especially if it came from my dad. That kind of seems like cheating, but people see my name or recognise me, and I am given stuff. It's a stupid thing to bitch over, but I bet getting whatever I want isn't nearly as rewarding as earning what I want. Despite Jennifer's failed attempts at being a mother, she did build a career for herself even though name-dropping my dad had probably helped her along.

Ugh, I don't know.

Plus, the idea of leaving Kitt now makes me want to, like, die or something just as dramatic.

"Of course it's not. I want you here, but more than that, we all want you to be happy."

"I'm not unhappy." Not in my daily life, but something is missing. I want to get so passionate that I put in every ounce of everything to make whatever it is a success.

How do you decide what you want to do?

"Besides, I have no clue what I'd do. I don't want to do anything with my degree. What would I do?"

He bites the inside of his cheek while he thinks. It's sexy.

"You're one of the most caring people I know. Doctor?"

"No, I wouldn't be able to keep a straight face if I had to look at people's *parts*."

He laughs and the arm on the back of the chair creeps down closer to my shoulders. I like that. The movie is forgotten. His focus is on me, and although I know it's temporary, I'm going to enjoy it.

"Actress?"

"Yeah, can't act." Although I'm doing a stellar job of acting like I'm not in love with him. In two years, only two people have guessed—Will and Peyton. *Though it must be obvious to Kitt now, surely?*

"Singer? You have an amazing voice."

"I can sing, but how cliché would that be? *Daughter of rock star releases first single.* Yeah, no one will see that coming..." I roll my eyes.

Kitt laughs again. It's rough and hot as hell, and it does things to my insides that make me want to go to bed—preferably with him, but B.O.B. would do, too.

"You can't choose a career based on what people will think."

"I know. Honestly, I don't want a career in music though. I think I prefer music to be something I love, not something I have to work tirelessly for."

He gives me a nod because he knows how much work it is even though, to him, it's more than worth it.

Lifting one eyebrow, he looks down at my body. "Model?"

"Looking good all the time really isn't where my talents lie."

"You could not be more wrong there."

Is it just me, or did it get seriously hot in here?

My mouth has gone dry, and I'm unable to form words. Nothing will come out. When he says things like that, he makes me feel nervous. I am usually confident and have no issues with speaking my mind. Around Kitt, I can be so painfully shy sometimes.

He could reject me, and I wouldn't have a clue as to how to deal with that.

"Oh, first one is about to be killed," I say, glancing back at the screen as the music turns chilling.

I'm not looking at him, but I can feel his eyes are still on me.

Keep watching the TV.

I want to kiss him again so bad that I have to dig my nails into the palms of my hands to refrain from reaching where they shouldn't. The need pulses through my body. My breathing takes on a new pace—bloody fast—and I feel lightheaded.

How's that even possible? You can't breathe fast and not at all at the same damn time. And I don't know if it's the breathing thing or not, but I feel like gravity has upped and fucking left. *How does he make me feel like I'm defying the laws of everything?*

Concentrate on the TV. He can't look at you forever. Even he will know the time has come to look away or risk being a creep.

Everything is fine. Totally fine.

It's so not fucking fine that I want to face-plant on concrete.

I'm itching to look at him. My skin feels too tight. I need…something.

He's so very close. I can feel his breath as his chest moves faster. *Is he having the same problems as me?* We kissed not even an hour ago, so I don't know why I'm so scared.

Well, I do. It took him five months after the first time to kiss me again or even acknowledge it.

Maybe I should pretend I need the bathroom and give us both a minute?

But my legs won't move. I will them to get up, but every single part of me wants him, anything that he's willing to give. And that's exactly why I can't.

I won't be the type of girl who hurts herself for a few stolen moments with a man who doesn't want more. There will never be anything casual about Kitt to me, so as much as I want to feel his lips, his...well, all of him, I won't allow myself, not unless I know he's in this properly.

Heartbreak won't look good on me.

Move your arse right now.

"Do you want a beer?" I ask, still staring straight ahead.

All I need to do is get him to snap out of it. He's the one causing the problem.

"No, thanks," he whispers in a husky voice that is just sex.

Well, shit.

With my heart thumping, I turn my head against my better judgement. It's not just his voice that is pure sex tonight. His eyes are burning.

You need to put a stop to this right now.

I squirm on the spot and kick my legs up under my butt. I'm aching. My nipples harden and strain against the light padding in my bra.

His head tilts a fraction, like he's getting in the optimum position to kiss me. I mimic the action but the other way.

Dangerous. This is dangerous. Abort. Abort!

What will you do if this is just a repeat of the last times he kissed you or crossed the line and then switched back to being your bestie?

Remembering how badly my heart aches for him is all I need.

"I'll get those beers," I say, jumping up like I've just been burned.

He didn't even want a beer. Tough now.

Kitt clears his throat, but I don't look back. I head to the kitchen, determined to get wasted and forget what almost happened back there. Again.

Ha! The idea that I could forget anything with him is hilarious.

But I'm making the right decision here. It would have been so easy to kiss him there, but afterward would've hurt worse than ever.

Relationships can't be this complicated, surely? Definitely not, or no one would bother with it.

I wrench the minibar open with so much anger and frustration that I almost pull the door clean off. I don't need a lecture about damaging property from my dad, so I make sure to close it nicely after grabbing two beers. A stronger drink sounds good about now, but there's nothing strong enough to stop the way my body is throbbing with need for Kitt.

I'm so sexually frustrated that I could scream.

When I turn to go back, Kitt is staring at the TV, like his life depends on it—or like it's porn.

Okay, things have escalated quickly, like they tend to do with us, and I need to do something to lighten it up. This can't be how we are around each other. I hate the uncertainty. If we can't be together, I can accept that, but what I can't accept is anything less than a best friend because that's what he's come to be to me. There's no one that I feel so comfortable around—present situation excluded—and we can't lose that because of a kiss and a near miss.

It's not worth it.

New rule: Unless he tells you he wants more with you, don't go there. No more Eiffel Tower kisses or kisses of any other kind. You're going to be strong.

I thump down on the sofa with full force, and he cracks a smile. Handing him a beer, I kick back and hope that he'll get on board with getting us back to normal. He will want that, too. We're too close to be distant.

"Thanks," he mutters as he finally looks up.

His cocky smirk is back—thank God—and he looks like my Kitt again.

That's all I need right this second. The rest, I can work out—or try to—later.

"I didn't open them. Can you do them with your mouth?" I ask.

He gives me a wink. "I can do anything with my mouth."
Yep, he's definitely normal again.
"Really, Kitt?" I say dryly.
"I've gotten women off with the first—"
I slap his arm. "We don't need to go there."
"Prude."

Rolling my eyes, I thrust my beer at him. That needs to be opened right the hell now. I'm having horrible, horrible mental images that are making me feel sick.

How much damage can bleach really do to your eyes?

Chuckling, he takes the bottle and pops the lid with his teeth. I'd be too scared of breaking one, so I'm never going to attempt it.

"Here, baby."
Baby?
Swoon.

18

KITT
MONDAY, MAY 11
GERMANY

We're back on the bus, and we have just entered Germany. Soon, we'll be arriving in Berlin.

Paris was incredible. The people and the fans have been amazing. I'm in love with the city. It was our first stop on the tour and the first time a kiss has meant so much.

France will always have my heart.

So will Texas.

Right now, Tex is sitting in her rightful place beside me.

Although we've not discussed the kiss at the Eiffel Tower and it's not happened since, we both know our relationship has changed. I'm okay to take things slow and figure it out though. As much as I'd love to spend every second with my hands all over her, we have to handle this properly, and that means taking our time.

I need time to get my head straight because it's all over the place, and it has been for a while.

I'm not sure if anyone else has noticed anything—Mark certainly hasn't—because we've barely left each other's side, but no one has uttered a word. Milo has been quiet on the subject, and that's because he tends to let people figure out their own shit and only steps in to help if asked.

"Peyton is coming soon, yeah?" Cooper asks Texas. He's obsessed with the pretty blonde and determined to fuck her, much to Peyton's disgust.

Texas glares. "Portugal. Leave her alone."

"Hey, I'll not do anything she doesn't want."

"She doesn't want anything."

"Please, everyone wants some of this." Coop gestures to his cock, making us all reach over to slap him.

Dickhead.

Texas twists her body, blocking him out, making it me and her. She is stunning.

"What's the first thing you're going to do in Germany then?" I ask her.

"Sleep. I'm tired."

Yeah, we didn't sleep much last night. Nothing happened, not because of lack of wanting, but we stayed up all night, talking about crap and not watching whatever movie came on next. I think it was around five a.m. when we finally fell asleep. She lay on my chest until we woke up a couple of hours later. I could do that every night and never get bored.

"Me, too," I whisper.

Did that sound like an invitation? Like I was asking her to sleep with me again? Because it kind of was.

Her mouth kicks up at the side, and her eyes turn playful. I start to get hard.

Do not stand up.

"Sounds good to me."

Yep, she definitely took it how it was intended.

"What are you two whispering about?" Mark asks, sitting down opposite of us.

Shit.

Tex is instantly on the lie, and she'll probably feel horrible about it. "All the room service we're ordering the second we get to the hotel."

I feel a stab of guilt as he looks at me like I'm not a daughter-kissing prick.

I don't think I've ever told one lie to my grandparents, mostly because they were so open and we had a truth-only rule, much like Mark and Texas. I'm the reason she's broken it, and that doesn't feel good.

But the truth isn't something Mark would take well. In fact, he'd fucking freak. And rightly so.

You made him a promise.

"Is that all you think about?" Mark asks.

She blinks before replying, "Yes. What are you planning on doing when we get to the hotel?"

"We have a meeting with Carl."

"Ugh, all of us?"

"No, Enigma. Jodie will be in Berlin this evening. Are you attending that meeting with Filthy Sound?"

"Absolutely. I'm going to tell her they've been terrible and see what happens."

She would as well.

I nudge her leg under the table. It's the only part of us hidden, so it's the only physical contact we can have, but I'll take it. Texas looks up at me through her eyelashes, and my breath catches.

I'm damn crazy about her, and there's nothing I can do to change that now.

Mark laughs. "She'll believe you over them."

"Oh, I know. I can't wait to get to Berlin."

Our trip to Germany is going to be short. It's two days, and we have shows on both of them, same as France. It's a similar story on the rest of the tour, except we mostly have one-nighters. There is a lot of traveling in a short space of time, and although I do worry about crashing and burning, this is the best way.

The album has been released, and we need to hit as many cities in as many countries to get it out there. I want Filthy Sound to explode. I want number ones. I want to make my—our—dream come true.

We will do it. I don't give up on something I want.

Texas will find that out.

TUESDAY, MAY 12
BERLIN, GERMANY

The first show in Berlin was everything we'd hoped for. The crowd was incredible, and the fans backstage were just as passionate about Filthy Sound as we are.

Carver Harvey, a big name in the industry, is hosting the after-party in his place in Berlin. There's a club in his cellar. He's well-known for his extravagance, so it comes as no surprise when I see the gold-plated walls encrusted with diamonds.

Tex is eyeing it up, like she thinks she'll get away with chipping one of them out.

The ceiling is pitch-black with hundreds of lights, making it look like the night's sky. The bar doubles as a tropical fish tank.

I wouldn't even be able to take a wild guess at the cost of it all.

"How is anyone this rich?" she whispers.

"Tex, you're this rich."

"I...well...whatever. Shut up. Still, I would never spend *millions* on walls."

"What would you spend millions on?" I ask.

She stops and thinks for a second. "Chocolate."

"Chocolate?"

"Uh-huh."

"You do know a large chocolate bar only costs like two pounds, right?"

"I'm not a princess! I know the price of chocolate and bread and milk and condoms." She gives me a smug little grin, turns on her heel, and heads to the bar.

I know the price of condoms, too. I have enough of them. None have been used since I started to grow even closer to her on the tour.

Wait, what the fuck? Is that right?

She's ruined me. She's actually ruined me.

I follow her in a daze. Growing up, I always thought the only person with the power to change me was myself. Without meaning to, without any knowledge of it, Texas has changed me.

I look around the room at the women dancing in tiny outfits. They're beautiful, there's no denying that, but that's where it ends. They're just beautiful. Texas is…there isn't even a word for it. She is my idea of perfection.

"You coming?" she asks over her shoulder. Her eyes are playful, and she knows exactly what her flirting is doing to me.

Damn tease.

Without thinking, I'm moving toward her, chasing her.

She stays by my side through shots and beer and some odd-looking blue cocktails that keep appearing.

As far as after-parties go, this one is awesome. Carver really knows how to do it right. I don't think there's a single sober person in the room, and most of them are dancing on the makeshift dance floor.

Despite her promise to her dad to take it easy, Tex is wankered and thoroughly enjoying herself. Coop is fucking some girl upstairs, and Milo's necking a girl over by the bar. Thankfully, these parties are the what-happens-here-stays-here kind.

My boys really are sluts. I'm so proud.
Was I ever that bad?

You know the answer to that. You have no idea what your number is.

Tex falls into my chest, laughing, and wraps her arms around my neck. Her body pressing up against mine is doing nothing to help cool my red-hot blood.

"Dance with me," I rasp into her ear, gripping her hips.

I remember the last time we danced together.

"Mmhmm," she murmurs against my skin.

The sound vibrates down south.

She's going to fucking kill me—or Mark is.

Texas and I have not spoken about keeping the things that have happened between us a secret, but we don't need to. Right now, we're not being very secretive. I'm so glad Mark and Jimmy decided to call it a night earlier. Will took some girl back to his hotel room, so I'm left with Milo and Cooper. Their allegiance is to me, so even if they see me with Texas, they won't tell.

Tightening my grip of her hips probably a fraction too tight, I slowly walk her backward. She looks at me with hunger in her eyes, and despite going backward, she doesn't stop watching me.

Bad idea.

We reach the middle of the crowd, which seems to have doubled in size, and I pull her flush with my body. Her hands go to my neck, and she sways her body against mine to the beat of the music.

It's hot and sweaty in here, but I couldn't give a fuck. Texas is maddening. I know I'm losing myself in her, and part of me doesn't care about the consequences. I want her badly, and it's becoming impossible to hold off.

She captures her bottom lip between her teeth, and my dick thickens. I run my hands around to her arse and below those sinful leather shorts. Texas should always be in leather.

I spin her around because she's too tempting, and I wrap my arms around her waist. This position was supposed to take some of the heat out of being pressed up against her, but she arches her hips and presses her arse against my crotch.

"Fuck," I hiss into her ear, digging my fingers into her waist.

Over the obnoxiously loud beat of the music, I hear her groan. Her head lands on my shoulder, and she rolls her hips again.

I close my eyes and bury my head in her neck. Lowering a hand, I dip inside the waistband of those shorts, and she claws my forearm. There are too many people for the size of the dance floor, so although we're surrounded, we won't be caught. Besides, the lighting is dull and smoky, hiding multiple sins happening in this room.

Lowering my mouth, I lick along her neck, and she bucks her hips, demanding more. I'm only too willing and so fucking ready to give her more, to give her everything.

Impatient, she pushes my hand, forcing it down. It's sexy as hell, and I waste no time in granting her request. I slip down further and moan as I find her hot and wet and ready.

"Yes," she cries, tilting her head to the side.

I take her mouth in a slightly awkward hot kiss just as my questing hand reaches its goal. With two fingers, I rub around the bundle of nerves that make her grind against my dick, and then my hand moves in frantic circular motions.

I'm so wired up and on edge. I want nothing more than to turn her around, get her naked, and push myself inside her—or to drop to my knees and taste her.

She digs her nails into my arm so hard that I feel the skin cut. Nothing is sexier. She comes apart super fast, moaning my name. I love how quickly I can get her to orgasm. When she's spent, her head falls back against my chest.

I reluctantly pull my hand away and kiss the side of her head. The crowd is still oblivious. Thank God.

Texas turns around, breathing heavily, and stares at me like we haven't just fucked up. She looks the way I want her to look at me, like we're everything.

"Tex," I groan.

"No. You can't take that back, Kitt."

Gulping, I lean my head against hers. "I know I can't."

"Do you want to?" The hesitation in her voice makes my heart clench.

I tilt my head to the side and close my eyes. Besides a career on the stage, Texas is the only thing I *really* want.

"No, not at all."

"Then, what's the problem, Kitt? I don't understand why we never talk about what's happening between us, especially after the Eiffel Tower."

She's hurt and frustrated, and it kills me, especially knowing that it's my fault. I want to jump in and go with this because nothing has felt so right since we started Filthy Sound, but it's not that easy.

"Let's go back to the hotel and talk. We can't do this here."

Her eyes widen as she looks around, like she's only just realised we're not alone. It feels good that everything and everyone disappears for her, too. That's the second time I've made her come in public. I give myself a mental high five.

"Yeah. Okay," she says.

We find Ted out in the hallway, chatting to a few other people. He tends to give Texas a little space when we're at parties. No one is going to harm her here, especially not with me near.

He takes us back to the bus and then heads back to wait for Milo and Cooper. Also, he clearly had his eye on a guy there. Him making sure the rest of my band gets back home is a shit cover-up for wanting to get laid.

I follow Texas into her room in silence. She's not said a word since we left the party, and I'm not sure what to say. I feel like I never know what to say to her. I'm good with women—hell, I'm great with women, but this one sends my mind spinning.

I'm a clueless, lovesick fool when it comes to her.

"Talk to me, Kitt." She groans in anger and pushes her hands through her hair, turning to face me. "Seriously, what the hell is going on with us? I want to talk about it. I don't want it to be something we ignore. I can't ignore it. You are so...argh!"

Raising my hands, I take a step back. "Whoa, where is all this coming from?"

Pausing, she looks up, like a deer caught in the headlights, like she's said too much. "I don't like not knowing what's going on. That's all."

"Really? Is that all?" I ask. "Because it sure looks and sounds like there's more to it." Like the *more* I'm feeling.

She stands taller and folds her arms, defiant.

Is this self-preservation? Like, she won't admit it first in case I tell her I'm not fucking obsessed with her.

"Put it this way, Texas. We're not going anywhere until you open up and talk to me. I hate how strained things have gotten between us, and I know you do, too."

"I'm just tired."

I so don't want to admit I like him first!

"Don't fucking lie to me! Tell me you need time, tell me you don't want to talk about it, but don't make up some bullshit excuse!" Turning, I pace.

I'm pissed off. So much for fucking honesty. She's the only person who can get me to explode in a nanosecond.

"I can't believe you, you know? You go on and on about how we should all be truthful, and then you turn around and lie to my face, Tex!"

"I like you, dickhead!" she snaps.

Time stands still as I freeze. Then, I very slowly twist my head toward her.

She *definitely* said she likes me.

I like her, and she likes me.

Finally, it's out there.

"You do?"

Embarrassed about blurting it out, she turns away from me.

"Texas?"

"Can we not do this now, *please*?"

It takes me three steps to reach her, and when I do, I suddenly have no idea how I've managed to stay away for so long. She turns and meets my eye.

Her breath catches as my chest presses against hers. I can feel her breasts through her thin cotton T-shirt.

"We are absolutely doing this now. After Paris, you know we're doing this."

"I hate you."

"No, you don't. You like me."

"A girl can change her mind."

"I like you, too, Tex. You don't have to be embarrassed. Wanting me is only natural."

She rolls her eyes. "Okay, I'm going to go now."

"No, I'm sorry," I say, gripping her arm. "I'll be serious now, I promise. Things have changed, and we both know it. I don't want them to go back to how it was. I want this…*you*."

She looks at me like I'm her whole world, and my heart soars.

"If I kiss you, are you going to yell at me again?"

Blushing, she shakes her head. "No, I definitely won't be shouting."

"Good," I say before capturing her lips.

19

**TEXAS
WEDNESDAY, MAY 13
BERLIN, GERMANY**

I wake up and still feel like I'm in one of my fantasies. Kitt is wrapped around me, and we're in my bed. He's making me sweltering hot, but I couldn't care less.

Kitt groans and tightens his arms around my waist. "Good morning," he whispers into my hair.

The fact that he's used the term *good* to describe this moment is hilarious. This is beyond amazing. Being in bed with him—although all we did was kiss—and being tucked in his arms is ten times better than I ever imagined. And I've imagined a lot.

I've got Kitt Daniels, and I feel like squealing.

"Good morning yourself," I reply, grinning like a lovesick puppy.

"Are you okay?"

Again, hilarious.

"I'm very okay. You?"

"Mmhmm," he murmurs as he tightens his arms, giving me a little squeeze. "I like this."

"Not complaining over here either. Although people will be getting up soon."

"And by people, you mean, your dad, and you're scared of what he'll say?" he guesses.

Correct.

"Er...kind of. I'm sorry. It's just that—"

"Don't sweat it, Tex. I understand, and for now, I want you all to myself anyway."

"I like that idea." *A lot.*

The thought of sneaking around with him turns me on—like in insane amounts.

His eyes smile. "Good. Let's have fun for now."

"Fun?"

He exposes the back of my neck and presses a kiss to the skin. I feel it *everywhere.*

"Hmm, lots of fun."

I turn over to face him because I'm so on board with that idea, and right now, I just want to get him inside me. Kitt wastes no time in pinning me to the bed with his body. I feel each bump of muscle on his chest. His shirtless form is something I've admired many, *many* times before, but this is the first time I've seen it up close and personal.

Kitt is perfect, and he's currently kissing my collarbone.

This is like a six-figure lottery win or walking into a hotel room to find Nick Bateman naked and handcuffed to the bed.

Through my Kitt-filled haze, I hear a toilet being flushed along the corridor, and I freeze. Yeah, he needs to get out of here before we get caught. But I don't want to move.

He must have heard it, too, because he lifts his head and scowls at the door, like he wants to kill it. "The one day someone else gets up early..."

"Rain check?" I say, wrapping my hands around his neck.

His eyes get dark. "Until tonight. I'm gonna rock your world, sweetheart."

"Cheesy."

"Not at all. I fuck as good as I sing."

"And who says we'll be fucking?"

Lifting his eyebrow, he says, "Texas, your legs are wrapped around my waist, and you've been squirming around on my dick since I rolled on top of you."

Oh. "Yes, well…"

"Well?" He smirks.

"Well, you should go." *Because I need a really cold shower.*

Laughing, he kisses my forehead and gets up. I want to whip his T-shirt away as he reaches down to put it on, but I need to cool down and let him leave. We can't have sexy sneak-around time if we get caught on the very first day.

Kitt gives me a smile over his shoulder and then leaves my bedroom. I fall back against my pillows and sigh.

I have him.

Watching the clock, I give it a few minutes after Kitt leaves, and then I head out of my tiny room and downstairs into the kitchen. No one is up, so whoever went to the toilet headed straight back to bed.

A door down the hallway opens, and I hear Dad groan. I guess he drank a little too much last night.

"Tex?" he mutters quietly. "Get your old man a strong coffee, please."

"Are you okay?" I ask entirely too loudly.

He winces and holds one hand up. "Inside voice. Fuck. I'm getting too old to drink like that."

"Yeah. So, why did you? You don't usually get so drunk that you're hungover the next day—at least when I'm on tour with you anyway. Not that it matters, so don't feel guilty. I'm not a kid. But is something bothering you?"

He sighs.

"Dad, we don't lie to each other."

Except, now, we do because I'm having a secret relationship with Kitt, and I agreed to keep it from everyone. I feel sick. My stomach turns over, and I look away from him.

I'm a horrible, shitty daughter.

Fabulous.

Don't think about the guilt you're feeling when he looks you in the eyes. You're not doing anything with the intention of hurting him.

"Lately, I've been feeling my age."

Dad's not really that old, but his lifestyle has been rough on him. It would have been on anyone. Plus, from a young age, he had a baby to raise alone.

"You don't have to work yourself this hard still. I'm confident you can live off the *billions* you have in the bank. Not even I could blow through all of that."

"The money isn't an issue, Tex. I've always done this, and I'm not sure I could give up music."

"You can still sing in the shower. I won't tell the label."

He rolls his eyes and sits at the table. "Coffee's taking a while…"

"I'm on it, I'm on it. Seriously though, if you need to take it easier, you can. Don't tour as much; don't release albums every five minutes. Plenty of old people do it when they've reached that special point in their lives where their bones creek when they move, and they can't handle their whiskey anymore."

"As ever, pumpkin, you're a delight."

"Hey, I'm being helpful here."

"No, I'm pretty sure you're mocking your old man."

I tilt my head to the side and give him an innocent smile. "Yeah, that, too. But, I worry about you, and I'm telling you to slow down."

"Mark's slowing down?" Kitt asks from along the hallway. He's pretending to have just come out of his room.

My heart jumps into my throat. I look over my shoulder, and another wave of guilt washes over me so hard and so fast that I almost lose my footing. Lying to Dad feels so wrong.

"He needs to. He's past it now," I say.

"I am not past it!"

"See? He's not past it," Kitt replies, not quite being able to look directly at me either.

Great.

I laugh a little nervously and turn away. We're off to an awful start if we don't want Dad to guess.

"Coffee, Kitt?"

"Please."

He walks past me, careful to leave as much distance as he can in the small space. Why would he go out of his way to avoid me like I'm contagious?

Is he trying to get us caught?

I'm glad he gave me a wide berth though because I hadn't realised how bad I would feel about this. It's like the happy Kitt rainbow over my life has dulled. Being with him was supposed to be pure, not tainted with guilt.

Because you know doing it like this is all wrong.

"You got up late," Dad says, shuffling over so that Kitt can sit down.

I bite my lip as I pour the first mug. Kitt is often up earlier than everyone else with me. He does his best lyric-writing at the crack of dawn apparently. Everyone knows that.

We have to be more careful.

Am I overthinking this?

Yes, because you're a mega bitch who's lying to her dad, and obsessively stressing over it is what you deserve.

Kitt yawns. "Yeah, didn't sleep too well last night."

I know that's a lie, and my eye twitches.

After he kissed me for ages, we fell asleep, and he didn't stir once. But, obviously, I'm not going to be pointing that out.

Dad's eyebrows lift. "Oh, yeah?"

Kitt laughs. "No, nothing like that."

"Now that I think about it, you're quite behind Milo, Will, and Coop. Did you not take the bet in the end?"

He'd better be *very* behind them.

Kitt runs his hand through his hair and shakes his head. "Nah, not really my scene anymore."

"Good for you. Not all of us feel the need to sleep with everyone because it's the done thing."

"And because you had an oopsy," I say, smirking at him.

Dad glares. "Yes, thank you, Texas. Babies and touring are difficult to juggle. You'd be better off concentrating at one thing at a time. If not, they turn out sarcastic as fuck and never let you live it down."

Kitt and I laugh.

"No baby plans for a while yet," Kitt says.

A while? By that, he'd better mean at least ten years. This body ain't going through childbirth for a really long time.

I still remember the video my personal tutor made me watch for sexual health and education when I was fifteen. I saw a woman's foofie split, and all of a sudden, the curiosity surrounding sex went right out the window. The next day, I made an appointment to get on the pill, and I take it religiously.

"Good. Suppose it does you no favours, keeping an eye on Texas at after-parties."

I almost choke. Stirring the coffee harder, I pretend I've not heard.

"She doesn't cause that much trouble. Honestly, I'd rather hang with her than prowl over women, like those dickheads."

He's saying all the right things. If we start to let Dad know that we're getting closer without actually saying the words, it will be much easier when we eventually tell him we want to start dating.

This could work. The lie is only temporary because Dad will know soon enough.

Justify it however you need to. You're still a liar.

"Glad to hear it because, as much as I trust Cooper and Milo, you're the one I trust with my daughter."

Bugger.

I turn around and see Kitt fail miserably in his attempt to smile. That hit him hard, too. His eyes are brimming with guilt.

Dad's phone starts to ring upstairs. He groans as he gets up to get it. Both Kitt and I are relieved. His posture immediately relaxes, and his fists unclench. The second Dad's out of sight, Kitt is in front of me.

How did he move so quickly? I gulp and tilt my head to face him.

"Are you okay?"

"I'm fine," I reply, breathless because of how close he is.

"Really? You're pale, and you look like you're going to hurl."

Wrapping my arms around my stomach, I shrug one shoulder. "I'm not good with lying to him. It feels…"

"Yeah, I know. He trusts me with you. Shit. But he won't take it well. You know that."

"I do. This isn't something we can just hit him with, but the alternative isn't easy. I've never lied like this."

He sighs and looks up to the ceiling. "I'm sorry, Tex."

"It's not all on you. We just need to find a way to start preparing him for us, like you could stop sleeping around, and then maybe in a few weeks, I can tell him I like you."

"I've already stopped sleeping around."

A smile creeps on my face. "Believe me, I've noticed."

"I'll handle this however you want."

I blink away a tear. "I hate lying. Why couldn't you have figured out you liked me after the tour, huh?"

Things would have been so much easier. For one, we wouldn't have all been cooped up together for months. Dad would have had space and time to work through his dreams for me versus reality.

"Timing, hey?" He smiles and places a kiss to my forehead.

Footsteps coming closer have him jumping back. He dashes over to the table and sits down.

I turn, so my back is to him because that, right there, him rushing off, is exactly why I hate this so much.

Focus on the good. You have Kitt Daniels!

But you could fuck up your relationship with the guy who gave you everything…

Whatever I do from here on out, someone isn't going to be happy, and that's hard to accept.

20

KITT
WEDNESDAY, MAY 13
BERLIN, GERMANY

"Good night, Berlin!" I shout, raising my arm in the air.

The crowd goes wild, begging for another encore.

Cooper removes his top and swings it around on the end of his finger. He's such a fucking show-off. "Until next time, motherfuckers!"

I jump on his back as we walk off. He's sweaty and gross, but neither of us gives a shit. Fourth show, and it just keeps getting better and better. I drop down off Coop's back, and he gives me a playful shove to the chest.

"Kitt, that was epic!"

"We were epic," Milo says, chucking his arm around my neck and rubbing his fist on my head.

I swat him away, laughing.

Backstage, Texas is waiting. I lock my muscles to stop myself from running to her. Mark is here still, and I can't do what I want to in front of him.

"That was awesome, guys!" Tex says, rushing forward.

She hugs Milo first, which makes him smirk.

She's doing it, so Mark won't suspect.

Cooper is busy, running his mouth a hundred miles an hour to Jimmy, so she comes for me next. I'm so ready to have her in my arms.

She gives me a knowing smile before I wrap her in a tight hug that tells her what I can't voice right this second—or at all.

I love you is possibly the hardest fucking thing in the world to say.

"I'm so proud of you," she murmurs against my neck.

"Thank you."

At the same time, we back up. I've not held her for nearly long enough, but Mark is watching, and it's making me feel sick. Because of him, I've just finished my fourth show.

"Come on," Milo says. "Shower and after-party."

Tex turns and walks beside him. "I'm so not showering with you."

He nudges her. "Ugh, you're no fun."

I don't know if it's because I'm with her now, but Milo seems to be winding me the fuck up at every opportunity.

"How did that feel?" Mark asks.

Grinning, I slap his back. "Indescribable."

"I remember that feeling."

I frown. "You've lost it?"

"No, but it becomes the norm almost. You'll look after her tonight?"

Dropping my eyes, I rub my chest. "You know I will."

Your idea of looking after her and his are two different things. He won't like yours.

"Can I ask you something?" He looks over and gives me a nod, so I continue, "If someone hits on her…"

"I want you to kill them," he replies, looking me dead in the eyes.

We stop walking, and I frown.

"I'm joking, Kitt. Texas is her own person. As much as I hate it, I can't stop her from seeing anyone. I just hope the person she chooses is the right one."

The right one. What does that mean? Someone like her ex?

Mark liked Xander. He was safe. He never challenged Texas, and he never did anything to piss her off.

I piss her off daily, and I'm never going to roll over and follow. I'll argue back, I'll push her, and I'll never have a nine-to-five.

Yeah, I have no doubt the right one in Mark's eyes is not me.

"Do men hit on my daughter a lot?"

"No, I'm usually with her. I think they mostly assume she's with me." *How do you feel about that?*

He laughs. "Good. Keep that up."

I plan to. Officially. Exclusively.

I've planted the seed. No need to go any further now. Tex's up next. In a couple of weeks, she'll tell him that after we've spent time together, she's starting to see me in a new light. Hopefully, it won't be a surprise for Mark.

This will also help with the pictures that seem to turn up every-fucking-where. Tex and I have been spotted together many times, and at the minute, no one has been reading anything to it. That'll probably change soon, but at least Mark knows we're together more at after-parties, so he won't question us.

Mark starts to walk, and I follow him. A dull ache is starting to spread across my forehead. There is so much riding on Mark taking this well, and there's not much room for error.

I can handle Mark being angry with me but not with her. I don't ever want to do anything to come between them. They're rock solid, and that's how it needs to stay.

Speaking of rock-solid relationships, I get my phone from my jeans pocket and dial my grandparents' house. I've not spoken to them in a couple of days. It's hard to find time to do everything, and they're always in bed by nine p.m.

"Hello?" Nan says. Her voice is sleep-filled and worried.

"So, I might've missed a few calls…"

"Kitt Daniels, you are not too old to ground. And do you have any idea of the time?"

"Sorry. I just wanted to check in."

"Your aunt showed me pictures. It looks like you're enjoying yourself."

"What's with the tone, Nan?"

"What's with the womanising, Kitt?"

Oh, fuck.

"That's not what I'm doing." *Anymore.*

"How is Texas?"

Nan loves Tex. She never had a daughter, and I'm her only grandchild, so she instantly took to my girl.

"She's doing good," I say. I mouth, *My nan*, to Tex as we walk into my dressing room.

Tex holds her hand out.

"Nan, I'm passing you over."

Tex takes the phone and flops on the sofa. Looks like I'm not talking to my nan anymore today. Leaving them to it, I get ready to go out.

I've just finished when Texas hangs up. Milo, Jimmy, Mark, and Cooper are in here now, too.

"Your nan said bye and to call her soon."

I take my phone back, and Tex's eyes narrow when I stroke the back of her hand.

Coop claps his hands. "Let's go get fucked up!"

Mark turns to me. "This is why I trust you with her."

I swallow a whole lot of guilt as I smirk. Texas looks away and wraps her arms around her chest. This is especially hard on her. She shares most things with her dad, and something this big, she wants him to know.

"She'll be fine with me, Mark."

An hour later, and we're drinking whiskey like it's water, sitting around a massive table with so many celebrities that I feel a little overwhelmed. Apparently, I'm one of them now. I don't feel it.

Texas is sitting so close that she might as well be on my lap, but no one bats an eyelid—except for Milo. He's smirking and periodically wiggling his eyebrows or pretending to slit his throat because that's what he thinks Mark will do to me when he finds out.

I mouth, *Fuck off,* and he throws his head back, laughing.

He's drunk already. His dark eyes look about three shades lighter with the pissed glaze.

Tex leans in, and her mouth is dangerously close to my ear. I shudder.

"You've been quiet tonight," she says.

"Guilt will do that to you."

It was only an hour ago that Mark said he trusted me. Now, my hand is on his daughter's thigh under the table.

"Why do you feel guilty?"

I'm struggling with it hard, and I'm not ashamed to admit it. Nothing will stop me from wanting her or enjoying being with her, but the guilt makes me feel sick.

"You know why. Mark took me under his wing, taught me everything I need to know about this industry, put us under the radar of the right people, gave us a spot on their tour, agreed to *support* our tour, and all he's ever asked in return is that we don't mess with you. I owe my career to him, Tex, and I couldn't even do the one thing he demanded in return."

She avoids eye contact. "Right."

I know she feels bad about this, too. She would never intentionally go against her dad's wishes.

"What does that mean for us?"

"Nothing," I whisper, trying to make this look like a normal, non-intimate conversation. "I'll deal with it the same way you are."

Chewing her lip, she closes her eyes and then looks up at me. God, I'll never get used to the way she sees me.

"Why does this feel like the end?"

"I don't know. It's not, Tex. There will never be an end, not between us. This. Is. *Not*. Over."

Her eyes fill with tears.

Fuck.

"Hey, don't. I want you, and I'm not giving you up. It won't be like this for long, I promise."

"Do you want to cool things until we're ready to tell him?" she asks.

I should want that. It makes sense; it's the right thing to do.

I shake my head. "I'm not good at selflessness when it comes to being with you. You're still my girl."

"Neither am I. So, we're okay?"

"We'll always be okay."

"Hey, motherfuckers, *tequila*!" Cooper shouts, raising his hands above his head.

The table cheers, and a few people get up.

"Cooper, where is your top?" Texas asks.

He frowns and looks down, like he's unsure. "Oh, yeah. I need to get that back." He turns on his heel and stalks off toward the toilets.

Tex turns her nose up and gives me a look. "I don't even want to know."

"You're probably going to on the way home."

"You drunk, Milo?" Tex asks as he stands and sways.

"Not yet, babycakes, but that can be rectified, right?"

"Oh, definitely. I'm so up for getting wasted tonight."

I cheer inwardly. Drunk Texas all over me later is exactly what I need to get this guilt off my mind for a while.

"Well, what are we waiting for?" He turns around and grabs two tequilas. He hands them to me and Tex and takes another for himself.

I chuck the tequila back and slam the glass on the table.

Texas is wincing as she stacks her glass on top of mine. "Jesus, I hate that stuff."

"Why drink it?" Milo asks.

She glares. "Why not?"

"Point taken."

"I got my top," Cooper says proudly, holding it up. He pulls it over his head and necks a shot. "This song is awesome."

It's a remix of Snow Patrol's "Run." The original is one of Tex's favourites. Her back straightens, and her eyes widen in recognition.

She looks between me, Milo, and Coop. "I want to dance. Who's coming?"

"You'll be coming if you give me a second," Coop says, lifting his pale eyebrow.

Clenching my fists on my lap, I take a deep breath. *Fucker.*

"Hilarious, but rock stars just don't do it for me," she shoots back.

I slowly turn my head. *The fuck is she on?*

Her mouth twitches with the effort of keeping a straight face.

"Lies, Texy baby. Come on, let's dance!" Cooper takes her by the hand and pulls her.

She falls on the table, laughing.

I'd help but it's funny.

"Coop, you crazy twat!" she squeals.

He reaches down, grips her around the waist, pulls her right over the table, and sets her on the floor.

"I would've walked around!" she says.

He chuckles. "I wanted to take you over the top."

I watch Coop take my girl to the VIP dance floor, and Milo drops himself in the chair next to mine. He stares at me.

"What?" I growl before draining the last of my SoCo.

"You good, man?" He's smug as fuck.

"Yep. Why?"

"You're loved up."

"Are you fucking twelve?"

He laughs. "No. Is it going well?"

"It's going well."

"But..." he prompts, frowning and scratching the dark stubble on his jaw. "You're not thinking of breaking things off with her, are you?"

He loves Texas, too, but in a very different way. Better be different anyway. He would also be in line to fucking castrate me if I ever hurt her. No one needs to worry.

"No."

"You're sure? Because if you're not, you have to end this now. You can't play around with her. She's not practice."

I get his warning, but he's pissing me off.

Gritting my teeth, I glare and lean closer. "She's my forever."

"All right," he replies, lifting his hands in surrender. "Gotcha. I used to have a forever. Now, I just have booze and women."

"Milo, if you miss her, do something."

He shakes his head. "She's the past."

Yeah, right.

"Which one is more me?" he asks, pointing out two girls at the bar.

"The brunette."

"You didn't even look."

"Neither did you. It doesn't matter, Milo, because you'll wake up in the morning and still want Lexi."

"You, sir, are a prick."

I throw my head back and laugh. "Sort it out. You still love her."

"Whatever. You love Texas."

More and more with every passing second.

21

TEXAS
FRIDAY, MAY 15
MADRID, SPAIN

We're in Madrid, and since the club in Berlin, I've barely seen Kitt. We've rain checked our rain check because he's been so busy.

Jodie is here, and she's packed a full schedule for Filthy Sound and Enigma. I've stayed back at the hotel with Ted because I have no desire to race all over the city, doing promo events and appearances. I'm passing on the show tonight because I'm drained.

Ted and I have been out a couple of times to get fresh crepes and eat amazing spaghetti, so I'm not totally alone. He knows about me and Kitt—obviously since he's my shadow—but so far, he's not mentioned it. He won't unless I bring it up, which I don't intend on doing because I'm already going a little crazy here already.

It's been two days. Get ahold of yourself.

I've realised that I'm not very good at being alone. I've always had my dad around along with his band, security, managers, and a tutor. There has always been someone, so when I'm in the hotel suite and Ted is in his, things are strange.

Silence shouldn't be loud.

I have a huge suite all to myself, and no one will be back for at least another few hours. At least I'm not cramped on the bus, not that I really mind that.

I'm going to enjoy this. What else can I do?

The show will be over now, but as usual, there's an after-party.

When I told Dad I would be passing on the show, he thought I was ill. Then, when he tried to insist on staying with me, I had to take it up a level to period pains. I've always known he would drop everything for me, but I'd never get him to.

I flick the channel over and settle on *Snapped: Women Who Kill*. That actually sounds good right now. About thirty minutes ago, I had practically the entire room service menu delivered, so I'm set for the night. I'm so pathetic.

Kitt is probably fending off beautiful women right now.

I shove another mouthful of cheesecake in and chew.

He wouldn't cheat, I know that, but it's not a nice image to have in my head. His fans get a little too handsy.

He can't even tell them he has a girlfriend, not that it would stop many people, especially the groupies. I feel like more of a secret now than ever.

I put the plate of leftover cheesecake down and lie on my side.

Peyton will have a lot to say, and I'm not ready to speak about it yet, so I can't call her.

Oh my God, get a grip! You're fine on your own for the night.

I finally get comfortable when someone knocks on my door. *Is there some room service missing?* I roll myself off the sofa and stand up. *This'd better be good. It'd better be chocolate or cake.*

I swing the door open and get a shock. "Kitt?" I mumble.

"Hey, baby." He tilts his head and smirks.

He must've come straight from the show. *No after-party for him?*

"So...I don't like it when you're not waiting in the wing for me."

"I don't really like being left behind."

He steps inside and closes the door. "You were never left behind, Tex. You could've come. We all wanted you there." He takes another step. "*I* wanted you there."

"Honestly, I wasn't in the mood to watch you flirt."

"I have to be friendly."

"I know that. You don't have to be so friendly though."

"As much as I like you jealous, I think I prefer you to be secure." He puts his hands on my upper arms. "There will never be anyone else for me. You're it, Tex. Can I spend the evening with my girl, please? I've missed her a lot."

"Well," I say, smirking and looking to the side, "when you put it like that..."

Kitt puts a movie on, and I grab a couple of beers from the fully stocked mini fridge. When I go over to the sofa and sit down, Kitt's arms circle my waist, and he pulls me onto his lap. Yeah, I'd much rather be here anyway.

I snuggle down and lay my head on his chest. His heart is thumping away, the hard and fast rhythm matching mine.

"I've been watching Twitter. Seems like you had a good show," I whisper, closing my eyes and enjoying this moment.

When his arms are tight around me, I feel strong, and I know everything will work out. Kitt makes me feel safe and loved, and I can't get enough of him.

"It would've been better if you were there."

"I'm sorry."

He kisses the top of my head and runs his fingertips up and down my bare arm. It feels so good. With closed eyes, I moan and tilt my head, searching for his lips. Kitt's mouth covers mine in a sweet kiss that makes my blood fizzle.

"Tex," he groans before running his tongue across my bottom lip.

I feel it *everywhere*, and I'm so close to coming on the spot. Shifting, I straddle his hips to gain better access. I'm too hot and too needy. The throbbing between my legs is almost unbearable.

He pulls back, holding my face in his hands. His eyes are wild, and it's such a turn-on to know it's because of me.

"What are you doing?"

"Isn't it obvious?" I mutter.

"You want to feel me inside you?"

Holy...

My throat is suddenly dryer than the fucking Sahara.

I nod because I've gone dumb.

The corner of his lip curves. "What else, Texas? Tell me what you want me to do to you."

There's a promise in his words. Whatever I want, he's willing to give me. Right now.

"I want you to undress me."

He wastes no time. Grabbing my hips, he flips us over, so he's hovering above me on the sofa. His erection is positioned perfectly, if it wasn't for our clothes.

"Lift up," he instructs as he reaches around to my back.

I sit up as best as I can, my stomach muscles aching as I hold myself.

Kitt pulls my top off and unclasps my bra. "You're fucking stunning."

His lips slam down on mine, and I'm flattened against the cushions. The kiss is desperate and exactly how I feel about having all of him. I've never wanted anyone or anything more than I want him now.

Oh wow, this is happening.

For two years, I've dreamed of what it would be like to be with Kitt. After sleeping with Xander, I wondered how different Kitt would feel and taste. Kitt has always been assertive, and that's something Xander lacked.

I like to be in charge, but I love to be challenged.

And Kitt is very challenging.

Right now, I'm not in charge.

His lips bruise mine with force. I can't get enough. We're too far away. I wrap my legs around him, and he presses his erection into me. I moan as electricity fires through my body.

His tongue enters my mouth and duels with mine. I don't give a single fuck. He can win because him winning at this is totally a win for me, too.

He rears back and looks down at me. His arms are shaking with the effort to restrain himself. Kitt is nicely toned, but holding himself up above me like this makes his arms look bigger.

Swoon.

"Texas, fucking hell."

My lips feel as swollen as his look. They're darker and glossed over.

"Are you okay?" I ask, blinking innocently.

"I have never wanted another woman like this. I don't...fuck, I can't even describe how much I want you."

I think I just came.

I breathe heavily and squirm below him. I'm so close. I just need him pressing against me again. "Kitt, please..."

Closing his eyes, he groans. "God, baby, that's it. Beg me."

"I need to touch you. Take your clothes off, Kitt. Oh my God, kiss me again. Do something, please. I'm so close." Seriously, one touch, and I'll be done for.

His dark blue eyes practically turn black.

I've seen him turned on, many occasions with someone else, but this is something else.

It's. So. Hot.

Slowly, he ducks his head and places a featherlight kiss on my collarbone.

Taking a deep breath, I arch my back, needing him closer. "Kitt," I whisper.

He repeats, kissing across my neck, and starts to trail down. His lips softly drag over the skin between my breasts, and I think I'm going to explode from the feeling.

I want him so bad that I feel like I'm going insane.

The sound he makes is so erotic as his hand travels south. I love how much he wants me. I've not even touched him yet.

"I want to lick you."

"What? On my vagina?" I freeze.

Oh God. Oh. My. God.

Kitt throws his head back and laughs loudly.

No.

No, no, no. That did not just happen.

What in the actual fuck is the matter with you?

I said that. I really, really said that. Right?

Of course I did. He's not laughing that bloody hard for no reason!

Pushing Kitt off me, I hide my face. I'm so bloody embarrassed that I want the ground to swallow me whole.

Actually, it's worse than that. Google *beyond mortified*, and this conversation will be the definition.

Shit, it's not like no one has ever gone down on me before. But Kitt hasn't. I never thought we'd even kiss again after he didn't mention the first time. He's not drunk now. He actually wants me, and my brain—although it's still up for debate whether I have one—isn't processing that well.

I want him so bad in every way that it's frying my mind.

The words slipped out.

Oh. My. God!

Kitt doubles over, laughing…and probably thinking he's had a lucky escape.

I need to leave, like, now and move to another country and change my name. The first thing I'm going to do when I'm settled in my new life is get myself tested because something is seriously not right.

I leap off the sofa, snatch my top, put it on, and head out. This is my room, but I don't care. I need to be elsewhere. It's not just my face that's on fire; it's my whole body. I've never been this mortified before.

"Where are you going, Tex?"

"To die!" I reach for the handle and yank it open.

"But I've not licked your *vagina* yet."

"Fuck off!" I shout before slamming the door behind me.

I've done some stupid things before, but that right there was on a new level. Covering my face, I walk toward the lift. I don't even care that Ted is in his room, and I should knock for him before wandering off.

You need to go somewhere remote where no other humans live.

I jam my finger into the call button and wait.

I can't believe I said that. I'm so embarrassed that I want to die. Things between me and Kitt are over now. I can never look him in the eyes again. Peyton would love this.

"Texas?" Kitt says.

I freeze. *Damn, he followed me.*

His hand circles my wrist, and he twists me around. "Hey."

"You can go now," I snap.

His hand tightens as I try to free my own.

"Let me go."

"Never, remember? Look, don't be embarrassed."

"Really? You heard what came out of my mouth, right?"

His mouth twitches as he fights his amusement. "I heard, but it's cool."

There is nothing cool about what I said. *Nothing.*

"Don't lie to me."

"All right, so maybe you wish you hadn't said it—"

"Maybe?"

He growls. "Get back in your room, Texas, now. I'm going to lick you, and then I'm going to fuck you. I don't give a shit if you're feeling embarrassed right now."

I want to be offended, but it's hard to be when he's looking at me like I'm his next meal, and my pulse is thudding so hard that I feel dizzy.

So, I've not had that much alcohol, but I still feel drunk. Swaying forward, I lean against him and close my eyes. His erection presses into my stomach.

"I'm an idiot," I murmur.

"You're an idiot for running away from me, not for how you reacted when I told you what I wanted to do to you. I love how you react to me."

I'm no longer a fan of it.

"Well, one of us should."

"Into bed, you," he says, reaching around to slap my butt.

There is no way I'm going to argue with that. I bite my lip and tug his hand toward my suite. I'm still beyond embarrassed, but it doesn't have to be a big deal. Maybe I'll replay the moment a million times and want to slap myself, but Kitt still wants to be inside me, and that is...well, a fucking miracle.

Kitt's smirk is back, and I slap his chest.

"You're a dick."

"You love my dick."

"How do you know?"

"You're about to prove my point." He spins me around and holds me against his chest.

His gorgeously defined chest.

Pressing his forehead against mine, he gives me a smile that makes my whole body ache. "You're perfect, Texas."

"Funny, I was going to say the same about you."

With a smile that melts my heart, he walks me back into the suite. We don't stop at the sofa, like before. He takes me into my bedroom.

He stands in front of me and watches with one eyebrow arched as I remove my top. Then, my hand goes to my zipper, and his breathing becomes heavier. He doesn't move, doesn't help. He just watches, and it's so sexy.

I step out of my jean shorts and push my underwear to the floor.

The tension between us is palpable, and all thoughts of my earlier slip-up have been forgotten. Nothing else matters but this moment.

Kitt unzips his jeans and shoves them to the floor. No boxers. My eyes dip down, and I think my heart stops beating at the sight of his erection. That's all for me. His fist grips the bottom of his T-shirt, and he whips it off over his head. The shirt makes a small thud as it hits the ground.

We're both naked and incredibly ready.

"Lie down on the bed," he whispers.

I take a step back, and when the edge of the bed hits my legs, I sit down. Placing my arms behind me, I go to shuffle back, but his palms land on my knees and hold me down. With a small smile, he nudges my legs apart.

Oh.

Kitt drops to the floor and places a kiss on the inside of my knee.

My heart jumps. I'm pretty sure if he does that again, I'm going to pass out.

His mouth reaches the apex of my legs, and I shudder. God, he's barely touched me, and I'm ready to come. His tongue flicks out, and I launch off the bed.

Fuck me!

He chuckles and uses his arms to press my hips down.

He swirls his tongue at maddening speeds, only to slow it right down and lick with the gentlest touch. My body is coiling, burning, and I'm in such a desperate need to come that it hurts.

"Kitt, please," I beg, grinding on his mouth as every nerve ending is set on fire.

He groans, and the vibrations tip me over the edge. I fall, loudly calling his name, and I ride out the most intense orgasm I've ever had.

Wasting no time, he shoves me back, slides on a condom, grips my thighs, and glides himself inside. He moans deep in his throat and tilts his head back. "Texas, you feel amazing, sweetheart. Fuck."

He stills inside me and bends down. I'm breathless and made of jelly after my orgasm, so when he kisses me, I barely register where he just was, not that I care much anyway.

Wrapping my arms around his neck, I kiss him back. His tongue battles mine, pressing hard and then retreating, teasing. When I feel it against the seam of my mouth, I suck, and he grunts, starting to move again. I meet his hips thrust for thrust. He's slow and deliberate, savouring the feeling. Every stroke stretches me to fit him perfectly, and I feel every ridge of his hardness pushing me to impossible heights.

"Kitt," I murmur into his mouth, feeling myself tightening again.

I dig my nails into the flesh on his back, and his rhythm picks up dramatically. Ripping away from my mouth, he pushes himself up onto his arms and closes his eyes as he starts a frantic pace, relentlessly slamming into me.

I grip on around his waist to stop myself from being shoved higher on the bed.

Fuck. Oh, fuck.

He's going to make me come again. I moan and scratch at his back as the intensity of him takes hold.

"Kitt!"

"Fuck, Texas. Fuck. Come with me, baby." He throws his head back as he pumps into me.

I watch him come apart, his eyes scrunched, his jaw locked in pleasure, and it's what makes me break under him. I let wave after wave tear me apart.

"Shit," I mutter, floating back to reality.

Kitt's hips grind mine as he rides out the last of his orgasm, and he collapses on me. Rolling over, he takes me with him, and I lie in his arms, snuggled close, breathing him in.

This is, without a doubt, my favourite place to be in the whole world. I could stay here for hours, doing nothing but lying all over him.

"Wow."

He chuckles. "Exactly. I've never come so fucking hard in my life."

Neither have I. "I never want to move," I whisper.

"Please," he says into my hair, "you'll want to feed soon."

He's got me there. I'm always hungry.

"Tell me you'll never get bored of this, Kitt."

He laughs, and his chest rocks underneath me. "Something tells me that's an impossibility."

I hope so.

KITT
SUNDAY, MAY 17
MADRID, SPAIN

Texas looks like she's been crying. I want to hold her and fix whatever made her upset, but Mark is here at the venue too. He's distracted because Enigma is opening in ten. I don't know how I'm going to wait that long.

"You good, man?" Coop asks, slapping me on the back.

I look between him and Tex, making sure she's okay. "Yeah, I'm fine."

"You don't look it. If you want the night off, I can handle vocals."

Now, he has my full attention. I laugh and thump his arm. "Good one."

"You know I'm a better singer."

"Yeah, you're really not, Coop, but thanks for the laugh." I turn back, and Tex is gone. "Where is she?"

"Where is who?"

"Texas."

Coop points. "That way, so pisser or one of the dressing rooms. Why? What's wrong?"

"Nothing. Just needed to talk to her about something. Be back in a minute."

Coop nods, and I follow the direction Texas wandered off in.

A few people stop me to fucking talk, but I quickly brush them off and find Tex in my dressing room.

I close the door, leaving us alone. "What's wrong?"

She spins around and drops her phone. Her eyes dart to the mobile.

"What?" I ask. I notice the redness surrounding her eyes and the way she's looking at her phone, like it's eaten all of her chocolate.

She bends down and swipes the phone. "Nothing. I just forgot something."

"You didn't bring anything." I step closer. "Want to show me what made you cry?"

"I haven't been crying."

"Texas. Phone."

Looking away, she thrusts the phone in my direction. "Open Safari."

I don't like this, but I do what she said. Images of me and a girl pop up.

For fuck's sake. "Texas, this isn't recent."

She turns back.

"Fine, it's recent but *before* you."

"I know that."

"Then, what's the problem?" I close down the page and hand the phone back.

"Nothing is the problem. I'm not stupid. I know your past."

"Then, you cried because..."

"I didn't full-on cry, dickhead. I'm fine, and we're fine, so give me a minute, and I'll be back out there."

I grab her hand and pull her closer. "I'm not going anywhere. You've got more talking to do, sweetheart."

She wants to be angry, but not even Tex can be that unreasonable.

She sighs in annoyance. "I don't blame you, but seeing you with other girls has always hurt, even more so now. I guess I wasn't prepared for that. I'll be all right, and I'll deal with it, like I did before, I promise. Want to give me that minute now?"

I shake my head and trace my hand down her cheek. She's soft, and she feels like forever.

"I don't want to leave you alone, so you don't have a choice."

She steps back, and her eyes narrow. My arm falls away, and I know we're about to have an argument.

"Yes, I do. You're not my fucking dad, Kitt."

Here we go.

"How am I a bastard for not wanting to leave my girlfriend when she's hurting?"

"Because I'm asking you to. Why are you being difficult?"

I laugh because...*fuck*.

"You think *I'm* being difficult? Texas, you have it down to an art form."

She folds her arms. "You need to leave."

"This is *my* dressing room."

"Fine, I'll leave." She pushes past me, her eyes firing bullets into my head.

Why the fuck did you ever think having a girlfriend would be a good idea?

Of all the things that could bring me to my knees—drugs, alcohol, fame—it's one infuriating little girl who turns out to be my kryptonite.

Well, fuck her.

If she wants to be unreasonable, that's fine.

I ball my fists at the burning sensation in my gut.

What the hell is wrong with her? I'm trying to fix this and make her feel better, and she's pushing me away. I can't help my past, and it doesn't bother me—I was single and young and in a band—but I can't help her because she clearly has an issue with my sleeping around.

I want to fucking throw something.

Calm down. You're soon going onstage.

"What did you do?" Milo's voice makes me jump. He's standing by the door, holding it open.

Twisting my head, I growl, "Why do you think it's my fault? She's crazy, man."

He laughs. "Love often is."

"I made a mistake."

"No, you didn't, and you know it. Don't ever let her hear you say that because you'll never be able to take it back."

Shoving my hands through my hair, I let my shoulders sag. "I don't have the first clue what I'm doing here."

Milo leans against the wall. "You're not the only person to feel like they're navigating a minefield. Some relationships are complicated and hard, but that doesn't mean they can't work. I let Lexi walk away. Things got messy when the band started to travel, and the more of a name we made for ourselves, the more she slipped away from me. I think I did the right thing because I would've only held her back. If you let Texas go, it will be the biggest mistake of your life—or the second. That little ninja tattoo is horrendous."

"Oh, fuck off, mate. Just because you're a pussy and can't handle a needle…"

Milo rolls his eyes. "I don't need any work."

"You're a dick."

"You ready to sing your little ninja heart out?"

"You ready for me to beat you with your drumsticks?"

Coop bursts through the open door. "What are you two wankers doing? Your mother's meeting over? Enigma is killin' it, and we need to get ready to smash it out of the park." He nods his head and walks back toward the stage.

Milo and I follow him.

"Coop, what would it take to get you to settle down with a woman?" Milo asks.

Throwing his head back, he holds his stomach and laughs. "Fuck. Nice one." Shoving Milo's head, he adds, "Angelina Jolie. That's it."

I roll my eyes. *He'll never change.*

"She ain't ever gonna look at you, dude. Give it up," I say.

"I'm way handsomer than Brad."

"You wish," I say, knocking him into the wall.

He retaliates and thumps my arm. It hurts, but hell would freeze over before I showed it.

"I love you two arseholes, you know that?" he says.

"I'm not doing a group hug," I warn.

Milo slaps my chest. "I'm with this guy."

"Let's do this," I say when it's time to go on. I can't wait. *Time to forget Texas for a while.*

I take off, running down the steps, like they're on fire. Running my hand through my damp hair, I growl. *That was horrific. Our fans deserved more.*

Two people try to approach me, but I put my hand up, and they soon back off. I'm not in the mood. I need to get out of here.

"Dude, wait up!" Cooper shouts. "What's going on?"

"I bombed. That's what's going on!" I snap.

"Whoa. Look, man, we might know that wasn't the best, but the audience lapped it up. They fucking loved us."

Yeah, shame there's only one person I need to love me right now, and she's not here. Because I pushed her away.

"What was that out there?" Milo asks.

Coop puts his arm out to stop Milo from getting any closer.

"What? I'm just wondering what the hell is going on. I thought you were cool. Are you sick, mate?" Milo asks.

"Something like that," I reply.

"Why didn't you say so? If you're not well enough to perform…"

I cut him a look. If I broke my leg halfway through a set, I'd strap it up and carry on until we were done.

You don't let your fans down. Period.

Maybe it wasn't a bad performance, but I wasn't on top of my game, and that's not okay by me.

"All right, I get it," Milo mutters, backing down.

"Look, let's get back to the hotel. Don't sweat it, bro. We rocked."

Who would've thought Coop could be so…normal?

His usual advice is to shag or drink any troubles away. I can drink it, but I can't shag it because I don't think Tex will be in the mood.

Right now, I could really do with losing myself in my girl.

I nod to Hank, who is standing within earshot, and then I turn to the boys. "Come on."

We have a couple of things to do before we can leave, like always, but I'm not up for any sort of party or anything where I have to be around people. I'm not good company right now, and the only company I want comes in a bottle.

When we get back to the hotel, Texas is sitting at the bar with her dad and Jimmy.

"What are you guys having?" Milo asks, assuming that I'm down with drinking there.

"If you're buying, I'm having beer and a couple whiskeys," Cooper says, slapping Milo on the back before heading to the table.

"Yeah, I think I'm going to hit the sack," I say.

Milo frowns. "Really? Maybe you should see a doctor. You're rarely ill, and even when you are, you still join the party."

It's not a doctor that I need. It's the girl sitting far too close to me for my sanity.

How do you deal with this?

I don't know if I should go over to her or not.

One thing I know is, I can't be around her when we're not okay.

"I will if I still feel like shit tomorrow," I say to pacify him. "Night, man."

He nods his head, and I walk away.

I can't sit around a table with her. Breathing the same air as her drives me insane. How I'll make it through to the end of the tour, I'll never know.

23

TEXAS
MONDAY, MAY 18
LISBON, PORTUGAL

We're back on the bus, and Kitt has barely looked at me once. I admit, I didn't handle the photo situation or our argument well, but he brings out emotions in me so strong that I can't control it. I hate arguing with him.

We're around the table, and he's focusing far too hard on his conversation with Milo. Coop is keeping me busy, listing all the women he wants to have sex with. It's gross, but at least I'm not focused on Kitt.

Well, I am.

Damn it.

We've arrived in Lisbon, and we are ten minutes from the hotel. I know that because I've been religiously questioning the drivers. I need to get off this bus. The atmosphere is tense although no one else has seemed to notice but me and Kitt.

He laughs, and the sound grates on my skin. *How is he laughing when things aren't okay with us?*

I grit my teeth and nod to Cooper.

You can do this. Soon, you'll be in the hotel, and you won't have to see him.

We'll work it out because we have to, but I'm too pissed off, and he's too...*him* to deal with it this second.

When the bus pulls up, I'm the first one off—almost. Ted rushes past me and gives me a stern look. I raise my hands. He's right. I can't risk my safety just because I want to get out of here.

We get checked in, and we're shown to our rooms. Like usual, I'm in a massive suite I don't need.

I lie down and curl up. My heart is heavy, and everything feels wrong. This is the start of our relationship, and it's not how it should be. The night we made love, we couldn't keep our hands off each other. It was perfect, just the way it should be. The contrast between then and now is crazy.

Just as I get comfortable on my bed because I don't intend on moving for a long time, someone knocks on my door. The guys are all out, so I have no idea who it could be. Maybe Ted, but he doesn't usually bother me unless there's a security issue.

I get up and pad across the thick pile carpet to the door.

"Surprise," Peyton says, throwing her arms up the second I open the door. "Missed me?"

"Um..." *Wow. Okay, I'm in shock.* "Yeah, of course. But, huh? Aren't you supposed to be here tomorrow?"

"Yes, but *surprise!*" Pushing past me, she heads into my room and looks around. "Nice. The label really does spring for the best suites."

Coop got the president. I think he's planning on having a lot of parties up there—and by parties, I mean, orgies. I'm not going anywhere near it.

"So, talk to me about Kitt. I want to hear, in detail, everything that's happened. Then, we're going to get you dressed—I love you, but you look like shit—and we're going out."

"I don't want to go out."

"I didn't ask if you wanted to. I'm telling you we're going."

This is why she's my best friend.

"Come on then. What's going on?" she says.

Groaning, I walk back over to the bed. I've not had nearly enough alcohol for this conversation. "Ugh, things were perfect—like, *perfect*. Then, we had an argument yesterday, and the drive here was awkward. I miss him, Pey."

"Talk to him then."

"He's avoiding me."

"Like you're avoiding him?"

I glare. "Piss off."

Her light-blue eyes smile. "You know I'm right. Talk to him, Tex. You'll feel better when you do."

"I hate it when you're right, bitch."

She purses her perfect rose-pink lips and tilts her head. "Is my pep talk over?"

"Did it start?"

Shrugging, she puts her hands on her tiny hips. "So, maybe I'm not the best at advice, but I can get you good and drunk like a bloody pro. Go change, Tex, because we're going drinking."

"Can't we stay here and drink?"

"Absolutely not. You might be that pathetic right now, but I'm not."

"You're all heart," I mutter sarcastically. "Fine, I'll get changed. No makeup, and I couldn't give a shit about my hair."

"Your hair always looks good, and you don't need makeup. But you do need to be in something other than ripped shorts and a Filthy Sound T-shirt."

I'm so fucking tragic.

"Don't judge. It's comfortable."

She holds her manicured hands up. "I don't think you're a loser, not at all."

"You're a horrible friend."

"You love me. Go change, and wear something sexy."

"Why?"

"Because I said." She shoos me with her hands.

"Oh my God, I'm going. I don't like the new more assertive Peyton, by the way." I leave her to it and go to get changed.

"Hurry up, Texas!" she shouts through my bedroom door as I close it.

I open my bag and take a quick look. Peyton said sexy, but I'm not looking to score, so I opt for my leather shorts and a white T-shirt that I tuck into them. I slip on a pair of black ankle boots, and I'm done.

It's not like I need to dress up. My name gets me into pretty much anywhere I want. I step back out of the room, and Peyton is just slipping on a thigh-length navy dress. Her lips are now Coca-Cola red. She's got sexy down.

She looks up, and her eyes hone in on my outfit. "See? This is why I hate you. How do you make a simple outfit look hot?"

I peek down at myself and give her a what-the-fuck look. That's really not what's happening here. And I'm cool with that. I'll never be super girlie or look like a real proper, sophisticated grown-up. I am who I am, and that won't change.

"Pey, if Cooper ever saw you in that dress, he'd never leave you alone."

She rolls her eyes. "Is it wrong I hope that happens?"

"What? Wait, you want..."

Hello, Twilight Zone.

"No! I mean, I'm sure a night with him would be out of this world, but I think I'd pay for it in the sense that he would never let me forget or live it down. But the man is undeniably gorgeous, and he oozes multiple orgasms."

I lift my eyebrow. *Has she been abducted?* "Peyton Best, is this something you want to find out?"

She scoffs. "No. Come on, let's get out of here."

I grab my phone and debit card, and we head to Ted's suite. He'll insist on taking someone else, too, since Peyton will be with me, but I don't really care who comes along. I never notice them anyway.

Peyton links my arm as we walk into the club. Ted and Marco, another addition to the security team, are right with us. Peyton has a harder time with security being so close. She always has. When we went out as kids, she would be hyperaware that we weren't alone, so she'd filter everything she said.

"Oops," Peyton says, nodding to the bar.

My face drops, but my heart soars. *Great.* Kitt and Cooper are here.

"My bad. I should've checked where they were first."

"Whatever," I say, shaking my head. "Just get me drunk—like, right now."

She claps her hands together. "Yay. To the bar!"

Linking my arm with hers, I can't help but laugh. She's such a perky glitter-and-rainbows person that it's impossible to be sad around her for long. Peyton is exactly what I need right now, and it's times like these when I realise how much I've missed her.

"When are you moving back home, Pey?"

"I have another year in production, and then I'll be back." She smiles brightly, and her gunmetal-blue eyes light up.

I know she gets homesick sometimes, but acting is what she was born to do.

We head to the bar. Kitt and Coop still haven't seen us. They're at the other end, sitting at a table. Cooper is his usual enthusiastic self, and my moody boyfriend is very moody. He's nursing a whiskey and sulking.

"You're staring," Peyton sings.

I look away. "Sorry." I can't help it.

Doesn't help that Kitt looks incredible in a simple blood-red T-shirt. His hair is messy, and although he's smiling, it's not real. We have that in common.

"If you want to make up with him, go and talk to him."

"I don't know what to say."

"How about you start with, *Sorry*? Or offer him a blowie."

"Yeah. How about you get me a drink first? Then, I'll figure out how to handle this."

She salutes. "Your wish…"

24

KITT
MONDAY, MAY 18
LISBON, PORTUGAL

Fuck.

Texas is here. And, somehow, a day early, so is Peyton.

Seeing Texas in those shorts and messy hair is torture. I ache to touch her.

They make their way over to our table. Milo is off dancing with a couple of girls, and Cooper's earlier hanger-on has fucked off with someone else because he wasn't giving her enough attention. He won't be interested now that Peyton is here anyway.

Peyton smiles. "Hello, boys."

Coop holds his hand up. "*Men*, darlin', and I can prove it."

She rolls her blue eyes. "I'm good. Thanks."

"Yeah, maybe that's the problem. I can help you be *real* bad."

Tex turns her nose up, but Peyton continues to argue with him. My girl takes the seat next to me and places her hands on the table. I want to reach for one.

Clenching my fists under the table, I give her a once-over. "I like the shorts."

"Thought you might, pervert."

"Ah, so you admit, you only wore them to drive me crazy?"

"I never attempted to deny it."

At least she's honest.

"Consider it, mission accomplished. I'm hard."

Her eyes flush with lust, and I groan. She takes an unusually long sip of her drink, scrunching her nose as she does. The thing reeks of vodka, so no doubt, she's got a double or triple.

"Drinking it away?"

She cocks her head and tilts her glass in my direction. "Yep. You?"

"I think I've got at least five on you. Shouldn't drink your problems away, Tex."

"Why not? You do. And if it's good enough for Kitt Daniels, why can't it be good enough for me?"

"Why are you on the attack?"

She drops her eyes and snaps her teeth together. "It's not easy."

"Oh, I'm well aware of that, but you don't see me being bitchy."

"I'm sorry, okay? This is so stupid, and I don't know how to make it better," she says.

"We're not broken. We had an argument. It's not like it's our first."

Her eyes go wide and afraid. "But it's the first time since we've been together."

"Are you pushing me away, Tex?" I put my drink down and take the glass from her hand. "Is that what this is about? You're preparing for the end? What part of 'I'll never get bored of this' did you not understand?"

I reach out and take her hand, not giving a fuck if we're photographed like this. "We are going to argue—every couple does—but that doesn't automatically signal the end."

She gives me a smile and moves her arm back. My hand drops on the table, and I clench my jaw shut. I'm aggravated, confused, and lost. My first instinct is always to make her okay. It's all her, but part of protecting her is giving us the start that won't fuck up her relationship with her dad.

"Sorry," she mutters. "There are tons of people here, and a lot of them are watching you."

"Fuck them. What are you thinking about *us*?"

"I think I overreacted, and I'm sorry. But you have to give me a little space if I need it. That doesn't mean I'm going to freak out. It just means I need to get my head straight. I'm not getting bored of this either."

"Fair enough." I can give her that. I hate to leave things on bad terms, leave an argument unsettled, but maybe that's better than having the cold shoulder for a fucking day. "We okay?" *You rational?*

She rolls her eyes. "Obviously."

"Good. Now, are you going to do tequila with me, or are you pussying out?"

"Bugger off. I'm not being beaten by a wannabe rock star."

"*Oh*," I say, clenching my heart and pretending to be wounded. "Coming from my wannabe groupie…"

Her arm flies out, and I block it, laughing.

The humour and fire are back in her eyes. This is how we're supposed to be, always like this.

"You're a dick, and I hate you."

I smirk. "I love you, too, baby."

She narrows her eyes, and then something catches her attention on the dance floor. "Oh my God, do you think she's actually going to sleep with him?"

I follow her gaze. Coop is pawing at Pey. No surprise there. But one thing that isn't at all the norm is Pey's reaction. She's pulling him closer. *About time.*

"Yes. If Coop wants to sleep with someone, he's going to."

"But they're so..."

"Different? Maybe that's a good thing."

Her eyes tighten. "Right, because people who are perfect for each other always have it easy. And it's not like it took you years to figure that one out." She groans. "Sorry. Sarcasm is kind of a default."

It's how she deals with anything she doesn't like, anything she doesn't understand, and anything that hurts her. It's why she jokes about her mum. She wouldn't admit that Jennifer giving her up has left her with serious insecurities that she feels the need to conceal with sarcasm. It's all a facade.

"Can we do that tequila now, please?"

Getting up, I say, "Sure."

I order two each, and we down them, one after the other. She hates the taste, but she'd never back down. Her eyes water a little as she sucks on the lemon. I pay too much attention to the way her lips cover the yellow skin.

Fuck, don't go there. You've got ages until you can get her in your bed.

"We doing another one, Kitt?"

I lift my eyebrow.

"Good." She giggles. "I think I'm getting a bit drunk."

Yeah, no shit. She's had at least two shots of vodka and two tequilas, and she's a lightweight, you know. I'm surprised she's not on the floor. Tex isn't a big drinker, so when she toughs it without the mixer, she's done for. I, on the other hand, could have whiskey in my cereal, and it wouldn't affect me.

Another important thing Mark taught me was, learn how to fucking handle your drink because, as soon as you start getting a name for yourself, they turn up for free. Not that I couldn't handle it before, but now, I'm pretty certain my liver is pickled.

"Come on, little drunk," I say, taking her hand and pulling her up. "To the bar."

Laughing, she rests against my shoulder as we walk. "We should just stay at the bar."

I lean against the chunky glass top, and she sits on the only free stool. Resting her chin on her hands, she watches me. Women look at me that way constantly. I've grown accustomed to it, but with Texas, it knocks my feet from under me every time.

"Your staring is weird," I say, glancing at her out of the corner of my eye.

Shrugging her shoulder, she runs her eyes over my face.

The bartender stops in front of us.

"Water, please."

Tex laughs. "I do hope you're not ordering that for me."

"Why? Don't you think you've had more than enough?"

"No, I don't. We're having fun here, and I like the buzz."

"You won't like it tomorrow when there's less buzz and more puke."

"I'm not that bad."

"I bet you a grand that if you keep drinking, you'll be sick tomorrow."

Her back straightens, and she folds her arms. "I'll take that bet. And another drink, please."

My grin widening, I order a couple of tequilas, too. "You ready to lose, baby?"

"I don't lose."

"We'll see."

We down another three shots, and I'm absolutely going to be a grand richer tomorrow.

She tilts her head back and laughs. "You're funny."

I haven't said anything.

I love my girl drunk.

She lays her head on my shoulder and sighs. "Sometimes, I wish my dad wasn't who he is. My life would be less complicated."

"You could be the most famous person on the planet or a normal person with a nine-to-five, and nothing about your life would be easy. Complicated is built in from the moment we're born. If something is easy, Tex, you don't want it."

"Tequila is easy, and I want that."

I laugh and lay my head against hers. "Yeah, your opinion on that one is going to change in the morning."

"I guess, by those standards, we're going to be together forever then? Because there is nothing easy or straightforward here."

"Do you honestly think I'm in this for anything less than forever? We said no getting bored, remember? I don't like to waste my time, Tex. It's why I kept women to one night and nothing more."

"You're always so sure of yourself and what you want."

"Yep." I down another shot and run my finger around the rim of the glass.

"At least you're not making it obvious," Peyton says, interrupting us.

Tex and I sit straighter.

Peyton rests her arms on the bar. "As far as covert goes, you both need a lot of work."

Tex rolls her eyes. "You've been dry-humping Coop on the dance floor."

"Yeah, that one kind of crept up on me." Her mouth twists from unsure to excitement. "He's yummy though. In a gross way."

"You often grind on the cock of someone you find gross?" I ask innocently.

Peyton looks at Tex while jabbing her thumb towards me. "Him? Really?"

I laugh. "The real question is, why would it be anyone else?"

Tex gives me a sultry smile. "I've developed a very useful tool. I can now block out the cocky."

I nudge her arm. "Shut up. You love the cocky."

Her eyes drift back to Pey.

Tex only left it there because she can't lie. She loves it when I'm cocky, and I love it when she's angry and unreasonable.

We're perfect together.

Coop wraps his arms around Pey's waist, and the blonde's eyes darken. *Oh, yeah, she really finds him gross.*

"Hey, man, we're going to take off. Can you get Tex back safe?" Coop asks me.

"Tex, you okay with that?" Peyton asks.

"Yep, I'm good," she replies. "You two go and have fun."

"We intend to," Coop replies, wiggling his eyebrows.

Peyton used to be immune to Coop's charms. He'd tried it on her so many times before, and every time, he would be met with a brick wall. I have no idea what's going on, but she's obviously had a change of heart. The way she's looking at him now is incredibly inappropriate for a public place.

"You sure?" Peyton presses, giving Tex a pointed look.

"Totally. Make sure he wraps up, yeah?"

Coop rolls his eyes and leads Peyton to the exit. Rule one for all of us is, where women are concerned, be careful. We didn't need to learn that from Mark, but seeing his struggles sure helped.

Texas gets off the stool and takes a deep breath. "We should leave, too. I'm tired."

I nod to Ted, who stayed behind for Tex, and Hank, who shadows me. One of the temps, Marco, left with Cooper. Hank is wise to Coop's shit, so when he can, he always makes someone else go with Coop.

Thank fuck none of them would talk about what they'd witnessed tonight.

"Come on." I take Tex's hand and raise it over her head.

She tilts her head back and laughs as I spin her on the spot.

Tucking her into my side, I hold on tight around her waist, and we follow Ted. At least this way, she's not stumbling, so those pictures won't be all over the Internet tomorrow. We will be anyway, but it's not like it'd be the first time, and we're not in some incriminating position.

We get back to the hotel, and Ted and Hank make their exit, knowing we want to be alone.

"Are you going to let me stay with you tonight, Tex?"

"Dumbarse question, Daniels." She shoves the key card in the door—the wrong way around—and frowns. "Huh?"

I whip it out of her hand and do it fucking properly.

She looks up. "Oops. Come on, bedtime."

Kicking the door shut behind us, I grab her around the waist, and she squeals. *Fuck, she's loud.*

"Shh," I playfully growl in her ear.

When I hug my arms around her waist, she giggles.

"I thought you liked it when I screamed," she says.

"I like it when I'm inside you, and you scream." And I fully intend to do that in about ten seconds.

"You still feel like a dream," she whispers as I walk us toward her bed.

"Really do have it bad for me, sweetheart, didn't you?"

She'll never know how good that feels. For the past few years I've known her, I've wanted her. How could I not? She's gorgeous and funny and challenging. I was okay with never being able to have her. I didn't think about it much, and there were always plenty of women willing to get down and dirty. But when she told me she'd liked me for a while, *fuck*, it was like she shoved open the door, and all these feelings came pouring out, feelings I hadn't known I had.

Stumbling under my arms, she laughs and nods her head.

God, I love this little pisshead so fucking much.

"Okay, into bed." I turn her around.

Her eyes are glazed over from the alcohol, and her cheeks have a light blush. I'm not sure if that's from the booze or the fact that we're going to be naked soon.

"Kitt, the room is spinning," she says seriously, like she believes there's a reason for it that isn't vodka or tequila.

"Close your eyes," I say, laughing.

Her eyes flicker shut, and she raises her arms for me to undress her.

My breath catches. I know what's under the material wrapped around her body, but it still makes my brain short-circuit when I see how beautiful she is.

Yeah, right here is where we belong.

25

**TEXAS
TUESDAY, MAY 19
LISBON, PORTUGAL**

Kitt is sleeping when I wake up the next morning. His arm is around my middle, and his leg is slung over mine.

And he's naked. *Win.*

I've missed this so much.

Get a grip. You were in a fight for one day!

Oh, shit, I'm one of those girls, the ones I make fun of for being so bloody ridiculous.

That's just great.

I've always prided myself on my ability not to need a boyfriend to determine my happiness, but the little bastard next to me has done that to me. When we're not okay, I'm not okay. *That's probably normal when you love someone, and they hurt you hurt, right?*

But Kitt isn't hurt. We only fought.

Yeah, fabulous. I can't even find a way to talk myself out of being a man-needy twat.

Kitt stirs in his sleep and tightens his arms around me, burying his head in my hair.

Best. Feeling. Ever.

"Are you awake?" I whisper.

"No," he mutters, his chest rocking with silent laughter. "Go back to sleep."

It's only six a.m., so we can afford another couple of hours in bed.

Kitt is breathing heavily, so I know he's drifted back off. I can't. My heart is thumping, and I have butterflies. He's here, allowing us some comfort. It's perfect.

My phone starts to ring on my bedside table, and I know what little ho is calling me at this hour. I can't wait to speak to her. I reach across, stretching my arm to the max, trying to grab it without disturbing Kitt. I scrape it closer with the tips of my fingers and swipe my thumb across the screen.

"Good morning, Peyton," I say with a grin. *Oh, yes, enjoying this already.*

"Don't use that tone, whore."

I laugh and relax back into Kitt's chest. "How was your night of hot sex with Jack Cooper?"

"You're a total bitch, and I hate you. But I'm also really sorry. I left you with Kitt, which confirms that I'm the worst friend in history."

I place a kiss on his knuckle. "Actually, it all worked out just fine."

"It did?"

"He's wrapped around me in my bed."

She squeals down the end of the phone. "Thank God! Should I let you go then? Do you have more *catching up* to do?"

"Like you're going anywhere before you tell me what the hell last night was. I thought you were absolutely not interested in Coop?"

"I wasn't, and I'm not."

"You have no idea how much I wish we were having this conversation face-to-face."

"Don't need to. I can practically see your fucking smile," she mutters.

"Nah, Pey, this is what besties do. Now, spill the beans. I want to know *everything*."

Well, I think I do. Coop is probably into some weird things, sexually, and I definitely don't want to hear about that.

"I don't know. We had a few drinks, a dance, and then all of a sudden, I wanted him. A lot. It hit me like a bloody bus and surprised the hell outta me because I know what he's like. I'm so not interested in being just another notch on the infamous man-whore's bedpost. But everything in my life has kind of been running away from me, and I've been feeling like I'm just along for the ride. Last night, I felt in charge. It was my choice, and I chose to have a one-night stand with a rock star."

"You've so made it," I say dryly.

"You're sleeping with one, too, lady."

I laugh, and that's when Kitt stirs again. He presses his erection into my backside, and I have to bite my lip to stop myself from moaning down the phone. I'd like to be sleeping with one right now.

"Pey, can we meet up in, say…twenty minutes?"

"Thirty minutes," Kitt corrects, groaning into my hair

I wince because Peyton definitely heard that.

"You got your thirty minutes, lover boy!" she shouts to Kitt. "Meet for breakfast, Tex, okay?"

"Yep, see you down there."

Kitt takes the phone off me and hangs up.

"Well, that was rude," I chastise over my shoulder.

He gives me an adorable smile that melts my heart into a puddle.

"I don't care. We're both naked here, and this body is driving me insane," he breathes, running his hand down the outside of my leg.

Closing my eyes, I tilt my head back and bite my lip to stifle a moan. I start to pulse between my legs. Damn, he's barely touched me.

"Kitt..."

His breathing gets heavier, and he curls his hand to the inside of my thigh. "I've never needed anything more than I need you," he says roughly.

"You said..."

His hand grazes my entrance. The touch is so light, but I feel it everywhere.

What was I saying? Did you even speak at all?

"I said, what?" he asks.

His husky voice drives me crazy. I'm too hot, too riled up, and I need to come. Right the fuck now.

"Kitt!"

He delicately rubs his finger in small circles. I need more. He knows that. I grind myself on his hand, and he moves it back, not allowing me what I want.

"Don't. Kitt, please. I need this. Please."

He groans in my ear. "So fucking hot when you beg. Touch yourself with me, baby."

Holy...

This would never have happened with Xander. He would never have even asked me to, but also, I didn't feel this confident before. It's like Kitt extinguishes any inhibitions I have the moment he kisses me. I love it. I love that I can ask for whatever I want, and he'll give it to me. And not only will he grant my every wish, but it also turns him on, too.

Without another thought, I lower my hand and touch myself. His fingers guiding mine is twice as erotic, and I feel like I'm going to explode the second his finger brushes mine.

"God, Texas," he groans.

It sends a bolt of pleasure from my toes to my core.

"Kitt, I'm close."

I grind myself on our hands, and Kitt presses his erection into my leg, breathing hard and biting down on my shoulder.

"Shit, that's it." My body shudders, and my eyes fall shut. "Kitt, I can't…"

"Let go. Come for me," he rasps, arching his hips against my butt.

I feel the dampness at the end of his cock, and that's what sends me over the edge. I ride out my orgasm on our interlaced fingers.

When my body goes slack, he pulls back. His eyes are dark with lust. "There is no need for anyone to leave this room until I've made you come—twice more."

"Oh, really, Mr Hotshot?"

"I'll give you my hotshot."

"Ew." I laugh, shoving his chest.

He rolls above me. "You love it."

I love you.

"Remind me why I like you again?" I say, narrowing my eyes.

He raises an eyebrow as he looks down south and licks his bottom lip. "I'm about to."

Sweet. Jesus.

"You should do it soon. I really, really can't remember."

Chuckling, he shakes his head as his tongue darts out and caresses my collarbone. I tilt my head to give him better access and let out a moan. Spurred on by my reaction, Kitt's hands are suddenly everywhere—in my hair, over my breasts, across my stomach, down the inside of my thigh.

I can't keep up, and it sends my mind spinning. All I feel is pleasure, and I never want it to end.

I squirm against the intense pulsing and close my eyes. "Kitt, please." I'm so turned on that I'm actually uncomfortable. I need him, his mouth, his fingers again—*anything*—right now.

His chest vibrates against mine, like he's laughing, but he doesn't make a sound, probably because he's busy taking my hardened nipple into his mouth.

"Relax. I'm going to take care of you now."

He pushes himself inside me, and my eyes roll back.

I'm still flushed when I meet Peyton for breakfast, and her smile tells me she's noticed.

"Really? You're giving *me* that look?"

"No judgement, remember?" she says before taking a sip of her coffee.

She's already poured me a large mug, and I waste no time. Morning sex with Kitt is my preferred way of waking up properly, but you can't beat coffee either.

"I'm not. I don't really understand how you go from never to one-nighter though. And I get that you want to take charge, and it's your body, yada, yada, yada, but *huh*?"

"Cooper is gorgeous and his body..." She pretends to fan her face.

"No, I get it. He is a beautiful man with a body carved from sin itself, but I've never gone ahead and slept with him."

"That's because you've been in love with Kitt since forever."

I'll give her that.

"As long as you know what you're doing, Pey."

"I do."

She doesn't.

"And that is?"

"Sex. We had sex, and that's it. Don't get me wrong, he was *unbelievable*, and I don't regret it, but I do know that I don't want a casual fling. It's not for me, especially since I no longer get much of a private life. Plus, doing something so intimate with Cooper more than once is a surefire way to get your heart broken. Doesn't really appeal."

"So, you just had sex once?"

She blushes and half hides her face by taking a longer sip of coffee.

"Oh my God, Pey, how many times?"

"Four," Cooper says proudly, sitting down beside Peyton.

Bloody hell, where did he come from?

My blushing bestie looks away and closes her eyes.

Because I'm her best friend, I'm going to thoroughly enjoy this. "Good morning, Cooper."

He flashes me a grin and throws his arm over the back of Peyton's chair. "Good morning indeed, Texas. How did you sleep?"

From the look in his eyes, I know he's spoken to Kitt already. Cooper knows.

"I didn't sleep much, Coop. Too busy having hot sex. I hear you were in a similar situation."

Peyton groans and gives me a hard stare. I don't even care. She would so do the same thing.

"Had a hot chick riding me like a cowgirl all night."

"All right," Peyton snaps. "We are *not* talking about this."

"Well, you might not, but Tex and I are."

"You really should have considered whom you were sleeping with before," I add, pouring some coffee into Cooper's mug.

"I'll remember that next time—if there were going to be a next time."

"We did agree on one night, but I'd change my shagging rule if you wanted to go again," Cooper says, leaning a little more toward her.

He's very much in her personal space now, but she straightens her spine, not letting him get to her.

"No, thank you. I won't be needing a repeat."

She smiles victoriously, but I know it's far too premature to think she's won against him just yet. This is Jack Cooper.

"Of course you don't need a repeat. You proved many times that I worked you over good and proper. I have scratch and bite marks to prove it."

And there we go.

She turns to me. "How do you put up with him?"

"I tend not to sleep with him."

Cooper laughs and looks back to Pey, waiting.

"I hate you both."

"You didn't hate me a couple of hours ago," he brags.

"Yes, I did. It was a pity shag."

Coop shrugs it off. "I got sex. I don't care."

Yep, he rarely loses.

"Anyway," he says before draining his coffee all at once, "I'll leave you to talk about my outstanding performance in the bedroom. Kitt wants us to go over a song he wrote for the new album."

They've not even finished the tour for this one yet, and Kitt is working on the next. He's never *not* thinking, never not typing lyrics on his phone or scribbling them in a notebook—except when he's in bed with me.

"Bye, Coop."

He gives me a wink and wiggles his eyebrows at Peyton before heading toward the lifts.

"That was interesting."

Peyton glares. "For you maybe."

"You knew the guy before. The gloating can't be a surprise."

"Ugh, I know. Seriously, the next guy I sleep with is going to be my husband. I'm never having casual again. I'm done with it."

"Yeah, right." I roll my eyes.

"I'm not kidding. I'm a born-again virgin. Sex just leads to having people like Cooper talking about the marks you leave behind. It should be more than that."

"I'll bet you five hundred grand that you'll give in to Coop again."

Her blonde eyebrows shoot up. "I'll take that bet, my friend."

Either way, it'll be worth it.

"How was Kitt?"

"Perfect. We're good now. Everything is great, and as soon as we're back in England, we'll tell my dad. We're going to let him see us grow closer, so it's not such a shock when we tell him we're together."

She tilts her head, and I can tell what she's thinking, but this will work out. *It will.*

26

KITT
TUESDAY, MAY 19
LISBON, PORTUGAL

I force myself to do something while Texas is out with Peyton because, frankly, I'm like a lovesick puppy, and I'm pissing myself off.

How can you miss someone you've only been separated from for an hour?

It doesn't make sense. But love rarely does.

Falling for Texas has made me throw my morals right out the window. I didn't exactly have an abundance of them before, but now, I'm betraying Mark and lying to everyone who matters to me. And though it makes me sound like a wanker, I don't care. I'm with her, and that's what matters.

They're going shopping, so that means I probably won't see her again until much later. Milo and Coop probably want to be out, lining up tonight's shag, but I'm making them work.

Milo is into it and happy to be here though, so I don't feel guilty. Coop...well, after last night, he's just happy.

Something has been simmering between him and Peyton for a while, and although they're probably not going to pursue anything, it'll be good not to feel dirty around them. The looks they give each other should be classed as sex itself.

I sent Tex a message a while ago, but so far, she's not replied. I very much hope it's because she's busy buying underwear for me to peel off her tonight.

"Are you sure this is how you want the chorus to go?" Milo asks after reading it through a couple of times.

I deadpan. "No. That's why you're here!"

"Is it shit?" Coop asks, not looking up from his phone.

My educated guess is that he's sending Peyton obscene messages and thoroughly enjoying it. The poor girl really should make better life choices.

"No, dick," Milo replies. "You could help, you know."

He chuckles. "Oh, I know."

I roll my eyes at Milo, and he shrugs.

"I vote we kick him out of the band," Milo says.

Coop scoffs. "Then, you'd have no band."

"Milo, focus."

Since Texas has had my mind tied up in figuring her and us out, I've not written much. I'm still constantly jotting down random lyrics, but I've got nothing solid. If we want to follow this tour and the album with something epic, I need to pull my finger out.

The show is over, and I'm back in my hotel room. Tex is messaging Peyton because, even against her better judgement, she's with Coop right now.

"I want to take you out tonight," I say, wrapping Tex in my arms.

She puts the phone down. "Yeah, I'll just get my mask. Come on, Kitt. You know we'd never get away with that."

She's right, of course. I can't buy a pint of milk without it being photographed, and neither can she. We can't risk going out on a proper date, not until we've told Mark. He can't hear it from anyone else. We owe him that much.

"Actually"—letting go of her, I step back, and she pouts—"give me a couple of hours, and then come to my suite at one."

Tilting her head with intrigue, she asks, "What are you going to be doing that you need me to leave and come back at one a.m.?"

"You'll see later."

"But I don't like surprises."

"You'll love this one." I give her a quick kiss because if I don't get my lips off hers straight away, I'll never get out of here, and I want to do something for her. So far in our relationship, I haven't taken her out to dinner. We've had a lot of room service on a lot of beds, but that's it.

Some things will have to be the same—room service—but I want to make it special, romantic.

I leave her room, head down the corridor and call Hank. He'll know what to do. It's his job to know what to do. Well, it's not, but he's very good at this sort of shit since he's been married since he was eighteen.

He answers on the second ring. "Everything okay? You need to go out?"

"No, I need a favour. It's for Tex."

"Go on," he says.

"We can't go to a restaurant because Mark doesn't..."

"You want me to set something up in your room?"

"Er, not exactly. I want you to tell me how to do it." I mean, I have the number for room service and the local pizza place, but I kind of need tonight to be more special than that. "What's good around here? I want decent food brought in, and I want something to make the suite not look like a hotel suite."

"I don't think they'll let you change the interior, man," he teases.

"I can fire you, you know."

"Oh, come on. It's good to see you whipped, but I'm not going to miss an opportunity to take the piss."

"Hank…"

"Leave it to me. I'll message you with some options."

"Thanks," I reply before ending the call.

It takes an hour and a half to hang the fairly light curtains all around the room, fill every surface with roses, set up a playlist for the evening, and look through a menu to see what I think Tex will want.

I've never done anything like this before, and I honestly didn't see myself doing it until my late twenties—when I planned on settling down—but she is so worth it. The plans I made are happening a lot sooner, but I wouldn't change anything. I'd rather feel this way for longer than screw around for another six years or so.

Texas terrifies me because she makes me want everything right now. Marriage, house, kids—I'd do it now. Logically, I know better. We're in the early stages of our relationship, and I have a ton going on, things I can't bail on and don't want to.

Doing anything other than singing in this band isn't an option for me, and Filthy Sound still needs a fuckload of my time and attention.

Somehow, I have to find a way to somewhat equally balance the two most important things in my life.

"Thanks, Hank," I say as he finishes up straightening one of the large black curtains. With them all around the living room, it looks like night in here, and the hundreds of fairy lights are like stars.

"Have a good night." He gives me a wink and then leaves.

I don't know how he managed to pull it off, but it looks awesome.

My palms start to dampen. I'm fucking nervous. She'd better like this.

When did I become love's bitch?

I wipe my hands on my jeans as someone knocks on the door.

I feel like I need a minute.

There's another knock, and I know for sure it's Texas. No one else is that impatient.

"Hey." She smiles as I open up. Her eyes go wide when she looks inside. "Kitt..."

"Come in," I say.

She doesn't move, so I take her hand and tug her inside.

"I've never seen you speechless, Tex. It's unnerving and, if I'm honest, something I thought was an impossibility."

Tilting her head, she gives me a look, and then she's back to being stunned. "I can't believe you did this. I mean, *Kitt Daniels* can be romantic. Who knew?"

I certainly fucking didn't.

"Do you like it?" I ask, rubbing circles on the back of her hand.

She takes the whole room in—the curtains that look like a starry night, the table laid out, the food and the wine waiting. "Kitt...I love it."

Finally, she looks up at me. Neither one of us has said, *I love you*, yet, but I'm not stupid. I see it in her eyes, and I feel it by the way she's holding me a fraction tighter than necessary.

I want to say it now. This is the perfect time, but she looks kind of overwhelmed already. And I'm scared. My fear doesn't come from a negative place—I know she'll say it back—but I'm having a hard time processing just how deep my feelings for her run, and I need to catch up with my heart. That bastard is miles ahead of me.

"Are you hungry?" I ask.

We're standing a good few feet away from each other, still holding hands. The intensity between us is maddening. I feel her everywhere. My heart feels her everywhere. It's thudding so hard that I'm considering calling 999.

"I am," she whispers, staring straight into my eyes.

"Good, because I ordered a lot. You look beautiful, by the way."

She's in a pair of those sinful leather shorts and a Filthy Sound T-shirt. Nothing is sexier than your girl wrapped in leather and your shirt.

"If I'd known what you've done, I would've worn something...well, else."

"No, I think you look pretty damn perfect in that."

She rubs her heart. "You seriously have to stop that."

Fuck, I love how I make her feel.

Stepping closer, I wrap my arms around her waist. Wherever we touch is electric. No one has ever made me feel like this. I can't get enough.

"I don't want to stop."

She gives me a little smile that means she doesn't want me to stop either. "What's for dinner? And where did it come from? You didn't cook, so..."

"Hank found this nearby restaurant that I wished I could have taken you to. Apparently, it's the best in the city. I had them deliver a couple of dishes."

"Do they usually do takeaway? And at this time?"

I shake my head. "I pulled a few strings."

"Ah, you've definitely made it now."

I give her a wink.

I have to say, it felt amazing. I've watched Mark, Will, and Jimmy get anything they want with one phone call, and to have that power is pretty damn cool. This is the first time that I've really done it. Other than to sing, I don't want much for myself, but I don't feel like a fucking diva if I'm asking for favours to make Tex happy.

"Thinking of calling Ferrari tomorrow."

She leans into my chest and tucks her head under my chin. "Mmm, good luck with that one."

With her pressed against me and her breath hot and heavy on my neck, I start to feel my jeans getting tighter around the zipper.

Texas arches her eyebrow and tilts her head as she feels me hard up against her, ready for action. "We've not eaten yet, Kitt."

"Sorry. Natural reaction when you're around."

"Feed me." She pouts, pulls back and turns away. "Then, when we're done, I want to be really dirty everywhere in this suite."

"Oh, come on," I groan.

She said it to drive me crazy, and she's real successful at it. Looking over her shoulder, she blows me a kiss.

Damn.

27

TEXAS
WEDNESDAY, MAY 20
ATHENS, GREECE

We'd arrived in Greece early in the morning, and I had a rare day alone with Kitt.

After going our separate ways to everyone else, we're wondering around looking for something to do together.

The sun is blistering above us, and I'm so hot. Not that I care. *Hello, date with my rock star.*

"So, where to first?" I ask.

He takes my hand and shrugs. "I have no idea. Do we need a plan? I've never liked making plans. They usually lead to disappointment."

"You never planned on being a rock star?" I ask.

"Nope. I was going to be a vet."

"Really?"

"When I was four, I had a fish, and I was devastated when it died. Figured, if I was a vet, I could bring him back. Only that didn't happen."

I roll my eyes. "And you were disappointed?"

"That was the last time I planned anything. The band happened, and I hadn't planned that."

"Wow, I never knew you were so deep."

"There's a lot you don't know about me, Tex."

"So, tell me."

"I'm not allowed some secrets?"

I shake my head. "No. I don't have any, so why should you?"

"Right. You don't have any secrets at all? Come on, Texas. Everyone keeps things."

"Hmm, you're right." I hold our connected hands up. "I've not told my dad about this."

"Solid call. I like my dick...almost as much as you seem to."

Bastard.

Dad won't castrate Kitt, obviously, but there will be lots of shouting and plenty of disappointment.

To this day, I've never done anything to disappoint my dad. I'm good at getting around him, but this is a stretch. He's not all that happy about me and boys, especially if they're a couple years older and rock stars. He's seen too many celebrities behave badly and treat their girlfriends like crap.

Fuck them all. Inconsiderate arseholes.

"We don't have long before we're back in England, and we'll have to tell him."

"I know," he replies. "Not looking forward to that, I have to say."

"You know what we'll say yet?" *Because I bloody don't.*

Kitt and I have been making sure we're seen together a lot more, but so far, Dad hasn't pulled me up on it. So, that means, he's not noticed us growing closer. There's a fine line between him suspecting our feelings toward each other are changing and him guessing exactly how close we are.

With the Band

We have to push a little bit harder. *But how hard?*
Answers on a postcard...

Kitt gives my hand a squeeze. "Now, *that* I might plan—well, my escape route at least."

"He's a pussycat really."

"Yeah...Tex, when it comes to you, he's a fucking lion."

"You could try not hurting me." *Please.*

"I don't intend to."

I'm not sure if he wants to add a silent, *But things happen*, in there or not, so I try not to dwell on it.

"Mini golf," he says.

"What?"

He lifts his chin toward a mini golf course, and it all makes sense.

"Er, sure."

In all honesty, that sounds bloody awful, but what we do doesn't matter. It's nice to be alone and do normal date stuff. Hopefully, no one will recognise us while we're here. We're banking on *not* because of the big sunglasses, but it's still a risk. He does look different in a long-sleeved shirt. He never wears them, but this way, his ink is covered.

We walk through the entrance and head to the ticket booth.

"Two, please," Kitt says, pulling some money out of his wallet.

The girl behind the plastic screen doesn't bat an eyelid. She takes his money and tells us where to get our clubs and where to go. I breathe a little easier, knowing how clueless she is.

"Have you played before?" I ask.

He smirks. "My grandad used to take me when I was a kid."

"Great. I'm going to lose."

"Now, that is not the attitude to have, Knight."

I turn and lift my eyebrow, having an idea. "You're right. I'm definitely going to win this."

"Why? What are you planning?" His voice is laced with suspicion.

"Nothing." Smiling sweetly, I grab a golf club and walk outside.

Kitt follows and walks beside me with his eyes firmly fixed on my face, as if he's trying to draw the truth out of me.

Not happening, buddy.

"Texas..."

I look up. "Yes? Can I go first?"

"Sure..."

"I don't know what I'm doing though. Can you help?" I make sure my voice is low and sweet, like a fucking damsel in distress. But I'm not. This is war—yes, over mini golf—and I don't intend on losing.

Kitt's midnight-blue eyes are trained on mine. "I can help."

He knows I'm playing, but he still puts his club down and comes over. The minute his chest presses against my back, I close my eyes. He takes a sharp intake of air and wraps his arm around my waist. His other hand starts on my shoulder and slowly caresses its way down until it covers mine. I feel goose bumps pebble under my skin at the contact.

Bugger, I'm supposed to win this.

Clearing my head from thoughts of having him take me back to the hotel, I say, "What do I do then?" Somehow, I manage to keep my voice steady.

His lips graze my ear with the gentlest touch. "Hold the club with two hands, here and here." He places my other hand in position. "Then, swing back, and try to hit the ball."

I slowly swing the club back, arching my back so that my butt presses into his groin. He groans, and his fingertips dig into my waist. It's working. I look at him over my shoulder and smile. As I swing the club forward and strike the ball, I push back a little harder. Kitt's short nails nip at my skin.

The ball rolls along the green felt and through the creepy clown's head.

"Yay! That wasn't too bad. Your turn, Kitt."

I step away from him, and he takes a quick worried glance around before adjusting himself.

I have this in the bag.

Gritting his teeth, he places his ball down and whacks it in frustration. It slams against the clown's cheek and rolls back.

I stretch my arms out and lean against my stick. Tilting my head, I say, "Oops. Want another turn before I hit mine home?"

He steps closer and glares. "Don't think I don't know what you're doing, Texas."

"We both know exactly what I'm doing, and we both know I'm going to be victorious."

"Fucking woman," he grunts under his breath as I walk around to find my ball.

I'm really enjoying myself, mostly because I'm driving Kitt wild, but then in the space of five minutes, three people come over for photos and autographs.

Kitt puts his arm around a girl. In turn, she thinks she's gotten the green light to feel my boyfriend up. She places her hand on his chest and smiles for the camera—the camera being her phone that I'm so very close to lobbing at her head. I click the button twice and hand it back to her.

"Thank you so much, Kitt! I love all of your songs! You're amazing!"

And thank you, Texas, for taking the photo…

No? Fine.

"Thank you. It's always great to meet a fan," he says.

I stand at the side and watch with a smile. This is a part of who he is, and although I might not like it, I have to be okay with it. He's not going to sleep with her or anyone else, so I let her have her two minutes.

Kitt finally says bye to her, and then his attention is back on me. It's always back on me, and that's what matters. He soothes that tiny jealous part of my soul with one look. It's me he wants.

"I don't want to leave yet, Tex, but…"

"I know. We can't play if you keep getting stopped. Let's go back to the hotel. I'm sure we can find something there to keep us occupied."

He steps closer and leans in. My eyes widen as I think he's going to kiss me. We're being watched now.

"I think you owe me for your behaviour today," he says.

I laugh. "My behaviour? I think I've been very nice."

"You know what you did. Do you have any idea how hard it is to hide a boner in public?"

Playfully shoving his chest, I giggle. "Come on, big boy, let's get out of here."

He slings his arm over my shoulders. "If you think I'm ever going to forget you calling me big boy, you're mistaken."

"Hmm, maybe I was joking though."

"Not in my head."

Kitt grips the steering wheel as we head back to the hotel. Ted is in another rental car behind us. He kept his distance, and I don't remember seeing him once, but that was probably due to the fact that I was lost in Kitt.

His hand rests on my leg, like it usually does when we're alone. "So, when did you start to drool over me?" he asks, smirking.

He knows it's been longer than since Christmas, but we've not had this conversation before in depth—for obvious reasons. Kitt does not need his ego inflating any more.

"Truth, sweetheart, yeah?"

Rolling my eyes, I twist my body to face him. I don't want to lie because we're supposed to be honest with each other. I'm not great at the touchy-feely stuff though, never have been. I was raised by my dad and the other two male members of his band. I was always encouraged to talk about what I was feeling, but they rarely did it, so I just followed suit.

"Fine. I've liked you for a while now. More than a while actually."

He frowns and suddenly looks very nervous, which is ridiculous since I'm the one who's pouring my heart out.

"How long is *more than a while*? How long before Christmas?"

"Um...two years."

With the Band

"Two years?" he blurts out, his mouth open. He equally looks at me and the road, constantly turning his head.

"We can have this conversation while you watch where we're going."

He cuts me a look before turning forward. "Two years, Tex?"

"Yeah, well, you look like that, and we've always gotten along really well."

"We have. Why didn't you tell me sooner?"

I laugh at that because, no, it's not like I would have told him. "Oh, come on! You're young and in a band. When we met, it was the early days for Filthy Sound, and you were living it up to the fullest. And by that, I mean, you were sleeping with everything with a pulse. You weren't ready to be in a relationship. It would have ended badly."

He swallows, and I can tell he wants to deny it, but he can't. Kitt doesn't want to admit that he didn't want me back then, but it's okay. I'm fine with it. Besides, he does now.

"It could have worked," he says.

"You don't even believe the words that just came out of your mouth. It's fine. Really. It didn't hurt that much."

"That much?" He slams on the brakes, like a fucking lunatic, and swings the car into a lay-by.

Ted pulls in behind us, but he must sense our safety isn't the reason Kitt stopped because he doesn't get out.

"Kitt!" I shout, grabbing the dashboard. "What's wrong with you?"

"Did I hurt you?"

I shrug. "It wasn't intentional. Forget I said anything."

"I can't forget it. Talk to me."

"It doesn't matter anymore. We're together."

"Texas!"

"What? There's no point in dragging this up. I'm happy with you."

"Tell. Me," he growls, fisting the steering wheel so hard that his knuckles turn white.

"Ugh! All right, yeah, it hurt. It hurt so fucking much every time I saw you with another woman that I wanted to die. The week before the tour was especially hard because it was the first time I saw you ready to shag someone else while I was in love with you. You didn't even see me that night, Kitt, but I was there. I left very quickly after I saw you with her. Every time, I told myself that I was okay, but I never was. Watching you kiss someone else, knowing she was soon going to know what it felt like to have you inside her, when I wanted you so badly, I felt like I was going to explode. There. Are you happy? Is that what you needed to hear?"

We're both breathing hard, and he's staring at me in horror.

Maybe that was a little too honest.

I see tears in his eyes, and I instantly regret what I said.

A simple, *Yes, sometimes, it hurt*, would've worked too.

I take a breath. *Calm yourself down. Now.* "Kitt, I'm sorry."

"No. You're not the one who should be sorry." He sounds breathless, in a painful way.

"Neither are you. You didn't know how I felt. You couldn't have known. If you're unaware, you can't be responsible."

"I'm so sorry I hurt you."

I groan and cover my face. "That's not why I told you." At this moment, I don't really know why I did.

"I know it isn't, but I *hate* that I've caused you pain."

"You didn't know. Things are good, and you make me *so* happy. Please, can we forget it?"

"I swear, I will never hurt you again."

"That's not a promise you should be making. We don't know the future."

"Not true. I'm looking at mine," he whispers.

Oh, sweet Jesus. That does things to me that makes me feel like I've suddenly defied gravity.

Letting go of the steering wheel, he leans over and presses his forehead to mine. "You love me. You said you're in love with me."

Yeah, great, I blurted that out as well. "I know I did."

Well done, you.

I'm such a fucking genius.

"Tell me again," he murmurs.

"Why? I've told you once, and you've not said it *ever*."

I have a moment of pure fear rush through my body. *What if he didn't plan on saying it because he doesn't feel it yet?* I want to hear those words from him more than I want anything but not if he doesn't mean it. I don't want those three little words to be whispered out of pity.

He smiles, and his thumb brushes over my jaw. "Texas, I love you. Of course I do. I love you more than I thought it was possible to love another person. I love you so much that it terrifies me."

My throat feels thick.

"Kitt, I love you." It's all I can manage to choke out.

"I'm going to kiss my girl now," he says, wiping a tear from my cheek.

"Okay," I whisper just before his lips land on mine.

He kisses me slow and deep, and it's filled with love and adoration.

28

TEXAS
THURSDAY, MAY 21
BRINDISI, ITALY

We pull out of the docks, and we're in Italy. The drive to Rome is going to take over five hours, so we've stocked the bus up, and we're ready for the journey. I'm tired, but that's touring. There have been so many late nights and early mornings, which I know will catch up with me eventually. I hope it doesn't until we're in England. When we're home, I'll sleep solidly for a day, I'm sure.

Kitt is opposite me at the table, and there's so much sexual tension that I can feel it vibrating off us both. Dad is up front with the drivers. Will and Jimmy are sleeping off hangovers. That leaves me alone with Kitt, Cooper, and Milo. Usually, that's fine, but right now, I'm tense and frustrated.

"All right," Cooper snaps, looking between me and Kitt, "what the fuck is really going on with you two?"

"What do you mean?"

"Come off it, Tex. I can feel it."

"You're delusional, mate," Kitt says, cracking open a beer. A beer at eleven in the morning.

"Am I? Fuck! Seriously, the sexual tension between you two is kinda turning me on. It's more than a one time thing."

I deadpan. "Coop, roadkill turns you on."

Milo and Kitt laugh.

"She's got a point, man. I think you just need to get laid. You're imagining things," Kitt adds.

"You haven't had it in two days," Milo says. "Do a girl tonight, and you'll stop seeing everyone else getting it on."

Cooper narrows his pretty baby blues, and I know he doesn't believe us. He knows Kitt and I have been intimate but he thinks just one night. As caught up as he is in getting the full rock-star experience, he notices much more than we give him credit for.

"You're right about the woman thing. But I'm right about those two," he says to Milo. "They need to shag for a week and get it properly over with because every time I look at them, I get a hard-on."

Kitt turns his nose up and slams his bottle down. "You did not just say that."

Cooper rolls his eyes and smirks. "Calm down. I don't want to bend you over, buddy."

"Can we please drop it before my dad hears?" I snap.

Understanding crosses Cooper's face, and he winks. "Got it. Your secret shagging stays with me."

Kitt growls. "We are *not* shagging."

Milo punches Cooper in the chest with the back of his hand. "Drop it, Coop. They said nothing is going on."

I don't know if Milo is aware of what's happening or not, but I suspect he is. I've seen him and Kitt talking privately. If there's one person Kitt can confide in, it is Milo.

"Fine," Cooper growls, annoyed that we all shot him down. "I need a beer. Anyone else want one?"

"No, thanks. It's not even afternoon yet," I say, eyeing Kitt's second beer.

He shrugs and takes a long gulp. I watch him drink, watch his Adam's apple as he swallows.

How does he make drinking erotic?

I take a deep breath as my hormones step into overdrive. *Turn away, Texas. You're making it obvious.*

If Cooper looks back now, his suspicions will be confirmed, but still, I can't stop staring. What I feel for Kitt is strong. The pull I feel toward him is getting harder to ignore or fight. I want more than a hidden relationship. I want Dad to know now, so Kitt and I can be together properly.

Sighing, I look away just in time. Cooper throws the bottle top in the bin and joins us at the table.

"So, what have you guys been working on?" I ask, steering the conversation to a safe territory.

"Kitt's got a few new things," Milo says. "They're a bit sappy though."

"Fuck off, dickhead. We agreed we need some—"

"Yeah, yeah, yeah," Milo says, cutting him off. "I didn't say they weren't epic."

"Wait, why do you need romance-y songs?" I ask, my heart somersaulting in my chest.

They have a couple of songs like that, but ninety-nine percent are not. They have about a million songs that are either funny, silly, racy, and catchy but only two love songs. One of them is a firm wedding favourite. Both were written by Milo.

"We've got to grow, Tex," Kitt says in a tone, letting me know he's borrowed Milo's words.

"Can I see?"

Kitt frowns, and his eyes flick to his sacred notepad that no one is allowed to touch. "It's not ready."

"So? That's not stopped you before."

"Well, it's stopping me now. I'm new to this love-song shit, okay? Milo is forcing me to think outside the box, so until I'm happy with them, no one but *Romeo* gets to see."

"If you're forcing it, man, it won't be good. Leave the love to Cupid over there, if you're not comfortable," Cooper says, tilting his head at Milo.

"I'm fine."

"Embracing *your* inner Cupid?" I say, smirking.

Kitt glares and swigs his beer, clearly uncomfortable with the subject. So, naturally, we stay on it.

"I wonder whom his muse could be…" Cooper says.

"Your mum," Kitt growls.

Milo laughs. "You've gotta appreciate a your-mum comeback every now and again."

"Fuck you, man. You ain't ever getting in my mum's bed."

"True," Kitt says. "She prefers it over the table."

Even though the thought makes my stomach churn, I laugh.

"You're a prick," Cooper barks.

"My mother probably would let you all take her over the table," I say, turning my nose up.

"Wait, we're allowed to do your mum?" Cooper asks. "I always thought she was a no-go zone."

Glaring, I reply, "She is. I'm just saying, she wouldn't say no." Hell, she would probably film it and leak it all over the Internet in a desperate bid for more fame and more attention.

Cooper sinks back into the seat and frowns in disappointment.

Well, tough. "Can we not talk about people *doing* my mother?"

"You started it," Cooper grumbles.

"Now, I'm finishing it."

The guys come through to join us for a drink, and Milo starts up a game of poker. Dad, Jimmy, and Will bundle in on the opposite side of the table. I just watch. I don't have the energy to focus on playing right now, so I get up to make a huge mug of coffee.

Dad follows me over to the minuscule kitchen and hands me his phone. "I didn't know you and Kitt went out."

My heart falls to my toes.

Stay calm. This is all a part of your plan.

The plan seemed like a much better idea when Dad wasn't questioning me though.

I take his phone. Okay, it's not bad. The pictures are actually really cute. They're from mini golf, and we're both smiling and messing around. Thankfully, there aren't any of Kitt helping me swing, but we weren't noticed until after that.

"Yeah, we got bored of hanging out in the hotel all day. I beat him."

Dad nods his head. "Is there anything else?"

"Such as?"

"I'm not blind. Does this mean anything?"

Oh God, I have to lie to him again.

My stomach burns as the lie forces its way past my lips. "No. Why?"

"I can see how you look at him, Texas."

I sigh. *Shit, keep cool.* "Dad, he's gorgeous. I'm not blind either. But you don't have to worry. Come on, what would he ever see in me?"

"Don't you ever do that to yourself," he snaps. "I won't have you tearing yourself down."

I'm a shitty person.

"Sorry," I mutter. "But it's true. He's a rock star, and he can have anyone in the world."

"Do you like him?"

"I might have a small crush. It's fine. I can handle it."

His face pales. "Are you sure?"

"Of course. We're good friends, and I won't ever lose that. And you never know. When he's old and past it, like you, and ready to settle down, he might just be able to convince me that he's good enough."

Dad laughs. "As a person, Kitt is one of the most decent. But his career choice in respect to him dating my daughter…"

"Yeah, yeah, I get it. Kitt isn't like other musicians, Dad. They're not all bad."

Gritting his teeth, he dips his head. He can't argue with that because he knows it's true. Filthy Sound respects the rules set out by him. Mostly. They don't do drugs, and they're not arseholes. But getting my dad to do cartwheels over me being with one of them will take time.

"Please be careful."

I roll my eyes. "Please. I can handle Daniels."

"But can you handle your heart?"

Nope.

"I can. Don't worry, Dad. I'm not going to get hurt."

"If you need to talk to me or if you want me to talk to Kitt..."

I almost laugh in his face. Like I want him to talk to Kitt.

"I promise, I will talk to you. But I swear to God, if you mention this to him, I will take you down, old man."

Laughing, he ruffles my hair, like I'm still two. "I had a feeling something like this would happen."

"Way to go, psychic."

"I'm serious, Texas. I don't want you getting hurt."

"And I don't want to get hurt. You don't have to stress. Kitt would never hurt me anyway."

I'm counting on that because he might as well be walking around with my heart in his pocket.

KITT
MONDAY, MAY 25
CZECH REPUBLIC

Things with Tex have been getting serious. Really serious. We need to tell Mark soon, before we get home, because, right now, I feel like we're standing still.

I've always been moving forward, and it bothers me more than anything else that Tex and I are stagnant. And with her, I want it all. I'm impatient. I don't care that we've not been together long, and it's a big secret. We've got to tell Mark and get it over with, so I can do something really fucking stupid that I won't regret and propose.

Like I said, I want it all.

She's it for me, and there's no point in waiting. Right?

I can feel the stress of it weighing me down. I didn't used to get so tired, and it's not all due to the crazy tour schedule.

In Greece and Italy we spent as much time together as we could. We skipped after-parties to go back to my room. We spent stolen moments kissing when no one was around. Everything was perfect.

But, now, we're on the bus, and I feel the distance between us. It's like thick iron bars are separating us. I'm back to acting like I'm not completely in love with her.

The idea of it makes me sick to my stomach.

I rub my eyes and sip coffee as Milo walks into the kitchen area from his bunk. He freezes. He looks at me and then his watch.

"Funny," I mutter.

"What are you doing up so early?" he asks, popping a cappuccino pod in the coffee machine.

"I couldn't sleep."

"Why? What's up? You've never had any problems with sleeping."

"Nothing's wrong."

He stops and turns on the spot. "Kitt, I swear to God, if you don't tell me what's going on, I'm going to punch you in the face. We've been friends since we were kids, so tell me what the fuck is going on with you, man."

I shove my fists into my tired eyes. "Texas."

"What's happened now?"

I lower my hands as he shakes his head and sits down, forgetting about his coffee.

"I can't spend one more day pretending like we're not what we are."

"Er, you're going to have to suck it up because you can't tell Mark yet. This isn't just about you. Think of me and Coop, too. The band, Kitt. Don't fuck this up."

I groan as I tilt my head back. Everyone I'm loyal to is sitting on the opposite side of the field of what I need.

You know you can never be that selfish. You won't put your needs before your boys, so grow a pair, and have some patience.

Watching him through narrowed eyes, I mutter, "I wouldn't risk it, but I don't like it. I want everything with her, Milo."

His eyes widen in surprise.

At the start of the band, we kind of made a pact that we wouldn't let women get in the way. It helped that we were young, and none of us wanted anything heavy, so I can see why my admission is a shock to him. He had to know that I wouldn't mess around and cheat on her, but he probably thought it would fizzle out.

We were supposed to shag our way through fans in our twenties before settling down in our thirties. I've managed only four years of casual sex before Tex ruined me.

"Mark is going to flip, and while I've got your back, I'd rather it happened when we're not all cramped on a bus."

"Tex and I have discussed that. Plan is to tell him when we get back home before we go to America."

"Sounds good, man."

"It's the best for everyone."

"Why do I get the feeling that you're not including yourself in that everyone?"

I sigh. "I want him to know. I hate the secrecy."

"Do you love her?"

"Yeah. She drives me fucking crazy, man. One minute, everything is great, and the next, I feel like I'm smashing my head against a wall. I can't keep up with this forward-and-backward thing. In private, we're either arguing or getting down to it. Recently, we've been more settled though."

"Wow, you do love her." He laughs. "And it's got to be the stupidest thing you've ever done."

"I'm not gonna argue there. Can't stop it either." *I've tried.*

"What can't stop?" Texas says, yawning, as she walks into the room.

She's smiling, but she's not cocky, so I know she didn't hear our conversation.

"Cooper," Milo says, covering my arse.

Thank fuck because I've got nothing.

He shakes his head. "If I have to listen to one more sordid bet..."

Texas folds her arms and narrows her eyes. "You're always in on those bets."

"I know, but it's getting boring. Not enough new material. Beating him at the same bet is getting old," Milo replies.

She looks suspicious as her eyes flit between us. Texas might be naive in a lot of aspects, but she can read people, and it doesn't usually take her very long to figure shit out.

"What are you doing up so early?" I ask.

"Ugh, I can't sleep. I either need someone to knock me out or a give me bucket of coffee."

Milo smirks. "Which one? I'm good with either, and I'm sure Kitt is, too."

Bastard.

"I'll make you a drink," I say to Tex. I kick Milo under the table.

"She hasn't decided yet, mate," Milo says.

I stand up and raise my eyebrow. "Are you going to knock her out?"

"Would you stop me?" he asks, his grin widening.

"Wouldn't *you* stop you?"

Texas looks between us both like we've lost our minds. I certainly have.

"That depends," he replies with a shit-eating grin.

"On what?" I bite out.

"On the consequences."

He's loving this, goading me.

"You honestly think any of us will stand back and let you smash your fist against her head?"

"This is a lovely conversation," Texas mutters sarcastically. "I think I'm going to go back to bed before you start discussing different ways to beat me up."

"No, we're done," I say a little too quickly.

Mark will be up soon, and I want some time with her where any flirting won't result in my nuts being squashed.

Texas smiles up at me and nods, and I can see Milo smirking.

Don't look directly at him.

"So, are you going guy-watching in Poland, Tex?"

Her eyes instantly flick to mine before returning to Milo.

If she answers yes to this question...

"Um..."

"Um?" Milo prompts.

"Oh, for fuck sake! Milo knows, Tex." I turn to him. "You can stop being a dick anytime you want."

Laughing, he shrugs. "I might not want to."

Of course not. That shit just comes naturally to him.

"Knows what?" Tex asks cautiously, still trying to hide something I've just told her is out in the open with Milo.

I tilt my head and say, "Come on."

Sighing, she leans on the table, closer to Milo. "How?"

"I could tell something was up with Romeo over there, so I made him tell me a while ago. You two are going to be in *so* much trouble if Mark finds out before we get home."

Tex lets her forearms drop to the table. "Well, it's a good thing he won't be finding out then, isn't it?"

Milo holds his hands up. "Hey, it won't be from me, but do you really think he won't? How are you going to hide it on the bus? I can feel the sexual frustration from here, so it's only a matter of time before your dad does, too. Hell, Coop senses it, and he usually only notices women who want him."

Milo has a point. The deeper Tex and I get, the more obvious it's going to be. I can barely take my eyes off her, and sooner or later, Mark will figure out why. Then, I'll be dead, and Texas will be in a convent. She'd probably go, too. I'm not sure if she's quite worked out that she doesn't need to do everything her dad says anymore.

"We'll be fine, and now, we have you," I say, smirking.

If he's going to be on my case about it twenty-four/seven, then I'm going to get something out of it.

He barks out a laugh. "If you think I'm going to be your lookout, you're fucking mental. I'm not giving Mark a reason to kill me, too. I'll keep your secret, but that's it."

Rolling my eyes as I make Tex's coffee, I reply, "I never asked that."

"Then, what are you asking, man?"

"If we make an I'm-going-to-rip-your-clothes-off face, let us know?" Tex interjects. "Is that right, rock star?"

I give her a look, not a ripping-off-clothes one. But she's hit the nail on the head. I feel the want every time I see her, and it's not going to be long before everyone else does, too.

Milo chuckles. "All right, but it'd be easier if you just didn't look at each other."

Do I look at her like that all the time? I can't *not*.

Either Mark is seriously stupid, or he trusts me too much to think I would ever go there. Either way, I'm a dead man walking.

"Impossible. Just look at this," Tex says sarcastically, pointing to her *The Walking Dead* T-shirt and black pyjama trousers covered in silver skulls.

Yeah, she's a geek through and through, but there's nothing she can't make look sexy.

"Come on, baby, you know zombies do it for me," Milo says, wiggling his eyebrows.

"Really, man? Right in front of me?"

Texas and Milo laugh, and I realise she's going to be siding with him to torture me. *So much for us being a team.*

"I like a jealous Kitt," Milo mutters not so quietly to Tex.

"Yeah, me, too," she agrees.

"I'm seconds from putting salt in your coffees, guys," I pipe up, stirring the drinks too hard.

"Well, I certainly look forward to watching you two navigate a secret relationship five meters from the person you want to keep it from and then having it blow up in your faces."

Texas shoves Milo's arm. "You're a horrible friend, Milo."

"You'd do the same for me, Texy."

"I'm so going to hell," I groan.

30

TEXAS
THURSDAY, MAY 28
GDAŃSK, POLAND

Since the Czech Republic, something has changed with Kitt. He's irritable and withdrawn, and I'm not the only one who's noticed. It's not like him. *Where has my cocky rock star gone?*

His mood is beginning to get on my nerves. I understand the pressure of the tour and our unique situation aren't exactly a laugh a minute, but he should be trying to make the most of it.

We're not checking into a hotel tonight because we'll be leaving in the early hours, so we're camping on the bus, and I'm starting to wish I could go diva and demand a suite somewhere.

Kitt is sitting near the front of the bus with his head in a notebook. He's not said a word to anyone for hours, and it's making me want to throw something at him.

This is more than being in the zone. He's pulling away from us. I can feel it.

I drain the last of my coffee, praying it would turn into something stronger. Unless he leaves his solitary corner, I can't talk to him. So, I'm left to fucking texting like a thirteen-year-old.

Are you okay?

Simple, but it says everything I want to say at this point. We'll see how this goes. I'm sure I'll have a few more words I want to use, if I'm not satisfied with his reply.

I hear the low buzz of his phone in his pocket. He looks down, but he doesn't move to pick it up.

He's not going to bloody answer it.

Seconds turn into minutes, and it becomes blatantly clear that he's decided to block reality for God knows how long. It wouldn't even be an issue if he'd told me that he needed a minute. I don't deserve the cold shoulder.

I curl my hand around my phone and look away.

Bellend.

"Want that drumming lesson now, Tex?" Milo asks. His eyes are wide and speak more than his words. He's asking me to go with him to talk because he knows more, and he's worried about me and Kitt.

I've got nothing better to do. "Yeah, but we have nowhere to play."

"First, you learn about the drums, and then you learn how to play them."

I salute. "Yes, sensei."

Milo and I walk upstairs to his room, and no one even looks up, not even Kitt. He's far too involved in whatever he's writing. My apology letter, I hope.

Milo is ahead of me and strides into his room with purpose. As soon as I'm in, he shuts the door and sits on the end of his bed. There is hardly any room in here, but we fit on the bed.

"Kitt can be a patient person. But he's different with you. I know he's acting like a dick right now, but cut him some slack. He's just trying to work his way through this."

"I don't get him, Milo. He says he's in, and then he won't even acknowledge me."

"He told me he's been finding it increasingly difficult to pretend like nothing's going on. Kitt is crazy about you, and he hates that he has to hide it."

"I'm not exactly doing a happy dance over here either. But I thought we were in this together."

"We are." Kitt's voice cuts through the room like razor blades against my skin. He grips the door handle, like he'll fall without it.

"It doesn't feel like it. Where were you last night? Where have you been today? I can count on one hand the amount of times you've looked at me since yesterday."

"Cooper's calling me," Milo says, leaping off the bed and pushing past Kitt.

I want to be able to leave, too.

"Talk to me, Kitt."

Groaning, he roughly rubs his hand over his face. "There's nothing to say. Remember when you needed space? Well, this is me needing the same thing."

"I also remember you chasing me."

"And I also remember you telling me not to next time."

"Oh my God, you're so frustrating!" I snap, shoving myself to my feet.

"And you're not? I love you, Texas. I don't have the first fucking idea how to handle everything you make me feel. Couple that with the fact that this is secretive, and I'm lying to the man who opened the door to my dream…"

"Yeah, *my* dad. Think lying to him is easier for me? Really?"

"I'm not saying that. Jesus. Talking to you is like—"

I hold my hand up. "Oh, don't finish that sentence. Come talk to me when you're done being a twat."

He moves to the side as I storm out. It wasn't that long ago he would have followed me.

What's happening to him?

This feels like the end. Dramatic, I know, but he's never pulled away from me.

In the five fucking minutes you've been together...take a look at yourself!

I'm an idiot. That's never been in question. God, I don't know how to handle this with him either. I feel like I'm treading on thin ice sometimes, too. As incredible as this feels, it's not been easy.

I spend the rest of the day sulking.

The guys go off to the show, and I stay behind—well, sort of. We're parked outside, and Ted is here.

"You look miserable," he says, stating the bloody obvious.

"This is quiet time, Ted."

Laughing, he raises his palms and kicks back, watching the football match on TV. I'm not in the mood for anything, and I don't want to end up snapping at him, so it's best to do our own thing tonight, and hopefully, tomorrow will be better.

Can't get much worse.

Unless Kitt ends things.

Great, think about that.

I wrap my arms around my stomach and curl on the sofa. He won't do that. We're a forever deal, but things are so shitty right now. One minute, we're happy, and the next...

How do we get out of this back-and-forth habit?

Chill. It's because your emotions are all over the place, and the situation is less than ideal.

But will that ever change?

Kitt makes me feel every emotion times a zillion. *Can being out in the open magically fix that?*

After two hours, Ted is falling asleep. His closely shaved head bobs, and then his eyes flick back open. He's trying to keep himself awake but failing miserably.

"Ted, go to sleep."

He rubs his eyes. "I'm okay. I'll make coffee."

"The door is locked, and no one can get around here, other than the guys. It's fine. You've slept when we've been alone before."

He gives me a long look that isn't about safety.

I sigh. "I'm okay, I promise. You can go to bed. I won't fall apart. Things will be okay."

"Are you sure, Texas?"

"Totally. Good night."

He gives me a smile and a nod, and then he disappears upstairs.

I bet I hear him snoring in under a minute.

I turn the after-football chat off because, no, and I blast through the channels without properly looking at what's on. TV is a distraction and one that won't work anyway. I turn it off, and I'm cloaked in darkness. The under-unit lights in the small kitchen area is all that will stop me from bumping into things when I get up.

The dark silence is oddly settling. At a time when everything is bright and busy, it's nice to sit still. Of course, sitting still means overthinking and obsessing, so I decide to call it a night. I stand up when I hear a noise, and it's not the soft snoring drifting down from Ted's room above. It's outside.

With my heart pounding in my chest, I clench my fists. It has to be one of the guys. They were all going to the afterparty because a friend of Dad's band is throwing it, but one of them must be here now.

I hope.

Unless it's a stalker.

Okay, you're ridiculous. You don't have a stalker!

The lock clicks open, and I breathe a sigh of relief. Whoever it is has a key. The door swings open, and Kitt stares up at me. His eyes are blazing. I've never seen anyone so pissed off before.

"What?"

He growls and turns around, tugging at his hair.

He's leaving? Um, no. I dash down the steps, off the bus and grip his arm.

"Texas!"

"What are you doing?"

Spinning around, he pins me to the spot with his hungry eyes.

Well, bugger.

"You know I've handled everything life throws at me with dignity and grace, including coming to terms with growing up without my parents. What I can't fucking do is handle you."

"You don't need to handle me. I'm not your bloody pet!"

"Don't I fucking know it," he hisses.

"You can be a real arsehole sometimes, Kitt, and I've had enough."

"You're walking away from me?"

Throwing my hands up, I reply, "Yes!"

"Why?"

"Come on, Kitt, you're not that stupid!"

"I don't speak crazy, woman."

"Crazy?"

Lifting an eyebrow, he replies, "Do you think you're being reasonable right now?"

"Do you want a slap?" I snap.

How am I the unreasonable one here?

"What the fuck do you want from me, Tex?"

How is that not obvious by now?

"Nothing," I reply.

"Bullshit!"

"What do you want from me, Kitt?"

His jaw flexes, and the muscles in his forearms bunch as he clenches his fist. He won't hit me. I know that much. He's angry though. Or frustrated. Or both.

He flies forward, knocking me back against the bus. My head hits the side with a thud as his lips slam down on mine.

He grips the hem of my top and rips it over my head. I've lost all logic thought, and I do the same, ridding him of his T-shirt. I feel like a wild animal. My mind narrows until all I can see is him, and all I want is to feel him inside me. He fumbles with the button of my jean shorts, and they soon land at my feet.

"Kitt, I can't wait." I'm desperate. My body is humming, greedy for the epic release I know he'll give me.

"That's the hottest thing you've ever said," he rasps, shoving his jeans to the floor. No boxers.

He steals my breath in a frantic kiss, and he pushes inside me. I cry into his mouth as he fills me completely.

Kitt grips my legs and lifts them up. I wrap my arms and legs around him and fuck his mouth the way he's slamming into me.

I'm loud and free, not caring if we're heard or caught. All that matters is each other and this moment.

Kitt grunts, angling me back, and I dig my nails into his neck.

Holy...

He's deeper. This new position is everything.

Oh, fucky fuck!

"Kitt, oh my God. I need more. I need..."

He seals his mouth over mine, drowning out my pleas and moans, and drives into me hard and wild. My orgasm slams into me, causing my body to shake, as I clench around him. He groans into the kiss, pumping harder, while he empties inside me.

His kiss slows until he pulls away, panting. Pressing his forehead to mine, he smirks. "So...that's what I want from you, Texas."

"Sex?" I ask. *I want more than that.*

He tilts his head against mine. "That was just sex to you?"

"No," I breathe. "That was everything."

"Exactly." He pulls out and helps me to get dressed. Quickly tugging on his T-shirt and pulling up his jeans, he chuckles.

I take a sweep of the area. It's dark, and no one is around. *Thank God. Shit.* My face heats. We could've been caught.

Kitt wraps me in his arms and holds me close. Suddenly, I can't remember why I cared about being caught.

"Let's get inside. It's getting cooler out here."

It's only when he mentions it that I realise I have goose bumps. Shorts were a bad idea. I'm even colder when Kitt moves away from me to open the door to the bus.

"Get in, you," he says with a cute subdued and lopsided smile.

When it's like this, I love it. I want to tell everyone, including my dad, because we fit together so well.

"Hey, do you think if the pressure of this being a secret wasn't there, we'd get along like this all the time?" I ask.

He closes the door behind himself and snorts. "Probably not."

I turn and cross my arms. "What? Why do you think that?"

"Experience."

"Meaning?"

Walking up the steps in one leap, he cocks his eyebrow. "I'm kidding, sweetheart. Are you ready for that? Really ready for your dad to know about us?" There's an unspoken, *Because I am*, there, too.

I want to say yes because I'm crazy about him, but I don't think I'm ready for all the questions and not being able to get any alone time with him.

"No," I say quietly. "I'm sorry, but I'm not ready."

"I'm sorry, too."

"It's not your fault. I'm your dirty secret, so we've got to keep quiet." I go for humour, but neither of us finds it funny.

"Don't. That's *not* what you are to me. We both know this industry, and everything will change when people know. Your dad has spent his whole life trying to shield you from as much of the paparazzi shit as possible, and that will end the second we're public."

I think I just fell in love with him even more.

"Look, I want more right now, and as much as it pains me to keep us hidden, I know, logically, it's best for now," he says.

"I hate being your secret."

"All I'm trying to do is what's best for you, Tex."

"You're what's best for me," I reply.

"I know," he whispers. "That's why I can never let you go."

Yep, definitely just fell in love with him even more.

"Promise me, you won't ever let me go."

He bends his head to look in my eyes. I feel like I'm falling.

"I *promise* you," he says.

And I believe him. It makes me feel a whole lot better about what's to come.

My life isn't very private at the minute, but I know that will get a whole lot worse when the whole world knows that Kitt is mine. I like that I can go out, depending on where I go, and not be hassled. Kitt can't do that.

We fall into my bed, and I curl into him.

He kisses the top of my head. "I want everyone to know how I feel about you, Tex. I want every guy to know that you're off the market, and I want every one of my fans to know that there's *no* chance of me shagging them. It happens at every after-party, Texas. Do you know how uncomfortable it is to have women hitting on me?"

I deadpan. Like I haven't been through the discomfort and downright pain of having to watch him with other women. And most of them, he took back to his room. So, yes, I'm somewhat fucking familiar with that feeling.

"Er, yes! Have you forgotten how freely you shared your man parts with everyone? And if you think women will stop making a move because you're taken, you are very mistaken, Kitt."

"This is heading somewhere neither of us wants it to, so let's move on. I want you and no one else. I want to be able to tell a person exactly why I'm not going to share my man parts with them."

"Didn't mean to get off track there. I'm sorry. I'm just saying that, even after we're out in the open, things are still going to happen. We're going to be followed more closely, our relationship is going to be under the microscope, we're going to be judged on whether or not we're deserving, and people are going to make things up if there's no new gossip."

He shrugs his shoulder, as if none of it matters, as if it will all be easy and we won't soon learn new things about our relationship every time we open a newspaper or click on the Internet.

I've had it my whole life. I've read things that I supposedly have done a million times over, and although I can laugh it off, it's different when people are making things up about someone you love. I detest the stuff written about my dad.

I'm not looking forward to Kitt being accused of cheating when he poses for a picture with a fan or people deeming me unworthy of him because I'm only a somebody, thanks to my parents.

Stop it. He chose you, and his opinion is the only one that counts.

"Three weeks, Tex."

"I can't wait to officially own you," I say, giving him a sly smile.

He cocks an eyebrow. "I would argue that, but I can't. You do own me, same as I own you. And it works out in my favour because you are minted."

"You're not doing too badly yourself now, you know."

"Yeah, I know." He looks like he's still having a hard time with accepting his wealth. Growing up, he didn't have much. His grandparents earned a decent amount, but they weren't even in a position where they could wall made of gold.

Kitt still struggles with his new wealth.

He's so sweet. The first thing he did when he signed with the label was pay his grandparents' mortgage off, so they owned their home. It was his way of thanking them for putting his needs before their own. They'd only had a small mortgage because they'd borrowed extra to extend the house and make room for a growing boy.

"You deserve it," I say.

He responds by kissing me until we're breathless.

31

KITT
FRIDAY, MAY 29
COPENHAGEN, DENMARK

"We have a huge problem!" Milo says.

Tex and I look up from her bed.

"Don't worry about knocking, mate."

"You have a sex tape!"

Texas bolts upright. "We have a, what?" Her voice is about a hundred octaves higher than usual.

"Sex. Tape," Milo repeats, as if she didn't hear.

She heard. And so did I.

I sit up because I cannot have this fucking conversation lying down. "We don't have a sex tape."

"Poland. Bus. Ring any horny bells?"

"What? But we...oh." I snap my jaw shut. *Yeah, CCTV outside the venue.*

Texas is whiter than Casper. "Oh-my-God," she mutters in one breath.

"Now, good news is, I've watched it, and—"

"You, what?" Tex's voice is back up there.

I wince.

"Milo, what the hell is wrong with you? You're like a bloody brother. It's completely unacceptable of you to watch something like—"

"Texas," Milo says, leaning forward, "take a bloody breath. You can barely see anything on the tape. It looks like arguing, which was hot, and then Kitt kisses you, and you disappear from sight."

Her eyes flick up to the ceiling. "Oh, thank you. But it was obvious that…"

"That he was balls deep in you? Yeah, babycakes, it was."

She turns her nose up at his colourful choice of words.

I give him the middle finger. "Cheers, mate."

"My dad is going to freak. Kitt, we have to tell him now. He can't find out like that. Oh my God, he's going to kill us both."

Grabbing her hand, I squeeze to offer her some comfort. "Way to stay calm, Tex."

She grips her fingers around my hand like a vise. "Why are you calm?"

Inside, I'm not. I feel sick, and my stomach has bottomed out. "We can't change it, so all we can do now is limit the damage. You've told him you have feelings for me, so we'll tell him now that we're together."

"And the tape?" Milo asks.

Sighing, I look up at the ceiling. *How could I have been so stupid?*

"We'll have to tell him that, too."

"Why is it even common knowledge?"

"There was an incident that night. A girl was mugged, so the CCTV was examined. Ted and Hank were with security reviewing the tape."

"So, my dad won't find out then?"

"He's in there now to review the tapes and see if he recognises anyone."

"What? Why?" Texas snaps.

Milo winces and rubs his forehead. "Because it happened outside our bus. It looks like they were trying to get in. This was not long after you two went inside."

Fuck.

People try to get out to the back exit all the time to catch us leaving. I should've been more careful.

"Well, that's it. Grab your passport, Kitt. We need to run to Mexico."

I clamp her hand down, stopping her from getting up. "You're being dramatic."

"How am I being dramatic? I don't want my dad to see that. Milo, stop him."

"How do you want me to do that, porn star?"

Texas growls and shoots daggers out of her eyes. "Someone needs to do something because my dad is going to freak."

"Ted's with him in the security room. The venue sent the footage to Ted. I think he's going to try to calm your dad down."

"You know," I say, "I didn't give Mexico enough thought."

Milo leans his back against the wall and folds his arms. "No one is running anywhere. Don't worry, like I said, you couldn't see much. Not once you got down to it against the bus."

Great.

I glare. "Easy for you to say, buddy."

"Yeah, it is, but I'm not the one who had sex against the bus, so let's lay the blame of that at you two's feet. This might be a blessing in disguise. Kitt, your mood swings are worse than puberty, and, Tex, you're being eaten alive by guilt. Have that conversation, get all the embarrassment and shame out of the way, and tell Mark you're solid. It is the only way."

Milo Sterling is making sense. Since he let Lexi go, I didn't think I'd trust him on the romance front again.

"I'm scared," Tex whispers. Her face is pale, and she looks about ready to pass out.

I turn to her, Milo forgotten. Lifting her chin, I kiss her. "Do you trust me?"

She nods her head. "Of course, but—"

"No. I hate the idea of him seeing that. It really doesn't look good on our part, but I don't regret a thing that's happened between us."

"I wouldn't regret bus sex either," Milo mutters.

I ignore him. "We'll make Mark see what this is, okay?"

"He's going to hate me."

"He could never hate you, Tex. You're his daughter." I brush her hair behind her ear, letting my fingers linger over her skin. She's so soft. "This will be okay. You have my word."

She swallows. "Okay. What do we say? The truth about everything?"

"We have to. We'll go back to the start."

"I like the start."

I smile. "So do I."

"Mushy as fuck. I'm out." Milo leaves the room and shuts the door.

I don't take my eyes off Texas. She's looking at me with so much hope that I feel like I'm suffocating. She believes I can fix this, and I'm not sure how Mark will react yet.

She believes you because you promised her, dick.

"Do you want me to do the talking, or do you think it'll be better coming from you?" I ask.

My head is starting to throb, and I want to ignore that this is happening, but Texas has gone stiff with fear, and she doesn't look good.

She's mine, and it's my job to make this okay. Somehow, I have to work this perfectly to convince Mark that we're real. He will find out about us through our fucking sex tape. It's going to take a miracle.

"What if he tries to send me away?"

"You're nineteen, Texas. You can do what you want and go where you want."

She drops her eyes and frowns, like she's only just realising that's true. "I don't know how I can stay around him if he wants me gone."

"Then, we'll ditch the bus and travel to each city on our own."

"What?" Her voice is breathless as her eyes whip up to meet mine. "You would do that?"

"Texas, there isn't a single place on this planet that I wouldn't follow you to. Whatever happens from today, we stick together. We show your dad how strong we are. We prove to him that I'm not messing around and that you're safe with me."

She sinks into my chest and wraps her arms around my neck. "I feel safe."

"I love you," I whisper, burying my head in her hair.

We won't have long before he comes storming in, so we need to be out of my room and downstairs. Damn it, I wish Copenhagen was a hotel city, but our stay here is short.

"Come on, we need to head down."

Pulling away enough for me to see her face, she says, "I love you, too, Kitt. Please let that be strong enough to not let my dad scare you off."

"Not happening. I don't scare easy, and if I want something, I'm going to have it. We promised each other forever, and that's damn well what we're getting. Now, downstairs. We have to talk to your dad about our sex tape. Think they'll give me a copy of that?"

She swats my arm, but for the first time since Milo barged in, she has colour in her cheeks as she laughs.

32

TEXAS
FRIDAY, MAY 29
COPENHAGEN, DENMARK

Kitt and I reach the bottom step when the door flies open and slams back on the metal wall outside.

My heart free-falls.

I don't want to do this. My legs are preparing to turn and get me the hell out of here when Kitt takes my hand. I feel his strength and courage seeping through, willing me to stay calm and do this right. No one else is in here, and I think that's purposely done. Ted or Hank probably rang ahead and made everyone leave.

"Texas!" Dad bellows. He rounds the corner and freezes when he sees us. His face is red, the tendons in his neck are protruding, and his fists are clenched by his sides.

Oh God.

He pins us both to the spot with a look of pure rage. "Sit. Down. Now."

We take a seat on the sofas with the table between, safer with a buffer. Kitt puts his hands out on the wooden surface and holds eye contact with my dad. Kitt's spine is straight, and he looks like a picture of calm.

How is he so composed? My back is hunched, and my arms are holding myself together.

On a sigh, Dad drops his arms on the table. "We need to have a chat." His voice is eerily cool for the situation.

It's the same voice he used on me when I *accidentally* put hair dye in this ho's shampoo bottle. She was trying to be his groupie, and…well, we all know how that ends. He was anything but calm when we got back to the hotel suite. And just to clear things up, I was *twelve* at the time.

"I want to know what was going through your head?" Dad asks. His question is for me.

I gape at him. *He wants to know what I was thinking about when Kitt was taking me against the tour bus?*

Out of the corner of my eye, I see Kitt's eyes widen, as if he can read my mind.

"He means, why did you do it, Tex?" Kitt says quickly, shooting me a what-the-fuck-are-you-on look.

Wow. Okay, close call. I shrug. "I-I don't know."

Dad swallows hard and says through gritted teeth, "You don't know what you were thinking when you gave your virginity away to a musician up against the side of a fucking bus?"

Oh…okay, next problem, not technically a virgin. Now, I get to either tell my daddy that I'd slept with my ex a year ago after I told him I hadn't or let him think that I'm such a classy bird that I got my cherry popped in a public place. *Decisions, decisions…*

"Um, Dad, that wasn't my first time."

Definitely better not to be the first-time bus whore.

I watch his face turn red. *Maybe it is better to be the first-time bus whore.*

He turns to Kitt. "How long has this been going on?" he growls.

Oh, shit, he thinks my first time was with Kitt.

Yeah, don't you correct that.

It might as well have been. It's the first time I *needed* it, the first orgasm through sex, the first time it meant so much more than a physical act.

Kitt's midnight-blue eyes briefly flick to me, and I silently beg him to go along with it. I know I'm not a slut. It's not like I've had the whole fucking band or anything, but I don't want my dad to look even more disappointed in me than he already does.

"A few weeks," Kitt says.

Wow. Yeah, it's not even been a month yet. How is that even possible?

"What exactly is going on?" Dad's eyes are wide.

I've known him long enough to know it's from fear as well as anger. In his head, he's seeing me crying after a coke and whore addiction story has broken about Kitt.

I shake my head because I, too, am scared—only, not about Kitt.

I clear my throat. "Well, we..." *Are in love and had wild sex against your band's tour bus.* "We just..."

"So, you have sex? So, you're just sleeping together?" He stands up so quickly that I almost don't see it. "My daughter is your *fuck buddy*?" he spits as he clenches his fists.

Okay, I made it worse.

He's jumped to conclusions.

Because you took too long telling him everything Kitt is to you.

Kitt stands, holding his hands up in surrender. If this situation wasn't majorly awkward and making me want to throw myself out of said bus anyway, my dad just uttered the phrase *fuck buddy*.

"No. It's not like that," Kitt replies, frowning. He looks genuinely disgusted that anyone would label us with that title.

"You're not together, but you're not fuck buddies," Dad says.

I bite back a laugh, earning a glare from Kitt. "Dad, please."

He turns to me. "This isn't how I brought you up, Texas."

"Am I supposed to die a virgin? Jesus, Dad, I've seen your band bring God knows how many women back to their rooms. I've even walked in on Will doing one of them in the dressing room! You really expect me to believe in no sex before marriage?"

He clenches his jaw when he knows I'm right. Dad might have done everything for me, raised me pretty much on his own, but I certainly haven't had a normal upbringing. Not that I minded. I've loved our life, and I'm sure, after years of therapy, I'll be able to forget Will and the redhead going at it on the counter.

He sighs and shakes his head. "I still wanted more for you, Texas. This isn't how it's supposed to be. And you should have been married before. And thirty."

"I'm sorry, Dad." Apologies are better, surely.

He paces, clenching his fists over and over. "So am I, Texas. Shit, who was I kidding when I thought it would be a great idea to raise a child on the road?"

I don't like where this is going. "There's nothing wrong with how you've raised me. I've seen most of the world. How many people can say that?" And I've met Guns N' Roses.

"And look where that's led? You shouldn't have been around this lifestyle," he growls.

"Oh, please. Look at all those other celebrities' kids. I think I've turned out pretty damn well, thank you." At least our sex tape wasn't released, and from the angle of the CCTV camera, you can't even see what we were doing once he slammed me against the side of the bus. Our clothes didn't come off until after that.

Winner right here.

"Look, we're not explaining this properly, and people are jumping to the wrong conclusions," Kitt says. He's the voice of reason when Dad and I aren't thinking about what's spurting from our mouths.

Dad freezes. "Then, please explain, Kitt!"

I look up between them. This isn't the calmish conversation it started as, and it's certainly not going how I want it to go. "Can we all sit back down first?"

They both glance down at me, but after a heartbeat, they do sit.

Kitt takes a breath and places his hands back on the table. I want to put mine over the top and show solidarity. Maybe it will show Dad what I'm having a rubbish time explaining, that Kitt and I are not messing around and that we sure as hell aren't casual.

"Paris is when I truly realised why certain things were bothering me—Texas looking at other men, for example. She started to get to me, piss me off, in ways she shouldn't have been able to."

I give him a look, but he's focused on my dad. *Charming.*

"We argued, and to make it up to her, I took her to the Eiffel Tower at night. Ted was with us," he adds before Dad can blow up on that one. "It's where I understood why things had changed. I realised I like her way more than I ever intended to."

Dad's eyes cut to me, and I sit up straight. There is so much judgement in his gaze, and I can't blame him for an ounce of it.

"You've been together since Paris?" he spits, his face turning red with rage.

I tap my knees under the table. "Yes. I've liked him for a lot longer than that, Dad, and I swear, this isn't some casual thing. We haven't jumped into this."

"That's not what it sounds like from Kitt's perspective. He said himself that he started to feel differently in Paris, and that's when you two started…this. That was…what? Nineteen days ago? Am I right, Kitt? Isn't that when you started to feel differently about my child?"

Kitt grits his teeth when I'm referred to as a child, but he lets it go. "Partly. I've always been close to Tex, but I never realised what that meant until Paris. I understand how this looks, Mark, but I'm crazy about her. We're together exclusively, and there's not one woman on earth I would risk losing her over."

Is it possible for your heart to explode? Like properly explode?

I almost have to fan myself. His words are too much. They make me ache in the best possible way. I can never get enough of hearing how much I mean to him, especially after wanting him for so long.

"I feel the same, Dad. We both appreciate that this will take some adjusting for you, and we owe you a huge apology for the way you found out. We probably need to have a few conversations about things we've discussed in the past, but I'm happy with Kitt, like lottery-win happy. So, please, can you try to be happy for us?"

Dad's mouth straightens into a grim line that makes him look harsh. It's not a great sign of things to come, but I'm not giving up on this. Whatever happens and whatever rubbish Kitt and I have to go through, it will work out because it has to. Dad will never be able to stay angry with me forever.

If he flies off the handle now, I know it'll only be temporary. He doesn't know me and Kitt together. All he knows is that I tend to wear my heart on my sleeve when it comes to the people I truly care about, and Kitt has a terrible track record with women.

It's easy to see why Dad's not doing cartwheels over this.

He rubs eyes that match mine. "I think, for the remainder of the tour, you should go back to London and stay with your mum."

My mouth drops in shock. *What the hell? Did those words just leave his mouth?*

Kitt leans forward. "Mark, can't we talk this through a little more?"

Yes! I like his idea. I don't want to stay with Jennifer, The Oven. I love it on tour, and I want to be where Kitt is. I have to be where he is.

"I don't think talking is going to achieve anything, *Kitt*," Dad spits through his teeth. He thumps his fists on the table.

Dad looks angry. His face is red, and his eyes are shooting daggers at the man I love.

Bloody perfect.

What did you expect? He saw you getting fucked against a bus!

"Dad, please," I beg. My eyes fill with tears.

He's never tried to send me to Jennifer before. Not once in my entire existence has he ever asked for help in raising me or dealing with a particular issue—even puberty. We kind of found our own way through it together, often having some very awkward conversations along with a tampon demonstration in a glass of water that I would *love* to erase from my memory. We've worked through every single issue without her, and now, when I'm nineteen, he wants Jennifer to take over for a while.

"Dad, I don't need parenting anymore."

His face hardens, and his jaw twitches. "You obviously need something, Texas, because the old you would never have lied to me or had sex in a public place!"

I turn my head, unable to stand the look of disappointment. "I'm sorry, okay? We didn't want to lie, but we needed to figure out what this was, and there's no way we could've done that if you knew. I'm not asking you to be okay with this right away, but can you look at this from our perspective?"

"No."

Well, great.

"Mark, you are the one person Texas would do just about anything to avoid hurting. This hasn't been easy for either of us, but she's struggled with this more than I think she's even told me." He looks at me and smiles, giving me strength and trying to keep me calm when he can see I'm starting to freak out over being shipped back to England with my mother.

Keeping something so big from my dad has been tougher than I thought. At first, it was fun. I loved the secrecy, and honestly, I was over the moon to be with him, but the guilt came thick and fast.

"But we did it because we were serious about each other. We know we planned to tell you and everyone else when we got back to England before leaving for America. I'm so in love with her, Mark. I *won't* ever hurt her. I'd die first."

Heart goes boom.

This time, because he makes me feel so loved, I could choke, and I cover his hand with mine. Dad immediately hones in on it, and the vein on his forehead protrudes. I don't care. This is unity. We are not asking for permission because we don't need it.

Oh God, I think I'm going to pass out from the pressure. I've never stood up to Dad like this before. I'm sure the pride will come after the paralysing fear has gone.

Kitt's thumb curls around my index finger.

God, I love him. "Please, Dad. I don't want to go. We can't leave things like this, and you know it. We've never even gone to sleep without sorting our issues out, so I really don't see what going back to England will achieve."

Every time I had a problem or Dad was stressing over the best thing for me, we'd talk it out because, together, we could get through anything. He was there every night I cried over my ex, and I was there when he struggled with a UK tour while I was taking my GCSE exams. Between rehearsals and appearances and performances, he was there with my textbooks, quizzing me and telling me I'd rock it.

"I'm sorry that we didn't tell you straight away when we figured out where this was going, but I was scared. Kitt doesn't want to disappoint you either, and it was hard for us to know that we would. You've said, there is nothing we can't get past, so I'm asking you to honour that because you and me both need our relationship to be solid. Please, Dad. I can't lose you."

"Texas," Dad says, closing his eyes and shaking his head.

"Come on, Mark. You know she doesn't want to go, and I know you don't want her to. Don't punish everyone for no reason. Don't do this because of me."

"It's not because of you. It's because of you *two*. How am I supposed to trust you around each other now?"

Maybe because you've just threatened to ship me off to my damn mother's house, and I would do anything to avoid an unscheduled visit.

"We'll earn your trust back, I swear," I say.

"I'll do whatever it takes to prove to you that I'm serious about her, however long it takes."

"You *really* want a girlfriend at this point in your life?" he asks Kitt, trying to psych him out.

Kitt squeezes my hand. "I didn't. This wasn't in the plan, you know that, but I can't help it. She changed *everything* for me, and there's nothing I want more than to make her as happy as she makes me."

Jesus.

I'm breathless and inappropriately turned on for the current situation.

Dad's eyes narrow, like he's unsure if he believes Kitt or not. He wants to because he wouldn't ever want me to end up heartbroken, but he doesn't like this at all.

"Dad, *please*. I…I love him, too. I feel the same as he does. And I love you. I need you both. Please, don't do this, Dad. Please."

"We'll see how it goes. If I still feel that I can't trust you in a couple of days, you're going to go to your mum's, Texas. I can't concentrate on this tour if you two are…"

His face pales, and I know what he's thinking. No one wants to know their teenage daughter is having sex.

"You can trust us." I'm not sure what he does not trust us with. *Restraining? Like that's going to happen. Does he want us to keep things quiet still?*

"I need to go and see Carl." He storms out of the room, slamming the door.

If he hadn't threatened shipping me off to Jennifer's, I would have made some sarcastic comment about him just leaving us alone.

"I'm sorry, Tex," Kitt says on a sigh. "I'd hoped that would've gone better."

"Well, he didn't cut any part of you off, and he's not booked me on the next plane to London, so it wasn't that bad."

"I suppose. God, I hate the way he looked at me. He's done so much for me, and now, he hates me."

"He doesn't hate you. He'll come around." I lay my head on his shoulder. "We just have to show him that we're not messing around here. It'll be fine."

"Yeah, I know," he whispers against my head. "Promise me something?"

"Hmm?"

"Don't give up on us. Now that I know what it's like, I can't go back to before you."

"You'll never have to go back to before me. Not ever."

TEXAS
FRIDAY, MAY 29
COPENHAGEN, DENMARK

Everyone has gone to bed, but I can't sleep. I watch the rain hit the window and drizzle down the glass. Today has been one of the crappiest so far. Dad hasn't looked at me since our conversation, and Kitt has kept a respectful distance.

"What are you doing up?"

My heart jumps at the sound of Kitt's sleep-filled voice.

"Couldn't drift off," I reply, not even bothering to look at him.

He sits down on the other side of the table and takes a sip from my freshly made coffee. The only thing he's wearing is a pair of sweatpants. I want to leap over the table dividing us, run my tongue over his chest and the sexy tattoo that runs over his right bicep and shoulder, and then have more wild sex—this time, *in* the bus.

"He'll calm down in couple of days. Guess seeing your daughter getting screwed against your tour bus kinda pisses you off."

I manage a smile. "You put it so tastefully. Technically, he didn't see anything though."

He shrugs one of his muscular shoulders. "I still think it's hot. Hank's sending me a copy."

My jaw falls on the table, and Kitt laughs.

"Uh-oh. If Mark catches you two porn stars out here…" Cooper says with the biggest, toothiest smile I have ever seen. He's loving this, of course.

"Not very good porn stars. You couldn't see anything," I reply, giving him the finger.

"Speak for yourself. I saw *a lot*," Kitt says, making me want to punch him.

I ignore him and focus on Coop. "No one would pay for porn you can't see."

"Unfortunately—or not—you could *hear* everything."

What the hell? My eyes pop out of my head.

Coop bursts out laughing. "Kidding!"

"I hate you, Cooper," I snap.

"Good thing really. Don't think your dad would have liked hearing you beg me to go harder," Kitt jokes.

I throw a pen at him, wishing it were a bloody knife. It was all I had. He's still holding my coffee.

"Hmm, maybe if you weren't such a little girl in bed, I wouldn't have to tell you how to do it."

"*Ou*," Coop says, laughing again. "That had to hurt, man."

Kitt raises his eyebrows. "Not really. I remember her moaning my name, and I still have the scratch marks on my shoulders to prove there was nothing girlie about it."

Coop smirks in my direction, and I want to throw them both out the window.

"Loved it, did ya?" Coop asks me.

"She did," Kitt confirms.

Do I even need to be present for this conversation? I hold my hand out. "Coffee."

Kitt's smirk rivals Cooper's as he hands me my drink back. "You both suck," I say.

Coop sits beside me. "Hmm...but do you?"

I have nothing left to throw besides my coffee, but if I'm going to have to deal with them, I need it. Turns out I didn't need anything to throw because Kitt chucks the pen I launched at him at Coop.

Ha.

Coop easily catches it, shaking his head and laughing. "So, what are you two doing now?"

"Sitting at the table with you," I reply.

"We're doing nothing, mate, so get your head out of the gutter."

Coop looks disappointed. "No more bang-bang?"

Kitt rolls his eyes. "No, no more bang-bang. Not until Mark gets his head around this. Or we're home. Or in a hotel."

Basically, no more bus sex.

"It'll be interesting, watching you two handle no shagging."

"We have some control," I mutter defensively. *Why does everyone think I'm a slut who can't help herself?* I *love* Kitt. It's not as if he's some random guy. He's the guy I trust with my life.

"Mmhmm," Cooper chants. "Well, first, it didn't look like you had much control on the big screen. And, second, now that you're having scratchy-back sex, you're gonna want it more and more. I mean, come on, how close are you to asking me to watch Mark's door like a hawk, so you two can get down to round two?"

I fold my arms. "I'm not."

Kitt smirks. "Bull. Unlike little Miss Liar over there, I would take her on this table in a heartbeat."

"Thank you. Just what every girl loves to hear," I reply sarcastically even though my body heats up at the thought. I need to get out of here before I say or do something I'll regret. "Cooper, can you let me up? I'm suddenly tired."

Again, Kitt smirks. "Your room is the first place he's going to check, Tex."

"The only action you're getting tonight is from your hand." And with that, I leave the kitchen area and make my way to my smaller-than-a-prison-cell room. *Arsehole.*

In the morning, everyone but Dad is out. Filthy Sound is in the arena, and I've no idea where the rest have been banished to.

Dad puts two plates of eggs, bacon, and toast down on the table.

We're about to have a serious conversation, one I've not had nearly enough coffee or sleep for.

I sit down and purse my lips. This will be about Kitt, but I'm not sure if the making of breakfast means he's accepting our relationship or he wants to soften the blow.

"Are you okay, Dad?"

He turns around but ignores my question. He sets down two mugs and the pot of coffee. Dad doesn't cook, so this is making me nervous. Finally, when everything is on the table and he can't waste any more time, he sits and faces me.

"This looks good," I say.

His lips try to curve into a smile, but he can't quite manage it.

"Are you going to start? Because there is obviously something you want to say."

Picking up his cutlery, he clears his throat. "I understand the manner in which I deal with your news affects our relationship, so I want to get this right. Jimmy said to discuss it *calmly* with you. So, this is me, discussing it calmly."

"Jimmy is wise. I didn't ever want to lie to you, Dad, I swear. I've liked—*loved*—Kitt for two years now. When I realised that he was starting to develop feelings for me, I felt like I'd won the lottery. I still do feel like that actually. But I knew you wouldn't like it, and I didn't want things to be tense and awkward for everyone here."

I take a gulp of coffee. *Don't stop now. You're doing great.*

"We were together for, what? Three weeks before you found out? And every day I lied to you, I was drowning in guilt. Kitt, too. He hated it as much as me. You're his hero and mine."

Dad's eyes fill with tears. But he must have known that already, surely?

"I love you, Daddy, and I'm so sorry I wasn't honest from the start."

He swallows hard. "There is this huge part of your life I don't know about. You never even told me you liked him before. Why didn't I know this two years ago?"

"Because you were working with him, and I didn't want my feelings to cloud your judgement. Kitt deserves everything good that's happening to him. Can you honestly say that you would have given him a fair shot if I'd told you how I felt?"

"I thought—*think* a lot of Kitt, pumpkin."

"That's not what I asked."

"I don't know, is my honest answer."

"You want to keep us apart, and we can't do that."

"You've been together *three* weeks, Texas."

I cut off a piece of egg. "I love him. I'm sorry that it's not been three months so that it's easier for you to understand. I didn't know there was a timeline for it, and even if there were, I don't care."

"Always doing things your way. I suppose I should be glad that you don't follow the crowd."

"You definitely should. You might not like all the choices I make, but at least you'll always know that, with the ones I make, I'm sure they are right for me."

"The bus…that was the right choice?" He grips his cutlery harder.

I swallow the food I'm about to choke on. "Oh, we are not going there. I wasn't slutting it up with some random. I was with my boyfriend."

"Boyfriend," Dad scoffs like it's a dirty word.

"I've had one before, and you liked Xander. Hell, you like Kitt more than him, and you know it. He's not the enemy, Dad. He wants the same thing as you."

Okay, maybe not exactly the same. Kitt doesn't want me to be celibate until my wedding day.

"Kitt is where I was when I was young and starting out."

"No, Dad, not anymore. He's changed just like you changed when I came along."

Wow, I'm one super cockblocker.

"You think he's ready for a serious relationship? To settle down at this age?"

"Yes, I do. I believe him. Anyone out there can sleep around. If he wanted, he could do it as a musician or a plumber. I trust him."

"I want to believe him, Texas, but you love him, and...fuck." He puts his cutlery down, takes a deep breath, and rubs his eyes.

Oh God, he's not crying, is he?

"Dad?" I say slowly. My heart is thumping. I don't want to see him cry, not ever.

"I'm okay. I don't know if I trust him with your heart."

"Well, I do. I might not deserve your trust right now, but please have faith that I know what I'm doing. Kitt is who I want to spend my life with, and so help me, we *will* be happy."

Dad laughs and blows out a held breath. "And you're sure you can deal with what will come next? The rumours? The time alone? The uncertainty?"

"One, I don't care what people think. Two, I have plenty of things I can do while he's off rocking. Three, I'm certain, just like I was when I told you that getting highlights was a bad idea."

He rolls his eyes. "I was young."

"Not really though, were you?"

"We're not discussing my hair, Texas."

"It's not about the hair. It's about me being right. Dad, I'm sure about me and him. And I promise not to leave you out of the loop again. I want to be able to talk to you about it. I'm happy. *Really* happy."

"That's all I want, Tex. But you don't ever hold anything back with me, even when he fucks up, yeah? I need to know, so I can set him straight. You're right when you said he won't hurt you."

I arch my eyebrow and twist my mouth. "So, he messes up, and I set my daddy on him?"

"Yes," he says, as if there's nothing weird about that.

We both laugh.

Good luck, Kitt.

34

KITT
SATURDAY, MAY 30
COPENHAGEN, DENMARK

"You good, man?" Milo asks, handing me another beer.

"Thanks," I reply. "I think so. Mark and Tex are cool, but he's still not said much to me."

"You're banging his daughter. What do you expect?"

"Really, Milo?"

Chuckling darkly, he sits down. "You had to know this was going to happen though, mate."

"Well, I was kind of hoping that when he found out, it would be because we'd sat down and told him. But no, I have to fuck her against a bus, and…" Groaning, I rub the dull throbbing behind my eyes. "I couldn't have done this worse if I'd tried. What the hell is wrong with me? This is Texas, not some random horny chick I'll never see again. The side of a bus, Milo."

He grins. "Yeah, I saw the footage."

Tightening my hand around the neck of the bottle, I glare. "Not helping, prick."

"Hey," he says, holding his hand up, "I'm not trying to be a wanker here, Kitt. I've seen it, and it's plain to see that this isn't some random screw. Everyone knows you two aren't just fucking. You've told Mark there's more with you and her, and you've not split up. He gets that. Let him get used to the idea of you being with his only child. You're overthinking. Give it some time. Besides, Mark can't just blame you. Texas was right there with you the whole way."

Yeah, I remember how with me she was. I ache to be with her again. It's been too long. I hate that we're back to being careful. I hate that I can't wake up beside her.

"If you have any great ideas on how I can fix this, please speak up."

"I think you need to talk to him again. Explain that, although you're sorry about how he found out, you're not sorry you're with her."

"Mark wants to rip my head off."

"Maybe a little."

"Has he said anything to you?"

"Not directly."

"Milo!"

"It's not my place to say. Stop being a moron, and go and sort things out with Mark before it affects Texas. You told him you'd do anything for her, so prove it."

I hop over the bench seat, slam my beer in front of him, and clap him on the back as I run past. He's right. "Where's Mark?"

"His room. Good luck," Milo says, chuckling to himself.

I run up the bus and make my way to Mark's room. Tex is in hers, and the pull to go there instead is strong. This needs to be sorted out first.

I walk two doors past and knock for Mark.

A gruff voice calls, "Come in."

Pushing the handle down, I let the door swing open. "Can I have a word with you?"

"There's no need, Kitt. I've spoken to Texas. I won't tell her how to live her life, but I want you to know that I'm watching you."

Smiling, I give him a nod. "She's it, Mark. No slipups, no freak-outs. I'll make her happy."

"Make sure you do. I'll still be watching."

"I know. Want the door closed?"

"Please."

I back out and release a breath. That was easier than it should've been. Suspiciously easier. Though his watching-you warning pretty much said everything he needed to, and I've already told him I'm in this for keeps.

Mark is okay—or as okay as we can hope for—about us, so I hover at Tex's door.

Will he be this okay?
Fuck it. She's mine.

For all of one second, I consider knocking, but instead, I let myself in.

She's lying on the bed, facing away from me, but she's not asleep. I know Texas when she's asleep, and right now, she's nowhere near peaceful enough.

Closing the door to give us privacy, I step closer and say, "I know you're awake. I need to talk to you."

Rolling onto her back, she smirks up at me. "Can't a girl take a nap?"

I shake my head and walk deeper into the small room. "Nope, sorry. I want to spend time with my girl."

"I love it when you call me that."

"I know. I love you, Texas."

Her eyes ignite. "Love you, too."

Crawling onto the bed, I climb over her. She's impossibly beautiful. Her dark hair is fanned in waves around her on the pillow. Her lips are begging to be kissed. I close my eyes, picturing them swallowing me.

Stop it. You'll get yourself frustrated, and you'll not be at a hotel for a couple of days.

"What are you going to do with me?" She bites on that lip.

"When we're in that suite, Texas, there isn't a thing I'm not going to do."

Her mouth parts. I take advantage and dive in.

Tex groans and grips ahold of my arm.

"I have to go and change, but I'll see you downstairs in a minute, okay?" I whisper before kissing her forehead.

She groans something that resembles, "All right," and pulls the covers over her head.

I won't be seeing her for a good couple of hours.

Feeling on top of the damn world, I quietly leave her room and go to mine to grab a change of clothes. No one is up yet because it's the arse crack of dawn, and they were all drunk last night.

I shower and change, eager to get downstairs so that I can see Tex. If she's not up, I'm getting her up. We won't have a lot of time together before Mark gets up.

When I get to the kitchen, Cooper is sitting at the table with his head in his hands, groaning like a caveman.

"Hungover, bud?" I ask loudly.

"Fuck off, bellend."

I laugh and sit down. "What happened with the last girl?"

His face is hidden, but I still see his smile.

"From that smirk, I take it that it went well."

"Oh, yeah, she was a beast. Milo won last night's bet though. His chick brought a friend."

"Great." *I really don't miss those bets.*

"How was your night? When I left with…Red, you were sobbing into a JD. 'Mark will never forgive me.'" His imitation of my voice is embarrassing.

"I wasn't sobbing."

He snorts and looks up. "You might as well have been. What's going on anyway?"

"Me and Tex are great. Mark is okay about it. He's *watching me* apparently."

He lifts his eyebrows. "So, Mark's cool?"

Shifting in my seat, I shrug. "I'm still in one piece. He wants her happy, and she's happy with me—duh—so there's not a lot he's willing to do. He won't hurt her by ordering her away."

"That was a close call. You're officially a dickhead for not telling me from the beginning. This could have affected me, too. Enigma could've pulled out of the tour."

"We still would've killed it, Coop. But you're right, and I'm sorry."

"Damn straight we would've. Don't sweat it, man. I've got your back—even if you think with your cock."

"Because you don't?"

"Not fucking arguing. I'm young and hot, and I can make women come just by looking at them."

The fuck is in my band?

"Yeah. Women like Peyton?"

His face falls, but just as quickly, his spark is back. "Now, she's fun. The poor girl is determined to prove she doesn't want me."

"Maybe she doesn't. Again."

"Please. I'll give her time. I can play the waiting game."

"Tex's best mate isn't a game, Coop."

"Fuck me, you're whipped. Pey made it a game, and I have no intention of losing."

"You're playing with fire."

His lips kick up into a slow grin. "I know. And if I ever need advice on appearing victorious from the flames, I'll come to you."

35

TEXAS
WEDNESDAY, JUNE 3
FORNEBU, NORWAY

I step up onto the bus, and it's eerily quiet. I know Enigma is practicing, but I have no idea what Filthy Sound is up to. My educated guess is, they're at some bar. Although Ted is always with me, it's nice to have a few quiet minutes, so I'm not going to call Kitt for a while.

Getting my MacBook Air out from under the storage seat, I sit down to finally catch up with some friends on Facebook. I use the term *friend* loosely because I've not known these people long enough to form a real connection to them, but we keep in touch.

It hasn't been that long since I last sent out my catching-up messages, but I'm so unbelievably bored that I might as well get ahead. There is nothing else to do. It's quite nice, but I'm definitely not used to it, especially while on tour.

Just as I lift the laptop lid, the bathroom door opens, and Kitt emerges—with only a towel around his waist.

Sweet. Jesus.

I didn't know he was still here.

Now, I know I shouldn't stare, but his damp six-pack is begging for my hands and mouth to run over it. I want to drag my fingers between the muscles all the way down to—

"Er, Tex?" Kitt says. He sounds amused.

Why wouldn't he be? I can't stop eye-fucking him.

"Texas!" Laughing, he clicks his fingers.

I reluctantly flick my eyes up. His grin cannot get any wider.

I blink, unashamed. "Yes?"

"If you're finished, I'll go get dressed. Didn't know anyone else was here."

And if I'm not finished?

His eyebrow arches. "Unless of course…"

"Unless of course, what?" I whisper. My body is on fire. I feel like pouring ice-cold water over myself to take away some of the heat.

Ted is only upstairs in his room. He could easily come down.

Kitt's eyes blister, and it's giving me heart palpitations. He slowly walks over to the table, getting closer to me. Working entirely on their own, my legs stand me up. It's like I've been taken over by a lust-filled hussy. I want him now—even on the table, for all I care—knowing anyone could walk in at any minute. I simply *do not* give a damn.

He stops when he's an inch away from me. His chest quickly rises and falls, and his mouth is ever so slightly open. Reaching out, he brushes my hair behind my shoulder, dragging his fingertips over my neck as he goes. It makes my insides turn all squishy.

I love it when he does that.

"Unless of course, what, Kitt?" I repeat even though I have a pretty good idea what *what* is.

He possessively kisses me, claiming me for his own, and I push him back and wrap myself around him.

Damn towel. I love and hate it, but right now, it's in my way.

Kitt catches my hand as my fingers curl over the edge of the towel. "Tex, I'm all up for spontaneous sex—in the inside of the bus this time—but..."

I gasp, and my face heats. Dad could come back and catch us.

"Upstairs, sweetheart. I want you laid out on my bed and ready."

My dad is suddenly forgotten. Kitt's words have me throbbing with need.

"Ready for, what?" I whisper breathlessly.

The corner of his lips kicks up, and his eyes smile. "Before I sink into you, I'm going to make you come on my mouth."

He doesn't need to ask me twice. I bound upstairs.

Looks like our no-bus sex pact is over.

Whatever. It was a stupid pact anyway.

THURSDAY, JUNE 4
FORNEBU, NORWAY

There are four people on the bus who aren't hungover—the drivers, Ted, and Hank. Milo is worse off than anyone. He drank the entire bar before rambling about something that had Kitt pulling him to the side. Then, he left with three women. Three! We're heading out of Norway towards Sweden.

"Look at this!" Will says with a chuckle.

My eyes widen. On the front page is a picture of me and Kitt outside the stadium as Filthy Sound made their way back to the bus. His arm is around my waist, holding me close.

Then, I see why Milo is laughing.

Kitt groans and shoves it away. "Really?"

"Kexas! Are they serious?" I say in disgusted shock. That sucks. They'll mash anything together. "And, oh my God, *why* didn't they go with it the other way around?"

Kitt laughs. "Titt? Great. Think we can put out a request to change it?"

"Oh, I'm going to."

"Read the shocking article," Coop says.

I flip the page, and my jaw drops. We've not been out in public yet. No one knows we're together, and I'm already fucking engaged to him.

"Quick work, Daniels," I say as I roll my eyes.

Dad looks over the article with a chilling silence.

What's going on inside his head?

"What are you going to do? I thought the plan was to keep it under wraps for as long as possible?" Milo asks.

"Ignore it," Dad says.

Everyone's eyes flick to him.

"Stories are in the paper every day. Ignore it until you're ready, and it'll die down."

He is determined to keep my life normal for as long as possible, and I'm all for it. Kitt and I will announce we're together soon, of course, but it makes sense to do it during a break in the tour. Hopefully, after that, things will die down, and we can get on with the second half of the tour.

I know what it's like to be mobbed on tour because something in your life has changed, and everyone has the right to know about it because you live in the spotlight.

Five years ago, Jimmy and Saskia suffered a tragic miscarriage, and the paparazzi were everywhere. It was the same when a girl claimed Will had forced himself on her. It was quickly proven that he hadn't. And again when Dad let it slip that he loved Jennifer. He'd meant as the mother of his child, but it was taken the wrong way.

Rubbish written by the pap is the reason my relationship with Xander was kept under wraps. It's the reason I want more time with Kitt without the media circus that is waiting in the wings.

"Tex?" Kitt says. "Is that what you want to do?"

I nod. "I think so. There's not long left until we get home, and—"

He leans over and plants a hard kiss on my mouth. "You don't have to explain. If that's how you want to handle this…" He folds the paper over, showing me that it's done and we're not going to give it another second of our time.

Dad smiles. "You've made the right decision. When we're home, I'll up security."

Can't wait.

"You ready for even more people in your house, Kitt?"

I have two reasons for asking this. Kitt needs to be prepared for the entourage my dad is going to have following me around. Kitt is used to Ted, but that's going to be upped. And my dad needs to know that I'll be over at Kitt's a lot.

He shrugs. "Doesn't bother me."

"It'd better not," Dad says. "Remember, I'm watching."

Cooper laughs. "One wrong move, and you're toast. And I can take centre stage."

I tilt my head. "You don't have the voice, Coop."

"My other qualities would more than make up for the fact that this pussy has a better voice." He looks down to his groin while jabbing his thumb towards Kitt.

"Gross," I mutter. "Are we anywhere near Stockholm yet?"

Milo snorts. "Tex, we left Norway five minutes ago."

"Then, can we chuck Cooper off?"

"Seconded," Jimmy says.

"You shits always pick on me, and you know why?"

We all wait.

"Because you're jealous," Cooper says.

Laughter drowns out the sound of the road.

"We certainly wouldn't want to be here without you, Coop," Dad says, slapping Cooper's back.

I blow him a kiss. "No, we love you and your delusions. Really."

On the table, my phone starts to flash with a notification, and then they come every few seconds. *Oh, great.*

"Looks like the article is out there," Kitt says, wrapping his arm around my waist, much like he did in the photo. "Ready for the crazy?"

I give him a look. "I'm always ready for the crazy, so bring it on."

The world can do its worst. We're stronger than anything they have up their sleeves.

36

KITT
FRIDAY, JUNE 5
STOCKHOLM, SWEDEN

Since the photo of Tex and I was released, the whole world has gone fucking crazy. *How can people be so invested in the lives of strangers?* But they are. Everyone is obsessed with us being a couple—whether they love or hate us. My critics say I'm not good enough, and Tex's critics say she's not.

It's a good thing we don't care what anyone else thinks.

Our Facebook and Twitter pages have exploded. There's something new online every minute, and it's the first question the paparazzi fire at us. They want confirmation, one way or another.

We've upped security for Tex now because the level of harassment is insane. It changed overnight, and I'm on edge every time she goes out in public.

It's been amazing for our record sales and catapulted the album up to number five in the charts, but I hate how much the extra attention is bothering Tex. It's shit like this, which is why Mark didn't want her with someone like me. I get it, too. Finally, I fully understand why he was against her being with someone in the spotlight. He wants to protect her as much as I do.

Mark spends his life trying to extinguish the media fire around Texas, and here I am, adding fuel to it. But I'm too much of a selfish bastard to let her go, not that either of us would allow someone else to influence our relationship.

Not even her dad.

The only people who know the truth are on tour with us, and they'd never talk. I think Peyton knows, too.

Mark has been watching me like a hawk, even more than before, judging how I'm dealing with the unwanted attention. He's not mentioned anything or given me any advice, so he either thinks I'm doing all right, or he's keeping his mouth closed and letting me work through it with Tex.

I feel like I'm on fucking trial. It's almost like he's waiting for me to screw up, and I'm downright petrified that, under his constant scrutiny, I will. It's a lot of pressure. I'm drowning under it, but I remind myself of what this is all for—Texas. My mind overworks, dreaming up every eventuality, and I stress over every little thing from a single line in a new song to being dropped by the label to Texas having enough.

Then, she smiles at me or says she loves me, and everything else turns to white noise.

"Anal?" Texas says, snapping me right out of my thoughts. We're sitting on the sofa together.

"What?" I blink. "What?"

"Ah, welcome back. No, by the way, to anal. I just wanted your attention. Tomorrow, you guys are on TV at seven a.m., so no partying tonight. I'll let you tell Coop."

"Thanks. Why seven? Couldn't you have booked it later?"

"Right, I control the breakfast show. Just because you're a rock star, Kitt, doesn't mean you get to make *all* the rules. Plus, I didn't book it. I, for sure, would have gotten it later because

I'm the mug who has to try getting your hungover arses to places on time."

"You manage us better than Jodie."

"She's super busy with a much better artist."

I narrow my eyes, and she laughs.

"I'm joking. You guys are getting bigger, so I think she'll soon get someone else to manage you guys full-time. She needs to concentrate on her train-wreck singer. That chick needs an intervention."

Jodie's other client is pop star Elody Wild, who's been in the industry since she was fucking conceived. The meltdown was coming, and she did not disappoint. Elody's breakdown means that Jodie is unable to be here the whole time. But Jodie was only ever our temp manager.

It's a good thing Tex is here because there's no way we'd make appearances on our own.

"I'm glad she's not here. She'd only moan about the volume of alcohol entering our bodies."

Tex twists and sits on my lap, almost kneeing me in my most important area. "Should I scold you for that?" she rasps.

I run my hands up her thighs, and I'm about to take her mouth when the bus door opens. Gripping her waist, I launch her off me, and she lands on the sofa, staring at me like I've lost it.

"What the fuck, Kitt?" she snaps, whacking my arm, as Mark, Jimmy and Will walk into the room.

Mark is immediately suspicious of Texas's action. I laugh, trying desperately to make it look like a joke. I'm not really sure how to explain to him that his daughter was straddling me five seconds ago.

He's accepted our relationship—although I do think he's been a little too cool with it. We get no hassle, but it won't take much for him to freak out again, and I know Texas will always choose him. From the second she was born, she's been a daddy's girl. I'm close to my grandparents, but I had a closer version of a normal childhood. The way Mark and Texas live and what they've been through makes their relationship a little different. It's strong as fucking steel.

"Hey, Daddy. How'd the sound check go?" Texas asks, settling back into the sofa after realising why I threw her like she'd burned me. Her cheeks turn pink, and she looks to the left of Mark.

The girl is shit at lying.

"Speakers cool now?" I ask.

Mark nods, mouth tight. "All good."

"I'm fucking starving," Will says. "Jimmy, cook some bacon."

"Why do I have to cook?"

Will rolls his eyes. "Mark, cook the bacon."

"Jesus Christ!" Texas says, pushing herself up and stroking my hand as she goes. "I'll cook! Besides Will, you all suck anyway."

"May I remind you, master chef, that you burned toast?" Mark says, pointing at Tex.

She turns and narrows her eyes. "I was distracted. The toaster didn't pop up on time."

"Blame the toaster, Tex? Really?" I tease.

The look she gives me tells me that if her dad wasn't here right now, she'd be telling me that I'd be outta luck for sex tonight. Unlucky for her—and lucky for me—she could never stick to a threat like that.

"You wouldn't even know which end to put the bread in, Kitt, so I don't know why you're taking the piss."

"Have you ever thought that I pretend to be an awful cook, so I don't have to do it?"

She takes a minute before replying, "No. I think you're just horrible at it, but please feel free to cook us all some bacon and prove me wrong."

Fuck, she's got me. If I don't do it, she'll think she's won, and if I do it, she'll have food cooked for her and still win.

And from the cocky head tilt and pursed lips, she knows it, too.

She puts her hands on her hips. "Well?"

With the Band

"Well, I'll sit right here and let you win while getting me meat." If I'm losing, I'm getting something out of it.

Out of the corner of my eye, I can see Mark watching us. He's intrigued, confused almost. He enjoys seeing how we interact because he can see that we're meant to be. But he's still *watching*.

"Fine. I'll make it. You're buying dinner anyway." She smiles and heads to the kitchen area.

"When have I not paid, Tex?"

"I'll treat you one day."

She bloody won't, but I don't want her to. I want to be the one who looks after her. And I will. Tex has a pretty strong personality, but I'm not backing down from that. She can kick and scream, but she's mine, and I'm taking care of her.

"Where's Milo and Cooper?" Will asks, flopping down beside me and throwing his hands behind his head.

"On the piss somewhere, I think. That, or screwing some chicks."

"Men are disgusting!" Texas shouts over her shoulder.

I watch Texas while she cooks. Her head is tilted to the side as she flips the bacon with one hand and looks at something on her phone with the other. She turns away, and I realise it's because she's reacting to something she's read.

Her shoulders slouch, and I'm on my feet. Something is up.

I walk over to her, stand close, and ask, "What's going on?"

"Last night, you cheated on me with this chick," she replies, shoving her phone in my face.

"Tex, no, I—"

"Don't," she says, ending my sentence. "I know it didn't happen. It's been twenty-four hours, and I can't count how many times one of us has cheated or there's been a new rumour. I can't keep up on any of my pages because they're being bombarded, and anytime I step outside this bus, people are there in crowds, waiting to fire questions and tell me how to live my life."

Shit. This never bothered her before, but like she said, it's been a day, and she can't keep up. She's already had enough. I can't wait to get this show over with, then we only have a quick stop in Finland before home.

"I'm sorry, baby."

She wraps her arms around my waist. "It's not your fault, Kitt. I need to stop looking so much. I'll ignore it. Doesn't matter what anyone else says anyway."

"You sure you're okay?"

Letting go, she gives me a playful shove. "I'm better than okay. I have you. Now, go sit down, and stop distracting me, or I'll never get this cooked to perfection."

I watch her for a second, looking for any signs of indecision.

There is none. She's still sure about us. She's still all in.

TEXAS
SATURDAY, JUNE 13
LONDON, ENGLAND

We're back in the UK for a week before going to America. I thought I'd feel less stressed here, but the storm surrounding our relationship is raging. It's pissing me off because I don't get stressed.

I'd just like to be a regular couple, even for a day.

Kitt is worried because I'm not as chipper as I usually am. I need to regroup and get my *fuck it* back. I need to hold my middle finger up and say, *Sod it*.

Easier said than done.

Kitt rolls over on my bed and throws his arm across my waist. That helps. "Are you really kicking me out?"

"Yep," I reply. "I don't want you to see me before I'm ready."

"That's a stupid idea. I like seeing you before you're ready."

Tonight, we're going to a red-carpet event, a movie premiere, and it's the first time Kitt and I will be together in public as a couple. It's time. Maybe once we've confirmed what everyone already knows, I'll do better with not caring.

While I'm with Kitt, I'll get more attention. It's always going to happen. So, maybe what I need to do is get used to how it is now. *Is this how Peyton felt when she joined the cast, and things got crazy?*

"Go, Kitt. Promise, I'll make it worth it later."

I watch the struggle in his eyes. He wants to stay, but he wants me to make it up to him.

"What will it be, Daniels?"

He kisses my forehead, rolls over, and catapults himself off the bed. "Until tonight," he calls over his shoulder.

I laugh and fall back against my bed. *Thought so.*

Time to get ready.

I'm torn. I want to be me because no one else can do it better, but I want to be what Kitt deserves.

Oh.

No, no.

What the hell is wrong with me?

Fuck the posh dresses. I'm going as me.

And if I ever think like that again, I'm going to stab myself in the head.

Shunning the long-length ball gowns, I slip on my deep red skater dress and black heels. I will be exactly who I am, and I don't care who doesn't like it. Let people say I'm not enough or that my clothes aren't red-carpet worthy. They don't matter. I have Kitt, and there will be alcohol.

I've grown up in the spotlight, but my dad sheltered me from much more than I realised until recently. Now, I'm jumping into it with both feet. There's no way I can keep as much privacy anymore, not since I'm with the heartthrob lead singer in one of the fastest rising bands.

"Damn it!" I snap, poking my hair in front of the mirror. I'm in the dress I want, but my hair is not going right.

Dad laughs from my doorway.

I frown at his reflection. "What's so funny?"

"You're stressing about your appearance, pumpkin. You're turning into a girl."

I glare at him and go back to the unruly mop on my head. "This is all your fault. Why did I have to get your stupid hair? Jennifer's hair is perfect all the time, and mine always looks like I've just woken up."

"You've never cared about your hair before, Texas. Why now?"

"Because it won't pin up properly!"

"And you think Kitt will care what your hair looks like?"

"No...but I do."

Dad walks into my room with a frown on his face. He pulls my hand away from my hair and gives it a squeeze. "If you care what the whole world thinks, I'll call a hairdresser in now. If you only care what you think, leave it alone."

"You're right," I reply. Sod the hair. It can be down. I give him a hug. "Thanks, Dad."

He hugs me back a little harder than usual and kisses my forehead. "Anytime. You look beautiful, by the way."

"Thank you. I don't really like the whole dress thing."

"There's my girl." He releases me with a smile. "I'm proud of you, Texas."

"Thank you. I'm proud of you, too. You're handling this Kitt thing a lot better than I thought. You even gave him a compliment there. He really wouldn't care what my hair is like."

"And I'll keep dealing with it just fine as long as he doesn't hurt you."

"He won't. This is more than what he had with other girls."

Lots and lots of other girls who I choose to forget about on a regular basis. A few pop up here and there to sell their kiss-and-tell stories, and those are the ones I feel sorry for. All they have of him is a memory and a couple hundred. Their time with him isn't even private anymore. I could never share anything that's just between us with the world, no matter what the price tag was.

"I understand that. I guess I've seen a lot of rock stars over the years. Each generation seems to…enjoy what the nature of the business has to offer more and more. I never wanted you to be a part of that."

"Never bloody will be. If Kitt didn't like me back, there was no way I would've let anything happen between us. I won't be Jennifer."

"Texas…" he warns.

"Whatever. You don't want me to be a teen knocked up by a touring rock star either. Good thing I'm not Jennifer, and Kitt's not you."

"I really wish I'd lied to you about your conception."

I grin. "But we have a no-lying-to-each-other rule."

A rule I have seriously pushed.

"Yes, we do. Remember that, Texas."

Oh, that's a warning. Whenever he asks a question about Kitt, he and I both know I'll have to give him a straight, honest answer.

"Kitt's here," I say as the front door opens and slams.

"I'm so glad I never took away his key," Dad says sarcastically.

"Play nice, please. He's important to me."

He groans and walks out, muttering something about hating me getting older. Clearly, he's still oblivious to the fact that I'm already older.

I take one last glance at myself and sigh. It's a shame I can't do this in shorts and flip-flops.

As I walk downstairs, I hear Dad and Kitt making small talk. They laugh, and the sound of my two favourite guys makes my heart swell.

Kitt's eyes focus on me as I come around the corner. Dad says his name, but Kitt's eyes don't move, and his mouth is open. Dad turns around, but I don't see his reaction to Kitt's ogling because I'm doing the same.

I'm used to Kitt being in jeans and a T-shirt. It's not often he's in a tux. He's so gorgeous that I want to bash my head against the marble floor. Or maybe jump him.

His black tux is a slim fit, and the top button of his white shirt is undone. He's never looked so sexy—well, except for when he's wearing just a pair of those slim jeans. Biting my lip, I walk the last few steps in a daze of filthy thoughts.

Dad clears his throat, and I stand up straight, embarrassed that he caught me and Kitt eye-fucking each other.

"Be in the kitchen," he mutters before making himself scarce.

Kitt steps forward until he's right in front of me. I look up, and the way he's staring at me makes my heart ache in the best way.

"Hi," I whisper. "You look good."

Kitt continues to stare. His eyes are glowing red-hot. Finally, he gulps and licks his lips. "Texas...shit. You're stunning."

"Do *not* get used to it. The dress thing won't be repeated often, and I think I'm going to fall over in these stupid—"

Kitt effectively ends my rambling by sealing his mouth over mine.

Usually, when he knows my dad is around, Kitt is extremely reserved when it comes to me, but right now, he's not holding back. And I'm not complaining. I hold on and kiss him back.

Twenty minutes later, we're in the limo. I have Ted with me and the new guy, Lars. Hank is here also. I get on with him well enough to feel comfortable having him shadow me, so my extra security isn't too bad.

"Do we really have to do this?" I ask, gripping Kitt's hand.

"Not if you don't want to," he replies.

"Hey, you're not supposed to give me an option. You know we can't just blow it off!"

"Sure you can," Cooper pipes in. "He's Kitt fucking Daniels, and if he wants to skip out on an event, he can. And I'll come with you." His eyes go wide. "Please, let me come with you."

Coop hates these types of things. Just give him the after-party, and he's happy.

"No one is skipping this," Dad says.

"Yeah, Coop," Jimmy adds. "And no more drinking beforehand."

Cooper scowls. "How else am I supposed to get through this shit film?"

"You don't know it's bad, idiot. You've not seen it yet," I say.

"There are no fights or car chases. That's how I know it's shit. At least you two can suck face to pass the time. What do I have?"

Kitt sticks his middle finger up and tightens his grip on my hand. Cooper, the bastard, did that on purpose. Thankfully, Dad doesn't react, and the incident is quickly forgotten. Plus, our limo has pulled to a stop in front of the red carpet, and it's our turn to get out.

Cameras are flashing, and actors from the film and celebrity guests are taking photos along the way. I'm terrified. There is absolutely no way I'm going to make it inside without falling on my arse. Kitt had better not let go.

"Let's do this. I call dibs on Elizabeth!" Milo says, causing Cooper to swear like a sailor. He wanted the star tonight.

"You can't just call a person, Milo!" I snap.

"Of course you can. Look up the shotgun rules, babycakes." He flashes me a smile and opens the door.

The screams make me flinch. We wait for everyone else to get out. Dad, Jimmy, and Will take their time, and I know they're looking for fans, so they can do autographs and pictures. They always make time for fans.

Milo and Cooper practically bound around in search of the best-looking women to approach. No change there either.

Kitt gets out next and turns around to take my hand.

I guess we're going straight in for it then. It's probably best.

I smile up at him when I'm standing successfully. *No tripping so far. Win.*

"Thank you," I whisper.

He leans in for a kiss. I manage to forget everyone else when his lips touch mine, but I sure as hell can't ignore the reaction. This is definitely what people who don't even personally know us want.

I'd like to be able to say that you can't be too invested in the love lives of people you don't know, but you absolutely can. I was devastated when Chad Michael Murray and Sophia Bush divorced. I was Team Brocas until the bitter end.

Kitt breaks the kiss after a second, keeping it classy and not allowing time for either of us to get carried away. Good thing really. We do not need any more of our private life on camera.

His name is yelled over and over, and hordes of women shout that they love him. Many of them shout that they love us, and I even hear, "Kexas," being screeched, too.

Lame.

This is insane. Keep walking. Do not fall and make a twat out of yourself.

He pulls me close under his arm and occasionally stops us to chat with someone or to pose for pictures. A few groups are holding Filthy Sound handmade signs—one saying, *I Heart Kitt 4eva*, which plain just makes me cringe.

He stops. "Hey, ladies."

They practically orgasm in front of us.

"Oh my God, we love you!" a girl screams in his face. "Will you sign our banner?"

"Of course." He lets go of me, takes the girl's Sharpie, and scribbles his signature over the banner that already has Milo's and Cooper's autographs on it. Their phone numbers are probably on the back by now, too.

"Do you want a picture?" he stupidly asks them.

Like they're going to say no.

"Oh my God, yes! We're so excited you and Texas are a thing. We just *knew* it!"

"Want her in it, too?"

The little prick.

I want to openly glare at him, but that'll make me look like a total bitch, so I smile.

The girls nod eagerly, and I smile as I turn awkwardly, so I'm in the bloody photo as well. Kitt holds me tight to his side and smiles at the pink leopard-print phone.

Another thing I don't like.

Find me a bloody pink leopard. Just one.

"Thank you," I say politely to the girls once the photo is done.

"See you around," Kitt says, taking my hand and leading us closer to the door.

I just want to be inside now. I was fully prepared to have photos for the press and paparazzi, but fans, too? Nope. That was not discussed. I'm not really that comfortable being around crazy fangirls unless I'm one of them. And I haven't been a fangirl of Filthy Sound ever. I know them too well.

We stop again and pose for proper pictures. Kitt kisses the side of my head, so I figure we don't have to hold back all affection. He isn't. I wrap my arms around that toned waist and smile.

This isn't so bad when it's just us. I need to quickly get used to the sheer amount of people interested in me and him as a couple.

Fuck it. I love him, and I'm not giving him up for anything, so I might as well get on board here.

Embracing my new official status as Kitt Daniels's girlfriend, I tilt my head toward him and pose perfectly for pictures that I'll no doubt see splashed all over social media tomorrow.

KITT
SATURDAY, JUNE 13
LONDON, ENGLAND

Texas handled the red carpet perfectly. She always does. I really don't give a fuck what anyone thinks about my relationship with her.

The film finishes with a round of applause from the audience, and Tex turns to me.

"That was awesome!" she gushes, clapping along with everyone else.

"Mmhmm."

It was good. The part I didn't like was where my girlfriend fanned herself when male lead, Aaron Conner, got naked.

"You liked some scenes better than others, huh?" I ask her.

My band laughs, suddenly interested in our conversation. They know exactly what I'm talking about because they know Tex is a little pervert.

She shrugs innocently. "It was a good scene. Very tasteful and classy."

"Yeah, the dude has a very classy cock," Milo deadpans.

"You wouldn't know, dipshit. Yours is probably covered in boils," Tex calls back.

Milo's mouth opens, but his shock is hidden behind amusement. He's as proud of her for that comeback as I am.

Cooper, laughing and pointing to Milo's cock, throws his head back and says, "Burn! Shit, man, you'd better not have any of that crap. We share a shower."

"Yeah, that's how STDs are spread," I reply sarcastically.

Mark clears his throat. "Although I do enjoy where our conversations go, this perhaps isn't the right place for it."

"Let's go get a drink," Will says, "and I can have a chat with Milo."

"Fucking hell, I have no diseases!" Milo exclaims, giving Texas a look over his shoulder.

Now that the movie is over, we'll have drinks and boring small talk where we'll congratulate the actors and director on a job well done. Then, it's the after-party, the real reason people attend things like this.

"Texas!" Peyton yells from across the room.

And I've lost my girl. They fly toward each other. We weren't sure if she'd make it and assumed not since we hadn't seen her come in, but she must've been late.

"Come on, use tongue," Coop says, watching Tex reunite with her friend.

They're hugging, not kissing like he wants.

"You're a dick, Coop."

"Oh, like you'd hate your girl getting down with another chick."

"I'm not you," I reply. Honestly, the thought of Texas's lips, or anything else, touching *anyone* else makes me feel violent. I don't share her.

"I need to get fucked up tonight," I say, nodding toward the bar.

"All right! Now, you're talking," he replies, slapping me on the shoulder and shoving me forward. "You getting Tex drunk, too? She's a fucking hilarious drunk."

I smirk. "Oh, yeah." Clumsy drunken sex with her is mind-blowing, and I'm definitely up for doing it as often as possible.

"Can't believe you've settled down, man."

"Neither can the old me, but she's worth it. Doesn't feel like a sacrifice with her. It feels right."

"Dude!" he exclaims, stopping dead and looking around on the floor.

"What? What's wrong?" I'm looking, too, but I don't know why or what for. *His phone maybe?* "Coop?"

"Your balls dropped off, man."

Oh, for fuck's sake! I stand up straight and punch his arm. "Wanker."

Cooper laughs, rubbing his arm. "Sorry, bud. Thought you'd swallowed a Jane Austen novel there."

I'm less annoyed that he's taking the piss and more proud that he knows who Jane Austen is. "It'll be you one day, Cooper."

"Bollocks," he replies as we reach the bar. "We'll have twenty-four shots of Sambuca, eight beers, and a glass of that pissy pink wine. That's what Peyton drinks, right?"

"Rosè, yeah. You remember her drink?"

He shoots me a dark look. "Don't go getting any ideas. I'm going to bang her again, but it's purely business."

"Business? Are you charging now?"

"Don't be a twat. She makes me come times a million, and I know I do the same for her. Why fight that?"

He turns back to the guy grabbing an obscene amount of shot glasses for a first round. None of us even like Sambuca.

"Fucking just got the talk from my uncle!" Milo growls, slouching on the bar beside me. "Where's Tex? She owes me."

"With Peyton."

"Pey made it?" He laughs. "Coop's going home with blue balls tonight."

"Least I still have some," he snaps back, nudging me.

I don't know how I've suddenly been brought into this.

"Whatever. Milo's right. Odds of you getting in her pants again are slim. Just look at your behaviour. She doesn't find that attractive, mate."

Coop stares, like he doesn't understand, and I roll my eyes.

"He's not right. The sexy blonde princess doesn't have to give it up again tonight. There are plenty of others willing. In fact, there are thousands who require no work at all. I click my fingers, and they lift their skirts."

"Ah, the easy ones," Milo sighs as he taps his heart with his fist. "God bless them."

To think, a month ago, I was one of them...

I never thought anything could get better than having *a lot* of sex without the responsibility of a relationship. I was so wrong that I want to laugh now, but I know it's something you have to figure out yourself. Milo kind of knows it from Lexi. Cooper? Well, I'll take great joy in watching him go through falling in love.

We down a couple of shots when Tex and Peyton join us. Coop immediately makes a play for the girl who I have a feeling is going to screw him up in the best way. Milo and Texas are deep into an argument about the validity of *The Lord of the Rings*. It's an age-old fight where Milo defends his favourite books and films, and Texas—also liking them—questions every point to piss him off.

She shrugs. "They should've just gone the other way around."

Milo's mouth is hanging open. "You've said some stupid shit on this topic before, Knight, but that—"

I tone them out and laugh at Tex trying to keep a straight face. Her lips twitch from the effort.

A shadow casts over my drink, and I look over at a very pretty woman I'm sure I'm supposed to know.

She leans her hip against the cool glass and rests her arm on top. "Hi, I'm Danniella."

Danniella who?

I nod. "Kitt. Nice to meet you."

"I saw you in Paris. You're phenomenal."

"Always good to hear. Thanks."

She sips her wine and smiles. "What are you doing after?"

My spine stiffens. She's fucking coming on to me in front of my girlfriend. To my right, I can feel I now have Tex's attention.

"I'll be going to my girlfriend's."

Her eyes flick to Texas, and she blushes. "Oh my God, I'm so sorry. You two are definitely a couple then? I thought, since you didn't mention it, you didn't really want her. I mean, why not confirm it if you thought she was worth it?"

I'm burning. My fists clench.

Don't hit a woman. You can never hit a woman.

Tex smiles, but there is nothing friendly in it. "Danniella. Fuck off."

"Stupid whore," Peyton mutters. "Who is she anyway?"

"She blogs or something like that. She's been linked to every male celeb who will sleep with her," Tex explains.

Makes sense. She reeks of desperation. I turn my back, effectively blocking the bitch from our group, and take a breath. My eyes lock with Tex, and she shrugs, like it was nothing. She downs a shot and immediately picks up her discussion with Milo.

I've never been prouder of her. But there's something in her eyes that I don't like. Doubt. Even if it's passing and she's no longer worried about us, she still thought it.

I pull her to the side when I get a minute.

"What?" She laughs nervously.

"Danniella…when she said I didn't confirm the rumours because I didn't think you were worth it, you believed her."

"No, I didn't, Kitt. Look, a part of me was angry because you didn't."

"You told me not to."

"I know that."

"So, how can you be angry, Tex?"

"Because I wanted you to *want* to tell everyone."

"I did want to!"

"I know, but you didn't."

Oh my God. "I didn't because you said not to. It was *your* choice."

"I know that, too."

My head is about to explode. "So…you're angry because I didn't tell even though you told me not to. Should I have gone ahead and made the announcement?"

"No, of course not."

"Fucking hell, Texas. I need another drink."

She presses her chest against mine, and I almost forget the argument.

"I'm sorry. It's unreasonable."

"Oh, is it?" I say sarcastically.

She glares. "You did the right thing. It's what I wanted, what we wanted. I wish we didn't have to hide away. But that doesn't matter now because we're together, and we're forever."

"Yeah, unless you keep on with that unreasonable mindfuck shit, and my head blows off."

She laughs and shrugs a shoulder. "You love it."

"I love you. And all your crazy."

39

TEXAS
SATURDAY, JUNE 13
LONDON, ENGLAND

Peyton, Kitt, Cooper, and I are sitting at one of the tables, drinking far too much. Since Dad left, I've upped my intake by about a thousand percent. Tomorrow is going to be hell.

"Stop it, dickhead!" I whisper, shoving Cooper's hand away from Peyton's arse.

She's deep in conversation with Kitt about the tour, and behind her back, a pervert named Jack Cooper is trying to touch her up.

He points to me with a cheeky grin and says, "You need to lighten up, sweet cheeks."

"You're such a twat, Coop," I reply, laughing at how dazed he looks.

The guy has probably had close to twenty drinks so far tonight. His blue eyes, which are a few shades lighter than

Peyton's, are glazed, and when he looks at me, it seems like it takes him a while to register who I am.

"You love me, Tex, so don't even try to deny it."

"Doesn't change the fact that you're a twat now, does it?"

Cooper adorably pouts his lip, and that right there is why he rarely gets into trouble for all the rubbish he causes. He has so much charm that it should be illegal.

"Are you going to put in a good word for me since you've been nasty tonight?" he asks, nodding his chin toward Peyton.

She hears and looks over, lifting a blonde eyebrow. "Every person on this planet could put a good word in, and I still wouldn't touch you again. Not even with Tex's."

I'm very pleased she wouldn't touch him with mine.

"Unlucky for you, Coop," Kitt says, hitting him around the back of his head.

Kitt wraps his arm around my waist and tugs me a little closer. We can do this now. I don't have to let go of him as we walk out the door.

"One day, love," Coop says, blowing Peyton a kiss.

Usually, I'd side with my bestie, but I'm one hundred percent behind Cooper on this—not because I think they should have sex again, but because I know it's inevitable. The tension and atmosphere between them is like it was when Kitt and I started to grow closer.

Laying my head on Kitt's shoulder, I ask, "Where'd Milo go?"

His chest shakes with the laughter. "Took a girl to the gents'."

I turn my nose up. "That's disgusting."

"You're not up for it?" Kitt asks. "Because I am."

"You want to have sex in a dirty bathroom?"

He shrugs and gives me a lopsided smile. "What can I say, Tex? I'm a rock star."

"Well, no."

Milo is such a classy bloke. But then, I had sex against a tour bus—and got caught. So, who am I to judge?

Kitt laughs. "He's going to knock someone up before long. I think he has even had more sex than Cooper."

"Whoa, whoa, whoa," Coop says, looking deeply hurt. "Let's not get ahead of ourselves there. I am the king."

"And to think, for a second there, I considered sleeping with you again," Peyton muttered.

Coop's head snaps back in her direction so fast that I hear his neck crack. "You've considered it for longer than a second. Pey, you can deny it until the day you die, but you know we're dynamite together."

She crosses her arms. "Doesn't mean I have to repeat it."

"You two are cute," I say.

Coop flashes me his signature grin. "Thank you, Texas."

"Hey, motherfuckers! We're taking the party to Whitney Blake's," Milo says, almost stumbling into the table.

There are no questions because we all want to see inside Whitney Blake's house. She's a mega rich actress and model, like way richer than my dad. She could probably buy my dad.

Kitt grabs my hand as we make our way outside. I wasn't prepared though. Cameras flash in our faces. Ted steps closer. The noise is deafening, and I wince.

People scream questions at us that I can only just make out.

"Kitt, did you know?"

"Texas, how did you react to the allegations?"

"Kitt, can we have an interview?"

Kitt's arm tightens around me.

What's that about?

Kitt frowns but keeps us moving forward.

"Keep walking. Almost there," Ted says. His voice is tight, and his eyes are everywhere. He doesn't like this.

There are so many people that the short walk to the car seems like miles.

Peyton, Milo, and Cooper are close behind. Hank and Lars surround them.

The back door to the limo is wrenched open, and both Ted and Kitt are ushering me inside. Only when we're all in safely do my shoulders sag.

I lay my head against Kitt's shoulder. "That was crazy."

"I know, babe. I'm sorry."

"It's not your fault."

"You okay, Tex?" Peyton asks.

She's sitting at the end with Cooper. His arm is around her, and she's leaning against him, like she trusts him to protect her. He might be a joker and a whore, but I trust him with my life, so she's right to do the same.

Milo lets out a string of swearwords as we pull into Whitney's drive. I think it's too big to be classed as a drive. This is a car park. Her house is massive and made of thick dark stone that gives it a gothic look.

I want to buy it.

Ted is happier now that we're on private property. It makes his job a lot easier, and he'll be able to relax. Steel gates keep out unwanted attention.

The car stops right in front of the door, and we pile out. The entrance is huge. A chunky double door opens as we approach, and two men dressed entirely in black welcome us with a smile. In silence, they both gesture with their hands toward a door.

Coop walks ahead with Peyton on his arm.

"Er, anyone else find this creepy?" I ask, gripping Kitt's hand. I'm still in heels, so I really can't be running if this is about to turn into a horror film.

"Yep," Milo replies. "Awesome, right?"

Oh, great. The door leads to stairs going down.

My eyes flash to Kitt, and he smirks. He's not at all worried. Music and laughter is coming from down there. *Do we really have to be in the cellar?*

My heels click on the limestone steps. I don't like this. The stairs curl around, and when we reach the bottom, I don't know why I was worried.

With the Band

The cellar is large, and the floor and walls are entirely stone. But that's where the creep factor ends. Carved solid oak has been used to create a bar and rustic seating areas. The DJ is at the far end, and staff is hurrying to lay food out on a long table at the side.

"I'm so glad you made it," Whitney says, hugging Milo and basically pressing her boobs on him.

She's old enough to be his bloody mother.

"Wouldn't have missed it," Milo replies.

"Texas, it's so good to see you. It's been a long time."

She hugs me, and I dig around in my mind to remember when we've met.

"Sorry, I don't remember."

Pulling away, she laughs and blushes lightly. "You were four, so you probably wouldn't. How is your dad?"

Oh my fucking God, she had sex with my dad! I swallow bile. *Do not throw up on her.* "He's great. Thank you."

"I see the tour is going well. Think you can sneak me into the O2?"

Kitt nods. "I'll make sure it's done."

"That would be fabulous."

You are not shagging my dad again.

"Anyway, please enjoy. Texas, we have to catch up soon."

I smile. "Definitely."

Whitney floats away to the next group who've arrived. Jesus, she's so elegant that she doesn't even walk.

"I'm disturbed," I murmur.

Milo's mouth is open.

Kitt kisses my temple. "Sorry, baby, but your dad is a legend!"

"I need a drink."

"I need to work on someone else. I'm not fucking someone your dad's had," Milo says before walking off.

Kitt's eyes follow him, and I'm starting to get suspicious of that. It's like he knows something that the rest of us don't. *What's up with Milo?*

Coop finds a table, and we're offered drinks. Whitney has everything—literally. Cooper spent five minutes listing every alcoholic beverage he could, and they have it all.

"What the..." My jaw hits the table.

Kitt's eyes follow mine. In the centre of the makeshift dance floor are five people dancing with costume deer heads and what I hope are fake daggers.

No, I'm not high.

Seriously, if I were a total bitch and wanted to be ostracised forever, I'd get pics of this and upload them to Facebook. I'm pretty sure Milo is one of the deer. I recognise his arms, but with no tattoos, it's hard to tell.

Kitt laughs. "Hands down, the best party."

Kitt and I have done far too many shots, and I can barely see straight. I don't know how he does it, but he *never* gets as drunk as the rest of us even though he drinks more.

"Where did Coop and Pey go now?" I ask.

They were on the dance floor—with their normal heads—a few minutes ago. I'm supposed to stop her from giving in and sleeping with him again.

Kitt laughs. "They went into one of those rooms upstairs."

"Oh, great. The *one* job I had tonight..."

"That's not the one job you had," he whispers in my ear, dragging his hand along my thigh.

The feel of his skin on mine steals my breath.

Yeah, screw Peyton. If you can't stop yourself from sleeping with someone, then you obviously don't want to resist them.

My phone vibrates on the table, and Kitt sighs. "All night, that's been going off."

I shrug. "It's your fault, rock star."

"Ah, here they are," he says, nodding to a rumpled-looking Peyton and pristine Cooper.

What did he do to her?

He's overjoyed and cocky, and she's frowning because she was supposed to resist.

I get up, grab my phone, and head over to her. "Drink, Pey?"

She glares. "No talking. I want a double."

"Whatever would we talk about anyway?"

"You're not cute when you do that." She links my arm, and I laugh.

My phone vibrates again. I need to look at it, or catching up tomorrow is going to be impossible. Peyton grabs it out of my hand and slips it into her bag.

Okay. "What the hell?"

She frowns. "Well, you're enjoying yourself. No need to check this."

"It's blowing up, Pey. I want to make sure everything's okay."

"Everything is fine," she says far too fast.

Something is wrong. Her pale eyes are shifty, and she can't look directly at me.

"Peyton Esmeralda Best!"

Coop's head flies in her direction. He's sitting with Kitt now at our table. "Your middle name is Esmeralda?"

"Fuck off," she snaps at him. "Enjoy yourself, Tex. Worry about this tomorrow."

Kitt gets up and holds his hand out. With a sigh, she hands it over. My heart is in my throat as I watch him unlock my phone. Peyton is being weird for a reason, and it has Kitt concerned. That means, I'm worried.

What's going on?

"What?" I ask, feeling ice settle in my stomach.

"Fuck's sake!" Kitt spits through gritted teeth. His jaw twitches where he's clenching it so hard.

"Show me," I demand.

Taking a breath, he hands me the phone.

"What the hell is this?" I whisper, shaking my head.

Kitt cups my cheek. "It's not true, baby. I swear to you."

"Yeah, I know that. Why can't people leave us alone?"

"What's going on?" Cooper peers over my shoulder.

"Some girl is claiming she's pregnant with Kitt's baby," I explain. "Apparently, it happened after that concert in February." That explains the weird questions when we left the premiere.

I look at the woman in question and gulp. She looks familiar. Kitt did sleep with her that night. Well, he went home with her, so I assume they didn't drink tea and play Monopoly.

"I know what you're thinking, Texas, so don't go there. I'm *always* careful. No exceptions. Right from the start, Mark warned us what could happen, so I've always checked condoms afterward, too. Her baby isn't mine."

"He's right, Texy," Coop says. "None of us would risk this shit. The woman clearly wants her fifteen minutes."

Kitt's eyes are wild. He's petrified that I won't believe him, but I do. This sort of thing happens too often. I've been through it with Will and my dad, too. Kitt would never risk getting someone pregnant. Dad definitely would've scared them half to death and made sure they knew to be overly cautious.

"Okay." I hand my phone back to Peyton and pull Kitt toward me. "This is no surprise. Some women do this. Next week, I'll be having an affair or something equally ridiculous."

He slides his hands around my back. "So, you're okay? We're okay?"

"We're better than okay. Neither of us can control what people say, but we can control what we believe. I trust you over anyone else, and I don't care what anyone says about all this."

"You mean, your dad?"

"He'll know she's lying, too."

He bends his head and kisses me. He's tense still, and I know it's because he hates things being written about him. He stresses so much, worrying that I'll eventually believe a rumour. I used to care what was written about me, but over time, it has become the norm. People will always have an opinion, and they will always say things to get attention or make themselves feel better. What I won't do is ever lower myself to a point where I believe lying strangers over the people I love and trust.

"Can we get out of here? I want you to myself," he murmurs against my lips.

"Definitely. I have some making up to do, remember?"

He smirks. "As if I'd forget."

40

KITT
WEDNESDAY, JUNE 24
NEW YORK

The last ten days have been hell. Half the world is behind me, and the other half thinks I'm a bastard for denying my child. People who don't know me or the women hell-bent on destroying my life are judging and picking sides.

Lindsay, my publicist, has released a statement, denying that I'm the father, and she's advised me not to mention it at all. She's also made it very clear that I'm not to be questioned on it during interviews or any other appearances. The woman is a legend, and as hard as this is, she's been making it a lot easier.

Texas has been hounded with messages of support, sympathy, or abuse. She is the true innocent person and the only one I give a fuck about. When someone says something about her, I feel like going fucking postal.

I hold her close as we walk out of the airport. Cameras click, and the flashes coming from so many make me wince. Texas looks up, and her eyes are wide. She's scared. There are more people here than what we were exposed to in England.

Ted and Hank pull closer, and Lars steps behind us. We have four other guys here, too, and they closely shadow Enigma, Milo, and Coop.

I'm bumped to the side as security fights to keep the crowd at bay. I clamp my arm around Texas and pull her in front of me.

Her name is being screamed almost as loudly as mine. It would seem that not everyone is here to shout shit though. There's a lot of, "I love you," in there as well.

But it's too much. I'm not naive. I know how things can get, but this is insanity. I step in line with her.

Texas smiles as she wraps her arm around me. She doesn't care what they say. I don't care.

You do care. You care that they're saying shit about the woman you love.

"Kitt, can I have an autograph?"

"Can we get a picture?"

"We love you!"

"You're a disgrace."

"How does it feel to know your boy fucks other women?"

I tighten my grip on Tex. She heard that, but it doesn't show. Her smile never falters as we push our way through the suffocating crowd. Ted's arms come out as a group beside us lunges forward. I'm jolted to the side, and Texas slips through my arm, crashing to the floor.

Fuck.

I taste bitter anger on my tongue as I bend down to get her. Ted is already there, and Tex is pushing herself up. Laughing, she shakes her head.

How can she laugh?

Ted practically elbows everyone else in our way. Mark takes charge of Tex and hauls her into the car. I'm left a few steps behind, feeling like shit. I stumble forward with ice in my stomach. Milo claps my back as I get in the limo.

What the fuck am I going to do?

Closing my eyes, I rub my hand over my face, trying to formulate a plan. It'd be nearly impossible to get everyone to believe that I'm telling the truth and to respect our personal fucking space. I'm public property now.

Texas scoots over and pulls my arm down.

"I'm so sorry, Tex."

"I fell over myself, Kitt. I've fallen over nothing at all plenty of times. That's no one's fault but Dad's and Jennifer's dodgy genes."

Mark looks over but doesn't bite. I can't tell if he's pissed or not. He's always watching, always judging whether I stack up or not. I usually think I do all right, but today, I failed.

I fucking let her fall!

"Kitt, please, don't beat yourself up over this."

Her hand reaches out, and I grip her wrist.

"You're bleeding."

And it's all your fault.

"Oh." She looks down at her grazed palm and winces. "Damn, I didn't even feel it."

"There a first aid box in here, mate?" Ted asks the driver.

"Kitt, there's barely even cut. You look like I've just sliced my head down to the skull."

All I can see is a thin string of red trickling from the graze. The blood sitting in the open skin has already started to clot, and it's not seeped out past a few millimetres, but *I'm* the reason it happened. She's right. It's a small cut that probably doesn't even hurt, but she's my girl, I *love* her, and it kills me that I've caused her to bleed. No one wants to see someone they love even have a headache.

I feel everyone's eyes on me, waiting for a reaction, trying to work out why this is so hard for me. Even Mark is dealing fine, and she's his daughter. But this isn't his fault.

"You're okay?" I ask.

"I'm fine. I've had worse."

That's not the point. This shouldn't have happened at all. It wouldn't have if there weren't so many people.

That fucking lying whore and her rumours.

She's going to ruin your relationship.

She's not. I won't let Tex go.

I've never felt anything so strong as what I feel for her. Texas changed the game for me, and I don't ever want to go back to the person I was before her. She's made me into the person I was always supposed to be. She was made to be mine. We're two halves of a whole, and the thought of living my life without her by my side makes my skin burn in rage. I'm fucking terrified that she'll decide she's enough. She's done this public property thing longer, since birth, but I've changed things for her, too.

Everything about Filthy Sound is hot news right now. We've exploded onto the scene. Last week, Cooper coughing on-screen for a morning show sparked a Twitter meltdown of fucking well-wishing and swooning. I've turned Texas from daughter of a rock star to girlfriend of one, and that is a lot juicer.

"Can we just get to the hotel, please?" I snap as I tug her closer.

Get ahold of yourself.

Texas sighs into my chest and holds out her hand, so Ted can tend to the cut that rips through my heart.

It's a fucking graze, you moron. She. Is. Fine.

We ride the rest of the way in silence. It isn't uncomfortable, but no one feels particularly chatty, not even Cooper.

Thankfully, the hotel is free of any gatherings outside, and we head straight inside and up to our rooms.

I had Texas's rooms cancelled for the rest of the tour, as we'll be sharing. Mark wasn't happy, but Texas is very good at getting around him. Once the door is closed behind us, I finally feel the tension evaporate.

"Are we going to talk about what happened, Kitt? You completely overreacted back there. Accidents happen, especially when I'm not looking where I'm going!"

"We were pushed, Tex. That's why you fell."

"I'd already corrected myself by then. I tripped a second later."

"And you wouldn't have done that if it wasn't for me."

She rolls her pretty hazel eyes that I love so much. "And it wouldn't have happened if I'd taken Milo's offer of a piggyback or been born to different people. Don't be ridiculous, Kitt. I'm supposed to be the mindfuck one, remember?"

I smirk. "Oh, you still are. And you know what fucks me up even more?"

"Go on…"

"These goddamn shorts." I trace the line where leather meets skin.

Laughing, she wraps her arms around my neck. "I don't even like them. I like the effect they have on you."

She smiles, and her eyes sparkle in a flirtatious way that makes my dick harden.

"All of you has that effect on me. It only takes a look. Fuck, waking up and smelling your scent before I even see you makes me rock solid."

Her breathing is thick and heavy, and her eyes gloss over with lust.

Fuck. I pounce.

41

**TEXAS
SATURDAY, JUNE 27
ONTARIO, CANADA**

It's been four days since the incident at the airport. Kitt shouted at a lot of people, and now, he has even more big, burly men with us. The photo of me tripping and making a twat out of myself is all over the web. If I become a meme, I'm going to lose it.

I try to stay positive because, really, there's nothing we can do, and I won't let anyone else dictate a thing in my life, but Kitt isn't okay. I hate the stress lines around his eyes, the permanent clench of his jaw, and the dullness in his eyes. I also stay positive because the way things have exploded is my fault. There wouldn't be half of the problems we'd been having if Kitt wasn't in a relationship.

When Kitt is seen with me, it becomes about our relationship and then about how I'm handling the news. He went to the shows in Tennessee and Illinois alone, and the crowds were mostly about him and the band. I'd stayed at the hotel with Ted.

I'm the trigger, but I can also defuse the bomb.

So, I know what I need to do. But the very idea makes my heart ache so hard that it leaves me breathless. Not only would I be away from Kitt and my dad, but I'd also be pretty much alone. I don't like being alone. I'd do it for him though. I see how crazy worried he is every time I have to go out in public.

He has to leave for sound check in ten minutes, and he's pacing our hotel suite.

"Kitt!"

"I'll have Ted bring someone else along with Lars and Hank for you."

"Kitt!" I snap. "Will you stop?"

He's turned into a version of my dad. And I think he might be worse. He won't let up on anything, and he's obsessed with making sure I'm never hurt again. Seriously, I only tripped and grazed my hand, but he acts like I was knocked unconscious.

"How can I stop? You were hurt!"

"I tripped."

"Because of the crowd, Texas."

Oh my God, we have this argument on repeat.

"There is always a crowd and always will be." I step forward. "Kitt, you have to get past this. My life will never be normal, and I'm fine with that. Why aren't you?"

"Because you were hurt!" he shouts. "You don't know how bad that fucking feels. I wanted to kill every bastard who'd hurt you."

I rub my forehead. No one hurt me, but he's not getting that.

"Kitt, I'm going home."

His head rears back, as if I hit him. "You're fucking, what?"

"Please, hear me out before you turn swear-y."

"You're not running. We have nothing to be ashamed of!"

"I'm not ashamed of you. I believe you when you say you've not done something, Kitt, and I'm on your side. But can you honestly say that you're enjoying the tour right now? Whenever we step outside, you're practically paralysed by fear of something happening to me. You should be living life to the fullest. Filthy Sound is everywhere right now, and that's what you have to focus on. Forget that woman because her lies will come out by her own choice or through DNA. Enjoy this, Kitt. Please, please go back to a few weeks ago when you were having the time of your life."

He steps closer, pressing his forehead to mine. He's determined and a bit pissed off. His eyes are burning a hole in mine. "The time of my life has you in it."

"I'm not going anywhere—well, except to England. But I'll be waiting for you when you get back. You have a month in the States and Canada, and then you're home for a while before Australia. It's not like you don't have time off coming up. This is how it works for a lot of people. Not everyone can drop everything and tour."

"I don't give a fuck how other people do things. I won't have you being chased away because of some fame-hungry bitch."

"She's not chasing me away. I'm choosing to do the best thing for you and the band. We can't be selfish, Kitt. This affects everyone."

He pushes away and stalks back and forth, his chest expanding in long, hard breaths. I hate to see him like this, but I keep myself locked in place, not sure if it's best to leave him when he looks like he's about to go off.

Kitt has never been the best at handling his emotions or even understanding them half of the time.

Soon after we first met, it was the anniversary of his parents' deaths, and he spent the whole night ignoring Milo's and Cooper's pleas to stop drinking and go with one of them to talk. He told everyone he was fine, and he ended up puking on himself outside the club before passing out.

He was supposed to be okay, like he's supposed to be okay now. When he can't control something, he spirals.

He reaches for the mini bar, and I know what's coming next. His coping mechanism has always been to drink. It's effective until it wears off.

"Do you think that will help?"

"Yep," he grinds out through his teeth. The muscles in his arms look like stone as he grabs a tiny bottle of Jack Daniels.

"Stop."

Spinning around, he steps toward me, and his eyes darken. And he erupts. "What the fuck do you want me to do, Texas? I'm *trying*. I'm trying to make things better. I'm trying to be strong for you. I'm trying to give you a fucking normal relationship, but obviously, I can't fucking do it, so just tell me what I'm supposed to do here!"

With my stomach tossing over, I pad closer, keeping my eyes fixed on his. Midnight blue softens, the closer I get, and some of the tension leaves his shoulders.

"Kitt, I love that you're so passionate and that you think from here," I say, placing my hand over his thumping heart. "But, sometimes, you have to think with your head. It will never be as magnificent or soul-searing, but on occasion, it's the only thing to do. You can't always lead with your heart. There has to be balance."

My throat seals closed, and tears prick my eyelids. "I know you, and I know you understand why I have to go home. The more you fight it, the more it hurts us. It's a *month*, and as much as I don't want to be apart from you for a second, you're worth it. You were worth the two-year wait, and you're worth this. I love you so much, and I need you to have the best tour experience you can. If that means I can't be an active part of it, that's okay with me because I know I'll get everything when it's over."

"Tex, babe," he rasps, slamming his chest against mine.

My arm is crushed between us, but I don't care. In his embrace, I feel strong—strong enough to leave for him. He can't do the right thing—he'd never be able to send me home—but I can.

"I know. Our forever will start when you get back."

His head dips. "No, Tex, our forever started in Paris."

Jesus. The things that boy does to me. I'm breathless and apparently struck dumb because I can't think of a single word.

"Cat got your tongue, sweetheart?" His hands trail down my back and over my butt.

My head falls on his shoulder, and I moan.

"Oh, I'll be making you scream in a few minutes. First, I want to make sure…"

I look up and curl my arms around him. "Yes, I'm definitely going home. No, it won't change a single thing between us. You're going to rock these shows the way I know only you can, and you're going to love every second in between. Have fun with your boys, and for the love of God, make sure you don't lose Cooper!"

He laughs and closes his eyes. His shoulders sag with relief. Leaving should hurt, but I know it's not about me.

"You shouldn't have to do that."

"But I will, and nothing will change us. It's fine, Kitt. Our plans will sometimes require…modification."

He presses a soft kiss to my mouth. "What will you do?"

"I'll stay with Jennifer for a little while."

His eyes go wide.

"I know, I know." But I don't like to be alone, and I'm due a visit there. "Just for a week or two, and then I'll go home and wait for you guys to get back."

"You've had it all planned since…"

"Yesterday. I hate that you're so stressed. This is your tour, Kitt, and you should be living it up. The start was so much fun, but it's not now. Is it?"

He opens his mouth and closes it.

"You can't lie to me, and I can't ruin this for you."

"You're not ruining it, Texas."

"You know what I mean."

"I do. I don't want you to go. Maybe we can do something though? Travel without the rest of them, arrive at different times?"

"Kitt, it won't work. The only answer is me going home, and you rocking the tour. When it's over, you'll come home to me, and we'll start our life together, the way we want."

"What does that look like, Tex? Because this right here is what my life is."

"This is your working life. I'm talking about *our* life. Me and you."

His lips part, and he takes a breath. "Are you telling me, you want to move in with me?"

"No. That would be ridiculous. We've not even been together for two months."

He smirks. "Doesn't mean you're not going to do it."

No, it doesn't.

His strong tattooed arms hold me close. "Texas, will you move in with me?"

I nod, and his lips find mine.

42

TEXAS
SATURDAY, JULY 4
NOTTING HILL, ENGLAND

In the grand scheme of things, coming to Jennifer's hasn't been the best choice. She's been acting like she's the perfect mother while being my friend.

Um, hello? Your sexual conquests are *not* a suitable discussion topic to have with your daughter!

I wanted to jab knives into my ears. She didn't stop, not even when I'd turned cold because I was seconds away from puking.

Kitt and Dad have been constantly messaging me since I arrived two days ago. I miss them both so much. I feel like I'm missing a limb, but it's only just bearable.

It helps that I still speak with them all the time. Kitt calls me every night and talks to me until I fall asleep. I'm not sure whom he's doing it for the most, but we both need to fall asleep with each other.

Jennifer is brewing a pot of coffee when I walk into the kitchen. Her hair, makeup, and outfit are flawless, and it's not even eight in the morning yet.

How does she do it? She must get up at six a.m.

"Good morning, Texas," she says, taking another mug from the cupboard for me.

"Morning."

"How are you doing?"

She asks me that every morning and evening. I think she asks because she cares, but I can't make myself believe it. Whenever we talk, I feel like there's an agenda.

Is she only doing it because she feels guilty for not being around? Does she only like me because I don't require feeding, changing, teaching?

"I'm okay. I've not seen much more about the woman's baby, so I think it's dying down."

She gives me a smile. "It always does."

She'd know. When it came out that I was living with Dad and she'd gone back to London, she got a lot of shit for it. People couldn't understand why she'd left me. I still can't even though Dad has explained. I can't say that I'm okay with it, but I don't hate her. I would never call her terrible names, like the way others did.

"Do you think you'll return on tour for the next leg? You love Australia."

"I'm not sure. As much as I hate being away from Dad and Kitt, I kind of want to find out what I'm good at. I don't think I'll do that if I'm forever tucked away in the tour bubble."

Jennifer flashes her perfect teeth in a Hollywood smile and hands me my coffee. "Let's sit in the drawing room, and we can talk through your options."

I don't know why the kitchen isn't good enough for coffee consumption, but apparently, it's not, so I follow her into the next room. It's huge, painted light grey with high ceilings, dark wood floor, stylish vintage seats, and a massive marble fireplace.

There is no TV. It's the only flaw.

She sits opposite me and puts her drink down. I keep hold of mine. There's not much that will get me to pry my fingers off my coffee until it's drained.

"Have you given it much thought?" she asks.

"To?"

"To what you'd like to do. Texas, you're beautiful and intelligent. You can do whatever you want."

"Yeah, no idea."

"Well, would you like to pursue something in the field of your studies?" The distaste drips from her words. She never liked that I studied something so gruesome.

"I'm not sure. I chose that because it interested me, but I don't think I want it to be my career."

"Lovely." She raises her eyebrows. "What about modelling? You have the face and the figure."

I blink. "Um..." My modelling background is limited to a few shoots with Dad over the years. I don't know if I'd have the patience to do what Jennifer does.

"Why not give it a try? There is no harm in having a go. It's the only true way to know if you enjoy something."

"Okay," I reply, not entirely sure how we got here.

She brightens, and her green eyes sparkle. "Fabulous."

Is it?

"I have a shoot at noon and then dinner with friends tonight. I would love it if you accompanied me. You've seen your dad at work a million times over. I'd like to share that with you, too."

I lick my lips. *She would?* I look down and mutter, "Sure."

God, why is this so awkward?

I have no trouble with talking to Dad about almost anything. With Jennifer, I want to keep things to safe small talk.

"Thank you, Texas," she replies, her voice wobbling with emotion.

Shit.

I'm not good with this. My skin is buzzing, signalling for me to get the hell out of here. But I won't let myself. I won't run from my relationship with her, not now that I'm trying the adult thing. No matter how hard it is to connect with her, I'll try. Maybe we'll both get something out of it, or maybe not, but it's worth a try.

Like modelling?

Yeah, I'll see how that one goes.

"It'll be nice to spend some time together," I say.

"I'm so pleased to hear that. I've wanted to show you off and take you to see what I do for years. Perhaps we can go shopping, too, and get you some new clothes."

I look down at my ripped denim shorts and System of a Down T-shirt. "What's wrong with my clothes?"

"Oh, nothing. I've always loved your sense of style, but you don't have a lot here, and I'd like to help you pick out a few things."

That's her way of saying she wants to choose my outfits because she's not happy with what I wear.

I shrug one shoulder. "Sure. I'm just going to try Dad," I say, holding up my phone.

I step out of the room, and the phone rings a few times before I hear Dad's voice.

"Texas, are you okay?"

"Yeah. Are you?"

"It's different," he replies.

"Things calmed down?"

He clears his throat, and that means they have, but he doesn't want to say because that'll be admitting that I was the problem. Dad has never seen me as a problem.

"Things are going well," he replies.

"I'm glad. It's not bad here either. Plus, Jennifer has, like, thirty bodyguards."

He chuckles. "Yes, she does go over the top there. But it allows me to sleep easier, knowing you're well protected."

"Always have been, Dad. Where are you now?"

"About to hit the sack."

"Oh, sorry."

"No, don't go yet. Have you spoken to Kitt?"

My heart stops. "Not yet. Why?"

"No reason. You always assume the worst. He misses you."

"I miss him, too."

"I know, love. Don't tell him I told you, but he has a countdown on his phone."

I laugh and bite my lip. "He does?" God, even from halfway around the world, he still makes me feel like the only person on the planet.

"He would kill me if he knew I'd mentioned it."

"I'm glad you did."

"Me, too. How is Jennifer? Are you enjoying your time with her?" He sounds scared to ask and scared for my reply. It would really hurt him if he thought I hated it here.

I lean against the wall because this is as shocking to me as it will be to him. "Actually, it's okay."

"Wow."

"I know. Not sure how or when it happened, but I feel different being here compared to when I visited before. I'm trying, and so is she. She's taking me to work with her today. Said she'd like to show me what she does, the way I've seen what you do." Nerves are buzzing in my stomach. "I didn't know I had so much hope for a relationship with her."

"Tex," Dad says on a sigh, "of course you do. She's your mum."

I clear my throat. "I'll let you know how it goes."

"Enjoy it. Anyway, I'm sorry to run so soon, but we have an early start. Unless there's something else you need?"

"No, I'm good. Just wanted to say hi. I'll speak to you later, Dad."

"Love you, pumpkin."

If he loved me, he would drop that fucking nickname.

"Love you, too, Dad."

I hang up and immediately fire a text off to Kitt.

How many days now?

His reply comes fast.

I'm going to fucking kill him.

I laugh and squeeze my phone. *God, I miss him.*

Sleep, rock star. I'll speak to you tomorrow…when we're a day closer.

I'm going off you, Tex.

No, you're not. Love you. x

He sends back a single kiss, which makes my heart race. He doesn't need any more than one letter to let me know how he feels.

"Everything all right?" Jennifer asks when I go back into the drawing room.

"Yeah, fine," I reply with a smile. "Dad's good, and so is Kitt."

"Glad to hear it."

I down the last of my coffee. "So, where to first?"

Her smile makes me wish we'd done this sooner. I'm not naive enough to think that one outing together will fix a lifetime of rejection and confusion, but it's a start. I want to understand her.

Kitt lost his mum before he was old enough to even remember her. It puts things into perspective. If Jennifer and I can work out a way to have a relationship deeper than the odd phone call and short visit, then I'm all in.

"Thank you, darling. We'll start with breakfast and shopping. Come, I know the perfect place. You'll love the food."

With hope in my heart, I return her smile.

48

KITT
SATURDAY, JULY 18
DENVER, COLORADO

I'm exhausted. Walking to my hotel room took every last ounce of energy I had left. I feel like we've been doing back-to-back shows for a year. It was always going to be full-on, and we chose for it to be like this, but it's not easy.

I ache in every bone, every joint, and every muscle. My thighs feel like they're bleeding from the inside. Not going to lie, I fucking love it, but it's taking a toll. Thankfully, after the next two shows, we'll have a day off.

That day will be dedicated to Texas.

It's been much harder than I thought. I used to think people were lying when they said they didn't have time to send a text. I thought it was an excuse because they'd had enough. But it's not an excuse. I miss her so much that I'm constantly looking for her. She should be here. I shouldn't have to get in this bed alone.

Chucking back the covers, I strip and get straight in. It's four a.m., so it's eleven a.m. for Texas. I lie down, and immediately, I'm being pulled under. My body sinks into the mattress, and my eyes feel like they're being weighted.

Groaning, I lazily tap the screen, missing her name a few times, and call her.

Come on, pick up.

I jab my free hand into one eye and then the next.

Stay the fuck awake.

Fucking hell, I miss her calls because I'm sleeping. It's almost midday over there.

What's keeping her?

The phone rings again, mocking me. I click it off and growl. This sucks beyond measure. I feel her absence every second. She might as well be living on another planet. I can't even get to her in less than ten hours, if I needed to.

Why would you need to, dick?

Tex isn't the most independent. She's on her own. Jennifer has never been much of a mum. The thought of Tex feeling lonely without anyone to talk to tears me to shreds. Everyone Texas holds dear and can confide in is in America.

Tomorrow, I'll get a snotty text about how I haven't bothered. But she won't directly say it. Oh no, that would be far too easy.

She'll ask what I was up to. *What've you been up to then?* She's not asking what I've been up to, not really. It's a woman's way of saying, *You're in the shit, you prick.*

With a deep sigh I feel right down to my feet, I close my eyes. I can't call again. I don't have the energy to force my eyelids open.

Hard work, I signed up for. I'm not afraid of it, and I never have been, but Tex is hard work on crack.

SUNDAY, JULY 19
PHOENIX, ARIZONA

"So, Kitt, can we talk about Texas?" Vanessa, the host, asks.

Even the sound of her name has my heart thumping.

We're on a talk show before heading to the arena here in Phoenix.

So far, Vanessa has covered pretty safe topics, such as the British accent, our favourite song to work on, and who gets the loudest screams—me. She knows not to broach the pregnant-whore situation. Lindsay and Jodie have taken care of that.

My statement is out there, and that's all the time I'm giving it until I'm required to do something else.

I sit forward, resting my arms on my legs. "Please do."

"She's back in England now? Do you miss her?"

"Yeah, she had a few things to do back home, but I'm hoping she'll be able to join me in Australia."

"What was it like to tell Mark Knight that you were dating his daughter?"

I laugh and sit back. "Terrifying, but it went a lot better than I'd thought. I still have all my body parts."

Cooper snorts. "Debatable."

I shove his arm.

Vanessa adds, "So, he was fine about it?"

"I mean, he didn't do cartwheels around the bus, but he can see how much I love her."

"Aw," Vanessa coos. "She's a lucky girl. And you're a lucky guy!"

Milo laughs. "He hit the jackpot, and he'll spend every day hoping she doesn't realise what she's done."

I roll my eyes. *Don't mention Lexi. It will make you the world's biggest tosser.*

"Cooper, what's the best part of being a rock star?" Vanessa asks, giving him a flirty smile.

I tense and feel Milo's body stiffen beside me.

Fuck. He wouldn't.

His eyes darken. "It's before the watershed, so I'll say the music, Vanessa."

Wow. His filter is on.

But I suppose, after saying fuck not once but four times on live radio, he's learned his lesson. Or he just doesn't want another punch in the gut for being a dick.

She throws her head back and laughs. "Thank you for censoring there, Cooper."

Oh God, he's going to shag her.

Milo chuckles, thinking the same thing.

Vanessa is in her late forties, but you wouldn't be able to tell. She must have a very good plastic surgeon who's stopped her aging at thirty.

Coop won't care that she's more than double his age and could've given birth to him.

If you're honest, you'll admit the pre-Texas you would've had a second look.

"How is touring together? Didn't you do most of Europe in a bus?"

"We did," I say. "It was incredible, but I have no desire to be stuck in close quarters with these idiots for a month again."

Milo scoffs, "He loved it."

"How are you enjoying the States?"

Coop grins and pats his stomach. "The food is amazing."

Vanessa laughs, keeping her eyes on him for a fraction longer than she does with me and Milo. He had better be discreet about this.

What am I saying? He's going to shout it from the rooftops.

"Well, thank you, boys." She turns to the camera and holds up our album cover. "Filthy Sound is at the Gila River Arena tonight at seven thirty p.m., and the album is out now."

We wait until we're told to move.

When they cut to a break, Jodie wanders over. "Thank you, Vanessa."

"You're welcome. It was a pleasure having them on the show."

Cooper's gaze locks on Vanessa, eye-fucking her in front of a roomful of people.

I clear my throat. "Yeah, thanks. We should be going though, right?"

We need to get Cooper out of here before he takes her on the fucking sofa.

Jodie's hand snatches Coop's upper arm. "Absolutely. We can't be late!"

Scowling, Coop lets Jodie pull him off the set.

"Honestly, Jack, I don't know where your head is sometimes. If you must, call her after you've given the performance of a lifetime."

She lets go, and he throws his arm over her shoulder.

"I plan to, Jodie! She's even hotter in the flesh. And I want to see her flesh. And call me Cooper!"

"I bet you're glad you took on a band, right?" Milo says to Jodie.

"Best thing I've ever done," she mutters sarcastically.

Four hours later, Enigma is performing their encore. I watch Mark in awe, still envious of the way he owns the arena and every person in it. Watching him is a privilege. I try to memorise how he does it, but it's not something that can be replicated. It's pure talent that bleeds on the stage every time he stands upon it. We all have our own way of doing things, and I'd never want to be a carbon copy of him, not really. But I can't help wish that I'd gotten there first.

I take my phone out of my pocket and send a message to my girl. She didn't text or try to call me back after my failed attempt last night, and I'm trying not to analyse why.

She's starting to get bored of your lifestyle. It was different when it was her dad. Everything about this is different for her.

Holding my phone in a death grip, I type. My heart is burning with the need to say what I want, but I hold back. Creating an argument isn't going to help us.

Going on soon. I miss you.

While I wait for a reply that might or might not come, I text my nan, too.

About to rock the fuck out of Arizona. Hope you and G are okay.

Milo slaps me on the back. "A watched phone never beeps."

"She's ignoring me."

"She's probably busy. Do you think all Tex is doing is sitting down, waiting for contact? She'll be off with Jennifer, partying, and sleeping with—"

Fucker. I plant my fist in his arm. "You're a dick."

He laughs and rubs the spot where I hit. "Come on, mate, get your head together. We need you focused out there."

My phone buzzes in my hand. "I'm all here, Milo."

I look down and sigh. It's from my nan. She can manage to reply early in the morning over there, but Tex can't.

Watch your language. I can still put you over my knee. We're fine. We love you, and we're so proud. Grandad says rock on or rock hard or something to that effect. Stay safe.

They will always be there. No matter what happens, what I do, how often I manage to get in touch, they will always be at home, and I will always be welcome.

I love you guys.

After I reply, I hand my phone to Jodie.

Blowing out a breath, I close my eyes to regroup. When the band started getting recognised, I made a promise to myself and the band. We will never let the fans down. As heavily twisted up I am over Texas and our dwindling relationship, I have to do this.

No one will ever leave saying our performance was shit. No one will ever want their money back.

I rock back and forth on my feet as the crowd counts down from ten. Adrenaline pumps through my body, replacing blood, thought, and breath. I survive on the buzz, the performance, and the crowd alone.

Nodding as I'm handed my mic, I walk ahead of Milo and Cooper and raise my hand in the air. The first wave of screams shakes the arena as we make our appearance.

"Are you fucking ready, Arizona?" I shout.

The second wave is louder, always louder. I laugh and face the crowd. It's packed to the rafters, every seat is taken, and every inch of space is inhabited. Flashes from cameras and stripes of colour from glow sticks attack my eyes.

"You can do better than that!" Cooper shouts. "Ladies, shirts up. Gentlemen…what the hell? Go for it!"

He lifts his shirt, too, and at least three women in the front row faint.

He's such an exhibitionist.

"Milo," I say, "'Quick'!"

It's the title of one of our most popular songs, and the crowd goes fucking wild.

This is my first love. Always will be.

44

TEXAS
MONDAY, JULY 20
NOTTING HILL, ENGLAND

It's been eight days since I've spoken to Kitt. I know what life is like on the road, so I know he's flat-out busy, but I'm still pissed off. Our talk-until-we-fall-asleep pact has been forgotten. Logically, I know better, but I feel like I've been forgotten.

We keep missing each other, and it's not getting any easier.

I press Cancel after another failed call and grit my teeth.

You're the one who left him and told him to live it up. You can't be surprised that he is.

Kitt means the world to me, and I want this experience to be epic for him, but I don't know how to keep our relationship solid when we never talk.

It's terrifying.

I understand I've been foolish and centred so much around him, but I can't change that. For the longest time, Kitt has been the grand ultimate prize, and he's not something I want to lose.

But how would we cope if things fell apart like this every time he was away?

I can give him space to do his thing, but I can't have radio silence, like we don't exist. There is no time off our relationship. No matter how much I love him, we're full-time or nothing at all. He has to make the effort to call at least every two days.

"Texas, darling," Mother drawls, "are you ready?"

I sigh and rub my forehead.

I actually enjoyed watching her last shoot; it was enlightening. There's much more to it than sitting still and looking pretty. So, I agreed to go again today, but after my failed attempt to get ahold of Kitt, I'm not feeling all that up to leaving the house. Human contact will not be good for me today.

"Sure," I reply, rolling over just as she comes into my room.

"Oh, Texas," she says, staring at me like I'm a hobo.

"What? Do I look that bad?" I look in the mirror. *Yes, I do look that bad.*

"We have to leave in ten minutes," Jennifer says. "Sit down. I'll do your hair and makeup."

She's going to make you into a mini her.

At least she knows what she wants and goes after it. I can't even get my fucking boyfriend to have a conversation with me. Perhaps a mini Jennifer is exactly what I need to be for a while.

I get up, pad over the thick pile carpet to my vanity table, and sit down on the romantic, chic stool. Not only do I not look good, I also don't look like me. Gone is the colour in my cheeks and the light from my eyes. I look lost and kind of like a scared child.

You weren't brought up to pin everything on a man!

Enough. Enough now.

Swallowing shame and uncertainty, I straighten my back. "What are you going to do with my hair then, Mum?"

"A few more curls. Your hair is naturally very beautiful, as is your face. We're just going to hide those sad eyes."

I tear my eyes away from her reflection. *Shit, it's obvious?*

"Don't be embarrassed, Texas. You love him, and you're allowed to be upset if things aren't happening the way you hoped."

"I just wish he'd call." I need to hear his voice. "But if you see me wallowing again, please slap me across the head. Get me looking human, and let's do this shoot."

She smiles and captures my long hair in her hands. "You want to try?"

I shrug. "Think I'll be allowed?"

"Do I think the photographer will want a mother-daughter shoot with Jennifer Star and Texas Knight?"

Laughing, I pick up a hairbrush and hand it to her over my shoulder.

She takes it and slowly drags it through my hair. "I've missed this over the years, haven't I?"

It would've been nice. Dad picked up the slack on that one, too. It's probably why I don't bother much with it. He's a brush-it-or-tie-it-up kind of man. There is no in between, no fancy updos.

She effortlessly curls my hair so fast that her arms look like she's doing the Macarena. It's stylishly messy and looks so good that I can't believe it's my hair. Some of it is up, and a few strands hang down, making it look like it's just been thrown together. It's the hair I hate on when I see it in a magazine because I could never get it to look right.

"Turn around, please," she says. She kneels in front of me. Twisting the mascara brush, she gently slicks some on my lashes. "Just a little lipstick, and you'll be done. I envy your looks, Texas. You always look so flawless."

I choke on the irony. "You've been voted Sexiest Woman of the Year twice, and you envy me for looking like I never try?" *Is she for real?*

Jennifer never has a hair out of place. Everything about her is symmetrical and painfully perfect.

"My looks take work, Texas. You're ready."

She stands up and smiles. I dip my head. We've turned into mother and daughter.

How the hell did that happen? The normalcy of it almost makes me feel uncomfortable.

"Yep, let's go."

My phone buzzes in my pocket.

"I'll get my shoes on. You deal with that," she says, nodding to my phone.

Heading to Vegas. Wish you were here.

Short and sweet. In the beginning, I'd get essays from him and reply with a full-length book. Now, we boil everything down to the least amount of characters we can get away with as we update each other on our single lives.

Heading to Jennifer's shoot. Hopefully speak later.

Tears spark behind my eyes. I don't remember the last time we said, *I love you.*

"Texas, we need to leave, darling!" Jennifer shouts from downstairs.

Wiping my cheeks with the back of my hand, I'm grateful that Jennifer didn't try to put foundation on my face and that she used waterproof mascara.

The driver takes us into Chelsea where Jennifer's shoot is. Houses around here are disgustingly expensive for the amount of space you get, but it's one of *the* places to be.

Ted is invading my personal space as we walk into the studio. "This will be interesting," he mutters.

"You'll love it, Teddy."

He gives me a look. "Just behave yourself today. I'm tired, so don't give me a lot to do."

"Oh, yeah? Good night, was it?"

"You're not cute. Go watch the modelling thing. I'll be here if you need me." He stops at the door and leans against the wall.

This really isn't his thing at all.

"Texas, this is Derek Woods," Jennifer says.

I know Derek. He's worked with Dad and Enigma a couple of times. He's one of the most sought after photographers in the UK, so of course, Jennifer's shoot is with him.

"Texas, last time I saw you was...oh, a good five years ago. You're beautiful, darling," he says. He air-kisses both cheeks.

I awkwardly make a kissing sound and smile. "Yeah, it was a while."

Okay, I can't do small talk.

"So, Jen-Jen, can we have you sitting front-to-back on the chair over there? Clara will come and get your top once it's off."

"This is a topless shoot?" I ask, my eyes widening in pure horror. *Why would she bring me to this one?*

In the corner, Ted chuckles.

"Nothing will be on show," Jennifer says, putting her hand on my arm in comfort. "All that will be visible is my back."

I laugh nervously. "Okay."

Derek's work is always very tasteful and classy, so I hope this will be no different. I'm not a prude, but I don't really want to see my mother's assets. I didn't even see them when I was an infant.

Jennifer changes into the leather trousers she was given and keeps her top on until she's over at the chair. There is no hesitation. She tugs her top off and hands it to Clara. Hair and makeup people descend upon her, so she sits perfectly still and closes her eyes. She's a natural.

No one is eyeing her up. They're all here for a job, and she's treated with the utmost respect. I stand behind the camera with Derek as he doles out instructions to *Jen-Jen*. Her eyes are alight when she's in front of the camera and not just because of the crazy amount of molten-hot lights beaming in her face.

Maybe I genuinely do want to try it.

"Beautiful!" Derek compliments. "You're perfect, darling. Head a little to the left. That's it! Hold it there."

Jennifer's neck is craned around for her to look back at the camera. If it's uncomfortable, she's not showing it.

"Okay, take five. Can someone bring me the Armani? Jen-Jen, you will love this dress. I'll need you over by the fireplace."

The set is reworked, so the lighting is perfect, and everything is in place for round two.

My feet start to ache.

"Great! We're done," he says after no less than seven bloody thousand clicks of his camera.

Okay, maybe less, but it felt like thousands. Jennifer has been photographed in a number of different outfits and poses.

"Oh, Derek, a couple with my daughter?" Jennifer asks. "Isn't she beautiful?"

"Judy, get her ready!" He clicks his fingers, and Judy appears.

I'm whisked away before I have time to speak, and then I'm shoved in a chair.

All right, looks like I'm really giving this a go now.

Whatever. You can't deny that you want to. You're intrigued, and after witnessing it, you know it's not seedy.

While I'm being pulled about, I can see some of Jennifer's photos on the monitor. They're all stunning. A lady, who I assume is from *Vogue*, as it's their shoot, is pointing to different images with Jennifer.

I'm a little nervous. I don't want her to look at mine. I'm no model.

"What's Texas wearing?" Judy asks.

Derek comes over and kneels beside me. "I've spoken to Jen-Jen, and she agrees that it would be perfect to get you in the same pose. Mother in leather trousers, daughter in leather shorts." He's animated as he talks.

With the Band

I feel hysteria rushing up my throat.

He wants you to go topless.

"I'm sorry. You want me to take my top off in front of everyone?" I splutter.

"Derek, let me," Jennifer says, floating over to us. "Darling, you saw my shoot. No one will be looking at you with anything but professionalism. It's discreet. This is *your* decision, Texas, but make sure you're making it because it's what you want and not out of fear."

A rather large part of me wants Ted to step in. He knows exactly what Dad would say—or shout—but the side of me just starting to emerge wants full control over every decision. Jennifer is right. This is not up to anyone but me. I'm an adult, and I can make my choices.

With my heart trying to shove its way through my chest cavity, I nod. "I want it to be done like my mum's. I don't want anyone to *see*."

Derek's toothy smile is triumphant, but he respectfully raises his hands. "Absolutely, Texas. We'll do this however you like. If you're uncomfortable at any point, please speak up."

"I will!"

Oh my God, what are you about to do?

"Why don't you get seated the way Jen-Jen did? And we'll set up. I'll let you know when to remove your top. Clara will be there to take it once you're covered by the back of the chair. Does that sound okay?"

Swallowing sand, I nod again.

Jennifer takes me over to the chair. She looks pleased but not smug, like I assumed she would be. "If you want that top back on or everyone but Derek to leave, you say. Derek might be the one running this show, but you are in charge."

"Okay," I reply. I step over the chair so I'm facing the back, putting my legs either side, and sit down.

"Are you sure?" she asks.

"I'm sure, Mum."

With a genuine smile that makes my heart further thaw toward her, she backs away, murmuring, "I'm proud of you for taking charge, Texas." She's not talking about the shoot. She's talking about my life.

You can do this. Reach down, and take it off.

I grip the bottom of my top and bring it over my head. Clara takes it along with my bra and backs off. Sitting half-naked, the wrong way around on a chair, in a roomful of people should make me self-conscious, but it doesn't. I feel strong. The surge of self-assurance makes my heart speed up. I sit straighter, letting my spine stretch out.

You can do this.

The lights are adjusted, and my back heats. My hair is played with, and my face is powdered...and whatever else they're slapping on.

"Are you ready, Texas?" Derek asks as my hair and makeup ladies retreat.

I look over my shoulder and hold my head up. "I'm ready."

I risk a glance at Ted. Surprisingly, he looks proud and also a little awkward.

"That's it. Hold your head there and smile. Lovely. Now, tilt your head down. Okay, slightly arch your back, put your hands behind you, and twist to the left."

I know I've got side-boob action going on, but I don't care. I follow Derek's instructions and pose how he's asked.

You like this. You fucking like it!

"Beautiful! Tip your head back and to the right—there! Hold that. Perfect. Stunning, Texas."

I want to hire him to follow me around and give me compliments all day because the man is amazing for self-esteem.

He lowers his camera. "Well, that was incredible. Would you like to dress and have a couple taken with your mum?"

The lady from *Vogue* gasps. "That would be wonderful! Jennifer?"

Mum smiles. "A mother-daughter article?"

She looks at me for my permission, and I shrug in a yes.

"Let's do it. Where do you want us, Derek?"

Once we're finished, we look back over the photos. They're amazing. Really amazing. I love them all so much. The ones of me and mum are awesome. We did a few serious and some funny ones where we're pulling faces. The individual ones has the *Vogue* lady—seriously no one has said her name and too long has passed for me to ask her—squealing and calling her boss. I end up answering a few questions, so we can do a joint interview.

I'm not even thinking about Dad's reaction because I'm on a high.

We get in the car, and Jennifer tells the driver to go to a cocktail bar because we're celebrating. I finally feel like I'm becoming *me*, and I won't give that up. It feels too good.

45

KITT
TUESDAY, JULY 28
DALLAS, TEXAS

I'm so ready for a break. I've loved every second of the tour so far—almost—but every bone in my body aches, and my heart is in shreds. I need to get back to my girl. The two weeks we have off before Australia and New Zealand have never been more welcomed.

I can't wait to get back out there and show our waiting fans what we've got, but we all need some R&R first. We'd burn out otherwise.

From now on, we'll be spreading tours out because I need more time with Texas. We're like passing ships in the night. The odd text here and there is all we've managed.

She's angry with me. So am I.

You're also angry with her.

Tex has more free time than I do, but she still only manages to text me in the morning or last thing at night. It's not all her fault, but we both need and deserve more.

We've been apart for six weeks, and it doesn't work. I can't do long distance with her. She's the other half of my fucking soul. What I'm feeling, I know she is, too. I can't walk around, feeling like I'm constantly lost, any longer.

So, as soon as we hit home turf, I'm demanding she gives us another chance. Not that she's told me we're over, but I know that's what's in her heart. I feel it in every text message. I hear it in her tone the few times she's left a voice mail. There's nothing emotional about any part of us, and I don't know why.

How can a month change something so permanent?

It's fixable. I know that. We need to get back on the same page and find a way of making time for each other. Neither of us has done long distance before, so this is a learning curve and a steep one. Now, we know what not to do.

It's now Tuesday, and we're flying home on Thursday. Tomorrow is the last show here in America.

I tap Tex's number and hold my breath.

"Hello?" she says on the fifth ring.

I close my eyes, and my dick hardens. "Hey, babe. Fuck, it's good to hear your voice."

"Yours, too. How's it going?"

"Last one tomorrow, and then I'll be home to you. I've missed you so much."

"Missed you, too." Her voice is shallow and lacking anything that makes me believe her words.

"Tex, are you okay?"

"Mmhmm."

I suck in a breath. "You're done, aren't you?"

Why the fuck did you say that? There's nothing you can do until you're back, so why are you goading her to say it? Three days, and you'll be in front of her and be able to fix whatever's wrong. You didn't have to make it fucking official!

"Kitt..."

"No, fuck, come on." I pace my room and grab the whiskey off the side table as I go. "I know things have been hard, and I've not called nearly as much as I wanted, but, Jesus, Texas, give it a bit more time. It's like you don't even want to make it work. Don't give up on us. I'll be back soon, and we'll sort this out."

I hear her breathless sobs down the other end, and it catapults me into darkness.

"Texas," I rasp, "tell me it's not over. Now."

"I-I can't. I don't know. Everything has changed. You'll see, Kitt. I can't do this."

"What does that mean? Why can't you? Fuck me. You're the one who started this. You don't just get to end it!" My chest is working overtime. I clench the phone so tight that the muscles in my hand burn. *Why did I start this conversation?*

"Stop! Just please finish the shows, and enjoy it. We can talk when you get back."

I laugh. "Are you joking? You expect me to leave it there?"

"You don't have a choice. Things are...crazy for me at the moment. I need to work stuff out. I can't do this right now."

The phone goes dead, and my heart follows. I drop it on the floor and launch the bottle of whiskey at the wall. "Fuck!"

What the hell is going on with her?

Something is wrong here.

Someone knocks on my door. Milo probably since his room is the one I just threw glass at. I stalk over and wrench the door open, breathing heavily. It's him.

"Shit," Milo says. "What happened?"

I turn on my heel and walk back. *Calm down. Get ahold of yourself.*

"We're over. She ended it," I mutter, staring off into space.

"What? She said that?"

"Just now on the phone. Apparently, she *can't*. And I pushed her to it."

"Mate, I knew you were finding it hard to stay in touch, but I didn't know it was this bad."

I can see it in his eyes that he's finally sure he and Lexi did the right thing in going separate ways before the band took off.

"I'm sorry." He sits down. "What do you need?"

"I need her. Tex is it for me." I lean down and put my head in my hands. "I don't know what to do. I'm thousands of miles away, and I can't do a fucking thing for three days."

I don't want to be split up for a second.

"Do you want me to talk to her?" he offers.

"It won't do any good. But thanks. I doubt she'll answer the phone to anyone now. She's everything. I love her. And now, I've got to figure out how to make it up to her. Tex might have ended our relationship, but I was the one who let it take a backseat to my career."

"You didn't have a choice, man. She had to leave. It was getting dangerous. Tell her she's not second. Make her believe you."

I tilt my head his way and lift my eyebrow. "I will, but...tips on how?"

"Er, no, but..."

"Yeah. Exactly. I'll never make this mistake again. Making her see she's first might prove difficult since difficult is practically her middle name, but I'll do it."

Sometimes, she makes getting into MI5 look like a picnic.

You'll be fine. It's not over. You both know that.

"Think she'll talk to you again if you try calling?" He smirks because he knows what she's like, and he knows how much of a hard time I'm going to have.

I've never been scared off by a bit of hard work before though. And nothing is more worth it than her.

"She has to. I'm not willing to give up on us. We have to work it out." Being apart isn't an option. "I want everything with her.

When we get back, she's moving in with me." She said she was, and I'm not prepared to deviate from the plan.

"That's going to be hard."

"It's not hard work when you're with someone you love."

Milo laughs, like I'm a clueless fool. When it comes to Tex, that's how I feel most of the time.

"Can I be there when you tell her to pack her bags?" Milo asks, smirking.

"Fuck off." I laugh.

THURSDAY, JULY 30
HOUSTON, TEXAS

I scroll through Facebook to have something to do. Texas has not answered or replied to my messages, and it's driving me insane. I can't concentrate on anything but figuring out what's going through her head, which is impossible since she doesn't seem to know half the time.

Don't obsessively look at Tex's profile. It will drive you crazy.

But I don't have to stalk her because she's everywhere.

My jaw hits the floor, and my heart sinks. A photo of her from the side, looking over her shoulder, kicks me in the gut. She's topless. You can't see much because of the angle, but she has no top on.

I read the headline.

TEXAS KNIGHT'S SEXY NEW PHOTO SHOOT

What the fuck?

I click the link and only realise I'm not breathing as my lungs burn, and black dots dance in front of my face.

"What did you do?" I mumble.

There's an interview with Tex and Jennifer. I almost don't want to read it. I flick down and look at the photos first. She looks different and not just because they would've applied all sorts of shit to her face that she doesn't need.

Texas is older here. She's in charge, matured, stronger.
Shit, she's a fucking natural in front of the camera.

Her posture in each one is self-assured and flirty. It's like looking at Jennifer, only Texas's beauty is on another scale entirely.

But she has no top on.

I follow the soft line of the side of her breast with my finger. She is perfect. *But why is she on show for everyone?* I close down the Internet browser and tap her name.

What the hell has happened to her since she's been at Jennifer's? A week or two was her limit before, and then she was supposed to go home. *What's Jennifer done?*

46

TEXAS
THURSDAY, JULY 30
NOTTING HILL, ENGLAND

The article with *those* photos has been released today. My stomach is rolling, making it impossible to eat. I don't regret doing it because I finally feel like an adult in charge, but I am worried about what Dad and Kitt will say.

Kitt. Damn.

I've tried so hard to forget about him. I won't let my mind drift there because, when it does, there is only paralysing fear and pain. One minute, I think I've made the biggest mistake of my life, and the next, I think it's for the best.

All I really know is, I miss him so much that I feel…wrong. Everything is dull. Everything that used to make me excited does nothing. Life has lost its colour, and all I want to do is lounge in bed or on the sofa. It's all too much effort.

Peyton is in town for a few days, doing some promo shit for the series since the second season is being aired in the UK soon. She's sitting opposite me in the eye-watering expensive restaurant. We've come for afternoon tea, but so far, I've only managed a couple of bites of the tiny, tiny cakes. She scans the magazine article with her mouth open wide. It's not the best sign.

"I don't know what to say, Tex."

"*Try*. My dad is going to flip, and I need to know what to say to him."

"Your dad doesn't get to make your decisions, Tex."

"I know that. Fuck, I proved that when I took my top off, but he's going to be disappointed in me. Again." The first time was bad enough, but he took that surprisingly well. This is different. This is me baring skin for the whole world to see.

"Maybe, but you can't live your life based around what your dad will or will not like. Tex, he might not like it, but it's not his decision, and you're going to have to deal with the fallout, if there is one. He won't stop loving you, so don't stress."

"See? I know you're right. Logic and all that, but you can see my side boob, Pey."

She laughs and wiggles her eyebrows. "Oh, I can see that! Don't worry. You have nice side boob."

"Not really what I meant."

"Drink your coffee. It'll calm you down. You and Mark will be fine. You always are."

Yeah, things do make more sense when I've had caffeine. Perhaps not naked things, but it's done now. Dad will have his tantrum, if he needs to, and we'll move on. I'm *not* looking forward to that conversation though.

It can't be worse than when he showed you the tampon.

No, nothing can ever be as bad as that.

"So…modelling?" She picks up a miniscule slab of coffee cake and takes a bite.

"Yeah. That one crept up on me. Mum asked if I wanted to try, so I figured, *Why not?*"

"Will you do it again?"

I shrug. "She's been asked if I have an agent, so she's been all over that. I have her as a guide, so I think I will. I felt different when I was doing it. I like that."

"Wow. Never thought I'd hear you call Jennifer Star your guide."

"Neither did I. This is what she's good at though."

"She's awesome at it. Are you ready for a modelling career? Didn't you come home to get away from the crazy?"

I top off my coffee mug and stare at her. "No. I don't care about that. People have always been super interested in me and Dad. I'm used to the attention. I'll admit, it's extra insane since..." *Kitt. His name is Kitt.* A name attached to about a hundred missed calls and dozens of unanswered texts. "But I left because he couldn't enjoy it."

"Right. And you ended it because you're scared that he's had enough, and you wanted to get there first."

"Bitch," I mutter. "He doesn't have time for me, Pey."

"Bullshit. You didn't talk about not having time. You didn't try to figure out a way to keep in touch that would work for you both. You ran, Tex. I'm not judging, and I'm *always* on your side. But what kind of friend would I be if I didn't call you up on your idiocy?"

"A better one."

She rolls her icy-blue eyes. "You don't believe that."

"Moving on...please?" *Because I can't talk about this anymore.* The ache in my heart grows daily, and it's sucking the life out of me.

"Fine. I know when you're done with a conversation. Let's get out of here and spend some time with Mummy Dearest."

I cut her a look. "She's trying, and so am I."

"Didn't say it was bad. Plus, the woman always has champagne on ice!"

I honestly think Jennifer lives on it. She chugs it down like it's water.

FRIDAY, JULY 31
NOTTING HILL, ENGLAND

I wake up to my phone blowing up. And I wish that was literal. I decided that the mature, rational adult thing to do about this topless, side-boob incident was to ignore it. So, I've been screening Kitt's and Dad's calls. Even Will, Jimmy, and Milo have tried to get in touch. Cooper just sent me a picture of himself with my photo. He looked so happy.

The ringing cuts off, and I sag in relief. Of course I know I can't put it off forever, and they're due home from the States *tomorrow*, but I'm a massive baby.

I throw my luxurious duck-feather quilt off and get out of bed. Jennifer buys the best of everything because she wants people to know she has the best of everything. The quilt is comfy as hell but creepy as fuck.

Arching my back, I stretch out the kinks, and my bloody phone starts up again. On a sigh, I pick it up. Kitt's name flashes across the screen. I gulp, and my hands start to shake. I'm going to answer and hear his voice for the first time since we broke up.

You can do it.

"Hello?" I say, trying to keep the pain from my voice.

"Are you okay, Tex?" He's breathless, worried.

"I'm fine, Kitt."

"*Vogue?*"

"You read *Vogue?*"

"Internet, Texas," he replies dryly. "Your pictures are *everywhere*. I read the article from there."

"Oh." *Fucking Internet.* "Yeah, well, I was watching Jennifer's shoot, and she wanted a couple with me. Turns out, they liked our pictures." *I like our pictures.*

"Right." He clears his throat. "Was it also her idea for you to take off your top?"

"Don't blame her, Kitt. It was my choice. Mine."

"I don't get it."

"Choice—as in, choosing from one or more options."

"I know what it fucking means!" he snaps. "What the hell are you doing? You shouldn't have left. I knew something like this was going to happen. Well, not like this because I never thought you'd do something like that!"

My hands shake for a different reason. "Excuse me? What do you mean by, *something like that?* Like what exactly?"

"Oh, come on, you have to admit, this isn't you!"

"Actually, I think you'll find it is me. I've changed, Kitt, grown up. I make my decisions, and I don't have to justify them to anyone. In fact, put my dad on while I'm at it."

Oh God, what are you doing?

Who knew I had so much conviction in my actions, and...well, balls?

"Texas..." His voice changes. He's no longer angry. I'm sure he is, but he's not showing it. "Look, I'm worried, babe. You break up with—" He can't say it, and that kills me. "You go home, and now, you're doing topless shoots. I don't get it."

"I went with Jennifer to her shoots, and on the second one, she asked if I'd like to have a go. I did, and you know what? I liked it. It was my decision to take my top off. She told me if I said the word, she'd get me out of there. I wasn't forced."

"No one made you?"

"No. I've been working some things out while I've been here. Jennifer and I are in a good place. I've been doing a lot more for myself even though I'm still staying with her. I've realised what I like, what I want to pursue."

"Modelling?"

"Yeah. I've been asked to do more. Jennifer is speaking to...people. I don't know. I'm good at it."

He chuckles low in his throat, and it's like music. My God, I have missed that.

"Yes, you are good at it."

"You like the photos?"

"I love the photos."

I can feel my heart melting. I was supposed to stay strong, not let him back in.

Who are you kidding? You never managed to get him out.

"Is my dad mad?"

"He's been very quiet."

"Shit."

Kitt laughs. "Yeah, I think so."

"Texas?" Dad's voice in the background makes me cringe. He's going to want to talk to me.

I take a deep breath and then another. This will probably go a lot better over the phone.

"Er, yeah, she's here," Kitt replies to Dad.

"Does he want to talk to me?" I ask.

"Texas, are you okay?" Dad asks. He must have snatched the phone from Kitt.

"Hey, Dad. I'm doing great. Looking forward to seeing you tomorrow."

Silence stretches for long seconds, and he finally clears his throat. "I don't know what to say, Texas."

"Nothing. You don't have to say a thing. I'm happy, Dad."

"We'll talk about this tomorrow. I'll come to Jennifer's. There are things I need to discuss with her, too."

That sounds like fun. Not.

"All right, we'll be home."

"Home?" he repeats in a low voice.

My heart takes a nosedive. "Not *home*, home. Her home."

"See you tomorrow, love."

He hangs up, and apparently, I'm done talking to Kitt as well.

You are definitely done talking for one day.

47

TEXAS
SATURDAY, AUGUST 1
NOTTING HILL, ENGLAND

Jennifer is throwing me a party—a party for taking my top off in front of a camera—and I finally see why she handed me over to Dad. I mean, I appreciate it and all, and it's thanks to her that I've found something I love doing, but it's a bit weird since she's my *mum*.

Peyton and her mum are still back in England, so her support right now has never been so appreciated. Dad will be coming here. He wants to speak to Jennifer, and I don't think it's going to be for a general catch-up.

Jennifer has a full set of serving staff on hand and three chefs. *Three.* For thirty people! I made her keep it small because I don't want a party, but the staff is overkill.

Whatever happened to ordering in pizza and everyone helping themselves to drinks?

Heaven forbid a guest of hers has to pour liquid in a glass. Can't have that now.

But this is how she does things, so I can deal.

Peyton is sitting on my bed, swirling neat Jack Daniel's around in a tumbler, and I've been watching her be off in her own world for the last ten minutes.

"So...what's wrong with you?" I ask. She goes to shake her head, but I add, "And don't tell me you're fine."

"Ugh. I guess it's being back home. I miss it. I miss people who are real and genuine. Maybe it's just me, but everyone in that industry seems to be out for themselves."

"I thought you made good friends with a couple of your costars?"

"I have, and they're both great, but one has been killed off, so I rarely see her, and Marissa's dating this new guy, so she's been busy."

"You don't want to date anyone?"

She shrugs and then takes a huge gulp of whiskey, scrunching her nose up as it burns. "I'm open to it, but I've not met anyone that I want to take things further with. It's not about having a boyfriend though. I just want strong relationships, like I had here."

"*Have*, bitch. I'm not going anywhere."

Laughing, she blows me a kiss. "I know you're not. Wish you lived in LA."

Me, too.

"Are you planning on staying there after the next season is wrapped up?"

"No, we'll definitely move back. But that's eight months away."

"Eight months isn't long."

"It's not. I'm being stupid."

"You're not. Hey, maybe I can come out there for a few weeks here and there. We could hang out when you're off, and I could celebrity-stalk while you film. Win-win."

"Make it happen! Now, let's go downstairs. We're being rude."

"You're only saying that because you're out of JD."

"And you finished your wine. I want some of that now, so move it, Tex!"

Downstairs is buzzing with activity. Everyone is chatting and laughing. Soft music is playing in the background. Classy fairy lights make gorgeous decoration to Jennifer's stunning house. It couldn't be more different from the after-parties I went to with Kitt, Milo, and Coop. This party isn't me, but the people here wouldn't like rock, shots, and dirty dancing.

Dirty dancing in a cage.

I tug the collar of my top.

"Rosè, Tex?"

"Please," I reply to Peyton.

It'd better be ice cold because I'm feeling hot. I miss the way Kitt makes me feel and the things he does to me. I miss everything.

Don't think about it. You. Are. Fine.

"Texas! There you are. Derek is here, and he has some exiting news!"

"They want me?"

She squeals. "You're going to be the face of Whitney Blake's clothing line! She loves your look."

"That's amazing!" I wonder if Mum knows that Whitney slept with Dad.

"Tex, that's awesome. We need to celebrate again!" Peyton hands me my wine. "To my supermodel best friend."

I nudge her arm. "Thanks, loser."

Jennifer laughs. "I'm very proud of you."

I kind of am, too. Soon, I'll be earning my own money. When I buy something, I'll know it's because of me. I never understood how good that felt before. I raise my glass with Jennifer and Peyton.

An hour later, the party is in full swing. There's about twenty more people than I expected, but I don't care.

Jennifer is tipsy and telling everyone who will listen—which is everyone since they seem to want to please her—about how proud she is and how well I'm already doing in the industry. It's a little embarrassing, yes, but this has never happened before. The parental pride has always come from dad. I like this from Mum.

There, I admitted it. I like it when my mum's proud, and I want a relationship with her. Dad has always been enough, but having them both is indescribable.

Peyton slaps my arm, takes my wine glass, and nods to the door. My eyes widen when I see Dad strolling inside, followed by Kitt.

Dad's eyes settle on me, and he points to the door. "I think you should get in the car now, Texas. We're leaving."

My face falls.

Jennifer stands forward, between me and Dad. "What the hell do you think you're doing, Mark?" she hushes sharply.

"What the hell am I doing? What the hell are *you* doing? She's a teenager, and you're her fucking mother! What were you thinking?"

I catch a glimpse of Jennifer rolling her eyes. "Oh, calm down. You're making a much bigger deal out of this. It's just skin."

"Our *daughter's* skin," he spits through gritted teeth. "How could you allow it to happen?"

"Texas is her own person, Mark. When are you going to wake up and realise she's not a child anymore?"

"Oh, so the passage to adulthood is exposing yourself to every fucker who wants to look?"

I flinch. *That's not how it was.*

"You're so close-minded," Jennifer says. "It's not seedy. She can make her own decisions, and she decided to take part in a *classy* photo shoot. The pictures are extremely tasteful, and this will do wonders for her career."

"Enough," I snap. "I think we should all calm down for a second."

"That isn't a fucking career *my daughter* is going to have!" Dad roars.

I step back and silently clap my hands together. "We're not calming down then," I mutter.

With the Band

Kitt is the only one who notices me, and his eyes tighten. He has about as much right to a say in my life as my father does.

How dare they barge in here and cause a scene. I fist my hands. "I said, enough!" I shout at the top of my lungs.

Three pairs of shocked eyes watch me, and I'm sure there are many more, but everyone else is behind me.

"Seriously, stop it. I can do whatever I want, and I don't need anyone's permission. And I certainly don't need to be told how to live my life."

"I beg to differ," Dad growls. "You've been flaunting your body, Texas. And I don't give a fuck about what people choose to do with their bodies, Jennifer, before you go on about that shit, but our daughter grew up not wanting to show off hers."

"I think you're missing the point, Mark. *She grew up*," Jennifer says, narrowing her eyes until they're tiny slits. "She isn't your little girl anymore. *Our* daughter is *nineteen*. She is an adult whether you like it or not."

Dad doesn't like that. His jaw twitches as he grinds his teeth together. It's always just been us. He's protected me from everything, even my mum. I step forward, not able to bear how hard it is for him. I'm the only child he's ever going to have. He pretty much raised me single-handedly while fighting to be the best musician he could be, giving us both a great life.

"Dad, I love you, and I love how you brought me up, but..."

"Yeah," he rasps as he wraps me in a big bear hug. He's shaking, and the desperation in his embrace breaks my heart. "I get it, Texas. I keep screwing up, don't I?"

"You're not screwing up. But you *have* to take a step back. Even if you don't agree with my choices, you have to accept them. Just like I have to accept that you slept with my new boss!"

Jennifer ushers people back into the kitchen, so I'm alone with Dad and Kitt.

Dad takes a step back. "I don't follow..."

"Whitney Blake. I'm going to be the face of her new clothing line." I bite my lip as it finally sinks in. *Shit! I'm the face of Whitney fucking Blake's clothing line!*

Dad's stunned. His eyebrows shoot up. "Oh. Well, er…I guess congratulations are in order."

"Thank you."

He smiles. "So, modelling, huh?"

I shrug. "Turns out, I like it. Plus, when they're not looking, you can grab some awesome clothes."

Rolling his eyes, he straightens his back. "Do you think you'll do…you know…"

"More topless? I don't think so. I wouldn't be comfortable flashing any more flesh than what I have done already."

"Okay." He dips his head. "I need a stiff drink, and I suppose I should speak to your mother."

"Yes, you should apologise for letting yourself into her home and yelling at her. She's been good to me, Dad. She's helped."

"I hear you." He looks at Kitt and then heads into the kitchen with everyone else.

Kitt sighs and looks up at the ceiling. "I screwed up by not keeping in touch, Tex, and I'm sorry."

Folding my arms over my chest, I stand my ground. The second we shared that first kiss I'd given him the power to rip my heart into tiny pieces, so this time around, he's going to have to get through iron gates and steel walls.

"Can we do this tomorrow, please? This is my party, and I'd like to enjoy it without crying."

Kitt blows out a breath, and his eyes flash with pain. "I want to stay and celebrate with you."

"We've never had any trouble partying together."

His lip kicks up into an adorably sexy smirk. "No, we certainly haven't. Will you do a shot with me?"

I've missed this. "I thought you'd never ask."

48

KITT
SUNDAY, AUGUST 2
NOTTING HILL, ENGLAND

Jennifer let us stay the night. Like we were fucking leaving anyway. Mark and I slept on the sofas in the living room. Texas was fun last night. Something's changed with her. She was more assertive and confident. Those aren't things she's particularly struggled with in the past, but now, she's as strong as iron.

It looks good on her.

But then everything—and nothing at all—does.

It's 5:34 a.m., and I can't sleep. Mark is awake, too, but so far, he's not let on. I want to go and find Tex, but waking her is never a good idea. Kind of how you never slash your own leg and then run into a lion's den. For weeks, I've missed her more than I care to think about, and now, she's so close that I can feel her presence.

Last night, she acted like our relationship never happened. We were friends.

Today, I need to fix that.

"Can't sleep either?" Mark says, breaking the thirty-minute silence.

I sit up. "No. Do you think she'll come home today?"

"She doesn't have a choice."

"Except that, at nineteen, she does."

Almost twenty. Mark needs to let her go.

He sighs, scrubbing his face with his hands. "I know." His voice is a scratchy groan. "I don't have to like it."

"You don't, but if you don't want to ruin your relationship with her, you'll do it with a smile."

"When the fuck did you grow up?"

Laughing, I look up to the ceiling. "About the time I fell in love with her."

He smiles. "Do you think she's really thought this modelling thing through?"

"Yes, I'm not a baby," Texas says, folding her arms.

Mark and I both jump at her sudden presence.

Jesus, she's beautiful. Even when she's angry. Especially when she's angry.

"I'm sure about my career, and I know things will change for me, again, but I'm prepared for that. This is my choice," she says.

"Do you think you'll be able to deal with the extra attention better than you did with these ridiculous baby rumours?" I ask.

"I dealt with that fine. You know that's not why I left."

"Bullshit," Mark says, standing up. "When someone is talking about the person you love, it gets to you. Maybe not right away, but it does."

"You speaking from experience there, Dad?"

Yeah, is he?

"There was a big fallout after Jennifer headed back to work, and you came with me. Your mother and I will never be together, but that doesn't mean I didn't feel anything for her back then. I hated people talking about it."

No one speaks for ten long seconds.

Mark clears his throat. "From those first articles that said you'd probably end up damaged, I vowed to make—"

"Dad, stop. We can't keep going over old ground. It doesn't matter what anyone has said about any of us. Their opinions don't matter. I just need us to be okay."

Does that stretch to me and her, too? Because I sure as hell can't do this without her.

Apparently, I'm a pathetic twat alone.

"She's right. We need to draw a line in the past right now and move forward," I say.

"And what does forward look like?" Mark asks.

I have no idea what she wants, so I look at Texas. The ball is completely in her court.

She sighs. "No more arguing. I want things to go back to normal."

Normal before or after we got together?

I take a breath, trying not to get my hopes up. "Does that mean you're coming to Australia?"

She shrugs. "I'm not sure yet."

"You want to stay here?" I ask in disbelief. Fucking hell, a month ago, she couldn't stand the idea of living with Jennifer, and now, she wants to make it permanent.

"I'm not sure, Kitt."

"What will you do here?" Mark asks.

"Well, there's that campaign for Whitney, for one. I have a job now. I can't chase rock stars around the world for the rest of my life."

She could. She doesn't want to. I love that she wants to do her own thing. I'd never want her to be unfulfilled, but I hate that the thing she wants will take her even farther away from me. She'll have shoots, and I'll have tours. It's just another excuse for her to say we won't work.

"You don't need to worry about me. I won't be removing anything in front of a camera again. You guys can go do whatever publicity you've got before Australia."

Oh, for fuck's sake. "Yeah, not happening," I say. "Cut the bitchiness, Tex. It doesn't suit you."

She grinds her teeth and straightens her back. "You can leave, Kitt. We're done here."

"You know what? I will go," I snap, getting up and pushing past her on my way to the door. *I don't need this.*

But shit. I do.

I freeze.

She wants me to leave her, to walk out, so she doesn't have to admit that breaking up with me was bullshit.

Don't leave. This is a mistake. She's testing you. Show her you're forever.

Mark is shaking his head at her when I get back in the living room.

"What are you doing?" she asks. Her voice is full of hate.

It kinda turns me on.

I smirk. "You're not getting rid of me that easy, sweetheart, so be as pissy as you want. I'm not going anywhere."

"Suit yourself. I'll leave," she snips as she walks away into the kitchen.

I give Mark a look. "Has she always been this…diva?"

"No, but I think we helped with that."

"Should I follow her?"

He shrugs. "Usually, I would say yes…"

I groan, and despite what my gut tells me, I follow her into the kitchen. There's no time to let her cool down. She's leaning against the island with her arms folded again. Thankfully, the island is nowhere near the knives.

"Shout at me, Tex. Get it all out, so we can move past this."

"You think that'll make it all better? Do you honestly think me telling you what a dick you were will take back every night I cried myself to sleep, every time I needed to speak to you and you weren't there, every day I thought I was going to go crazy from not seeing you?"

"Tex," I whisper.

Fucking hell, she's killing me.

"Don't," she turns around, wiping her eyes. "I can't go there with you again, Kitt."

"What?" I feel like I'm free-falling. "You can't give up."

"Me?" She spins back around, and her tear-stained face rips me apart. "I'm not the one who gave up, Kitt. You are! You told me we'd be fine, and then you stopped calling. You promised you'd call, and you broke that promise. Do you have any idea how much that hurts?"

My God, she is impossible sometimes.

"I tried, Texas. This wasn't like any other tour I'd done. This is *our* tour. It's so much more involved. We've had appearances of some sort every day, performances at night, and travel in between. You know that."

Her eyes pierce into mine. "You made me a promise."

And there it is. Doesn't matter what happened, what reasons I had for missing calls, because I broke something I'd vowed I never would. We're not supposed to break promises, not with each other. She's big on that. So am I.

"I love you," I say numbly.

I've lost her.

You can't lose her. You'll lose yourself.

She looks up to the ceiling and takes a breath. "I love you, too, but it's not enough. Not anymore."

"Not anymore. What's changed?"

"Me."

"It's only been a month, Texas."

She laughs without humour. "Feels longer. A lot longer."

"Well, it's not. What happened to, as long as we love each other, we'll be fine? Was that just me?"

"No, but I can't do it again. Nothing is going to change. You're back off on tour in a couple of weeks, and then where will we be?"

"You could be in Australia, too. You know that."

"And what? Be a rock star's girlfriend for the rest of my life? I can't do that, Kitt. I have commitments now."

"I don't want you to do that. I want you to do whatever makes you happy, model if it's what you want, but there's no reason why you can't do that with me."

She shakes her head. "I don't…"

"What? You don't want to? Is that really what you're telling me? After everything we've been through, you're throwing it away because things are hard. I get that this isn't the ideal situation, Texas, and we've both made mistakes—hell, we still will—but we can figure it all out together. Nothing is perfect. All relationships take work."

"Yep, ours takes something beyond work though."

"I don't give a fuck what it takes! I love you, and I'm not letting go. You're making things more complicated. I should've been prepared for that. Not sure why this is a surprise."

"Excuse me?"

"Everything is always exaggerated with you. If you really wanted this, too, you'd be willing to try."

I shouldn't just blame her. We're equally responsible for the intensity of our relationship and how we handle it. But I'm the only one fighting here. She's all too willing to let go. Again.

She's doing that self-preservation thing she's perfected for her relationship with and expectations of her mum. "You really are a dick."

With fire in my veins, I smirk. "That the best you've got, baby?" I'm goading her now. I need to get her to lower that fucking wall she's built around herself. I step closer. "Give whatever reason you need to convince yourself that you're making the right decision, but we both know this isn't over. We're not temporary, and you know it. Get on board soon, Texas, because I want my girl back."

Turning around, I walk away.

For now.

KITT
MONDAY, AUGUST 3
NOTTING HILL, ENGLAND

I'm due back on tour in two weeks, and I have a bunch of promo shit to do. In that very short time, I need to remind Texas of who we were. I don't know what's happened with her, clearly a lot, but somehow she's got lost.

She's convinced we're over.

I know we're not.

But how do you get through to someone so stubborn? I've thought about tying her up until she realises that what she's doing is stupid and irrational, but then I figure that would be overkill. It's a solid plan B though.

Sighing, I lay back against the sofa. We're back at our flat, and I'm going out of my mind.

"Well, you look fucking awful," Milo says.

I narrow my eyes. "Cheers, mate. I feel it. She is *not* happy with me."

"You're surprised?"

"You're not helping."

"Oh," he says. "I didn't realise I was supposed to be."

"God, I can't wait until you have women troubles."

He laughs. "I bet. What are you going to do?"

"I don't know. I need to make it up to her and show her I'm all in, but she's being difficult."

Maybe she's testing me. I let things turn to shit before, so perhaps she's protecting herself by making sure I'll fight this time.

"If anyone can make her listen, it's you. For some weird reason, she seems to like you."

"You're a prick, Milo."

He smiles triumphantly.

"That wasn't a compliment."

"Why's Milo a prick?" Coop asks, strutting into the room in only his boxers.

It's far too early to be seeing so much of him.

"Kitt's still having Texas problems, and apparently, I'm unhelpful," Milo explains.

"Just fuck her, and then everything can go back to normal. I miss her on tour. It's not the same without her," Coop says.

"She won't let me close enough to do that," I say. "But thanks for the advice...I think."

He shrugs. "Don't give her a chance to say no."

Did he just suggest... "Er, yeah, it's actually not okay to do that, Coop."

Milo laughs and shakes his head.

"You know what I mean, dickhead," Coop deadpans. "You're letting her push you away. Don't."

Groaning, I run my hand over my head. "It's not quite that simple. People are always around."

"So, get her alone," Milo says.

"Yes, great," I say sarcastically.

Their advice is stupid. I need suggestions on how to get her alone, how to make her realise we're perfect together, how to convince her we deserve another shot.

"How?"

"Oh." Coop slaps his hands together. "I'll invite her somewhere, and you'll show up, too."

"You want to put yourself in the firing line?" I ask.

She's going to be pissed at us both. Tricking Texas isn't something she'd be okay with.

"If it'll sort it out, yeah. Joking and shit aside, you belong together, and right now, Miss Grumpy Pants is the only one who's denying it. I'll take one for Team Kexas."

"That's *not* becoming a thing."

We might be Kexas in magazines, but it's not happening here.

Cooper laughs. "You don't like it?"

"Fuck off, and arrange something with my girl."

"You're welcome, brother. You're welcome." He goes back into his room, but seconds later, he appears with his phone glued to his ear.

"Hello, darling, I've missed you." He's all smiles, taunting me.

She's probably telling him she's missed him, too. His eyes glow as he watches for my reaction.

Milo is enjoying this too much. He flits between watching Cooper and watching me. I fold my arms.

"Uh-huh. Well, we both know he's an idiot, but he's an idiot who's in love with you."

I glare. *What the fuck is she saying?*

"I know you do, Texy."

He knows she does, what?

I take a deep breath. This is doing my head in, and they've only been on the phone for five bloody seconds. Texas will know I'm here, too, because Cooper's voice is loud and animated. He is enjoying this too much.

"Meet me somewhere today? We can talk, and I can perv on your tits."

Arsehole. But at least he's making this meeting sound more genuine.

Coop laughs. "I'm kidding." *He's not at all.* "Okay, sounds good. I'll see you later."

"When and where are you meeting her?" I ask as soon as he chucks his phone on the sofa.

"Wouldn't you like to know?"

"Don't fuck with me, Coop."

"Why not? There's nothing else to do around here. I'm bored, and Pey is refusing to give us both what we want—oral."

Milo rolls his eyes. "You're a twat."

"Hello?" I snap. "Can we stay on topic? Where are you meeting her?"

"We're having lunch. I'll text you the details. I need a shower. Can still smell last night's chick's perfume."

Nice.

Cooper heads back into his room, and I exchange a look with Milo.

"He's definitely more disgusting than me, right?" Milo asks.

"I'd say, you're pretty even."

"Fuck off! I might sleep with more women than he does, but I'm more of a gentleman about it."

"You wish!" Cooper shouts from somewhere in his room.

"See?" Milo says, gesturing in Coop's direction.

"Yeah, I'll give you that one. I wonder who will tame him," I say.

"Cooper with a girlfriend? Nope, I can't even imagine it."

Laughing, I sit back and wait for Cooper to get ready. This had better work because there is no way I'm leaving this country without being back on with Texas. I'm willing to do whatever it takes.

Ten minutes later, Coop barges out of his room, dressed in tight leather trousers and a black T-shirt.

"You robbing something?" I ask.

He points at me. "I pull this off, tosser."

"No, you look like a giant dickhead," Milo says.

"He's right, man," I add.

"Do you want me to help you?" Cooper asks. "Because, right now, I'd be telling Texas to run."

"All right, all right." Holding my hands up, I smirk. "You look...dark."

He deadpans. "Good enough. I'll text you when I'm there. I actually want to see her for a bit before I'm on her shit list."

I salute as he grabs his phone and heads out the door.

"Think you'll win her over?" Milo asks.

"I have to, man."

We belong together. There's no way either of us will last long without the other. I'm tired of feeling like I have half of a heart, of waking up with a hole in my chest, of feeling like I've accomplished so much but have nothing.

There are replacements and make-dos for a lot of things in life. Love is not one of them.

50

TEXAS
MONDAY, AUGUST 3
NOTTING HILL, ENGLAND

I leap up the second I see that blond head. My God, I have missed Cooper.

He looks around, light eyes scanning the crowded small restaurant. He settles on me, and his smile melts my heart. Opening his arms, he dashes past a table of two gawking women. I waste no time in jumping into his arms. Everything about him is home. They all are.

None more so than the one who's broken my fragile heart a hundred times over.

The last occasion is down to you and your fear.

But I can't feel the way I did when I broke up with Kitt again. I wouldn't survive.

"I missed you, girl," he says, sweeping me up in his strong arms and squeezing the life out of me.

"I missed you, too," I whisper, sinking into his chest.

His body tenses. He grips my upper arms and pulls back. "What the fuck then, Texy?"

I groan. It was only a matter of time before things turned serious. "Can we sit? I think I'll need wine for this conversation," I reply, looking away and taking my seat.

The table is square, and instead of sitting opposite, Cooper plonks down to the side. I have a feeling he wants to be closer, so he can grab me if I run. I'm not going anywhere. If I've learned anything from the topless incident, it's you can't run from inevitable conversations.

"Let me sum up," he says. "You come back to England, you break up with Kitt, you go off the rails, you pose topless."

"Yes, great, let's do bring that up as often as possible," I reply sarcastically.

"I ain't complaining about the topless thing—although it would've been nice to see some nipple."

I glare. His eyes widen, but his lips quirk.

Holding his hands up, he says, "We're moving on. I get coming back here. You needed time and space, and you wanted Kitt to rock without worrying. That's sensible. But why did you break up with him? You know women were going to come out of the woodwork when you guys came out."

"They're not the problem, not even the one who claims to have his baby. I trust Kitt, and I know he has a colourful past."

The pregnant bitch hasn't been heard from since, but as of yet, she's not retracted her story. People are bored of it now anyway. Kitt will prove he's not the dad in due course, and that'll be it.

"I'm not seeing the issue, girl. You're going to need to spell it out for me."

"It was too stressful for us both. This tour is crazy full-on, and he had no time. I found myself being consumed by him and what he's doing and when he'd eventually get around to calling me back. And I wasn't worrying that he was doing someone else. I knew that would never happen. I didn't like the person I was becoming, Coop. My life became planning when he'd be done with appearances, sound checks, performances, and everything else that goes along with it. Then, when he'd call or I'd wake up and find a quick 'I'm sorry' text, I'd feel so deflated. I love Kitt *so much*, but I don't want him to be the only thing I love."

Something thick lodges in my throat.

Don't you dare cry.

I'm avoiding the whole thing as much as possible. I won't let myself think about him too much because the pain leaves me breathless. Logically, I know I can't skip to the end, but right now, I can't deal with it. I wish there were a switch you could flick to fast-forward time. But I don't know if I'll ever be over Kitt Daniels. He's my first everything.

"You don't love *me*?" he says, holding his heart and faking hurt.

"Really, Coop? You know what I'm saying here."

"I do, and I also know you're putting too much on him. Breaking up with him for that reason is dumb. Hear me out," he says as I go to defend my decision.

I slouch back down, closing my mouth.

"If you don't want Kitt to be your main focus all of the time, then don't let him."

"That's it?"

"I thought it was sound advice. You scared of buttons? You don't touch buttons. You don't want the cooker to burn you? You don't touch the cooker."

I stare at him, dumfounded. "Coop, have you taken anything?"

"No, I'm giving advice. You make things way too complicated, and I don't know if that's all the estrogen or what, but it doesn't need to be that hard."

"Sexist pig."

"That's not sexist. My mum and sister are the same, and me and the old man aren't, so I've taken an educated guess."

"Whatever." I can't argue that right now. I'm so over arguing, and I genuinely have no idea how online trolls picj fights all the time. *I mean, what the fuck must be wrong with you?*

"All I'm saying is, don't let pride get in the way of happiness. It ain't worth it, and when you're old and looking back, you'll wish you'd chosen to be shit-eating happy."

So, I don't know how eating shit and happiness go together, but Cooper is right. I suppose.

"He's desperate to work this out, Tex. I've never seen him like this before. Honestly, I search for his balls nearly ten times a day."

"Men are allowed to be upset following a breakup, Coop."

"Yeah, yeah, I know. Will you talk to him?"

"Are you just here to do the bidding for your mate?"

He narrows his eyes and leans forward on the table. "I'm here to make sure you're okay. I'm here because I missed the fuck out of you. But, yeah, I'm here for him as well because, as much as I think he's been a whiny prick since you two got it on, he's a mate. I love him like a brother. Please put my brother out of his misery and make up. And my misery, too."

"Your misery?"

Coop rolls his baby blues. "He really has been a nightmare. You wouldn't believe how many sappy songs I've vetoed."

"How difficult that must have been for you…"

He shakes his head, dead serious. "Texy, you have no idea."

I give him a look because what Coop's been feeling is nothing compared to how hard missing Kitt has been for me. I didn't know emotional pain could be physical. I feel it in every inch of my body.

It *sucks*.

"Where is he?" I ask.

"He'll be outside in his car by now."

I freeze. "He's here?"

"Like he was going to stay at home if there was a chance you'd speak to him. I'm good to wait here if you want to go out there. A chick just walked in, and I want her to sit on my face."

"What the hell?"

With the Band

Cooper laughs. "Joking. I've got weeks of making you do that face at me to catch up on. I'll just sit here and have a beer."

"I honestly think there's something wrong with you, Jack Cooper."

"You, too, Texas Knight? Now, go see my boy, please."

I don't want to seem too eager, and I'm not entirely sure why, so I take another sip of my water, wishing I'd ordered something stronger. Then, I pick up my bag.

"No promises, Coop. I don't know what I want yet."

Sitting back, he tilts his head to the side and gives me a look that I know means he doesn't believe me.

Okay, so you obviously do know what you want, Kitt.
But I don't know if I can go through this again.
Screw you, fear.
Just go and see him, and you'll know how you feel.

Turning, I head out the door. The car park is private, so we'll be alone. Plus, Kitt's black Range Rover has tinted glass. He looks like a bloody drug dealer but a private one. As I approach, the door opens. Kitt must have seen me coming.

My heart starts to do somersaults.

"Hi," I say, jumping up and sliding onto the seat. I slam the door shut and bite my lip.

Oh my God, he looks incredible, and he smells edible. Being so close to him is the most beautiful kind of torture.

With a charming smile, he murmurs, "I was about to say that."

I bite harder. I want to reach over. All I have to do is crawl onto his lap, and everything will disappear. There will be no pain, no wanting, no fear. He has the power to make everything better. But, more importantly, I think, he has the power to cut out my already weeping heart.

We lapse into a somewhat awkward silence that radiates off every surface. I don't know if he wants to kiss me or run. I don't know what I want to do either.

Kitt groans. "I hate this. I don't know what to do, Tex. Can you tell me what to do here?"

"I don't have all the answers. I wish I did."

Most of the time, I feel like I don't have *any* of the answers. And that's because I don't. The biggest decision I had to make until Kitt was whether I should have streaks of red put through my hair or not. I went for not.

I might do that soon.

Thumping his head against the headrest, he sighs. "Then, can we skip to the part where we're together again?"

"Come on, you know we can't do that."

Closing his eyes, he looks down, his fists clenched by his sides. "This is awful, Tex. For both of us. Fucking hell, just let me back in. I don't understand why you're doing this. There's nothing we can't sort out, but you're acting like this is irreparable. I don't get it."

"No, you don't! That's exactly why I can't pretend like the last few weeks haven't happened."

"Well, you're not telling me! How am I supposed to get on the same page if I don't even know what fucking book you're reading from?"

"I don't know, okay? I don't know," I snap. "See? This is why we don't work, why we will *never* work."

He sucks in a breath that makes my heart drop. His eyes are full of pain. Tears well at the sides, and I want to die.

What have you done?

"Kitt…I…"

"You should go," he says breathlessly, gripping the door handle for dear life. "I need you to go."

I don't want to go. I want to take my words back, but I can't. They're out there now, and nothing will change that. Nothing will change that look on his face when I broke his heart.

"Please, Kitt, I didn't mean…" I wipe a tear from my face and shuffle closer.

I want to touch him, but he's breathing heavily and staring straight forward. I'm scared that if I reach out, I'll break him.

"If you feel anything for me, Texas, please do what I asked. I need you to leave," he whispers. His voice is low and rough.

Usually, I love that, but right now, it's laced with pain. He's hanging on by a thread.

Without looking, I reach for the door handle. I hate myself. Shoving the door open, I get out, slam it shut, and sprint for my car, holding my stomach so that I don't come apart. I can't even go back inside and tell Coop I'm taking off.

My knees buckle under the weight of guilt and heartache, and I fall against the door of Jennifer's spare car. "No," I cry, feeling like my legs are made of lead.

"Texas?"

Cooper is by my side in an instant, holding me up. "Damn it, what happened?"

I grip his arms, pulling him closer, and I cry. I can't hold it in. I can't be strong anymore. I sob and bury my head in his chest. "It hurts, Cooper. It hurts so much that I think I'm dying."

He holds me tight and kisses the top of my head. "No, you're not. It's going to be okay. What did he say?"

I shake my head. "It was me. I hurt him, and—oh my God, what did I do? I can't stand it, Cooper." My chest shakes, and I feel so, so heavy.

"Shh, it's not your fault. Maybe this was a bad idea. We shouldn't have sprung it on you."

"I told him that we'd never work."

Coop rubs my back. "Do you mean that?"

I pull back and take stuttered breaths.

Just keep breathing. In and out. Just get yourself home, and it'll be fine. Hold it together a little longer.

How could I have let things get so out of hand?

"Tex?" he says, frowning.

Cooper raises me up on my wobbly legs. He keeps his arms extended in case I fall again, but I won't let myself.

"I need to go, Coop," I sob, shaking my head and holding my stomach tight.

All you have to do is get in the car and drive home. You can drive. You're fine. You're fine.

And maybe if I tell myself I'm okay often enough, I'll believe it.

That's a thing, right? People start to believe all sorts of shit if it's repeated over and over again.

You. Will. Get. Through. This.

51

KITT
TUESDAY, AUGUST 4
OXFORD, ENGLAND

It took a good four hours to stop feeling like her words cut me to pieces. She didn't mean it. We're not over, and that scares her, so she lashed out. Texas wants to be able to control her emotions when it comes to me, but it's impossible. We can't be controlled.

Cooper took her home, to her dad's, and I went back to the flat that I share with the guys. Tex and I should be looking at Rightmove now, searching for a home together.

I couldn't leave things, so I went to her house.

Mark stares at me, like he wants to tell me to do one. Not happening. I'm not leaving.

"I need to see her."

"I don't know what's going on, Kitt, but my daughter was brought home in tears and—"

"Yeah, I know. I'm here to fix it and show her that she's being stupid."

His eyebrows flick up.

"She's stubborn, but so am I."

Sighing deeply like it hurts, he steps aside, and I walk in.

"I don't want to see you putting any more tears in my daughter's eyes."

"Neither do I." Turning, I take the stairs two at a time. I tap on her door and count the seconds. *One, two, three—*

She opens the door, and her eyes widen.

"Please don't slam the door in my face, Tex," Blocking it with my arm as she tries to slam it, I plead with my eyes. *Let me in.*

She groans and looks away. "What do you want, Kitt?"

"There was too much pressure. I'm sorry, Tex, I shouldn't have turned up at the restaurant without warning, but I'm kind of desperate here. I don't know what to do. I only know that not being with you hurts so fucking much. I won't keep pushing, but please, please, if there's any part of you that thinks we can be saved, give me a shot."

Her eyes drop to the floor, and I feel her pain, too. This is hurting her just as much.

So, why is she doing this?

I couldn't stay away from her for anything in this world. There is no amount of pain she could cause me that would stop me from loving her.

Right now, her refusal to look me in the eyes is from her shame. She's feeling guilty because of what she said. She might have forgotten that I know her, but I fucking haven't. She looks up. Her hazel eyes stare past me, and her chest is moving fast as she tries to control her reaction to me being so close.

"Stop trying so hard to be okay. You're not okay. Neither of us is. I'm not angry about what you said anymore. But we need to talk about this."

"Do you think it's going to get us any further? I don't want to keep hurting each other."

"We won't. Please?"

She finally meets my eyes, and I feel like I'm flying again. No matter how we are, she still has the power to make me feel weightless.

"Tex, I fucking love you."

Her eyes sharpen, and she takes in a breath. "I still love you, too. You know that, right?"

I nod because I do know. What we have isn't something that fades—ever.

"Is that enough for you?" I ask.

"I want it to be. Kitt, every missed call and unanswered text made me feel like…a groupie, like I was disposable. I should've known better, but I was hurting and scared. You throw women away and the thought of you letting me go that easily…" Taking a breath, she swipes away a tear.

Shit.

"I gave up too easily. I'm sorry for that. Kitt, I can't lose you, and I know I'm being stupid right now because I'm the one who ended it, but you're not disposable to me. Ever. God, I was terrified that you'd find someone else, so I panicked."

"Texas…" *Fucking hell, she can rip me apart with her words.*

"No, don't. I'm not blaming you, not anymore. I'm so sorry that I was such an unreasonable bitch."

"You were trying to protect yourself," I mutter.

"Yes. It's dumb, I know. We both got hurt, but I didn't know what else to do because I've never lost, or thought I've lost, something that I love so much before."

I step forward and cup her cheek in my hand. "Let me in, and we'll talk. This is fixable. Whatever you're feeling, we can work through. But I can't do it alone."

She considers me for a minute, and the intensity on her face shows how big this is for her. She's terrified. My girl is an overthinker, so fuck knows what she's dreamed up in her head as the result of us getting back together. Obviously, it's not a pretty picture.

"We need to be able to find more time for us when you're on the road. I promise I won't freak out again, but I need something to work with. I've never wanted anything more than you so total silence kind of sends me... Well, you know."

"I know, and it's done. We'll figure it out. I've already said I won't do another loaded tour. I'll have more breaks, travel by plane. I'll do anything I can, so we're not apart for as long. I promise you, babe."

"I want you to be as supportive of my career as I am of yours."

I wrap her in my arms and tug her close. "Already am."

She laughs. "Are we crazy?"

"Who isn't? I love you."

She responds by pushing up on her tiptoes and planting her mouth on mine.

FRIDAY, AUGUST 7
OXFORD, ENGLAND

Texas is with Jennifer, having a meeting about her modelling Whitney's clothes line, and then she's going to go shopping with Peyton, so I take the time to do something I've been thinking about since I fell in love with Tex.

Me and Tex are doing good. We've talked, shouted and cried. It will take time for us both to be secure in our relationship again, but we're both determined to get there.

I follow Mark into the massive kitchen.

He starts to make us coffee. "I'm not sure what time she'll be back. When Peyton and Texas are shopping, it can go on for a while."

It goes on for a while because Peyton loves to shop. Tex will be in hell.

"Yeah, I know. I actually want to talk to you."

He slowly turns on his heel, his jaw clenched, and I know where this is going.

Holding up my hands, I laugh. "No, she's not pregnant."

His back slumps with relief. "Good."

"I wouldn't do that to her, Mark. She has all these plans. I'll wait at least a year before I put a baby in her belly." I smirk and sit on a stool.

It's only because he knows I'm joking that my legs are still attached.

"Is there anything in particular you want, Kitt?"

"Yeah, actually. I want to marry your daughter. So, if I can get your blessing, that'll be great."

His jaw drops, and his eyes bulge. He stands stock-still, like he's not sure he heard me right. Or he's trying to figure out who to call for the number of a hit man.

"You all right there, old man?" I ask, leaning forward.

I'm treading a very fine line here. He could say no. It's not going to change anything. There is nothing he could say that would stop me from proposing to her, but I know she will want him to be okay with it.

"You want to marry her?"

"Of course I do. How are you surprised by this?"

He coughs. "Because you're twenty-two, and she's nineteen."

"All right, so we're young, but that doesn't change a thing. We're still going to be together until the end. I'm not saying I want to get married right now, unless she does, but I want to put a ring on her finger."

"Why now?"

"Why not now?"

He cocks his head. "That's your answer?"

"I don't really know what else to say. I love her, and I want to marry her. That's my reason. What more do you need?"

His back straightens, and he folds his arms over his chest. Mark wants to say no. He wants Texas to live at home with him longer. He's not ready for another big change where their relationship is concerned, but he also can't do anything he knows she wouldn't want.

He's scared she'll say yes and move out, and he knows it'll happen.

"When were you planning on doing it?"

"Before we leave for Australia."

"Why so soon?"

I smirk. "Because you'll probably be sick of me when we hit the road again, and I'm not going to give you the opportunity to change your mind. I'm looking for a yes from both of you, so I'm not taking any chances."

"What if she says no?"

"She won't."

"What if I do?"

"I'm going to marry her, Mark. You know that, too. I'd rather do it with your support, and so would Tex, but I will make her my wife."

He stares at me for a long time. His hazel eyes search for answers to every doubt he has. I hold his eyes, sitting tall. She is all I want, and he'll never find anything else inside of me other than Texas.

Finally, he breaks our gaze. "When she was six and asked why her mum didn't live with us, like her friends who all had two parents together, we ended up having a huge discussion. She got upset...*for me* because I didn't have anyone to parent with. I had to do it all alone. And when I told her I was happy to do it alone, she promised me she'd live with me forever. Of course, that would never happen, but she was so sure. I would love more time with my daughter, but I would never ask her to put her life on hold or give up her happiness for me. So, if she wants to marry you, Kitt, you have my blessing."

Thank fuck for that.

The weight of the damn world lifts off my shoulders.

Shit, I get to marry the girl of my dreams. Like I said, it's happening anyway, but it's better with the old man's approval.

WITH THE Band

"Thanks, Mark. And I don't expect her to move in with me straight off. You're both going to need time to get used to it."

"Oh, she'll want to move in with you. You'll be engaged, Kitt. You should live together."

Well, I know that, but I'd never push her. Not that much anyway. Not when it comes to her relationship with her dad.

"You've had enough of her already?" I joke.

He laughs. "I'm just looking forward to watching you try to handle her."

I have a few tried and tested ways. None I can discuss with her daddy.

"It's fine. I'll drink."

Folding his arms, he takes a step closer, like he's putting me on trial. "What does this mean in the long-term? You'll be touring, and she'll be..."

"She'll be wherever she wants."

"You're fine with her staying behind?"

"Mark, all I need is for her to be happy. Whatever we're doing, we'll figure it out. And I won't cram the whole world into a summer next time. I love my career—it's all I've ever wanted to do—but it will never come before her. Nothing will."

He gives me a nod, and I think he's content with what I've told him. I've never had to put so much fucking work into a relationship before. Mark and Texas aren't easy, but I love them both. In very, *very* different ways.

"Better not. If she sheds one tear over you, I swear..."

"Got it," I reply. "Anyway, shouldn't you be worrying about your next move? Your nineteen-year-old daughter will beat you down the aisle. Don't you think it's time to settle down?"

"I'm about to get rid of one woman, so I think I'll enjoy the peace for a while."

"Mark, if I ask you a personal question, do you promise not to—"

"Ask me if I'm gay, and I'll break your neck."

415

I laugh and take the mug of coffee he's finally made. "Looks like I'm not the only one to question."

"No, my sweet little girl has. My whole adult life has been about Texas, and although I wouldn't have had it any other way, she's at a stage in her life where she doesn't need me to parent her. I'm looking forward to...how do I put it?"

"Shagging around?"

He chuckles. "Something like that."

"You're doing it backward, you know?"

"Play and then settle? I know, but I knocked up a groupie, so I had that situation to deal with first." He shrugs and grins.

I love how open and lighthearted he and Texas are about what happened.

"No one around to teach you rule one about wrapping up...which I'm thankful for."

"You're welcome. I did it all for you," he says dryly. "How are you going to propose? You'd better make it good."

"I'm not sure yet. It'll be good. I could write it on a napkin, and she'd still cry."

My girl can get a bit emotional when it comes to us. And when she's hungry. Or tired. Or her favourite program ends on a cliffhanger. Or Netflix doesn't have the next series to her latest obsession.

"The summerhouse," he says. "Do you remember the first time Texas and I met you, and you gave us that CD?"

I nod.

"Well, after I listened to it, Texas stole it. Every day, all summer, she would be out there, with the doors open, playing your album. It was on repeat. When I found out about you and Texas, she told me that Paris wasn't the start for her. I realise now what she wasn't telling me. It was back that summer, two years ago, when she fell in love."

Fuck me, I love her.

"The summerhouse?" I clear my throat.

Jesus, the things that girl does to me.

My throat is lodged, and I feel like I could fucking cry. But I won't because that would be humiliating in front of Mark.

"I can make it easier and not be here. Will wants to let off some steam in Dublin before Australia."

Translation: Will wants to sleep with Irish chicks.

"Thanks for not being a wanker about this."

He laughs and sits on a stool, finally comfortable and over the shock of me wanting his daughter forever. "Thank you for never breaking her heart."

It's a threat and one that is completely unnecessary because the only thing I would never do for that girl is hurt her.

I dip my head. "You got it."

epilogue

TEXAS
MONDAY, AUGUST 10
OXFORD, ENGLAND

"What do I get for the rock star who has it all?" I ask Milo and Cooper.

We're out shopping for Kitt's twenty-third birthday, which is in three days, and none of us have a single clue. I'm so grateful that I get to spend his birthday with him before he goes to rock Australia. I'd hate to be separated on special occasions.

So far, Coop is the only one suggesting things to get, but as you can imagine, it's all highly inappropriate.

"Sex coupon?" Milo says.

I roll my eyes because that was obviously coming at some point.

"He can have sex with me anytime he likes. He doesn't need a coupon."

"Oh!" Coop says, slamming his hand down on the table in the café.

Great, we've managed a few minutes alone, and now, he's drawing attention to us.

It's not that bad here. We're in a fucking expensive coffee shop where a drink costs about the same as the rent for a one-bed flat, but that does mean people aren't all over us.

"You could get him a coupon for sex with someone else."

I can, what?

Milo and I look at him, waiting for that to sink in and for him to realise what he's just said.

Cooper stares back.

"Really, Coop? You think I'm giving my *boyfriend* something that'll grant him a shag with another woman? And do you think Kitt would even want that?"

Because he wouldn't.

Despite having hundreds of women willing to do anything with him or to him, I know categorically that he would never stray. He loves passionately, and he's fiercely loyal. Kitt would never risk my heart and our relationship for anything.

He puts me above a career he's wanted since childhood.

"All right, just thinking of ideas." He mouths, *Wow*, as if I've said something ridiculous.

"Can we get back on track, please?" I put my head in my hands.

This is hard. I want his birthday to be perfect, I want to show him how much he means to me, but I don't know how. Since we started our relationship, Kitt has gotten real good at the romance thing, but I'm still lacking in that department.

"Why is this stressing you out so much, Tex?" Milo asks. "Kitt doesn't want things. You've given him everything by being with him."

Coop's eyes are back on me. "Wrap yourself up for his birthday."

I ignore the pervert and reply to Milo, "He's always going that extra mile for me. I want to do the same for him. If I'm all he wants, how do I give him more than that?"

"Anal," Coop says.

With the Band

"Oh, seriously!" I snap, trying to look annoyed, when I want to laugh.

Cooper shrugs and leans back in his chair.

Out of the corner of my eye, I see Milo freeze. He's staring at the door with his eyes wide, his mouth open, and his hands gripping the table.

I follow where he's looking. A cute girl with dusty-blonde hair and eyes brighter than turquoise is planted to the spot, watching him like she's just seen a ghost.

Okay, who is she?

"Milo, you all right?" I ask.

But he's not hearing me.

The girl takes a few steps closer after a deep breath. "Hi, Milo," she says so timidly that I'm scared she's going to cry.

"Lexi," he whispers back as he stands up.

Cooper's eyes shoot up.

Seriously, I'm the only one who has no idea what's happening here.

"You're here," he says.

"I never left, Milo."

Oh, there was some hostility there. Something big went down between them because the atmosphere is palpable.

"Lexi! I've missed you, babe," Cooper says, smirking at Milo.

He's cut down by a look that screams murder, but that's exactly what he was going for.

"Are you free, Lex?" Milo asks nervously. He looks unsure of his own words.

Lexi looks like she wants to say no and run away. She looks sad and scared, and it kind of makes me want to punch Milo because whatever happened between them, he broke her heart pretty thoroughly.

"I am. I just came in here for coffee before heading home."

Milo looks back at me. I'm not sure if he's seeking permission or maybe some help.

"Of course. We've got this. You go with…"

He shakes his head. "Sorry. Texas, this is Lexi, my childhood friend."

Why do I think he's using the term friend very loosely?

"Lexi, this is Texas Knight. She's—"

"I know who she is. It's nice to meet you, Texas."

Perfect. She's seen my almost topless picture.

I shake her hand, and that's when Cooper stands up. Tugging his arm, I bring him closer to me because I have a feeling if he tries to hit on Lexi, no matter if he's only doing it to piss Milo off, Milo's head might explode.

"Lex," Coop says, dipping his head.

Lexi gives him a smile, and I'm happy to notice that he has no effect on her. Milo notices it, too, and his posture relaxes a fraction.

"See you later," Milo mutters to us, but his eyes stay fixed on Lexi. He walks around the table and stops beside her.

"Um, we can go to my place. It's not far," she says.

Coop and I watch them leave, and then he turns to me. "Bet he shags her again."

I roll my eyes. "I need to know everything."

"Childhood sweethearts," he says. He takes a swig of his coffee. "When we started the band, it demanded his time, and they grew apart. Then we got to tour in clubs and pubs and shit. He broke it off because they were barely ever spending time with each other."

"Wow. So, they were around, what? Twenty when they broke up?"

"Yeah. It wasn't long before we met you."

"Is that why he's a slut?"

Coop's mouth kicks up at the corner. "Yep. Cliché, right?"

"What about you?" I ask.

"Rock. Star."

"Come on," I deadpan. There must be more to it than that.

"Come on, what? I'm young and gorgeous and killer in bed. There's not a woman in this world who could get me to settle down in my twenties."

"All right. Fine. Now, Kitt's present?"

"Threesome? Me. You. Him. I ain't touching his, but you will love it."

"Know what? I'm going to call Peyton and get her advice."

"Now, there's a woman I would settle down with. In about ten years."

"She'll be thrilled," I mutter dryly. "Let's get out of here. People are starting to look."

"Where to?" he asks, getting up.

"Home. I'll have to think about his present. Again." At this rate, I really will have to wrap myself up.

"You'll find something."

I'd ask what Cooper is getting for Kitt, but I'm sure it's a sex toy of some sort.

When I get home from shopping, Dad is by the front door with a small suitcase. He gives me a grin, and there's a secret behind it.

"All right, what's going on?" I ask.

Dad smiles. "Me, Will, and Jimmy are heading to Dublin for the weekend before Australia."

"Huh? Since when?"

"Since now. You'll know why soon."

"Oh God. You've not knocked up someone else, have you?"

"Why is that your default?"

"Because it's fun to remind you of your fuckups."

He steps closer and pushes my hair out of my face. "You're my daughter. You've never been a fuckup, and if I hear that language coming out of your mouth again, you'll be grounded."

"And here I was, thinking that we've made progress in our relationship. I'm not a kid, remember?"

"Just because you've stopped being a child doesn't ever mean you'll stop being *my* child. I don't care if you're nineteen or ninety. You're stuck with me and my slightly overbearing, overprotective ways."

Slightly overbearing?

I hug him tight. Although we've had a rocky road, trying to navigate an adult father-and-daughter relationship, I wouldn't change a single thing about him. Not for anything.

"I love you, Dad."

"Love you, too," he replies, hugging me back and kissing the top of my head. "Something's in the summerhouse for you. I'll see you on Monday."

"Presents? Shiny things?"

Laughing, he shakes his head and picks up his duffel bag. "Be good." He holds his hand up. "Before you say a word, no, I will not get anyone pregnant."

I pat his head. "That's the spirit. Have a nice time."

"Summerhouse."

Saluting, I reply, "Going."

It's bloody freezing and drizzling with fine rain—thank you, England—as I go out the back and dash down the path. Holding my hand out, I block the water from getting in my eyes and shove open the door.

My feet root to the floor. "Oh my God," I whisper as my eyes fill with tears.

Kitt is standing in the middle of the room with a big bunch of roses. The wooden summerhouse is filled with flowers and fairy lights. The wood burner is on, making it toasty. Pillows and blankets are laid out in front of it. He has snacks and beer on the coffee table.

"Hi," he whispers.

"Hey," I reply, still looking around. The summerhouse is small, but he's decorated it beautifully. "What are you doing here?"

He smirks. "I'm here for my girl."

His girl. Gets me every time.

I look into his eyes, and I'm falling, just like the very first time. Like Paris, the cage, the bus, every time I've awoken in his arms and been on the end of frantic and passionate kisses.

I thought the time apart would heal my heart, and I'd get over him. It hasn't, and it couldn't. I love him more than I ever thought was possible.

"I've made a lot of mistakes, Texas, and my biggest regret is letting you get on that plane to come home. I should've fought harder."

"No. Stop," I say, taking a step closer to him with butterflies in my stomach. "It was the right thing for us both, and you know it. We needed space. You had to finish being a rock star, and I had to find out who I was. Let's not go over old ground. Forward, not backward, remember?"

He grins. "I know who you are even if you're not always sure."

"Yeah? Who's that?"

He closes the distance and takes my face between his hands. Staring into my eyes, he whispers, "You're Texas Knight. Beautiful, compassionate, funny, loyal, driven, and passionate. You love completely, and you'll do anything for the people you care about. You love music and dancing and Netflix. You give as good as you get, and you always put one hundred percent into everything you do."

"If you want me to cry like a baby, continue!" I say, unable to wipe my eyes, as he's holding my head hostage. I don't mind in the slightest.

With a smirk, Kitt sinks to one knee, and I think my heart gives up altogether. He stares up at me with love and adoration. Maybe with a few nerves mixed in.

Oh God, oh God.

Oh. My. God!

Don't hyperventilate. Don't faint and miss this moment!

"Texas Knight, my whole world changed when I fell in love with you. You forced me to reevaluate everything. You made me question everything, and the answer was always you. I love you so much, and I want to spend the rest of my life with you. Marry me, baby?"

I'm dreaming. Right?

I open my mouth to scream, *Yes*, but nothing comes out. This moment is something I've dreamed about for years, and it feels a million times better than I ever imagined. I swallow thick emotion and nod my head because my voice really isn't working.

Kitt's smile is bigger and brighter than I've ever seen it before. He jumps up and tackles me in a bone-crushing huge hug. "Fuck yeah!"

I attack his lips, kissing him with every ounce of love and happiness I feel right now. I'm soaring. Kitt ends the kiss way too soon and reaches into his pocket.

Oh God. He has a ring.

I already love it.

When he presents the diamond to me, I'm breathless. It's beyond beautiful. It's a chunky rectangle that sits high with smaller round diamonds around it.

"Kitt," I whisper breathlessly.

No one has ever been this happy before, I swear.

I blink a few times to clear the tears blocking my view of the ring that means I'll marry this man one day.

"Do you like it?"

"I love it. I love you."

He sucks in a breath and presses his forehead against mine. As much as I love looking at the ring, I love looking at him more.

"It was my mum's. My nan's originally. My grandad worked two jobs to be able to afford a ring he felt was equal to Nan's beauty. It meant so much to them both. They knew they would hand it down, so when my dad told them he wanted to propose, she gave it to him. It's why my nan only wears a wedding ring now. And when my mum died, the ring was given to me." He takes a breath. "Texas, from the moment that ring was passed down to me, it has belonged to you."

"Oh my God, I love you."

I wipe my tears and press my lips against his. He kisses me back with so much passion that I feel like my heart is going to explode.

Can you love someone too much? Because this is so overwhelming that it almost hurts.

Kitt pulls back again, and I'm beginning to hate him for breaking our kisses. But then, he slides the ring onto my finger, and I let out a proper girlie little sob.

"I want to marry you now," he rasps, staring at the ring on my finger.

"We kind of need someone to officiate, or it's just a primary school marriage."

Looking up, he smirks. "I don't think I'll ever find enough words to describe how much I love you."

"You could just take me to bed and show me."

His eyebrows shoot up. "Well, I am a big believer in actions speaking louder than words."

I grip the hem of his T-shirt and pull him closer. "Then, action me up real good, rock star."

acknowledgments

This book has been one of those never ending books that takes a lot of time and patience. Unfortunately, I possessed neither.

So, I want to say a huge thank you to my girls who have gotten me through late nights and long writing sessions. Kirsty, Zoë, Hilda, Chloe, and Rachel, you girls keep me sane!

To my husband, Joe, and our son, Ashton, thank you both for being so understanding when I was chained to the laptop.

A big shout-out to the bloggers who have signed up to promote this release. You work long hours, often with nothing in return, and I don't think I'll ever be able to express how much that means.

That brings me to my readers. Thank you so much for your love, support, and all of the amazing messages you send that make the late nights and (many) moments of pure stress and anxiety totally worth it.

You're all my rock stars.

about the author

UK native Natasha Preston grew up in small villages and towns. She discovered her love of writing when she stumbled across an amateur writing site and uploaded her first story, and she hasn't looked back since.

She enjoys writing contemporary romance, gritty Young Adult thrillers and, of course, the occasional serial killer.

Made in the USA
Charleston, SC
25 February 2016